MISSION TO LOVE

BROTHERS IN ARMS

SAMANTHA KANE

SK Publishing

For my extended Family—Readers, Authors, Editors, Cover Artists—
all the people that make this magic possible.

❀ Created with Vellum

CHAPTER 1

S imon hesitated at the step off the gangway onto the quay. It had been less than two months since he'd last set foot on English soil, yet it seemed like years. A Barbary Coast prison could do that, he supposed.

"I'm starving," his oldest friend Daniel Steinberg said peevishly from behind him. "Hurry up, Simon. Between the weather and Harry getting me shot, I never thought we'd make it back from this voyage. Whenever I set foot on a ship it turns into a disaster." Despite the bullet wound in his thigh, Daniel still looked as smart as always, trim and fit and dressed tiptop, only a slight limp giving him away. Simon, on the other hand, looked like something the cat had dragged in after mauling it.

"Why," Simon, said, rounding on Daniel, "did you have to bring Harry? Just because you're shagging him does not mean that he has to go everywhere with you."

"Yes, actually, it sort of does," Harry Ashbury said smoothly from behind Daniel. "And, also, it's my ship." He was annoyingly tall, and still looked annoyingly rugged and good-looking despite a torturously rough crossing. The eye patch he wore from a decade-old injury made him more appealing than not.

Focusing on Harry rather than how wonderful the rather dark and dingy quay looked kept Simon's emotions from overwhelming him. He was quite sure he'd never seen a more wonderfully dilapidated, decaying, moldering piece of brilliance in his life. Every piece of rank grayish-green, sway-backed, slime-encrusted board announced he was home. And there were even a few pieces of new timber here and there where repairs had recently been made to this section of the wharf. No doubt Ashbury's doing. His trading company offices were along this section if he remembered correctly.

"But he is so annoying," Simon said to Daniel, ignoring that it was Harry who actually responded to him. "Was he this annoying during the war?"

"*You* have always been annoying," Harry said, impatience finally creeping into his tone. "I remember that quite clearly."

"Yes," Daniel agreed, switching allegiances as quickly as a debutante changed dance partners. "I'm beginning to wonder why I was in such a lather to rush off and rescue you. Everyone was in tears over poor Simon's fate. I pity your poor jailors. You most likely annoyed them to death."

"Really?" Simon asked with exaggerated interest, gritting his teeth against the memories of exactly what his jailors did to him in the few weeks before Harry and Daniel showed up to rescue him. Peckish or no, Simon wasn't going to put up with Daniel's notoriously sharp tongue. "Do you think so? Did they look annoyed to death when they shot you? I wish I'd annoyed them into shooting you both."

"Stop it, both of you," Harry said, his voice cracking like a whip. "I have put up with your bickering for the last week because you were both suffering from your injuries. But even I have a limited store of patience." He sighed. "Simon," he said in that quiet, soothing tone Simon really hated, as if he were speaking to a bedlamite. "I know you've been through a great deal and this is difficult—"

Simon cut him off. "Don't be tedious," he snapped. He stepped onto the quay, ignoring the shiver that raced down his spine as the fresh brand on his back tightened and stung painfully. The unusually hot weather intensified the brackish smell of the water and he gratefully took a deep breath of the rank perfume. He would have preferred cooler weather. He'd had enough of the heat in Africa.

He waved down a hackney with a stiff arm and limped toward it.

"Where are you going?" Daniel asked in alarm, grabbing his arm.

"Home," Simon said, shaking his hand off. "I still have one, don't I?"

"Of course. As far as I know." Daniel didn't sound as confident as his words would indicate. "You were paid up before..." He trailed off.

"Before I was kidnapped?" Simon finished for him. "Yes, I was." He climbed up into the hackney, refusing to show how tired he still was, even after a week of lying about the ship's cabin.

"Come home with us," Daniel urged, refusing to let Simon close the door. "Let us take care of you."

"I can take care of myself," Simon told him firmly, tugging the door. "Contrary to popular opinion." He got the door closed and called his destination to the driver, and the carriage took off with a lurch that nearly left his stomach on the wharf.

He had to close his eyes on the ride. For starters, he didn't have his land legs back and was quite queasy. He was tired of casting up his accounts across the English Channel, so he was determined to hold onto them across London. And he really couldn't handle being home again. He could admit it now that he was alone. *Finally. At last.* He truly loved Daniel, and he found Harry to be a more than tolerable companion, but all he'd wanted for the last week and a half was to be blessedly, quietly, alone.

He hadn't been alone since he'd been thrown into the hold of a stinking ship with a sorry lot of other kidnapped bastards on their way to slavery—if they were lucky—on the Barbary Coast. Most had been snatched to be sold and then hopefully exchanged for ransom. A practice that had all but died out among the Barbary pirates thanks to the efforts of the Royal Navy and the Americans.

But there were still a few who dallied in it. The truth was that the victims taken with Simon weren't the kind who would fetch a high ransom, or any ransom at all, most likely. Which meant slavery. They had to earn their price somehow.

He'd lived with a background symphony of hopeless sobbing, painful cries, grunts, groans, begging, weeping, cursing, beatings, rapes, and all manner of violent trespasses day and night for almost two months. He'd had to defend himself countless times—an almost impossible feat after he'd been beaten by his jailors for imagined transgressions several times. And after Daniel and Harry had rescued him, he'd had to listen to Daniel's apologies and recriminations and platitudes. Which had been all well and good for the first day or two, but by day three Simon had been ready to jump ship, or throw Daniel overboard. And Harry knew it. Damn Harry and his all-seeing eye. The fellow was far too observant.

All Simon wanted was to be alone with his thoughts. Was that too much to ask for a poor man who'd been kidnapped, beaten, tortured and rescued?

Alas, it was not to be.

CHAPTER 2

"**O**h, Christ on a crutch, not you," Simon complained when he saw Sir Barnabas James sitting on the uncovered sofa in his apartments. Seeing his former commander from his military days dampened his joy at being home again, but only slightly.

"It is good to see you, too," Sir Barnabas said with that slight crook to his upper lip that could pass for a smile, but could also be interpreted as a smirk. Simon had never been able to read him well. Not like Daniel. But then, Daniel and Sir Barnabas had been lovers for years. Even a spy as gifted in subterfuge as Sir Barnabas couldn't contain all his secrets in the throes of passion, Simon supposed. Or perhaps he could and he only let Daniel know what he wanted him to know.

The rest of the furniture had been uncovered as well, although there was still an air of disuse about the room. Sir Barnabas had opened a window, but it remained miserably hot and stuffy. Simon sat down hard on his favorite chair and put a hand on his aching forehead. Dust motes flew into the air around him from the neglected, well-worn cushion. His apartment wasn't palatial by any means, but it suited him well.

Comfort meant more to him than status. It always had. It was why, of course, he had never pursued a career or played the market for longer than it took to make enough money to live satisfactorily, if not well. What use did he have for useless objects and closets of unworn clothes? He just needed rooms that weren't drafty, a trusty stove, a soft mattress, and a fine jacket or two. All right, and several pairs of good boots. A man had priorities, didn't he?

Anyway, when he wanted gilt and fine furnishings he only had to go to Daniel's, or Freddy's, for heaven's sake. After all, Freddy was a duke. Simon practically choked on the gold dust in the air at his ducal estate, Ashton Park.

"Given yourself another headache with too much thinking again, have you?" Sir Barnabas asked with feigned concern. Simon didn't need someone to interpret that for him.

"You'd think you'd have some sympathy for a man in my condition," Simon whined. He dropped his head back to rest on the chair.

"What condition?" Sir Barnabas asked, crossing his legs.

Simon lowered his hand and stared at Sir Barnabas incredulously. "Just released from forced captivity? Kidnapped by Barbary pirates?" he reminded him. "Beaten? Tortured?"

"Hmm, tortured, were you?" Sir Barnabas said, his brow furrowing in what appeared to be real concern. "The cat o'nine? Fingernails all pulled out? The rack?" He leaned from side to side, observing Simon up and down. "You don't look any taller."

"You should see the brand on my back," Simon told him wearily. "I'm tired, Barnabas. I haven't the energy or, frankly, the wits to play guessing games with you, so just tell me why you're here."

"Did they really brand you?" Sir Barnabas asked, and this time the concern was unmistakable. Simon tipped his head to the side as he met the other man's gaze and he was touched by what he saw there.

"Yes, they did. And no, it wasn't your fault."

"I wasn't going to take the blame," Sir Barnabas said, surprise on his face. "I certainly didn't tell them to kidnap or brand you. I'm very sorry it happened, however, as you were doing me a favor at the time."

"Most sympathetic human beings would feel a bit guilty about that," Simon explained to him, rolling his eyes.

"Would they?" Sir Barnabas said, mere curiosity in his tone. "How utterly foolish of them. Although I do find guilt a great motivator in my line of work."

"I'm sure you do." Sir Barnabas was in charge of a shadowy department at the Home Office, although the favor that Simon had been doing for him had been personal. "How is Mrs. Jones?" he asked, using the pseudonym Barnabas had given to his lover when she came to work for him as his housekeeper and was trying to keep her identity a secret. She insisted on continuing to use the name for reasons known only to her, and Barnabas supposedly. Simon squirmed a bit, trying to get more comfortable. His back was hurting like the devil tonight after that carriage ride from the quay.

"Brilliant, of course," Sir Barnabas said with satisfaction. "She refuses to marry, naturally, either myself or Lord Wetherald. Considering her last husband was a treasonous abuser and whoremonger, I can't blame her. We are content with our present arrangement."

Simon was surprised Sir Barnabas had revealed so much personal information, and it must have shown on his face. "As you said," Barnabas told him, "you were kidnapped doing us a considerable favor in an effort to bring about the capture and ruin of her late, unlamented husband. If nothing else, I felt you deserved to know the results of your efforts."

"Ah, yes. Daniel told me that Lord Wetherald killed him. That must have hurt. I'm sure you wanted the satisfaction."

"Trust me, satisfaction was achieved." The smile Sir Barnabas sent his way made it clear the double entendre was intentional. "What are you going to do now?"

"Now?" Simon asked in confusion. "As in, right now? This moment? Sleep, I should think. The passage over was rough; my back is aching; Daniel, as you know, talks far too much, and he got shot again, so I haven't gotten much sleep since I was *rescued.*" He put undue emphasis on the last word.

"Yes, I heard about that," Sir Barnabas said. This time Simon was quite sure it was a smirk and not a smile. "Harry is good in a fight, but he never did that sort of thing in the war."

"No, thank God," Simon said, "or we'd all be dead and it'd be King Boney of England, wouldn't it?" Sir Barnabas actually laughed. "Daniel had to spend more time rescuing Harry than rescuing me. Although Harry did dispatch his fair share of pirates, I'll give him that. But he's a battering ram when a lock pick would have been more efficient."

"Did you really blow up Menard's compound?" Sir Barnabas asked. "Professional curiosity. I would be greatly obliged not to have to waste manpower on that particular threat anymore."

"Consider your manpower saved," Simon said, waving his hand negligently. "I blew the powder kegs meant for the mines. Menard and most of his minions are dead."

"Well done," Sir Barnabas said, and Simon got that same thrill he used to get during the war when his superior praised him. He silently scolded himself for being a ninny. He didn't work for Sir Barnabas now.

There was a loud knocking at the door and a flurry of activity as it was thrown wide. Several men Simon hadn't noticed before materialized out of the shadows in the hallway, but Sir Barnabas waved them back as Mrs. Veronica Tarrant came bursting into Simon's apartment.

"You're back!" she exclaimed as she flew across the room. Right before she threw her arms around him he saw a trail of people following her through the door. "We thought we'd never see you again!" she exclaimed tearfully. Everything Very said seemed to end in an exclamation point.

"Simon, old man," her husband, Wolf, said, offering his hand in greeting. Simon had to reach around Very to shake it since she wasn't letting go. Simon and Wolf had worked together during the war, both of them spies in Sir Barnabas's network.

"Sir Barnabas," Wolf said coolly, turning to the other man who was already at the door, hat and gloves in hand. Wolf had never forgiven Sir Barnabas for the things he'd done under Barnabas's orders during the war. Sir Barnabas accepted his resentment with the stoicism peculiar to command, as if it was a requirement of his position to bear the blame for his men's misdeeds.

"Ladies," Sir Barnabas said, bowing his head respectfully. "Mrs. Tarrant."

The jibe made Very pull away from Simon with a frown. She grabbed Wolf's arm before he could say anything. "Sir Barnabas, you really must stop trying to bait my husband," she scolded him. "It is good to see you, too. Give Mrs. Jones and Lord Wetherald my love."

She grinned at him. Very was a tall, robust woman, with dark hair and rosy cheeks and the combative temperament of a Valkyrie. Unlike her husband, she had come to terms with Sir Barnabas and his past. Simon had often thought that if she and Sir Barnabas had met in another time and place, they would have ruled the world together.

Sir Barnabas just crooked his lip and raised a brow at her public reminder of his very personal, unconventional romantic entanglements.

"Indeed," he said. "Good afternoon." He bowed his head again, and like a shadow fleeing the sun was gone in a breath.

CHAPTER 3

"What did he look like?" Mrs. Christy Manderley asked, leaning forward in her chair and pinning her dear friend Daniel with a sharp look. She could feel a frown creasing her forehead and didn't care. "Was he gaunt? Pale as death? Bruised? Battered? Starved? Had they shorn his hair? His glorious hair?" She bit her trembling lip. She had loved Simon's hair. The feel of it in her hands as he kissed her. The color of it, like wheat after the rain.

"For God's sake, are you done?" Daniel snapped impatiently. "You know, you could have met us at the dock. We did send word of our arrival."

"No, I couldn't," she said, taking a deep breath and leaning back in the chair, pretending a calmness she was far from feeling. "It wouldn't have been seemly. And you didn't answer my question."

"Which one?" asked her ex-husband, Harry Ashbury, his voice full of amusement. "The one about his glorious hair?" She turned and glared at his smirk. "You never told me my hair was glorious when we were married."

"Because I didn't think it was glorious, then or now," Christy told him plainly, not meaning to be unkind. "Ours was never that kind of marriage."

She knew other women had always found Harry attractive, men as well, but he had always just been Harry to her. She thought him tall and gangly and awkward, and since he'd come back from America, his missing eye was difficult for her. Sometimes she still had trouble knowing where to look when she was speaking to him. Everyone thought him tall and handsome and dashing and mysterious. *What rot.* Now that she thought about it her lack of attraction to Harry should have been an indication of their unsuitability.

"And what about your current marriage?" Daniel asked sarcastically, tapping his fingers on his desk. "Not to Simon, I might add. Does Robert have glorious hair, Mrs. Manderley?"

"Yes." The fact was her husband did indeed have glorious hair. Not in the same way as Simon's, whose hair was soft as silk and blond. Robert's hair was thick and slightly coarse, a dark chestnut color that gleamed like copper when the sun hit it just right. She did like his hair on a sunny day.

"Christ," she heard Daniel mutter, and she looked back at him and blinked a couple of times to bring him into focus. He had his head on the desk and was gently bouncing it against the polished wood. "She's daydreaming about both of them."

"Oh, stop being so melodramatic," she told him with a dismissive sniff. "You should have pursued a career on the stage." She knew Daniel quite well now, after spending months in his company in Scotland waiting out the divorce with him and Harry. What an odd little family they'd made together.

Harry choked with laughter. "Spying is somewhat similar, my dear," he said.

"You are not amusing," Daniel told Harry, but Christy could hear the affection in his voice.

She wasn't sorry she'd divorced Harry so he could be with Daniel and she could marry Robert. She and Harry had married so young, and been so ill suited. Their Scottish divorce had hardly raised a brow in London since Harry had deserted her the day after their wedding and when he returned ten years later she was seven months pregnant.

Everyone assumed the child was Robert's since they'd married immediately after the divorce was final, but of course little Christian was not Robert's. He was the son of a lowly coachman whom Harry had paid well to move to America and keep his mouth shut. Really, Harry was the best friend Christy had ever had, or ever would have, Robert included.

It was really too bad that she'd had the misfortune to meet and fall in love with Simon at the same time she'd met and fallen in love with Robert. Life was really terribly unfair, wasn't it? Ten years alone without a single gentleman of distinction anywhere, and as soon as she got pregnant from a misalliance— a very disagreeable lapse in judgment—two perfectly wonderful gentlemen appear. Really, how was she supposed to fall in love with just one? It was probably just as well that Simon hadn't wanted her. It made the choosing that much easier.

Robert had seen her tendre for Simon before he'd asked Christy to marry him. She had put that aside as any woman with a conscience would have done upon marriage. Robert had never asked her about it nor indicated in any way that he did not trust her or suspected she still had feelings for Simon. She would not betray his trust in such a fashion. But surely asking about Simon's well-being after such an adventure as he'd recently survived was not a betrayal of trust?

"Christy, stop worrying about Simon," Daniel told her. He rose from his seat and limped over to gingerly lower himself into the chair beside her. He'd gone and got himself shot while rescuing Simon. It was a good thing he hadn't been too injured to get Simon away from those awful pirates. "He was a little weak and a little worse for wear, but he will recover," he assured her.

"What does that mean, worse for wear?" she asked. She didn't even try to temper the shrillness creeping into her voice. "What is worse and who was wearing it?"

Harry smiled at her and she calmed a bit. He always played straight with her, as he put it. In other words, he told her the truth and didn't treat her like a simpleton or a child, as most men did. It was true men tended to treat women with a certain level of disdain, but Christy was frequently subject to a higher degree of it. She assumed it was her appearance. She was petite, with piles of black hair and big blue eyes, and her rosy cheeks stood out against her white skin. She looked like a caricature of a china doll. It was quite vexing. She hated it. She fervently wished she looked like an Amazon, like Mrs. Tarrant. No one treated Veronica Tarrant like a simpleton. If they did, she knocked them silly, Christy was sure.

"I just meant that he was tired, a little bruised, thinner, yes, but not starving," Harry explained. "And as far as I could tell, every hair was still on his head." He glanced over at Daniel, and in that glance Christy could see that he wasn't telling her something.

"What?" she asked, reaching out and gripping Daniel's arm. "What aren't you telling me?" She shook his arm. "Tell me. Tell me right now."

"They branded his back." Daniel sat back in his chair with a sigh. "A big awful slash of a brand down and across his back." He slashed his hand in the air to demonstrate, and Christy's gaze fixed on his hand hanging in the air. Curiously, the longer she stared, black crept in around his hand, surrounding it until the sight of it winked out completely.

"Christy? Christy, are you all right? Can you hear me? Damn it, Daniel, did you have to tell her like that? You know how sensitive she is." Harry's voice seemed to be coming from far away.

"Sensitive? Christy?" She heard Daniel snort in disbelief.

"There was a time I might have believed that corker, but I've lived with the woman. She's as sensitive as I am, which is to say, not at all."

She felt something press against her lips.

"Here, drink this. Whiskey usually does the trick."

"I never faint," Christy insisted, hating how weak her voice sounded. She shoved ineffectually at the glass pressing against her lips, mumbling her words. "You are forever trying to pour spirits down my throat," she protested. She took a sip just to get him to leave her alone.

"Well, this is the second time you've fainted in my drawing room, not that I'm counting," Daniel corrected her. "And if you'd stop fainting on my carpet I wouldn't waste my good whiskey on you."

She looked up at him dubiously as Harry helped her back up into her chair. Daniel was finishing the whiskey in one swallow.

"I think you pour the whiskey for yourself and use me as an excuse." Christy patted her hair into place and curled her hand into a fist when her stupid fingers wouldn't stop trembling.

"Guilty as charged," Daniel said unrepentantly.

Christy would love to be that blasé about her own transgressions, but the world was not weighted equally when it came to the trespasses of men and women. She ought to know. Her mother-in-law still hadn't spoken a single word to her in almost eight months of marriage, and refused to acknowledge Christian's existence even though dear Robert had given him the Manderley name. There would be no forgiveness from that quarter.

She pushed aside those useless thoughts and forced herself to confront the ugly news that had upset her so a moment ago. Really, she was being ridiculous. She hadn't even gotten queasy at childbirth. The only other time she'd fainted was when she'd nearly been kidnapped by would-be assassins, and honestly it was more likely that not eating that day had caused her temporary lack of control rather than fright. Her nature was far too practical for fainting.

Not that her husband knew that.

Poor Robert had rescued her from her kidnappers that night almost a year ago, and to him she was still the delicate flower who fainted in fright. She simply hadn't been able to bring herself to correct his first impression. That was the woman he'd asked to marry him, and if that was the woman he wanted, then that was the woman he deserved, no matter how irritating she found the role she was forced to play. Robert was the dearest, sweetest, most wonderful man on earth, who had offered for her hand at a time when she was desperate. How could she disappoint him by showing her true colors?

"How bad is the...the brand?" she asked, her voice only squeaking a little on the last word. She blinked away the spots in front of her eyes. She would have to remember that Simon seemed to be her weakness. It wouldn't do to show that in front of Robert.

"Bearable," Harry said quickly, grabbing the glass from Daniel's hand and frowning at him when he saw it was empty. He shoved it back at Daniel, who just shrugged.

"You are both being very tiresome," Christy snapped, pushing Harry's hands away as he ostensibly tried to comfort her, or hold her steady or some such nonsense. "If you'd just tell me what was going on instead of prevaricating, perhaps I wouldn't think the worst and act accordingly!"

"I see," Daniel drawled, pouring himself another whiskey. "Somehow, in typical female fashion, this is our fault."

"Don't 'typical female fashion' me," Christy said, narrowing her eyes at him. "This *is* your fault." She slashed her hand through the air. "You were trying to assault my sensibilities with those theatrics and you know it. Now stop it."

"Motherhood has made you shrill," Daniel said. He flipped

his coattails out masterfully before sitting down behind his desk.

"Don't be a fishwife," she snapped back. She turned to Harry, who was laughing at them, as usual. "Now, how bad is it? You told me you'd deal it plain, didn't you?"

"I did," he said, clearing his throat. "I'm sorry. It isn't pretty. But it's healing, which is good. The ship's doctor had a salve that worked wonders. Says he uses it for the men who are served the lash." Christy shuddered. "But he's still very tender, and from what I know of burns it will be a constant reminder of his ordeal."

"That's terrible," Christy whispered, her eyes filling with tears. "Poor Simon." She pounded her fist against her thigh. "I wish Sir Barnabas James to Hades! Why did he have to get Simon involved in his personal vendettas?"

"Don't blame Barnabas," Daniel said with a sigh. "Simon was looking for trouble, and he would have found it somewhere with or without Barnabas's help. I was actually relieved when I found out he was doing something for Barnabas. That usually means a fair bit of backup."

He ran his hand through his hair, an uncharacteristically frustrated gesture for Daniel. "Christ, it's hot. I wish I'd known what the two of them were about. I could have solved the whole problem without any of this mess."

"Or not," Harry said. "You don't know that. It could have been you we were rescuing. What's done is done. And no one is to blame. Understood?" He looked between Christy and Daniel. "Understood?" he asked again when neither one answered.

"Understood," Christy muttered.

"I don't have to answer to you," Daniel said mulishly. "Are you going to go see him?" he asked Christy, changing the subject.

"Oh," she said, startled. "Oh, no, I shouldn't. No." She shook her head vigorously. "I don't think he'd like that. Do you? No.

That wouldn't be a good idea." She paused. "Should I? No. Really? Why?"

"I think he'd like to see you," Harry said. "I'm not sure it's a good idea either, but I do think he'd like to see you."

"Why?" she asked again, worrying her bottom lip. She'd bitten the poor thing into a sorry state of affairs the last few weeks. "I mean, why isn't it a good idea?"

"Are you truly asking that question?" Daniel asked incredulously. "Let's see. One, you're married to Robert." He ticked the item off on one finger. "Two, you're married to Robert." He ticked off another finger. "Any way you look at it, that seems to be the main issue here."

"I'm surprised you feel that strongly about my marriage," she said, genuinely taken aback at his vehemence. "I mean, you have so many friends who are...who are..." She searched for a polite way to put it.

"Engaged in illicit liaisons with persons who are not their spouse? Engaging in them with their spouse? Wait," Harry said, holding up his hand, "engaged, in the company of their spouse, in illicit liaisons with persons who are not their spouse. There," he offered helpfully, dropping his hand. "I think that's it."

"In love with more than one person was what I was going to say," Christy corrected, blushing.

"Yes, well, we are not in Rome," Daniel said sternly. "We are English, after all."

"That makes no sense at all," Christy said impatiently. "What have the Italians got to do with it? I don't even know any. And you and Harry are lovers, and heaven knows that sort of thing isn't English at all."

"It is far more English than most Englishmen admit," Harry said with a chuckle.

Daniel tried to steer the conversation back. "Do not go see Simon. That was the point I was trying to make."

"Well then, say what you mean," Christy told him, exasperated. She slumped in her chair. "And I won't. I said I wasn't, didn't I? That's why I'm here, not that you two are being very helpful."

"Where *is* Robert?" Daniel asked. Christy could tell he meant why wasn't Robert keeping an eye on her. She ground her teeth together. Daniel was worse than the old squire's wife back home.

"He's working, of course. He's been gone almost all the time for the last several weeks. A difficult case, he says. He assures me it isn't dangerous, but I know it is. He's a constable, after all." She clasped her hands with a sigh. "I really didn't think how hard it would be to be the wife of constable. It is worrisome, isn't it?"

"I'm sure he's fine, Christy," Daniel told her, concern in his voice. She sat up straight as she smiled at him. They might bicker like family, but he cared about her, too, and it warmed her heart. He and Robert had been friends since they were children growing up together. He worried as much as she did.

"Of course you're right," she told him brightly, hiding her concern. Between Robert's mysterious case and Simon's kidnapping and Christian's teething, Christy hadn't had a decent night's sleep in weeks.

"Stay for supper," Harry told her.

"Yes, stay." Daniel tried to cross his legs and winced.

"Oh, Daniel," she said with a little tsk. "Do remember you got shot."

"Yes, Daniel," Harry said, "do remember."

"There is a distinct lack of sympathy in this room," Daniel grumbled.

"Well, Harry already lost an eye," Christy said prosaically. "What's a little shot to the leg?" Daniel's problems seemed so simple.

"Madam," he said, raising his refilled glass of whiskey, "I couldn't have said it better myself."

CHAPTER 4

"Manderley! What's the problem here?"

Robert sighed and took a moment to compose his features. He wiped his forehead before turning around to face the senior constable at the scene.

"Nothing is amiss, sir," he responded with a polite nod of his head in greeting and a slim smile. Always polite, that was him. Nary a word of complaint or rebuke from Robert Manderley, no sir. He was a man's man, a good sort who'd do the work his superiors were incapable of doing.

He sighed. The hot weather had them all on edge. He tucked his handkerchief away.

"Take care of that, eh?" Mr. Clythehorn turned away with a dismissive hand and Robert instinctively responded with a, "Yes, sir."

Now what the bloody hell had he agreed to? He really needed to pay more attention. Christy was rubbing off on him.

At the thought of his sweet wife, he smiled to himself. Christy was always lost in her daydreams it seemed. It was a wonder she remembered what day of the week it was and where she'd put the baby.

He looked back at his assistant, Thom Longfellow. Thom just nodded at him with a wink. Good, Thom had it under control. Good man, Thom.

Robert returned his attention to the body on the ground. This one made ten. Ten young pickpockets, scruffy lads of the streets with their throats slit, left to bleed out in back alleys where they wouldn't be found until the stench gave them away, and the rats and the elements had made it impossible to identify them. This one was the exception. This boy had only been dead perhaps a day, maybe two at the most. The hot temperatures did not mix well with dead bodies, however, and while still identifiable, the stench was almost unbearable.

The murders weren't crimes of passion. There were no signs of struggle, no evidence of a sexual nature to indicate the boys had been violated either before or after death. There was nothing.

Robert narrowed his eyes and stared harder at the surrounding area, willing some evidence to appear and point to their killer. What madness was afoot in the stews of London? Not madness, he suspected, but foul play. This case had the sense of executions more than murders of circumstance.

He sighed. Whatever the solution was, they'd best find it and quick. They couldn't keep the murders from the public for much longer. He was surprised that no one had put two and two together so far, but the sad fact was the murder of boys like these was merely a passing footnote in the brutal history of these streets.

God! It was at times like this that he longed to be at home, at his wife's side with Christian on his knee, the baby's laughter bringing a smile to Christy's face and peace to Robert's world.

But it was not to be. None other than Sir Robert Peel of the Home Office was breathing down their necks to solve this case before he found himself before the Parliament answering uncomfortable questions. This was the sort of thing that led to unrest and riots and gave the government a bad taste in its mouth. The memory of the riots surrounding Queen Caroline's death just a few years prior were still fresh in the memories of many in the government. Sir Robert Peel had been appointed to avoid more of the same. It wasn't concern for the young lives cut short that motivated them, but the fear of political careers cut short.

Robert whipped his hat off his head and thumped it against his thigh in frustration. His growing dissatisfaction and jaded opinions about his superiors wasn't going to help solve this case, or his career.

"Stumped again, eh, sir?" Thom asked. "Tsk. We gots our work cut out for us, sir, we have." He crouched down and tipped his head to the side, observing the body. "This one's laid out different than the last two. You notice that?"

"I had not," Robert said, shaking his head in disgust at himself. "I should have. Good eye, Thom."

He walked over and crouched down beside Thom, observing the body as Thom was. His assistant should rightly be the chief constable on the case. He had the most experience and was an excellent policeman, skilled in detecting the sort of information many less experienced men missed. But Thom was uneducated and ill spoken. He'd grown up on the wrong side of the law, and the law never let him forget it. He was still considered by many of Robert's compatriots as nothing more than a lackey and informant. Robert had pegged him as more immediately and enlisted his aid as his assistant. Robert had initially taken a great deal of gruff from some of the other constables about it, but he'd silenced them with his exemplary case completion rate and meteoric rise in the department. He knew he had Thom to thank for that, and he made sure to compensate Thom appropriately.

Unfortunately, their partnership had garnered unwelcome attention lately, and some of the other constables had been complaining to his superiors about it. Several had tried to lure Thom away with higher compensation or other bribes. So far Thom had remained loyal.

"See? He's got one hand behind his back. Awkward like." Thom demonstrated, twisting his arm behind him.

"Perhaps he fell that way," Robert suggested, tilting his head as he imagined the boy falling down, his throat slit, losing control of this body and his limbs.

"Nah," Thom disagreed. "Yer fall like that, yer arms are out to yer side, just swinging in the breeze like, right?" He demonstrated again. He walked over and gently lifted the boy's head. "Head's not smashed in, neither. He fell like that, smash his head, wouldn't he?"

"The others didn't smash their heads, either," Robert pointed out. "I don't think any of them fell. I think they were placed."

"Placed, that's the right word," Thom agreed. "Like they passed out drunk and they friends set 'em up so's they wouldn't puke themselves, right?"

"Yes, exactly," Robert mused. "But this boy is on his back. Not sitting up in a doorway. I had noticed there was no doorway."

"Well, there is," Thom said, pointing. "Right over there. Almost as if they couldn't get to it. Maybe interrupted by something, or someone? Dumped the body sooner than they liked, maybe?"

"Maybe," Robert said. "But what is the significance of the arm behind his back?"

"I think he was rolled over," Thom said. "Like he was on his stomach first. Come 'ere." He gingerly pressed on the boy's chin, turning his face. "Look at his cheek. That's, what'd you call it, post-mortem. No bruising. Just scraping dead skin."

Robert looked. "Right again, Thom. Perhaps I should just go home to Christy and let you solve this one." He smiled ruefully and Thom chuckled.

"Now, they wouldn't be letting me do that, would they?" he asked. "I get to do a sight more investigating with you than I ever would with them. And when you're on the mark you gets the job done right, you do." He patted Robert's shoulder. "New married. That messes up a man's thinkin', don't it?"

"Why did they roll him over?" Robert wondered. "Here, help me."

As gently as they could, he and Thom rolled the boy's body over. Robert caught and examined the hand that had been under the boy. It was dirty, of course, but also blood-stained. The cuffs of his thin jacket were stiff with dried blood.

"Did they slit his wrist as well?" he asked incredulously. He pulled on the stiff material, getting it out of the way so he could see the damage that had caused the bleeding.

"No, sir," Thom said. "They tied him up." A quick check showed the other wrist was in the same condition, rubbed raw by rope burns.

"None of the others were tied up," Robert said grimly. "Either our murderer is running out of willing victims, or these boys are getting wise to his tricks."

"Either way," Thoms said, standing and dusting off his hands, "I don't think this is the last of 'em."

Robert very much feared Thom was right. Knowing the circumstances of the boy's death didn't get them any closer to the murderer. Perhaps it was time to ask an old friend for help.

"ROBERT! COME IN." Daniel stood up behind his desk as Robert crossed the room and then shook his extended hand.

"Daniel. How are you?"

"Fine, fine," Daniel said. Robert's suspicions were raised immediately. One fine was usually above board. Two meant something fishy was going on. He sighed.

"Did I just miss her?" he asked in resignation as he sat down in the chair Daniel indicated with a wave of his hand.

Daniel hesitated as he sat. Just for a moment. Most people would have missed it. His face gave nothing away. "Who?" he asked.

"Christy," Robert said. "I don't know why you all feel as if you need to conceal her visits from me. I know she comes here, and I don't mind. Really, I don't."

"Well, we did just return from Africa," Daniel said. Robert's head jerked up at that news and Daniel closed his mouth, cutting off his next remark. "You did know we were in Africa, correct?"

"I forgot." Robert could feel his cheeks warming with embarrassment at the lie.

As if he could forget that Simon Gantry had been taken prisoner and held captive in Africa. Hardly a day had gone by that he hadn't caught Christy crying about him. And the truth was that even though Gantry had been his rival for Christy's affections—and still was—Robert had worried about him every day as well. But he had honestly forgotten that they'd only just returned the day before and that Daniel might not be up to helping him at present.

"Good God, Daniel, I'm so sorry. What an imbecile I am." He stood up. "You must be exhausted from your journey. I've no right to impose right now. You must excuse me."

"Sit down. Now you really are being an imbecile." Daniel shook his head. "Honestly. I was about to say it was only that Christy wanted to stop by and welcome us home and check on our well-being. She was not here for nefarious purposes." Which meant, of course, that she was there for nefarious purposes.

"Is Gantry here?" Robert asked as he took his seat again, trying to keep his voice neutral, yet concerned for Gantry's welfare. Which he was, naturally. He didn't wish the man ill.

Not necessarily. Certainly not kidnapped by Barbary pirates and sold into slavery ill. A nasty cold, perhaps. A setback on the exchange would be nice. Perhaps a bit of balding. That sort of thing.

Daniel began to drum his fingers on his desk. "No. He went directly to his apartments."

"So he survived the ordeal in good shape then?" Robert asked, more relieved than he liked to admit. Because yes, damn it, he had wished the man ill many, many times over the last year. Guilt had weighed heavy on him while Gantry had been a captive.

"As good a shape as you'd expect," Daniel said. "Good enough to go home and spurn my offer of hospitality."

"I dare say he'll show up for breakfast," Robert said wryly. "He usually does."

"Perhaps," was all Daniel said. "If you aren't here to welcome us home, why did you come?"

"I came to ask a favor, but honestly, it's too soon," Robert said. "I can handle this on my own."

"Does it have anything to do with this difficult case Christy mentioned?" Daniel asked, not looking at Robert as he fiddled with a small tray of pen nibs on his desk.

"What did she tell you?" Robert was surprised she'd mentioned it.

"Just that you'd been working long hours because you were on a difficult case," Daniel said with a shrug. "That's all I know." He drummed his fingers on his desk again. "I wouldn't mind helping," he offered nonchalantly.

"Helping with what?" Harry asked as he came into the room. "Evening, Manderley."

Robert stood. "Good evening, Ashbury," he said. Most people would be surprised how well he got along with Christy's ex-husband. The truth was, Harry and Christy really only lived as man and wife for less than twenty-four hours. For ten years of their marriage they'd lived on separate continents. It would be foolish to be jealous of him. And since his predilections had led him into Daniel's arms, even more so. Harry Ashbury had never been a serious contender for Christy's affections and they all knew it. Not like Simon Gantry.

"What was it that Daniel was offering to help you with?" Harry asked.

"Nothing," Daniel said quickly before Robert could answer. "Nothing at all."

"Well, it was something," Harry said, amusement in his voice. "I clearly heard you offer to help. You don't do that often. I can think of three things you'd make that offer for: Christy and the baby, something to do with haberdashery, or someone needs killing. So, which is it? Since Christy was just here and didn't mention anything, I wouldn't try to use that one."

"Well, no one needs killing," Robert assured him. "As a matter of fact, I'm trying to stop another murder, not cause one."

"Not haberdashery then," Harry said. "This sounds equally intriguing. Go on." Just then Daniel got up and Robert watched him limp around his desk.

"What happened to you?" he asked, frowning.

"I was shot," Daniel said with a sigh. "Thank you for noticing."

"How did you get shot?" Robert was shocked.

"Well, they were pirates, Robert," Daniel explained. "They tend to do that sort of thing when you try to steal their property."

"I...I hadn't thought about that," Robert admitted sheepishly. "I just assumed you'd negotiate with them for Gantry's release."

At his comment, Harry laughed. "Daniel does not negotiate," he said, still chuckling. "He lets violence dictate his terms."

"It wasn't I who blew up the compound," Daniel said. He sounded a bit put out to Robert. "That was Simon."

"I daresay he was a tad upset with his captors over his less than stellar accommodations," Harry said. His words alarmed Robert. What had happened to Simon in captivity? "And I can't help but think he's working for Sir Barnabas again. That's the sort of thing I'd expect from an agent. Menard won't be a problem along the Barbary Coast anymore."

"Gantry works for Sir Barnabas James?" Robert asked, confused. He'd had no idea Gantry was a spy. Was there nothing the man couldn't do? Handsome, suave, well-dressed, lethal? And irritating. Excessively irritating.

"No. Or yes. Who knows? Neither one of them tells me anything," Daniel said with irritation as he gingerly lowered himself into a chair. "Now tell me what you need my help with."

"I'm not sure I like that look in your eye," Harry said. "Please try to remember you are injured." Daniel pretended he didn't hear him.

"It's this damn case," Robert said, letting his frustration show as he slumped in his chair. "It has me at a standstill. A brick wall, if you will. Ten boys murdered in the last three weeks. Pickpockets, street urchins, youngest about thirteen oldest eighteen at least."

"My God," Harry said, shocked. "We've heard nothing."

"We've been out of the country," Daniel reminded him.

"No, you'd have heard nothing anyway," Robert told him. "Boys like that are a dime a dozen. No one pays attention. But pretty soon someone is going to put two and two together and the press will come sniffing around and we'll have a full-blown panic on our hands."

"Superiors breathing down your neck, are they?" Daniel said with a wry chuckle. "All right. Let's go through the facts. Tell me how, where, when."

"Throats slit, and their bodies moved and left propped up in doorways in back alleys all over the east end. We haven't found the murder sites yet. But the dates and locations of the body drops seem random. The victims were left sitting in such a way that it's only the stench that gave them away eventually. No defensive marks at all. Until today. Today's was different."

"How?" Harry was leaning forward in his chair, as interested as Daniel.

"He wasn't in a doorway, for one. Just dumped in the alley as if the killer was in a hurry. Thom Longfellow thinks they were interrupted or surprised and so dropped the body."

"Still working with Mr. Longfellow?" Daniel asked, nodding absentmindedly. "Good, good. Good man. What else?"

"His wrists were abraded, from a rope we believe. He was tied up before he died. None of the others were. Not a mark on them except for the killing blow. But this boy clearly struggled and was subdued prior to his murder."

Daniel's eyes met his. "That's not good."

"No," Robert agreed. "That's not good at all."

"I don't think I'm the man you should be asking for help," Daniel said, surprising Robert and, from the look on his face, Harry. "Come on. Let's go see Sir Barnabas."

CHAPTER 5

"I've already been to see Simon," Sir Barnabas said without looking up from the papers on his desk. "Don't ring a peal over my head about it. He's fine." He looked up and blinked twice, and Robert got the impression it was an uncharacteristic reveal of surprise.

"Constable Manderley," Sir Barnabas said politely. His gaze cut to his secretary standing nervously behind them. "What a surprise."

Even Robert, who didn't know Sir Barnabas well, could tell the innocuous remark was meant as a severe set down for the secretary rather than any sort of greeting for him.

"I'm sorry, sir," his secretary said, his voice smoothly modulated. He'd been trained well. Robert would have been shaking in his boots over that look. "He wasn't on the list, and since he was accompanying Mr. Steinberg, I assumed he was permitted."

"Never assume," Sir Barnabas said, smiling at Robert. Because of the smile it took a moment for his words to register. Robert stiffened his spine.

"I do beg your pardon," he said, proud of his cool but polite tone. "If I am interrupting I will make an appointment and come back another time."

"Don't be rude, Barnabas," Daniel snapped. "I daresay it is not overly dramatic to say someone's life depends on it. The constable needs to have a word with you, please."

Sir Barnabas assessed Robert for a moment, then he relaxed back in his chair with a sigh and threw his pen down on his desk. "Fine. Let's get this over with. I won't get a moment's peace if I don't. What happened to you?" He turned his razor-sharp gaze on Daniel and barked out the question like it was an order.

"I got shot. If you've been to see Simon, then I assume you already know this and chose not to come see about my welfare." He held up his hand and stopped Sir Barnabas's denial before he could say a word. "Don't bother to deny it."

"I wasn't going to," Sir Barnabas said. "People love to regale one with their tales of woe when it comes to physical injuries. I thought I was being polite by asking. You have now rendered the niceties of polite discourse unnecessary. My thanks. What do you want?" he asked Robert, turning his predator's eyes upon him with the speed and accuracy of a hungry hawk.

"Me? Oh, yes. Well, I am working on a case, you see," Robert said, trying to gather his thoughts. He'd heard that Sir Barnabas James could scramble a man's wits with a look and hadn't believed it until this moment, but then he'd never been the recipient of one of his infamous looks before. He'd avoided these particular hallowed halls at the Home Office. "Boys. Murdered boys, that is. In the East End."

"Working a case? As a constable? How unusual," Sir Barnabas said sarcastically. "Let me put all the nation's business here aside while I listen to the fascinating details of your case." With each word Robert's temper flared hotter.

"You, sir, are even more intolerable than Daniel led me to believe," he said stiffly, standing up and putting on his hat. "It is apparent you have no desire to help a lowly constable such as myself solve the murders of poor, unimportant boys from the streets when you could be saving the empire and gaining favor. Don't let me keep you from the nation's business. I shall go about mine. Good afternoon, sir."

He turned to leave, unsettled by his uncharacteristic show of anger. He had only taken one step when he was halted by the sound of a slow clap behind him.

"Bravo," Sir Barnabas drawled. "Damn me if you don't sound just like Wetherald. Really, Daniel, I get speeches at home from Ambrose that always embroil me somehow in trying to save the world. Now you're bringing it to my office as well? Is this a conspiracy against me? Doesn't one of your doltish friends need rescuing? That's at least entertaining more often than not."

"You are in fine form today," Daniel told him. "Much more churlish than usual. Any particular reason you'd like to share?"

"Hastings," Sir Barnabas said. "Again. Always Hastings. The man is a thorn in my side."

"Fire him," Daniel told him. "Problem solved. Now help Robert."

"You know I can't fire him," Sir Barnabas said impatiently. "I've invested a great deal of time and effort in training him. He is privy to state secrets. To *my* secrets."

"Kill him," Daniel said dispassionately.

"Daniel," Robert protested, taking his hat off and going back to sit down. "You can't just kill a man."

"Why not?" Daniel asked. Robert was quite concerned at the genuine look of puzzlement on his face.

"I take the blame for that," Sir Barnabas said, and Robert looked over to see a flash of regret on his face as he watched Daniel.

"Now who's being melodramatic?" Daniel asked. "I like Hastings, by the way, so I won't do it."

"You don't work for me anymore," Sir Barnabas reminded him.

"No, I don't. Does Simon?"

The question seemed to take Sir Barnabas aback. "No," he answered, and Robert believed he was being truthful. "Why?"

"He blew up the compound, Barnabas," Daniel said wryly. "We could have slipped out unnoticed, but he decided he needed to blow up the damn compound and free everyone."

"Don't look at me," Sir Barnabas said defensively. "I'm not the one with a bloody conscience. Look to those bleeding hearts you surround yourself with. Or yourself, who took it upon himself to be the avenging angel of St. Giles, with Simon your ever-faithful hound, following in your footsteps? You of all people shouldn't have been surprised by his act of martyrdom."

"Martyrdom my arse," Daniel grumbled. "I'm the one who got shot for it."

"You're getting slow in your old age," Sir Barnabas said sadly. "It was bound to happen."

"Wait. You're the Angel of St. Giles?" Robert asked, confounded. At his question both Daniel and Sir Barnabas snapped their mouths shut, and it was quite obvious nothing short of an act of Parliament would get an answer out of them. He didn't need one, however, since their silence spoke as loudly as any words could.

The Angel was a shadowy figure that had haunted the streets of St. Giles for several years, ruthlessly meting out justice when the law was unable or unwilling to do so. The constabulary had been unable to discover his identity and the criminal class had been unable to stop him. Robert was flabbergasted to discover it had been Daniel. And apparently Simon, of course. Add avenging angel to his list of accomplishments.

He did not wish to discuss Simon's heroics again. Was there ever a man as perfect as Simon Gantry? As handsome and heroic and irresistible?

"What exactly did Hastings do?" he asked, bringing the conversation back around.

"Disobeyed an order," Sir Barnabas said. "He killed a man he was supposed to bring in alive. I needed to question him. He had valuable information. Hastings has a nasty habit of killing first and asking questions second."

"I...don't think that's possible," Robert said, frowning.

"What an excellent constable you must be," Sir Barnabas said sarcastically. Suddenly his face cleared and a smile broke that was almost as frightening as it was attractive in a predatory, feral sort of way. "Indeed, quite excellent," he said thoughtfully. "Trained in the proper methods of suspect apprehension and interrogation, I presume. You do have an impressive arrest record. A veritable young star among the city's constabulary."

"How do you know that?" Robert asked.

Sir Barnabas went on as if he hadn't spoken. "Hastings has already made contact with some informants concerning the murders," he mused. "At least seven of the boys were well-known couriers for various employers. The spy network is being slowly choked off. The last boy, however, was not a courier. He was the spy. But no one seems to know who he worked for."

"What? Spies?" Daniel said incredulously. "You knew why we were here? You're already working this case?"

"Of course," Sir Barnabas said, raising one eyebrow in a very superior look. "Don't I always? Didn't you expect me to? Isn't that why you came?"

"So are you taking my case away from me?" Robert asked, his teeth clenched in anger. It was his case. Those boys were his. No matter what Sir Barnabas said, Robert would find their killer. This spy nonsense made no difference.

"Of course not," Sir Barnabas told him. "You have been first on the scene at all the murders. You and Mr. Longfellow have gathered all the evidence. You have detected patterns. No. What

I am proposing is a partnership. I shall send Hastings to you, and you shall work together."

"Oh, Barnabas," Daniel said, trepidation in his voice. "I don't think that's a very good idea."

"Will he have information that can help me solve these murders and prevent more deaths?" Robert asked Sir Barnabas.

"Yes."

"Then send him to me tomorrow morning," Robert said, ignoring Daniel's warning.

"With pleasure."

Sir Barnabas's smile reminded Robert of a snake. He just hoped this decision didn't come back to bite him before they were done.

CHAPTER 6

"You want me to what?" Simon asked, rubbing his eyes. "What time is it?"

He'd only just gotten out of bed and wasn't sure he'd heard Daniel correctly. They were standing in the middle of his apartment and Daniel was, as usual, dressed quite smartly. Simon wasn't even sure if it was morning or night. He was still in his nightshirt, his dressing gown barely tied and hanging open. He didn't care how disheveled he looked. It was only Daniel and Harry, after all.

"It is eight o'clock in the evening. You have been sleeping for almost two days. I want you to go to Robert's tomorrow and help him and Hastings solve this murder case he's working on," Daniel told him. "Aren't you going to offer me a seat? My leg is throbbing."

"Since when have I had to offer you a seat?" Simon asked, completely confused. "Don't you usually just take one? Look at Harry." He pointed at the other man who had made himself at home on Simon's sofa. "Has the world gone mad?" He spun around in a slow circle. "Am I even home from Africa or is this a fever dream?"

"No fever dream," Harry said. "Have you got a fever?" He stood up. "Come here, then." He walked over and put his hand on Simon's forehead, and Simon swatted it away.

"No, Nana, I'm fine," he said. "And no, I will not go and offer to help Manderley solve some murder with that bedlamite Hastings. Are you drunk?" He sniffed Daniel's breath, and this time it was Daniel who swatted him away.

"No, I am not drunk, unfortunately," Daniel said. "Let me start at the beginning. I don't think you were awake enough to understand that part when I arrived."

"I don't even have a recollection of any beginning," Simon said with a yawn. He wandered over to the sideboard and poured himself a cup of tepid tea. It would do for now. His back was aching something fierce. He supposed he ought to get used to that.

"You're limping," Harry said from beside him. "Do you need something for pain? Laudanum?"

"Absolutely not." Simon had no desire to become a slave of another sort, one to that drug. "It's just stiff when I first get up," he lied. "You know how that is." He winked and then made himself walk without limping so much and sat down in his favorite chair. It hugged him comfortably.

"Robert is working on a murder case which, it just so happens, Barnabas and his office are also working on," Daniel told him. "Ten boys murdered in the last three weeks. Couriers masquerading as pickpockets, that old ruse. Robert was unable to go any further with the case, I suggested going to Barnabas, Barnabas suggested Robert partner with Hastings, whom he had assigned the case—presumably as punishment for killing another suspect—and now I need you to go and watch over the two of them and solve the murders before Hastings gets Robert killed or worse."

"There's something worse than getting killed?" Simon asked curiously.

"I was wondering the same thing myself," Harry said.

"You are both being very obtuse," Daniel told them irritably. "Bring me an ottoman. That one there," he told Harry. "My leg is quite sore."

"Why didn't you say so?" Harry admonished him. "You've been traipsing all over London today, first to see Barnabas and now Simon. You are in no condition to be doing so much. You ought to be at home in bed."

"Where he'd be doing nothing, I'm sure," Simon remarked drily. "But clearly I'm in the pink of health and perfectly fine to be jockeying about solving murders. Right. Tell me again, which one of us was kidnapped and tortured by pirates?"

"Are you going to live on that story forever?" Daniel said. "It's already growing tedious."

"I've been asleep for two days, you say?" Simon asked. "So that story is two days old. I can see what you mean."

"You know if I were able I'd be more than happy to keep an eye on Robert and Hastings myself," Daniel told him.

It was true, Simon did know that. Daniel liked nothing more than to root out evil and extinguish it. It was absolutely his favorite hobby.

"But I can't. This leg is giving me a devil of a time. That idiot ship's doctor should never have left the bullet in. I think it's beginning to fester."

"What?" Harry said, sitting bolt upright, worry creasing his forehead. "You didn't tell me that." He stood up. "Simon, take over this nonsense with Robert and Hastings. Daniel, I'm taking you home. Simon will report any news on the case." He walked over and gently scooped Daniel up in his arms.

"What in the hell are you doing?" Daniel demanded, but he wrapped his arm around Harry's shoulders just the same. Now that Simon was paying attention, he did sound tired.

"Fine." Simon gave in with another yawn. "I will present myself to Robert tomorrow with some concocted story about why I suddenly feel the need to solve a murder. Do as Harry says and don't worry about a thing. I've got everything under control." The knot in his stomach at the thought of seeing Robert Manderley again gave lie to his assurances, but Simon made sure his outward demeanor revealed nothing of the turmoil inside him.

"You never have anything under control," Daniel said over Harry's shoulder.

"Then why did you come to me?" Simon asked, crossing his legs and taking a sip of tea as he watched Harry somehow open the door without dropping his burden.

"It seemed like a good idea at the time."

"That was your first mistake." Simon smiled as the door closed on Daniel's dismay. Then he set his teacup down and closed his eyes to get some more sleep. He'd need it if he was going to keep Manderley safe for Christy.

ROBERT GLANCED over Hastings's head at the approaching figure and then had to look again, sure his own fevered imagination had produced a waking nightmare. Unfortunately, it was harsh reality.

"Good afternoon, gentlemen," Simon Gantry said pleasantly when he reached their side, leaning on his cane. "How are you all this fine day?"

His declaration that is was a fine day was so convincing, Robert had to look around the dirty alley, made odorous and infernally hot by the unusually warm weather, just to make sure he hadn't taken leave of his senses.

"Gantry," Hastings replied, saving Robert the trouble of acknowledging him. "What are you doing here?"

Yes, thought Robert. *What are you doing here? And how did you find us?* They were lost in the bloody bowels of the East End, at the first body drop location. The sun had barely risen and most respectable gentlemen were still abed.

"I heard you two were working on a rather interesting case," Gantry said. "I thought I'd pop over and see if I could be of assistance."

"Hmm," Hastings said. "Just like that, eh? Thought you'd pop over? Sir Barnabas doesn't trust me to show up and do as I'm told then?" His words were clipped.

"I haven't talked to Sir Barnabas," Gantry said, yawning. "At least, not about this. No, I spoke with Daniel and Harry."

Robert gritted his teeth. "Did you?" They were the first words he'd been able to speak since seeing him.

"Oh yes," Gantry said, grinning. It was clear he knew exactly how irritated Robert was at his arrival. "Daniel suggested I stop by and see if I could help. As you know, I've a bit of experience with this sort of thing."

"You've only just returned from what must have been a harrowing and life-threatening situation. I appreciate the offer, of course, but you mustn't put yourself out on my account," Robert said with as much sympathy as he could muster. His emotions were rather jumbled at Gantry's appearance. Christy would be happy again, now that he was out of danger, and for that Robert was relieved. But the old jealousy wouldn't leave him alone. Yet, there was a part of him that was quite glad to see the other man, despite their past rivalry.

"No trouble at all, old man," Gantry assured him, his smile never faltering. Robert noticed it didn't reach his eyes. "Has Hastings killed any promising leads yet this morning?"

"Not yet." Robert bit back a smile at Hastings scowl.

"I am tired of being treated like a recalcitrant schoolboy," Hastings complained. "You've both been in the field. You know that situations arise in which unfortunate events occur. Death is often one of them. I much prefer when it is someone else's and not my own."

"I jest," Gantry said, slapping Hastings on the back. "I'm sure you had a valid reason for killing whoever it was. The point Barnabas is trying to make here is that as one of *his* agents, you need to be better than that. Death is not an option; it is the *last* option when he deems it so."

"Oh, really? Did someone forget to tell Mr. Steinberg that?" Hastings asked sarcastically. "His death toll is legendary."

"Yes, well, that was Daniel's specialty, wasn't it?" Gantry said with a shrug. "He was rarely told not to. Come now," he cajoled. "Helping the good constable solve a case like this surely isn't a punishment. It's well within your purview and is a good exercise of our logical abilities. So let us put our heads together and find the culprit. Yes?" He was so persuasive that Robert found himself nodding along with Hastings in answer to his question.

Robert turned away so as to hide his consternation at being reminded yet again of the lethal nature of his childhood best friend. He'd had no idea of Daniel's wartime activities nor his vigilante past time here in London the last few years. The idea of Daniel as a lethal killer shocked him. Daniel was small, trim, immaculately dressed at all times, almost fussy in his mannerisms and attire. Not the sort of man who made one think of assassins and violence.

It was easier to think of Simon in such a capacity. Robert had seen his abilities the year before when together they had chased down and apprehended one of the miscreants who had set fire to Daniel's house, trying to kill him and Harry and Christy. Simon had easily caught the man and brought him down with several well-placed blows despite being the worse for drink. The man had not landed a single blow. Then Simon had handed him over to Robert to bring in. In his current condition, Simon was perhaps not up to the task, but when in fighting form he was a good man to have at your side, it was true.

Tall, strapping—Mr. Gantry's form was the result of well-built musculature and not padded clothing. Robert had seen it that night. Simon had worn nothing but a pair of tight pants and a half-open shirt as they raced through the streets of London after the fire starter. There was a time Robert had thought Daniel and Simon involved in a sodomite relationship, as was Daniel's way. He knew now they were no more than close friends. It was Christy with whom Simon had been intimate. Christy, Robert's dear, beloved, sweet wife.

"Are you all right, Constable?" Simon asked, and Robert realized he'd been staring at him.

"Yes," Robert said.

He looked away only to find Hastings watching him closely. Hastings's face told him nothing, but Robert had the feeling the agent missed very little.

"Shall we continue?" he asked Hastings. "Mr. Gantry can catch up as we discuss what was found that day."

"Of course," Hastings said, his voice devoid of any judgment.

"Where is Mr. Longfellow?" Gantry asked, looking around.

"Here I am, Mr. Simon." Thom stepped out of a doorway with a big smile. Simon returned it, and the two shook hands like old friends.

"I say, Thom, you look well," Simon told him. "How is Lottie? And the children are well?"

"Fine as fiddles, Mr. Simon. Thank you for remembering them at Christmas. I ain't heard from you and Mr. Daniel much the last year or so. Is everything all right?"

"You two know each other?" Robert asked in disbelief.

"Oh yes," Simon said. "Thom is an old informant of ours. We recommended him highly to the department, as did Sir Barnabas. He would have made an excellent agent, but he didn't want to stray far from the fold. Too many mouths to feed, eh, Thom?"

"Isn't that right, Mr. Simon?" Thom asked with a laugh. "And Lottie with another one on the way."

"I didn't know," Robert said in dismay. "You didn't tell me. Congratulations, Thom."

"Yes, congratulations," Simon said, shaking his hand again. Thom blushed.

"Well, we don't discuss the missuses much, do we, Mr. Manderley?" Thom said. "We likes it all business."

Robert took that as a rebuke, though he was quite sure Thom hadn't meant it that way. Was he all business? Perhaps too much? He'd been so focused on proving to the world that he hadn't made the wrong decision in becoming a constable. So many had seen it as a step down socially. Some of his mother's friends had cut her and they'd stopped receiving invitations. And many within the police saw him as a dilettante playing at solving crimes and not as a dedicated officer. Robert no longer fit in either world, and so was determined to prove something to both.

"Have we seen it before, Thom?" Simon asked him, and Robert realized he meant the murders.

Thom shook his head. "No, sir. Not part of any organization we've dealt with previous. New crop of young'uns. And I don't think they's spying for the French, neither."

"Americans?" Simon asked. Robert was taken aback. He hadn't thought of the Americans.

"I doubt it," Hastings said. "They've got their own troubles brewing. Indian troubles. Always trying to grab more territory from the surrounding colonies. It's a terrible mess over there. They haven't time to build a new network here, or the care to do so."

"We'll make a list of potentials then," Simon said. Thom immediately pulled out a pencil and paper and made a note. Robert tamped down the jealousy surging in his breast. Thom was his assistant. Not Simon's. At least not anymore. Time to take back control of this investigation.

"Excellent idea, Gantry. Thank you for the suggestion," he said politely. "Good idea, Thom. Make a note of that."

Thom stopped writing and looked between Robert and Simon, wide-eyed. Hastings looked on, clearly amused.

Gantry didn't miss a beat. "Why don't you tell me how you found the body—or show me—and I can tell you if I had any similar experiences? Comparing notes is always a good starting point. Has Hastings already done the same?"

"No," Hastings said. "We hadn't gotten that far."

"Another excellent suggestion," Robert grudgingly admitted. "How long did you work for Sir Barnabas? After the war, I mean?"

"Officially?" Simon asked, following Robert as he walked toward the doorway at the end of the alley. "Not at all. But I've unofficially helped with several missions over the years. I had no desire to put myself under Barnabas's thumb again."

"Hear, hear," Hastings mumbled behind them.

"I can't figure out what your relationship is with Sir Barnabas," Robert said. "You and Daniel both seem to hate and admire him in equal measure, and the feelings seem to be mutual."

He slowed down. Simon was limping. It was very subtle. More a stiffness than an actual limp. He obviously wasn't as recovered from his adventure as he'd like people to believe. So what was he really doing here? A man would have to be insane to leave his bed half infirm to help solve a murder case that had nothing to do with him.

"Yes, a mutual admiration society," Simon said wryly. "That's our little triumvirate." He sighed. "War makes strange bedfellows, that's all."

As Robert escorted Simon and Hastings to the first body drop location, he couldn't help but think that murder made strange bedfellows as well.

CHAPTER 7

"Christy?" She startled at Robert's voice behind her. "I'm sorry," he said immediately. She quickly stood and turned to face him. "I wasn't expecting you to still be awake." He smiled and walked over to kiss the cheek she turned up to him.

"We've kept supper warm for you," she said. "I didn't want you to have to eat alone again."

"I don't mind. I hate to keep you from your bed." Robert carefully avoided her gaze and she didn't try to force him to look at her. She wished conversations between them weren't so awkward. They'd been married for months. At what point would things get easier?

"I wasn't tired," she lied. "And Christian only just went to sleep."

"I'm sorry," Robert said, and she knew he meant it. "His teeth are still bothering him?"

"Yes." She bit her lip, not sure what to say next. "Teething. Still."

"Yes." Robert checked his pocket watch. "It's late." He put his watch away. "I don't mind if you wish to go to bed."

"No." He looked surprised by her vehemence. "I mean, I'm fine. Come, I'll get your supper."

"I'm sure the maid or the cook could take care of it," he said.

She bit back an irritated retort and took a deep breath before responding. "I sent them to bed. I can get it. It's no trouble. Would you like to eat in the dining room?"

"The kitchen is fine," he said, following her.

They didn't speak again until Robert had a supper of roast pork and potatoes in front of him. She poured him a glass of ale and herself a cup of tea, and joined him at the kitchen table. "How was your day?" she asked, trying to make conversation.

"Good, thank you," he said politely, wiping the corner of his mouth. "I'm working with a gentleman from the Home Office on a case of joint interest to our two departments. A Mr. Hastings. You might remember him from the situation last year. One of Sir Barnabas's men." He slowly cut a piece of pork. "Mr. Gantry stopped by and offered to help with the case as well," he said, not looking at her.

Christy had barely been paying attention until he mentioned Simon. She choked on her tea. "What?" she asked after she stopped coughing. By now Robert was looking at her and she knew she was giving herself away with a painful blush.

"I said Mr. Gantry was helping with the case," Robert said, sitting back in his chair, his supper apparently forgotten. "He has a great deal of experience with this type of thing."

"He does?" Christy felt like an idiot, but all she could muster were inane questions as she tried to digest the fact that her former lover was now working closely with her husband.

"He, too, used to work for Sir Barnabas," he reminded her. "According to Daniel and Harry, he might still be working for him," he added. "There is some speculation that he blew up the pirate's compound in Africa as part of a mission for Sir Barnabas."

"But I thought he was doing Sir Barnabas a personal favor

when he was abducted," Christy interjected. "It wasn't official Home Office business."

"That's what I was told as well, but since it is Sir Barnabas James and Daniel, who knows what the truth is? You know as well as I that they both lie as easily as they draw breath. It is the nature of their calling."

"How can you say that about Daniel?" she demanded, offended on his behalf. "He is one of your oldest and dearest friends."

"That is true," Robert said, picking up his knife, "but I am not blind to his faults. I love him in spite of them."

"And if Simon is working for Sir Barnabas, what does that matter?" she asked, crossing her arms. "The Home Office is a respectable department of the British government, is it not?"

"Indeed it is," Robert said. He wasn't looking at her again. "If Mr. Gantry is working for them, that is his business. I can only speak to what I know of Sir Barnabas's reputation and what I have personally seen of his behavior, both in his position and in his personal life, mostly concerning Daniel and Mr. Gantry. He is not a man to be trusted, and I'm afraid that is most likely true of the men who work for him."

"I think you are wrong," Christy said firmly. She could see that her words shocked Robert. He was used to the quiet, mousey Christy who was a delicate flower afraid of her own shadow. Well, in this matter she would show her true colors. She couldn't sit here and let him disparage Simon in such a manner.

"From what I know of Mr. Gantry, he is a man of impeccable honor and courage, and if he is working for Sir Barnabas then he has good reason to do so. If he is helping you to solve your case, whatever it is, then he must be doing so for altruistic reasons and none other, I am sure. But as for Sir Barnabas, I am sure you are right," she added to assuage his pride, as most men needed some sort of salve when told they were wrong.

"I'm sure you know better than I," he said, "as you are better acquainted with Mr. Gantry." Since he wasn't looking at her she didn't know how to take his comment. Did he know what had happened between them? Did he suspect how intimate they had been? That she still desired Simon?

She bit her lip. When would she learn to keep her mouth closed? What a fool she was, to jeopardize her marriage to a good man who had saved her over a man who had not wanted her.

After his supper, Robert was clearly surprised when Christy followed him into their bedchamber and stood there expectantly. "Is something wrong?" he asked.

"No." She could feel herself blushing. She'd never initiated intimacies with Robert before, not since their first kiss anyway. But after her defense of Simon, she felt she ought to do something to belay any suspicions Robert may have.

And of course, even thinking in such a manner made her feel guilty and tarnished. She'd felt like that ever since Robert had offered for her, because she'd wanted Simon instead. Robert had never done anything to make her feel less than cherished, like a lady and a wife should be. But she knew the truth. He deserved so much better than she. The least she could do was perform the one thing she appeared to be good at. At least two other men had found her so, anyway.

"I can help you undress," she offered. She frowned. She didn't care for how quiet and unsure she sounded. She cleared her throat. "Let me help you," she said firmly. She took a step toward him, but stopped when Robert took a hasty step back.

"Why?" he asked warily.

"You don't want me to?" She was disappointed, of course. She'd foolishly thought Robert was the one man she wouldn't have to convince to take her to bed, being her husband and all. Her first lover and Simon had both needed a bit of cajoling. She sighed. At least she had experience in that area, too.

It wasn't as if she and Robert had never had relations. He'd come to her room every third Tuesday of the month since they'd married. He'd awkwardly told her the first time that he didn't want to inconvenience her with his needs or cause her undue distress. She hadn't said a word because as far as she knew this was normal behavior for ladies and gentlemen who were married. She must be the abnormal one with her almost constant desire to have a man between her thighs. She was a wanton disgrace, which, really, she'd known all along and was sure Robert suspected. On the other hand, she'd heard ladies talking behind their fans about men's baser urges and their inability to turn away a willing woman. She just needed to make Robert understand she was willing.

"It's not that," Robert explained hastily. "It's just, you've never offered before. You don't need to help me, I don't mind. You must be exhausted."

"I don't want to go to bed," Christy told him. "I mean, I do. I want to go to bed."

"Then go to bed." He sounded exasperated. "I have no desire to detain you."

"No desire at all?" she asked a little desperately, not sure exactly how to let him know what she wanted without using crass language which both Simon and the coachman had enjoyed but she rather thought would shock Robert insensible.

Robert pinched the bridge of his nose. "I've had a very long day, Christy," he said. Was that a note of desperation in his voice as well? "Go to bed and I'll see to myself."

She started to turn away but stopped, lecturing herself all the while to straighten her backbone and show a little gumption, as Daniel was always telling her as it concerned Robert.

"No." Robert closed his eyes tightly. "I want to help you undress. So that we can..." She hesitated. "So that we can go to bed. Together." She realized she was wringing her hands and immediately dropped them to her sides.

Robert's eyes opened wide as he stared at her in astonishment. "Together?" he asked. "As in, together?"

"Yes." She didn't lower her head or look away, exactly. But she didn't meet his eyes, either, staring slightly over his head at the door lintel. She'd recently had the wood painted a very pleasant shade of robin's egg blue. She liked it very much. Robert said she had an eye for color. He liked everything she did.

That thought gave her the courage to meet his eyes. She did bite her lip while doing so, but she couldn't help it.

"Christy," he said gravely. She didn't like the sound of that. "You needn't do anything you don't want to. I'm not upset with you, you mustn't think that." He walked over and took her gently by the shoulders and kissed her forehead. "I meant what I said. I'll never inconvenience you with my needs. That also means you don't need to try to please me in that way if it doesn't please you."

"What if it does please me?" she asked, the question bursting out of her despite her misgivings. "Sometimes...well, a month is a very long time to wait to be...to be close to you. Like that."

Robert looked a little flummoxed. "I...well, I never thought that you would feel that way. I mean, I know that you had bad experiences with men in the past, and I didn't want to make you feel the way they did." He grimaced and shook his head as he stepped back away from her again. "I'm sorry. I never meant to bring up your past like that. It was uncalled for. Forget I said that."

"I'm confused," Christy said. "You don't want to because of my past? Because I've been with other men? Or because you think I don't want to be with other men now? Ever again?" Which couldn't be further from the truth. Oh, how could two people be married and not know anything about one another? What a bother this business was. They knew less about one another now than they did when they got married, it seemed.

"I thought you might have a distaste for it now," Robert said. "I didn't want to force anything on you."

"Oh, Robert," she said, laying her hand on his heart and smiling up at him sadly. "I suppose if I were a lady that would be true. But the truth is, I enjoy it. I probably shouldn't admit that, but it's true. The physical act between a man and a woman pleases me. I like it. With you." And she did. If it wasn't the thrilling, passionate encounters she'd had with Simon, what of it? Robert was tender and kind and passionate in his own way. Perhaps he'd be more so now that he knew she wasn't disgusted by his baser nature.

Her nerves stretched taut as she waited for Robert to respond. He stared at her for what seemed endless minutes, his face unreadable, which in itself was unusual enough to make her nervous. Normally he had a very expressive face and she practically knew what he was going to say before he said it. Perhaps Robert had been showing her someone else as well, someone not true to his real self and this unreadable stranger was the man she'd married. The thought both frightened and intrigued her.

"I don't know what to do," he finally confessed, his brow wrinkling. "I want to take you at your word. Believe me, Christy, I do. Fervently. But I fear taking advantage of your gentle nature and your eagerness to please." He held up a hand to stop her before she could respond. "I know you feel you have something to prove to me, though God knows why." He reached out and took both her hands in his, bridging the gap between them. "You are a lady, Christy, and have always been so to me. If I have ever done anything to make you feel otherwise, I am truly sorry and deserve your spite and rancor, not this gift you are attempting to bestow upon a most undeserving husband."

Christy squeezed his hands and laughed. "On the contrary, you have always treated me like a lady and a cherished wife, my dear. That is why I wish to treat you as a cherished husband.

Now, come to bed with your wife. I'll not take no for an answer."

Without waiting for him to find another reason to reject her, she stepped close to him and reached for his cravat. He grabbed her hands to stop her, but she met his gaze with her determined one and he gave in, letting go and giving her free rein by tipping his chin up. A thrill of victory coursed through her veins. *She'd won.*

Christy slowly unwrapped her prize. Robert was very fit for a gentleman, she supposed due to his livelihood as a constable. He'd told her once he sparred with other policemen in the boxing ring, and he had played cricket and gone riding and hunting with Daniel and Harry when he'd come to visit them in Scotland while they'd been waiting on the divorce. He'd always been the sporting type, which pleased her. She enjoyed his muscular frame. Many gentlemen grew soft with age, and she wouldn't mind when that happened to Robert, but she knew he wouldn't grow fat. He simply wouldn't allow himself to do so. He hadn't the temperament or the disposition for it.

She smoothed her hand down his arm after she helped him off with his jacket, the linen of his shirt warm from the firm, strong arm beneath it. She hurriedly laid his coat aside and reached for the buttons of his waistcoat, eager to divest him of the rest of his clothes before he remembered to extinguish the candles. He always came to her in the dark. She supposed it was another effort not to offend her delicate sensibilities. If only she had the courage to tell him she her sensibilities were lusty rather than delicate. But that was perhaps not what a husband wanted to hear about his wife.

When Christy began to tug the tails of his shirt from his breeches, Robert put a firm hand on hers, stopping her. "Let me do the rest," he told her. "You go and undress, and I shall meet you in your room."

Christy tried to hide her disappointment. She'd been

enjoying the spontaneity of their encounter, but Robert always preferred to plan ahead, whether it was marital intimacies or a Sunday carriage ride in the park. Since this was for him, she would acquiesce.

"Of course," she said, smiling at him. "Join me as soon as you can. I shan't take long."

Robert took so long to come to her room, she began to fear that he'd changed his mind. She'd lit every candle in the room, hoping he wouldn't take the time to blow them all out. She'd even placed some in out of the way places so as to make it inconvenient for him to do so. She felt like a wanton seducer doing it, but she didn't care. When he did finally come he began methodically walking around the room extinguishing them, and she finally spoke up.

"Please leave them burning," she begged. "I like the light. I want to see you."

Robert froze in the middle of reaching for a candle and looked over his shoulder at her in shock. "I don't wish to embarrass you."

"I won't be embarrassed if you won't," she teased. She held out her hand. "Come."

She was covered up to her chest, her arms on top of the blanket. Her bare shoulders made it clear she was nude. Robert pulled aside the covers just enough to get in but not to expose her bare body. He was still wearing his dressing gown. "Aren't you going to undress?" she asked.

"I don't—"

"Robert, for heaven's sake, get undressed," she said, her patience wearing thin. He looked startled and her heart began to pound. She'd let the mask drop too much. "I mean, don't worry about me so much," she stammered. "We are married, after all. This isn't our first time together. I will not be offended nor frightened by your nudity." She held her breath, hoping he'd accept her explanation.

"Of course," he agreed. He turned away and slipped the dressing gown off, laying it over the back of a nearby chair. Christy had to fight to control her breathing. His back was beautiful. Long, sinewy, well-muscled, a sculpture worthy of Michelangelo's David. And he was hers. *Hers.* In a way no one had ever been or would ever be again.

When he finally slipped under the covers she went to him willingly, gladly, eagerly, forgetting the past several months of hesitation and awkward caresses. She took him in her arms and kissed him possessively, putting her mark on him, telling him the only way she could that she adored him and that he was hers.

Robert kissed her back, wrapping his arms around her and pressing her full against him. She realized it was the first time they'd ever been that close, skin to skin. Robert had always kept his nightshirt on when he'd come to her or insisted she remain half dressed. She'd attributed it to shyness on his part, but was it some sort of misplaced chivalry? She was determined to show him tonight that she had no boundaries when it came to physical intimacy. They were married, and whatever they did in the privacy of their bedchamber was perfectly acceptable to her. Actually it was more than that—it was extremely agreeable.

She used her weight to roll him onto his back and climbed on top of him, stretched out so that she felt him from her breasts to her toes. He was hard, and she couldn't help but rub against him in hedonistic delight.

"Christy," he gasped against her lips. His hand slid from her lower back to her hip. She wasn't sure if he meant to stop her or encourage her, and she didn't think he was sure either. So she did it again. His fingers dug into her hip deliciously and pushed her away for a brief second before pulling her back in, and this time he rubbed back against her. She moaned, and he stopped. "Are you all right?" he asked breathlessly.

"I am better than all right," she said, her teeth clenched

against the sheer delight of his touch everywhere. "It's perfect. Don't stop." She pressed kisses from his mouth across his cheek and then gently bit his earlobe. This time he moaned.

"Christy, what are you doing?" he asked. She'd never heard him sound like that before, rough around the edges and a little out of control. Robert liked very much to be in control.

"I'm not exactly sure," she admitted. "Whatever feels good, or crosses my mind. I'm not thinking very far ahead at this point."

Robert turned his head and captured her mouth again, delving inside to tangle his tongue with hers. He'd never done that before. She'd always initiated their more passionate kisses. He slipped his hand into her hair and cupped the back of her head, holding her captive to his kiss, and she let him, encouraging him with a moan of surrender that made him tighten his grip on her hip and pull her into him again. She slid her legs open and straddled his hips so his penis was nestled against her sex. She felt hot and wet, and she gasped at the vibration that resonated through her at the contact.

Her breasts ached. She broke the kiss with a gasp and sat back, her hands pressed to Robert's chest. The covers slid down her back, exposing her, and she watched as Robert looked at her body. She enjoyed his perusal, so she sat up straighter, trailing her hands down his chest to his tight stomach. His hard penis was now pressing against her sex in just the right way, and she moaned, her head falling back as she closed her eyes. Even the touch of her hair on her back felt deliciously erotic.

"Touch me," she begged.

"Where?" Robert asked. He had his hands on her hips. He was holding her so tightly she knew she'd have marks in the morning, and she loved it. She wanted it, wanted the proof that at last Robert had shown a passionate desire for her.

She grabbed his wrists and lifted his hands to her breasts. He held them so gently, barely touching her, and she huffed in exasperation, dropping her chin to her chest as she glared at him.

"Harder," she demanded. She put her hands over his and showed him what she wanted, squeezing tighter, and the pleasure made her squirm on top of him. They both groaned as her movement ground her sex against his in a most pleasing fashion.

She moved his hands and rubbed his rough palms over her sensitive nipples. She began to rock against his cock, and she grew breathless. She had to let go of his hands on her breasts to put them on his stomach again, and the change in position caused her to lean forward just enough to let the tip of his cock slip inside her.

"Yes," she cried out, pressing back and pushing more of him into her passage.

"Christy," he groaned. He pinched her nipples and she gasped. It felt as if there was a string traveling directly from her breasts to her sex and he'd just plucked it, like the string of an instrument. Suddenly his hand was on her hip. "I don't want to hurt you," he said, his voice deep and rough with the effort he was making as he held still.

"It doesn't hurt, it feels good," she told him. "Please, Robert. Please," she begged.

She fought his hold until she'd pressed back and taken him fully inside her. She smiled at the joy that rushed through her, lifting her hands to look at them, expecting to see light shooting from her fingertips like candle flames. She felt wicked and wonderful, and she hadn't realized until that moment how much she had missed that feeling.

"Christy." She looked down at Robert and saw that he was offering his hands to her. She took them, used them to balance herself as she rode him like a stallion. She could see on his face that he wasn't disgusted with this side of her, this wanton woman who used him so decadently. He was mesmerized by her, and his smile was as joyous as hers.

It only took moments for Christy to peak—it had been so

long since she'd experienced such a rush of pleasure—and she cried out. She tried to keep watching Robert, but the last thing she saw before she closed her eyes and lost herself to her own joy was Robert's eyes closing as well as he thrust his head back into the pillow and came apart beneath her.

CHAPTER 8

"Gantry."

"Constable." Simon eyed Manderley warily. They were in his office at the police station. The constable had been late for work. Simon and Hastings had been waiting for almost a quarter hour.

Hastings was pacing like a caged tiger, as usual. Honestly, the man was good in a fight, but so far he'd proven all but useless at the more mundane elements of secret service and police work.

"Where have you been?" Hastings demanded. "You've kept us waiting."

"Have I?" Manderley seemed almost insultingly unconcerned. As a matter of fact, he seemed rather delighted with the whole thing. "Do accept my apologies."

"Of course," Simon said smoothly, cutting off Hastings irritated retort. "I hope all is well?"

Simon was perched casually on the corner of Manderley's desk. He didn't want to directly ask about Christy, that wouldn't do. But he'd been twiddling his thumbs here imagining all kinds of dire situations that might have delayed Manderley at home. He was beginning to think it was not a dire circumstance that had caused his lateness but something far more pleasurable, and a great deal more distracting for Simon to think about.

At his question, the constable turned and focused a sharp look on him. "Everything is fine," he said. "Why do you ask?" The question seemed to bear more weight than it ought to as Manderley continued to stare at him.

"No reason," Simon replied. "You are usually punctual, that is all."

"Sir." Longfellow stood in the office doorway, addressing the constable as he glanced between him and Simon. "I've got the information on our dead body from the other day." He held up a piece of paper. "Someun' came to claim the body at the morgue." His comment broke Manderley's concentration on Simon.

"Did they?" Manderley asked, taking the paper from Longfellow. "Well, then, who was he? And who claimed him?"

"His name was David Foster, and the lady what claimed him said she was his ma, Alice Gaines. The names are legitimate."

"Gaines?" Simon asked. "That name seems very familiar." He tapped his walking stick on the floor while he turned the name over in his mind. "Geoffrey Gaines, Alfred Gaines, Tibby Gaines," he said under his breath, listing all the people he could recall knowing with that last name. "Oliver Gaines." He stood up. "Oliver Gaines." He looked over at Longfellow. "Is Alice Gaines married to Oliver Gaines?"

Longfellow grinned. "She was, sir. But Mr. Gaines turned toes up about two years ago. Rumor has it the wife had summin' to do with that."

"Who is Oliver Gaines?" Manderley asked with commendable calm.

"A former soldier, informant, and French courier," Simon said. "He's also been known to assist the Russians on occasion."

"Past tense," Hastings corrected. "How did you know him?"

"He informed for me, of course," Simon told him. "Nasty little fellow, but useful. He was married to a madam with a

house over in Bermondsey, adjacent to a gin shop. The afore-
mentioned Alice Gaines, I presume, although she went by Fat
Linnie on the street. I never met the woman. I long suspected
that much of the information he sold was actually gathered by
her and her girls in the course of their work."

"To Bermondsey, then." Manderley picked up his hat and
gloves, which he had only just removed. "Come along,
gentlemen."

"WHY ARE we just standing around here?" Hastings asked for the
tenth time, huffing out an impatient breath as he shoved his
coat out of the way and put his hands on his hips. There were
times when it was painfully obvious that Barnabas had
recruited him off the streets, straight out of the orphanage. He'd
taught him to speak and dress like a gentleman, but his mannerisms too often gave him away. Luckily, in their line of work that
was more often a help than a hindrance.

"Because it behooves us to get the lay of the land before we
go charging in there demanding answers." Manderley answered
the question this time. They'd been taking turns. "One can learn
a great deal by simply observing, Mr. Hastings. I suggest you
give it a try."

Ouch. That was a direct hit. The constable's patience must be
wearing thin. Simon had thought he had an endless store of it.
Apparently not. He rather enjoyed discovering a chink in
Manderley's armor. Practically perfect paragons were decidedly
boring. And Manderley was perfect, or nearly so. Simon had
almost forgotten how perfect he was. But he found that it didn't
bother him like it used to. As a matter of fact, he rather liked it.

"I'll have you know I'm one of the best agents the Home
Office has got," Hastings retorted. "I'm being wasted doing these
endlessly idiotic chores instead of real work in a ridiculous
effort to punish me for killing someone who deserved to be

killed. Now, how is that fair? Or efficient? To waste an excellent agent like myself in such a manner?"

"So you keep telling us," Simon answered, looking at his thumbnail. He'd snagged it on something, damn it. Now he was sure to put a run in his silk waistcoat. He'd worn his best today, for some reason. Curse Daniel and these favors. "If you really were one of Barnabas's best agents, I daresay he wouldn't keep punishing you by putting you on secondary duties such as this. Perhaps you should be asking yourself different questions, instead of questioning his directives."

He looked up at Hastings and raised his brows with a smirk. He was being deliberately antagonizing, but he was bored, too. He was a smart enough agent to know that Manderley was right, however. He knew from experience that good information came to those agents who waited patiently.

"I am quite sure that I shall be delighted to inform Sir Barnabas that I do not require anyone's assistance if you two do not stop bickering like schoolboys," Manderley said quietly.

Thom Longfellow had been ignoring their conversation, silently observing the house, and at a signal from him Robert stepped up beside him, waving Simon and Hastings back. They both melted into the shadows as a large carriage stopped in front of the gin shop across the street.

The carriage was just a tad too large and a bit too fine for this area. Nothing too ostentatious, mind you. But it was in good repair and obviously belonged to someone of means. No hangings were hiding crests on doors or other telltale markings. It would have been absurd to find a peer's equipage here, and frankly it would have disqualified the occupants as thrill seekers rather than persons of interest in the current case.

But this carriage—this was the sort of thing they'd been waiting for. It sat outside the madam's house for a good five minutes, the coachman simply perched on his bench while the passengers remained hidden inside. There was a corresponding lack of movement in the house.

"Well, that's interesting," Hastings murmured. "Just seeing the sights here in Bermondsey, are we?"

"Indeed," Manderley agreed in a whisper. He touched Simon's arm softly, stepping in closer, and Simon nearly jumped out of his skin at the shiver that raced down his spine at the contact. What rubbish was that? He knew it was Manderley behind him. He must be more on edge than he thought.

"What do you think?" he asked, his voice coming from right next to Simon's ear, his breath a tickle against it. Simon shivered again and scolded himself silently for his foolishness.

He turned his head and whispered into Manderley's ear, "They're waiting to make sure no one is around before they show themselves."

He hadn't realized how close the other man was. Simon could suddenly feel his body heat against his side from shoulder to hip. It was nerves, obviously. He hadn't seen action since Africa, and that had been a nightmare from beginning to end. His back began to ache as if on cue.

"Then we shall make sure not to reveal ourselves," Manderley whispered back, and Simon couldn't help but glance at him as he spoke. The constable's lips were quirked in an anticipatory smile. He was enjoying this, enjoying the chase, the mission. Some of his excitement bled into Simon and his nerves settled.

"Indeed," Simon said with a similar smile as Manderley's gaze met his. He'd clearly caught Simon's attempt to imitate his earlier remark to Hastings and amusement flashed through those eyes.

"Why don't we just rush the carriage and find out who they are and what they're doing here?" Hastings asked impatiently. "All this waiting is foolish, if you ask me."

Manderly sighed, and they were so close his breath rushed

across Simon's lips like a phantom kiss. Simon jerked back as if he'd been burned.

Manderley's brow wrinkled quizzically, but he merely shrugged and stepped away. "Because we will get no answers that way," he explained patiently. "Most likely they would get away in their carriage, and there's a high probability someone would get shot. I do not wish to get shot today."

"It's that sort of cowardly attitude that allows criminals to boldly walk the streets of London," Hastings remarked snidely.

"If you weren't an immature boy who is being petulant about having his wishes thwarted, I'd call you out for that," Manderley said mildly. "But rest assured I am not pleased with your remarks, sir, and shall take exception to them at a more appropriate time."

"You're an idiot," Simon said more bluntly. "Honestly, are you really the best the Home Office is producing these days? Rush in, start shooting, and get no answers? No wonder Barnabas sent you to Manderley for more training."

"This snooping about business is not my specialty," Hastings whispered angrily. "Normally I just kill them. That's my job."

Simon understood then. "You're the new Daniel."

"Whatever that means," Hastings said dismissively. "I'm not shagging Sir Barnabas, that's for damn sure."

"What?" Manderley burst out in an aggrieved whisper. "Why does every conversation with you people somehow end up at shagging?" He put a hand on his forehead. "I can't believe I just used that word."

"It's a good word," Hastings said. "Fucking is for the lower class, or so Sir Barnabas tells me."

"Good Lord," Manderley whispered to himself, shaking his head.

Simon decided to try a new tack. "Hastings, think of it this way: Sir Barnabas is trying to round out your skill set. Clearly you are proficient at the killing skills, and now he would like you to become more proficient at the snooping about skills. Even Daniel had to learn this side of the business. That's all this is. So look, listen, snoop, and learn. Less shooting—"

"And killing," Manderley interjected.

"And killing," Simon agreed. "And more snooping. That's all. I'm sure you'll be allowed to get back to killing soon enough."

"Yes, well, I suppose you're right," Hastings said with a sigh. "Snoop away." He leaned back against the building and looked up at the dark sky as he blew out a breath. "I'm more a man of action, you know."

"Yes, we know," Manderley said. "You mentioned that." He tapped Simon's shoulder. "Something's happening."

"The sun's gone down completely," Simon said, squinting to see across the street. Only a few candles had been lit in nearby buildings and the windows were so grimy the light was useless. Not many stars, either. "That's what they were waiting for."

Two men stepped out of the carriage, one tall and large, built like a bull. The second was small and round. The bull came first and looked all around before he helped the smaller man out of the carriage.

"A bodyguard," Thom Longfellow surmised. Simon had been thinking the same thing. "I know him."

"I recognize him, too," Manderley said. "Coggins, Ernst Coggins. He works on the docks, but can more often can be found working as a bodyguard for anyone with the money to pay him. Much more lucrative work. He's a monster with his fists, and isn't above using a knife when bare knuckles aren't enough."

"So it would be easy for a foreign visitor to find him on the docks," Simon guessed.

"Why foreign?" Manderley asked. "What do you see?"

"His clothes, for one," Hastings said. "They look German."

"Dutch," Simon said. "I think, anyway. Are there many Dutch around here?"

"No," Manderley said with a frown. "Not that I know of. I will of course check with the local constabulary tomorrow."

"Good idea," Simon said.

"Yes, wonderful idea," Hastings said sarcastically. "I'm learning so much. But do you suppose, just maybe, we could do something, oh, I don't know, now? Before they leave again? Possibly?"

"Brilliant idea," Simon said. "Why didn't we think of that? Can you go around to the back of the building? Thom, why don't you join him? Don't go inside yet. And do not kill anyone. I mean it. Don't kill anyone. Just find a spot where you can overhear what goes on inside. I'm going to do the same. If the opportunity arises, try to get inside and get a better look at the face of the little one." He pushed Hastings lightly toward the end of the alley. "But—"

"Yes, I know. Don't kill anyone," Hastings threw over his shoulder. "I've got it. Christ. You're as annoying as Sir Barnabas."

CHAPTER 9

As soon as Hastings left the cover of the alley, he disappeared from view. Simon knew he was somewhere out there making his way across the street and behind the gin shop, but couldn't see him.

He really is good, he thought. But somewhere along the way something had gone wrong, and killing had become Hastings' default method for solving problems—and missions, which wasn't really the best option in their line of work as a general rule. They dealt in information more than death these days. Such was peace.

"He's a good lad. He just needs a firm hand," Manderley said, as if reading Simon's mind.

"I think the hand has been too firm," Simon said with a frown. "Maybe what he needs is a lighter touch."

"What do you mean?"

"I mean Sir Barnabas isn't the confiding or nurturing sort."

Manderley suddenly pressed his back against the brick wall and stretched his arm out across Simon's chest, pressing him alongside him. Simon almost laughed at the protective gesture, as if he needed anyone's protection. Even with his back aching he could still scale this brick wall with nothing but his bare hands and feet in just a few seconds and race unnoticed across the rooftops to make his escape. He very much doubted, despite his obvious good health and physique, that Manderley could do the same. The gesture was touching nonetheless.

Simon reached up and held onto Manderley's arm as he leaned forward just a bit and peeked around him at the street. The bodyguard had moved forward and was knocking quietly at the front door. A signal knock. Two short raps, followed by a pause, a knock, a pause and a final knock. The sound echoed on the street.

"Why is it so quiet here?" Simon wondered in a whisper. "I've never known a London street to be so quiet. It's eerie."

"It is." Manderley looked at him. "Even the rats are avoiding that house."

"For a bawdy house it's not very bawdy."

A candle appeared in a second floor window, and they watched its progress down a flight of stairs. It disappeared right before the door opened.

"It is I," the little man said. His accent was Dutch. Simon had been right. He liked being right.

"Of course it is," a woman answered, sounding irritated. "Get in 'ere then. Yer late."

"I was detained at the dock by customs," the man said, his educated voice faint as he moved inside. His bodyguard followed. The door closed and they couldn't hear what he said next.

"Interesting," Manderley said, "but not enlightening. Come on." He grabbed Simon's lapel with one hand and pulled him away from the wall.

"You're enjoying this, aren't you?" Simon asked in a whisper as he watched Manderley peek around the corner, checking to see if anyone else was on the dark street.

"Yes," the constable said, his voice agitated. "Normally I don't go skulking about. It's quite invigorating."

"Yes, skulking is one of my favorite pastimes," Simon agreed. He gently pushed in front of Manderley. "Why don't you let me lead, seeing as I've a bit more experience with being underhanded?" He motioned Manderley to straighten up. "Don't be obvious. At least, not more than can be helped. Act as if we have business here."

He walked out of the alley, avoiding what little light there was, stepping carefully. Then he reached back and put his arm around Manderley's shoulders and gave a quiet laugh. He pulled him along as they started walking away from the gin shop.

"Where are we going? What are you doing?" Manderley asked, looking over his shoulder.

"For God's sake, I said don't be obvious," Simon hissed through his smile. "We are gentlemen slumming around this evening looking for entertainment. Now act jovial and randy, and walk with me as if we are sharing whiskey and confidences."

"Why can't we simply sneak around like Hastings?"

"Because you are not as good at it as Hastings, and frankly neither am I. I am better at second story work and subterfuge. This is the subterfuge because I don't think you can do second story work."

"What is that?" Manderley sounded confused but very intrigued.

"Climbing up on roofs, that sort of thing," Simon told him.

He made an abrupt turn down a side street and Manderley stumbled into him. He tried to grab Simon's jacket but missed, and his hand slipped inside and caught on Simon's waistcoat. When he tried to pull away he'd somehow gotten entangled in the chain of Simon's watch. They stood there barely six inches apart, and Simon could feel Manderley's heat and his breath and he could smell the cologne he wore, and Simon's heartbeat quickened and he felt his cheeks flush, and he was appalled. Utterly, completely appalled at his reaction. This was *Manderley*. The upstanding constable. Christy's lawfully wedded husband. A paragon of virtue.

Once again Simon felt like dirt on the bottom of his own boot. Why did his damned libido rise like a demon phoenix from the ashes at the most inopportune times and with the most inappropriate people? What had he done to deserve such a curse? His inability to control his desires had caused him nothing but pain and trouble since his misspent youth and he had learned nothing—*nothing*—from the tragedy of his youthful marriage, apparently, because here he was wanting someone completely wrong in the worst possible place at the worst possible time again. Would he never be satisfied until he'd killed them all?

He took a moment to calm his clearly overexcited emotions. No one was going to kill Manderley or anyone else simply because Simon found him attractive. Honestly, Africa had scrambled his brains.

"Hold still," he told Manderley, and he was very proud of how calm he sounded. "Don't break my watch chain."

Manderley dutifully held still, but instead of letting Simon untangle them, he reached for the chain with his free hand and expertly extricated himself.

"I'm terribly sorry," he said, sounding every inch the proper gentleman with nothing on his mind but skulking and watch chains. "How clumsy of me." Suddenly he laughed and threw his arm over Simon's shoulder. "Come on then," he said gaily, tugging Simon farther away from their mark.

After another block Simon cut to the right again and Manderley followed. Off the main street now, Simon kept to the shadows and doubled back to the gin shop, making an oblong sort of circle that brought them to the doorway of the empty building beside the shop. The carriage was so close they could have jumped on the rear for a ride.

Simon caught Manderley's eye and motioned that they would stay close to the building, in the deep shadows, avoiding the coachman's attention. He pointed to a window on the side, where the light of a candle or two could be seen flickering through a curtain. Manderley nodded.

Simon went first and crouched under the window. He didn't look back to see if Manderley had followed him successfully. He knew he would. Robert Manderely wasn't the sort to fail, even if he was new at this.

As he'd expected, the constable slid down beside him. "I can't hear anything," he whispered.

"We've got to try to open the window," Simon said. They were very close, whispering, trying not to be heard by the coachman, who couldn't see them in their position, but there was a slim possibility he had excellent hearing. Worse coincidences had led to dire situations, and Simon had learned to be cautious.

He counted off three on his fingers, and then he and Manderley stood up and tried to push the window up. Breaking the seal caused a nice creak, and the two immediately ducked back down.

Almost immediately the curtain swung aside and someone was peering out the window. "Anyone there?" the woman asked sharply.

"Naw." It was the bodyguard. He didn't even check the window, which couldn't have been open more than a mere slit if that. They'd only broken the seal. But if he'd pushed on it, it would have given and they'd have known someone was out here.

When the bodyguard let the curtain drop and moved away, Simon let out the breath he was holding. He looked over at Manderley, who was grinning madly and he just shook his head.

This time it was Manderely who counted three off on his fingers. They stood again, and when they pushed the window it moved silently. They opened it just enough to hear what was being said. Too much would have caused a rush of cool air to stir the curtains or be felt in the room.

Once it was open enough, they crouched again. They were so close their thighs were touching. Simon forced himself to ignore Manderely's proximity and focus on the task at hand. Skulking was much easier when done alone, or at least with someone you were not overly attracted to. He and Daniel made the best skulking partners.

"Where are the messages now?" the Dutchman was asking, clearly agitated but trying to hide it.

"I told you, they're safe," the woman—Simon assumed Alice Gaines—said, her tone gloating. "You'll get them when I gets my money."

"How did you learn of the network?" he asked her. "The boys are overlooked by British authorities, who suspect nothing. Yet I am to believe a whoremonger discovered the truth? This is not possible. Which one of them revealed himself to you?"

"You'd be surprised what I know," she said smugly. "You and all the rest of them gentlemen spies around here. The docks are crawling with the likes of you. And sooner or later everyone makes their way into a bed 'ere, ain't that the truth?" She laughed throatily. "Everybody needs a tumble now and then, and Fat Linnie's is the best place to find it around 'ere, every-one'll tell you that. And there's some what can't shut their mouths when they're fucking. Lord, the way they talk!" She laughed again. "So I began to deal in more than the flesh, if you take my meaning. It's been very lucrative."

"You could simply have blackmailed me to keep the informa-tion secret, rather than dismantle my network and highjack my messages," the Dutchman said. "You have gone to a great deal of trouble. Are the boys working for you now?"

"Naw," she said dismissively. "They couldn't be trusted, could they? Turn on one employer, they'd turn on another. I've got girls what likes to take care of that business for me. Got no love for the male of the species. Fuck 'em for money, kill 'em for fun." She laughed, and Simon cut a quick glance over to Manderley, who, even in the dim light, looked pale at that revelation.

"You have killed the boys?" The Dutchman sounded as horrified as Manderley looked. "They were innocent couriers. Most had no idea what they were delivering."

"No, but I do," the woman said. "Kill me, and that information goes straight to the Home Office. I'm sure they'd be very interested in knowing about a good old-fashioned assassination plot. You don't run into that very often, do you?"

There was a pause, and Simon heard some footsteps, the woman. "That's right, I can read," she said. "I know exactly what you've got planned. So here's my proposition. I want in. I went to a lot of trouble to cover our tracks. Even went to the morgue and picked up one of them boys to throw 'em off the scent. There's money to be made here, and I've got my own network, see? Girls what no one suspects. That's how I took care of them boys. I figure you can get them some papers, and we can slip into places where you need eyes and ears, and maybe a blade. Am I right?"

Another pause. "Go on," the Dutchman finally said.

Suddenly there was a commotion upstairs. A woman screamed angrily, and a crashing sound indicated a door being slammed. Then a man yelled and pandemonium broke loose.

"What the bleeding 'ell?" Mrs. Gaines cried out. Simon heard her steps run across the room and she yanked open a door.

"There's a man up here," a woman yelled from upstairs. "He was creeping down the stairs, spying on ya. He locked himself in a room with Dilly, and it sounds like they're tearing it apart."

"You brought someone else!" Mrs. Gaines yelled accusingly.

"No," the Dutchman said. "We must go. I cannot be found here."

"Hastings," Manderely whispered, looking about frantically. "What do we do?"

Simon grabbed his arm and put a finger to his lips. Hastings could handle one woman, no matter how deadly she was. He was an assassin for Sir Barnabas. He knew his way around a fight.

"I'll contact you again," the woman said, her voice muffled by the sound of footsteps.

"The same method," the Dutchman said, his voice fading. The front door opened, and Simon pushed Manderley down on the ground. He followed suit.

"We need to follow them," Manderley whispered furiously. The sound of a carriage whip could be heard and then the thunder of horses' hooves.

"With what?" Simon asked.

Just then there was the thud of feet behind them, and Simon rolled over, ready to defend himself. Hastings crouched at their feet, looking battered, his hat gone and his jacket torn. Thom wasn't far behind, grinning like a fool, though he didn't look like he'd climbed into the boxing ring with an alley cat.

"Run," Hastings said. "The whole house is coming after us. A house of she devils." He slapped Simon's boot and then took off, jumping agilely over the fence. Simon heard the sound of women yelling and footsteps pounding. He rolled to his feet and gave Manderley a hand, yanking him up.

"Run," he said, and they did just that, Thom close behind them.

CHAPTER 10

By the time they returned to the house with a detachment of officers and agents, it was empty. The disarray left behind indicated the women vacated hastily.

Sir Barnabas didn't say a word as he stood there looking around the empty house. Only the one finger tapping against his thigh gave evidence of his agitation. "Tell me again exactly what they said." He looked at Simon.

"I don't work for you," Simon said. The casualness of his reply astounded Robert. He knew they were old acquaintances, but Sir Barnabas James was one of the most powerful men in England. The only man he answered to was Sir Robert Peel. Surely even Simon couldn't get away with that level of disrespect.

"My dear, misguided Mr. Gantry," Sir Barnabas said in a silky voice, all the more frightening for its even tone, "now that this has become a matter of national security, everyone works for me. Including you. Welcome back to the Home Office. Now, tell me again what they said."

"The pay had better have improved then," Simon said insolently. "Last time I was paid approximately nothing. My price has gone up."

Sir Barnabas took a deep breath through his nose and his eyes narrowed just slightly. "Why are you here again?" he asked. He looked at Robert and demanded, "Is he working for the police?"

"Steinberg sent him," Hastings told him. He was sitting on the edge of a table, looking bored. He still had dried blood on the corner of his mouth. Robert pulled out his handkerchief and handed it to him, pointing to his own mouth. Hastings shrugged and licked the corner gingerly before wiping it.

Sir Barnabas pinched the bridge of his nose. "I see. Why?"

"I think because he was worried about the constable," Hastings said.

"What?" Robert asked, surprised. "Surely Daniel knows I can take care of myself."

"Ordinarily yes," Simon said with a sigh. He pointed at Hastings. "But not with such an unpredictable companion."

"Thought I'd get you killed I reckon," Hastings said with an unrepentant grin. "Or kill you myself." He shrugged. "Either way."

"So, still doing favors for approximately nothing?" Sir Barnabas asked Simon, who had the grace to blush.

Robert was furious. "That is ridiculous, and if you had told me when you first arrived that that was why you were there, I would have sent you right back to Daniel. I do not need protection from Hastings or anyone else." He stood up straight. "I am a very good police officer, regardless of what you apparently think of me. I have an exemplary arrest record, and I have, on occasion, been able to get myself out of a scrape or two. I do not need you to come riding to my rescue. Good God, man! You've only just been rescued yourself from a Barbary prison. You are in no condition to protect anyone. While I will admit that your advice and experience were much appreciated this evening, on more than one occasion *I* had to protect *you*."

"That is false," Simon said, clearly fighting for calm. "I let you think you were protecting me, but frankly I thought your efforts were amusing considering my own extensive skill set at getting myself and others out of scrapes, as you put it. Between your complete lack of experience at skulking and *your*"—he pointed at Hastings—"predilection for attempting to kill someone everywhere you go, I am the only reason we have this information."

"That is going a bit far, old man," Robert said with dignity. "I was beside you the whole night. I insisted on watching the house instead of barging in there in the first place, and I was certainly the one who managed to open that window. With your back you can barely open a door."

"What do you know of my back?" Simon asked. "Did Daniel tell you?"

"No one told me anything until you, just now," Robert said. "You've just confirmed what I've been observing for two days. I don't know what's wrong with it, but it's clearly hurt. I assume from your ordeal in Africa."

"Damn it—"

Sir Barnabas cut Simon off. "They branded his back in Africa. Now, while I am thoroughly enjoying watching you gentlemen flirt, let us get down to business, shall we? Exactly what information were you both instrumental in getting this evening?" He looked at Hastings. "I don't suppose you heard it, too? Or is that asking too much?"

"I know the Dutchman had a network of spies and the whores killed them all," Hastings said. "And since one of them tried to slice my throat and gave me a good beating in the process, I believe it. If you can turn that one, you'll have a prize."

"Useless. What else?" Sir Barnabas was tapping that finger again.

Robert had been rendered speechless by Sir Barnabas's accusation. He had never flirted with a man in his life. How could arguing with Simon be misconstrued as flirting? One was an art, the other was the result of unfiltered emotion. Robert had never mastered the art of flirting. And branded? Like cattle? Or a slave? The very notion turned his stomach. How was Simon even on his feet?

"Apparently she's got all the messages she intercepted from the couriers," Simon told Sir Barnabas tightly. "And according to her it tells quite a tale. Embedded spies and assassination, as we said. We don't know who, we don't know when, we don't know where."

"She wants to join forces," Robert said, feeling he should add something to the conversation. "She wants to give him her network of spies, her girls, since she's eliminated his. But," he added, "I don't think that's plausible now and I'm sure they both will realize it. We didn't hide our arrival here. They know someone overheard. The only salient information we gleaned was to be on the lookout for a new network of female spies. Ergo, they are no longer as useful as they might have been had we not learned of their existence."

"What do you mean?" Simon said.

"The Dutchman said the boys were overlooked by the British authorities, who never suspected a thing. That's what made them a valuable network. The women, particularly young women, would have been the same. Would your first suspect be a woman, Sir Barnabas? A serving woman, most likely? A maid or cook or washerwoman?"

"No," Sir Barnabas admitted.

"Doesn't matter," Hastings said. "They've got a use for those women, even if they can't use them as spies anymore."

"What?" Robert asked, puzzled.

"Assassins," Hastings said, looking at Robert's now bloody handkerchief. "They've gotten very good at killing, haven't they?"

Robert looked around the room and he saw his own dawning understanding on the faces of Simon and Sir Barnabas. Finding a female assassin, God knows where in London, hunting God knows who, was an impossible task. Gargantuan in scope and a logistical nightmare.

"Then we shall find the Dutchman," Robert said to himself.

"What?" Sir Barnabas asked sharply.

"We all know finding the assassin is impossible right now. But finding the Dutchman should be much simpler. Yes?"

Sir Barnabas smiled at him. "Yes." He turned and spoke to a man who had been standing off to the side, taking notes. He pointed at Robert. "He works for me now. Notify his superiors. Until further notice." He turned back to the room. "Mr. Longfellow, I'll need you to keep working the murders. I'll notify your superiors that you are to take the lead on the investigation. You three." He pointed at Hastings, Robert and Simon. "Your priority is finding the Dutchman."

He turned and began to walk out of the room. "Clean this up," he said to his secretary, who snapped his fingers. Men immediately began moving silently through the house, removing everything. Robert was stunned at the efficiency of it.

"But—" He started to protest Sir Barnabas's highhandedness, but Simon stopped him with an outstretched hand.

"Don't bother," he said, resigned. "He gets what he wants. And isn't it what you want? To find the Dutchman? To catch the killers?" He shrugged. "When it's over, we'll all go back to our lives and he'll clean up any mess he's made. It's how he operates. His interest is immediate. He can't worry about the future when so much is at stake in the present."

"Exactly," Sir Barnabas said over his shoulder. He turned his head and once again pinned them all with his predator's gaze.

"Watch your backs, gentlemen. They know they are being hunted. And they are not used to being the prey."

He looked at Hastings. "They know you now. Soon they will know all of you. It is inevitable." He turned away and put his hat on. "Find the Dutchman as quickly as you can."

CHAPTER 11

Robert knocked at Simon's apartment door. It was late, passing two in the morning. He ought to be at home in bed with Christy. But he'd sent a note by the house telling her he had to go by the police offices and fill out some paperwork in order to officially transfer to Sir Barnabas's command. Always there was paperwork. Very rarely did superiors think of it when they issued highhanded commands like Sir Barnabas had. He sighed. So why was he here?

He tapped on the door again. He was here because Simon had looked unwell when they'd parted earlier. He'd been noticeably limping, which was highly unusual. He'd done a very good job of hiding his weakness the last couple of days. Robert had only noticed it because they'd been in such close proximity for a prolonged period of time tonight, in unusual circumstances. He felt an obligation to check on him.

He was still shaken by Sir Barnabas's revelation. He couldn't even imagine the horror of being branded like an animal. He knew slavers did it and had always considered it an abomination. But he'd never known someone who'd experienced it. It must have been excruciating. They had to have held him down for it. If it had been Robert, he'd have been fighting like the devil. He'd noticed some scarring on Simon's face, some still an angry red from recently healed wounds, some fading already. He'd fought, too. Robert knew he had. He was lucky. A wound like a brand in a Barbary prison? That would have been the death of a lesser man.

"Who the hell is knocking at this time of night?" Simon demanded as he ripped open his door. He stood there with his robe half tied and falling off one shoulder, his pants only half buttoned. He was barefoot and he held a pistol at his side.

Robert took a step back.

"Oh, God. It's you." Simon's stance immediately went from aggressive to drooping. He ran his empty hand through his hair.

Robert saw that hand was shaking. He looked down and saw the hand that held the pistol was shaking as well. He stepped closer, leaned down and gingerly took it away. "Here," he said softly. "Let me have that before you shoot your foot off."

Simon laughed weakly. "Wouldn't that be a marvelous ending to a wonderful day?" He turned and walked away, leaving Robert to catch the door before it hit him. "You might as well come in."

Robert followed him in, closing and locking the door behind him. "Thank you, I will."

"Why are you here?"

"You look awful." Robert looked around. There was a blanket in a heap on the floor by the sofa, and an almost empty bottle of whiskey next to a half-full tumbler on the table beside it.

"Thank you," Simon said. He grabbed another glass from the shelf and then limped over to the sofa and dropped down onto it, wincing. "I feel much worse than I look, if that's any consolation."

He poured some whiskey in the second glass and shoved it in Robert's direction and then added some to the glass on the table before he picked it up. He saluted Robert.

"To whatever brought you here." He took a deep swallow. He was quite pale and his hair was damp, as if he'd been sweating. The evening was almost cool considering the recent heat wave, and the apartment felt cold and damp.

"I came by to check on you," Robert said. He moved aside some pillows and sat down next to Simon. "You didn't look very well when we parted this evening."

Simon leaned back against the sofa cushions and perused the whiskey in his glass dejectedly. "There was a time I always looked very well indeed," he mused. He smiled wanly at Robert. "Those days are long past, I'm afraid."

"Nonsense," Robert said, taking the glass out of his hand. "I think you need less of that, however, and more sleep."

Simon closed his eyes and let his hand fall to his lap as his head dropped slowly against the back of the sofa. "God, what I wouldn't give for more sleep."

"When was the last time you slept?" Robert asked in concern. He hadn't thought he looked too exhausted today. Just a little tired.

Simon laughed wryly. "Right before you knocked." He opened one eye and looked at Robert as his mouth quirked in a smile to match the laughter.

Robert felt himself blush. "I'm terribly sorry," he said, starting to stand. "Then I shall take my leave."

He was surprised when Simon grabbed his arm and pulled him back down. "No," he said quickly. "Don't leave." He sighed and let go. "I didn't say it was a restful sleep." He ran his hand over his face in an age-old gesture of exhaustion. "I haven't had a restful sleep in years. Definitely not in the last few months."

Robert felt a bit at sea. He wasn't used to such confessions, especially from men. He didn't know Simon that well. They'd both been involved in helping Christy and Harry last year when Harry's family was trying to kill her for his money, before they knew Harry was still alive.

And he'd rejected Christy and let Robert have her. Robert mustn't forget that. His wife had wanted Simon, who had not wanted her.

Looking at Simon now, Robert thought Christy would be surprised to see him this way—vulnerable, weak, ill. But she would know what to do. Robert was sure of that. Christy always seemed to know what to do. She liked to pretend to be gentle and soft spoken, easily swayed, but the truth was Christy was much more like the woman who had been in Robert's bed last night. God, was it only last night? He tried to do what he thought she might in this situation.

"Why?" he asked. "Why haven't you slept?" He placed his hand on Simon's thigh comfortingly. "Go ahead. You can tell me."

Simon looked at Robert's hand on his thigh for a moment and then held his hands up in front of him—they were shaking. "Look at me," he whispered. "How they would laugh if they could see it."

"Who? Who would laugh?"

"Everyone." Simon let his hands drop. His eyes closed, and to Robert's horror a tear fell from the corner of one. "They won't leave me alone at night, those bloody memories. Giselle, the war, those goddamn pirates." A sob escaped, and was all the more devastating because Simon didn't try to cover it, didn't hardly react to it. Just continued to sit there, his shaking hands in his lap, his shoulders slumped dejectedly.

"Simon," Robert whispered.

"Don't call me that," Simon whispered brokenly. "Don't call me that unless you're going to hold me."

Robert was frozen, shocked at Simon's words, but even more so by his immediate reaction, which had been to gather Simon in his arms and hold on tight, so the memories couldn't get past him to hurt Simon anymore. At least not tonight.

Where had that come from? His thoughts of Christy, perhaps, and what she would do.

"Hold me, Manderley," Simon whispered, so quietly Robert barely heard him. "Please hold me. Right now you're all I've got. Everyone else has gone and left me here alone."

That was enough to spur Robert into action. He didn't think anymore, but just wrapped an arm around Simon's shoulders and pulled him into his embrace, squeezing him tightly. Simon wrapped his arms up and under Robert's, his hands gripping Robert's shoulders tight enough to bruise.

"Don't let go," Simon said. "I might slip away tonight."

"I won't," Robert promised. "I've got you. And my name is Robert." Whatever demons haunted Simon, they weren't going to get him tonight.

SIMON DRIFTED in and out of sleep. The pillow under his head was abnormally firm, but it smelled divine, like Robert's cologne. He took a deep breath and hugged the pillow tighter. The pillow hugged him back. Then it rolled him onto his back and crawled on top of him and kissed him.

He kissed his pillow back. This was quite possibly the damnedest dream he'd ever had, but it was most definitely better than any he'd had recently. His pillow was a man, with a scratchy morning beard and a hard cock that he ground into Simon's. Simon moaned and slid his hand over his pillow's hip to his firm derriere and up his back to his nice, thick hair. The caress made his pillow hump him deliciously, and Simon let the dream go for reality.

This was no pillow. He spread his legs and ground his cock against his lover's. They were dressed. He wrapped both arms around broad shoulders, both hands in that thick, luxurious hair now as the kiss went from languorous to passionate.

He opened his eyes and nearly shouted in shock to see

Robert on top of him, kissing him so roughly. Robert's eyes were closed, his face flushed with sleep and desire. He sucked on Simon's tongue and Simon moaned, reaching down and cupping his buttocks to pull their hips in tight, grinding against him.

He was so damn close. He didn't want Robert to wake up and realize what was going on before he came. It was selfish and quite possibly self-destructive and he didn't care. He hadn't had this in so long.

He began to climax and he dug his fingers into Robert's firm flesh, grinding against him. "Robert," he groaned into his mouth.

Robert pulled away and blinked, confusion on his face. Before he could face reality, Simon kissed him again passionately. It only lasted a moment before Robert jerked up onto his hands, his hips pressed hard into Simon's, and on his small clothes Simon could feel the damp, damning evidence of their morning encounter.

Robert stared, dumbstruck, into Simon's face and then he scrambled off of Simon, nearly unmanning him in the process. Robert fell ungracefully to the floor and banged his elbow on the table, knocking over a glass of whiskey still sitting there. Simon realized the sun was up already. The room was brightly lit.

"I'm sorry seems inadequate right now," Simon said hesitatingly. "Especially because I'm not really sorry. So I'm sorry for that, too."

"I don't even know what to say right now." Robert sounded like men during the war who were shocked insensible after their first battle. His eyes were large and his breathing was fast and he looked like he'd watched his dog die. Repeatedly.

Simon rolled onto his side and propped his head on his hand. He was actually feeling remarkably better than he had in recent memory. He was of the school that sex tended to make everything better, although he had indeed seen it make everything worse. It was a dichotomy he had yet to resolve. "Well, the truth is at first I thought I was dreaming and you were some sort of sentient and very ardent pillow."

"I don't know what I thought," Robert said tonelessly.

"Really? Well, I confess I realized it was you before the dénouement," Simon said without an ounce of contrition. "But by then I was past the point of no return. You see, it's been a very long time since I've had that sort of passionate, voluntary encounter with a man." He pushed aside thoughts of the involuntary encounters he'd endured while immobilized and injured in Africa. If he thought about those he'd go mad, and he was feeling far too satisfied to endure self-inflicted torture today.

The look Robert gave him said he'd noticed the distinction he'd made. "I have never been with a man like that," he said. "I know you may not believe that, considering Daniel is one of my oldest and dearest friends, but it's true. I've never even been tempted. I had never even been with a woman until...until my wife." He put his head in his hands. "Christy. What am I going to tell her?"

Simon sat up then. His stomach churned a bit and he chose to attribute it to last night's whiskey and an empty stomach rather than guilt over cheating on Christy with Christy's husband. Or rather, forcing Christy's husband to cheat on her with him. Although forcing was a strong word. It was the right word, but it was strong.

"Don't tell her anything. It would only hurt her and she doesn't deserve it. We deserve to carry the burden of treating her very shabbily with this morning's nasty little mistake. At least I do. If I'm correct, and I know I am, you scrambled away like I was hot coals before you climaxed." *Oops, there was the bitterness and self-loathing talking again.*

"It wasn't a nasty little mistake," Robert said quietly. "But it was a mistake."

Simon forced himself to stand. He was very stiff and his

back was screaming. He'd been numb when Robert was riding him roughly, but every ache was making itself felt now.

"Did you really not know it was me?" he asked, and then could have bitten his tongue off. How pathetic he sounded. When had he become this pathetic, broken man?

"I knew," Robert whispered. "I knew, I think, from the start." He heaved himself off the floor. "I need to clean up." He cleared his throat. "And then we are going to go about our business."

"Yes, sir," Simon said sarcastically. "Whatever you say." He pointed to the washstand. "Over there. Just give me a minute to change and we'll be on our way."

"Pack a bag," Robert told him as he headed for the washstand.

"What?" Simon stopped and turned back to him, sure he'd misheard.

"Pack a bag. You're coming to stay with Christy and me."

Simon stumbled and sat in the nearest chair. "That is not a good idea."

Robert was wetting a cloth in the basin. "Perhaps not. But you are in no condition to protect yourself here. I had a great deal of time to think last night while you were sleeping, and I realized that we are all vulnerable. I'm going to ask Sir Barnabas for some men to watch the house. I don't wish Christy to fall victim to someone coming for us, nor little Christian."

He looked quite pale as he wiped his face with the damp cloth. He paused a moment after drying and then self-consciously began to take off his jacket. "It is simply more expedient for you to stay with us," Robert was explaining. "It is easier to watch one house than two."

Simon watched in fascination as Robert stripped down to his bare chest and washed. He blushed and didn't look at Simon. He was trying so hard to be matter-of-fact about the whole thing, and Simon found it rather endearing. He had to bite his tongue not to offer to help. Robert was splendidly built. He'd felt like it, on top of Simon. Christy must enjoy that. She'd liked Simon, when he was healthier. He was a bit thin still from Africa.

"It's going to be very awkward," Simon told him. He ignored the excitement and anticipation that roared through him at the thought of being in Christy and Robert's house, in close proximity to the two of them. Good God, he loved to torture himself.

"It is," Robert agreed. He looked rather grim. Simon chose to ignore it. He briefly considered how many things he was ignoring in order to get his way this morning, but all he could think was, *it's about damn time I got what I wanted.*

CHAPTER 12

"What is going on?" Christy asked, trying to be calm as a line of men entered the house and began snooping everywhere. Robert, Simon and another man who looked familiar followed at the back.

Robert stopped at her side and kissed her cheek when she held it up. She tried to keep her eyes off of Simon but couldn't. When she looked at him, she found him staring at her. The jolt that went through her when their gazes met was like lightning.

"It is for our protection, my dear," Robert said gently. "Don't be afraid, please. The case we are working on has simply gotten a bit out of hand, and Sir Barnabas and I thought it best if he had some men come by and secure our home."

There was a great deal of information in there, and Christy sorted through it while the maid took the gentleman's hats.

"You remember Mr. Gantry?" Robert said, his voice even.

Simon stepped forward and took her hand, holding the tips of her fingers politely and bowing over it. She almost laughed aloud at how proper his greeting was. At one time he had stripped her naked and taken her roughly on a sofa in Daniel's drawing room. Now they were strangers.

Her eyes pricked with tears and she blinked. "Of course," she said firmly. "How do you do, Mr. Gantry?" She forced herself to look away, at the other man who was watching them closely.

"And this is Mr. Hastings," Robert said. "He works for Sir Barnabas James."

"Ma'am," Mr. Hastings said, his greeting identical to Simon's.

"Please, gentlemen, join me for tea," Christy said, indicating the drawing room, where one man was checking the windows. He pulled out a hammer and nails. "What on earth?" Christy exclaimed as he began to nail them shut. "My windows!"

"They'll be fixed when it's all over," Mr. Hastings told her.

She turned to Robert and narrowed her eyes. "Sit." She pointed at a chair. "Now, explain to me what is going on. And none of that business you just gave me at the door."

She crossed her arms, blocking his escape. He looked uneasily at the other men at her outburst. So be it. She'd made the decision not to dissemble with him any longer. They were married, and it was about time he found out who she really was. She glanced at Simon, who was trying to hide a grin.

"I told you, don't worry—"

"Robert Manderley," she scolded. "I am a full-grown woman. When a man comes in and starts nailing my windows shut for my protection, I think I deserve a full explanation."

"I agree with her, Manderley," Hastings said. "Shall I do the honors?"

"No," Simon said quickly. He indicated the door. "We'll just go and find our rooms."

"Your rooms?" Christy could feel herself grow pale. "You're staying here?"

"Yes," Robert said. "I hope you don't mind, Christy. You see, we all need to be cautious. And it's just easier to protect us all in one place. Not to mention we've a bit of a time constraint on this and it will make it easier to consult with one another on the case."

"No, of course, that's fine," Christy said hastily, recovering from her shock. *Simon, in her house. Sleeping. Bathing. Naked. Breathing. In her house.* "I'll have Nell show you to your rooms." She waved the maid in. "Show Mr. Hastings to the green bedroom and Mr. Gantry to the red bedroom," she told the maid.

She bit her lip. She knew it wasn't wise to put Simon next to her and Robert, but she so desperately wanted him to be close.

"Excellent," Robert said stiffly. "Gentlemen, if you'll excuse us. I need to explain to Mrs. Manderley exactly what's going on."

"Of course," Simon said. He bowed and left the room, and to Christy it felt as if some of the air had left with him. She sat down, slightly lightheaded.

"I am sorry about showing up like this without warning you," Robert said, sitting down next to her and taking her hand in his. "The fact of the matter is—" He paused and waited for the man to finish nailing the windows shut.

"Sorry, sir," the man mumbled as he left the room, tipping his hat at Christy as he went. He shut the door behind him.

Christy looked at Robert, waiting. "The case has turned dangerous, Christy."

Her heart sped up and she clutched his hand. "What has Sir Barnabas James to do with it?" she asked fearfully. "You know I don't trust him, Robert."

"I know, but in this instance we must." Robert sighed and rubbed the back of her hand with his thumb. "I'll be working for him until this mission is over."

"But why?" she asked, her fear escalating. "What has he to do with these murders?" She didn't know very much about the case. Robert didn't like to discuss his work when he got home, but she had gotten him to talk about this case a little because it had troubled him so.

"The victims were caught up in a spy ring, it seems," Robert told her. "We're not sure for whom or what they were up to, but it isn't good. And we've got to find out. We believe they are planning something dastardly, and that it's going to happen soon. And so Sir Barnabas took over and commandeered my services for the duration of the mission because of my familiarity with it."

"And Simon? I guess you were right; he was working for Sir Barnabas." The idea distressed her. He'd fallen back into his old ways, it seemed. She'd known he'd been drinking heavily before he was kidnapped; apparently he'd been spying again as well.

"Actually, no, he wasn't," Robert said. "You were right. He offered to help with my murder case at Daniel's suggestion. Frankly, I think Daniel was giving him something to do to take his mind off his recent travails." He sat back, his shoulders slumped. "He isn't doing well. Not sleeping. And he sustained a terrible injury to his back there."

"He was branded," she whispered, as if Simon could hear them. "Daniel and Harry told me."

"Of course they did," he said wryly. "Why did I think they hadn't? Those two tell you far too much."

She scoffed. "If not for them, I wouldn't know anything. You fear offending my delicate sensibilities far too much."

"I'm beginning to see the error of my ways," he told her. "Never fear. But yes, back to Simon. His back troubles him, more than he admits. You can clearly see he isn't himself yet. I thought perhaps if he came to stay with us you could nurse him back to health. Or am I asking too much?" The look he gave her was searching. "We haven't discussed it, but I know his failure to ask for your hand hurt you."

She was startled that Robert would speak so plainly after all these months. She took a deep breath, wanting to be honest, but not wanting to ruin the fragile new feelings and trust she felt growing between them. "It did. And I do still have feelings for him. Particularly in his present circumstances. How could I not?

Naturally I will gladly tend to him. But you must know that he will resist admitting any weakness."

"You know him so well?" Robert asked.

"I know enough of men," she said, standing up. "I don't know very much about *him* at all. He was very kind to me when I was at my lowest." She reached for his hand again and smiled at him. "But you were my white knight, my darling, not Simon. You are my husband, not him. I am worried about you."

"Me?" Robert asked. "I am fine."

"Just make sure you stay that way," she warned him.

CHRISTY KNOCKED at Simon's bedroom door. She figured she might as well get this over with. Avoiding him wasn't an option, not in her own home. So she had better learn to deal with him and figure out how to conceal her feelings while somehow nurturing him back to good health.

Easy as a camel through a needle's eye, she thought, rolling her eyes. Never had Nanny's favorite Bible verse seemed so appropriate.

"Come in," Simon called out. He looked startled to see her at his door.

"I wanted to bring you some fresh linens," she said. "Things are a little different here than at Daniel's or Ashton Park, I'll wager." She smiled to take the sting out of her words. "We've only one maid, one cook, and Nanny. Cook will have something warm for your breakfast, and we'll have supper at eight, if you're here, that is. I understand the case is a difficult one."

"Yes," he said. "Thank you." He walked over and took the linens from her. She hadn't been able to go more than two steps into the room, not trusting herself. He looked so tired and wan. Thin. There were dark circles under his eyes. His walk was stiff. "I really don't know what our schedule will be."

"That's fine," she said.

An awkward silence descended.

"Christy—" he began with a sigh, but she cut him off.

"Don't bother." She smiled. "Robert and I are very happy. And we have Christian now. I'm sure you made the right decision for all of us." She reached out to put her hand on his arm, but changed her mind. "Can I get you anything else?"

"No. No, thank you," he said, the awkwardness only getting worse. "Is Robert ready to go?"

She nodded. "I think so. He's in his study. It's at the bottom of the stairs, on the left. The door is open. You should see him."

Simon turned and put the linens down on the corner of his bed, and then smiled politely at her and bowed slightly. Then he walked past her and out of the room. She'd been holding her breath, keeping her composure tightly controlled until his exit. Then she allowed herself to slump down onto the bed next to the linens. She put her face in her hands.

"Oh, Lord," she whispered. "This is going to be awful."

LATER THAT AFTERNOON Christy was heading into the butcher shop when she was hailed by a strange man dressed all in black who called out her name. One of Sir Barnabas's men had accompanied her, but he was several steps behind, carrying some packages for her from the other shops she'd visited. More people in the house had meant more food.

The stranger that approached her was small and thin with a high voice. She stopped and waited.

"Run!" A small blonde woman in front of the shop began waving wildly at her and shouting. Christy frowned in confusion. She didn't recognize the woman.

There was a commotion behind Christy, and she turned back to see the agent who had accompanied her toss the packages aside and push several people out of the way as he struggled to get to her. At the same time the small stranger lunged, and Christy recoiled.

Suddenly another man—a tall, thin one—dressed exactly like the first emerged from the crowd around her and grabbed the small man, yanking him away. Christy glanced up, and her gaze met the tall man's for a brief second. Her heart was racing with fear. Who were these people? Then she noticed the small man go limp right before he was dragged back into the crowd and they both disappeared.

When she turned back, the blonde woman had disappeared as well. It all happened so fast Christy had no idea what was going on.

"Mrs. Manderley," the agent said, out of breath as he grabbed her arm and shoved her behind him. "Are you all right?"

"I…I'm fine," she said, her voice—indeed her whole body—shaking with fright. "Who were those people? What's going on?"

"Let's get you home," the agent said gruffly. "Then I'll send for Mr. Manderley and report what's happened."

CHAPTER 13

"**Y**ou're sure no Dutch ships were held up by customs yesterday?" Robert asked the harbormaster. He felt he was on more solid ground today. This sort of mundane footwork was his specialty.

"No, sir. I'm quite sure." The harbormaster looked down at his ledger. "We had sixty-two ships dock yesterday. Three were Dutch. Their main cargo was passengers, and we had no issues with them."

"Let's try a different approach," Simon said. He was sitting by the window, staring down at the wharf below. He turned to look at the harbormaster. "Which ships were held up in customs yesterday? Not Dutch ships. Any ship, regardless of registration."

"Oh, brilliant," Hastings said, perking up. He'd been getting quite bored with each successive dead end today. "Just because he was Dutch doesn't mean he's actually working for the Dutch, does it?"

Robert sighed and closed his eyes. "That throws another obstacle in our path, Hastings. It doesn't help narrow our search."

"Of course it does," Simon said. He'd been short with Robert ever since they'd left the house. Robert knew he and Christy had spoken alone upstairs. Apparently it hadn't gone well. Robert had been tempted to seek Christy out and make sure she was all right, but in the end he left her to her privacy.

"Fine," he agreed with as much patience as he could muster. "If you please, harbormaster, can we get a list of vessels held in customs yesterday and where we might find them today?"

The harbormaster frowned at them. "On whose authority? I don't want to get in trouble for handing out that information to anyone who comes asking."

Robert pulled a letter from Sir Barnabas out of his jacket pocket. "I believe this will assuage your fears, sir."

The harbormaster took a moment to read it and then nodded. "I'll make a note that it was on Sir Barnabas James's orders, then." He signaled to an assistant. "Bring me the customs list."

The assistant came back within minutes. Robert was mightily impressed with the organization at the port authority and would make a note of it in his report. All the same, he wanted to snatch the list from the harbormaster's hand. They were the ones who needed it, after all.

"Fourteen ships in all held up by customs yesterday, gentlemen. All but six were cleared and sent on to dock." He handed the list to Robert. "You'll find the name of the ship, its country of origin, cargo, final destination, and current docking location and duration of stay."

"Thank you." Robert turned to go.

"You can't take that with you," the harbormaster said.

Robert stopped and took a deep breath before he turned back to the harbormaster. He saw Simon watching him with a smirk. He hadn't moved. He clearly understood the mechanizations of bureaucracy better than Robert.

"Do you need a copy?" the harbormaster asked impatiently.

"Yes, please," Robert replied, handing the list back.

"Bloody hell," Hastings mumbled behind Robert, who wholeheartedly agreed. *Still.*

"Language, Hastings," he reprimanded at the harbormaster's scowl.

"It will take a few minutes," the harbormaster said, handing it back to the assistant. "We do actually have work of our own, you know."

"Just point me to a desk, and if you'd be so kind as to lend me the use of a pen and paper, I will gladly copy it myself," Robert offered with a placating smile.

"That's fine," the harbormaster said, clearly appeased. "I'll have my man copy it. He's a quick, steady hand." He nodded and the young assistant hurried off.

"Thank you again," Robert said, glaring over his shoulder at the other two.

"Yes, thank you," Simon chimed in, sounding moderately sincere.

"Thank you," Hastings said, making a face at Robert. The harbormaster marched off, disgusted with them all.

"You don't do yourself any favors by making enemies of men like him," Simon told Hastings, surprising Robert. He hadn't thought Simon was very interested in the proceedings, either.

"Why?" Hastings asked belligerently. "I still think this is a waste of time."

"Because he may not have the information we need today, but he might in the future, on another case," Simon told him. He stood up slowly. His back must still be bothering him. Perhaps their activities last night had been too much for him.

Robert blushed and turned away to hide it. He'd actually meant the sneaking about at Alice Gaines's, but as soon as he'd had the thought, their other activities entered his mind. That was this morning, however. It was a good thing he had no intention of repeating their liaison, since he was fairly certain Simon's back couldn't take it.

"I think you are both being unnecessarily negative," he said, joining the conversation just so he could get away from his own thoughts. "This information may yet prove quite valuable. We don't know yet."

"You are right, of course," Simon said with another sigh. "I'm being morose today. Forgive me." He flashed a smile, but caught himself and looked away again. As unbelievable as it seemed, he appeared self-conscious about what had happened between them as well.

"Fine," Hastings said impatiently. "I'll go and trade pleasantries with the harbormaster and try to hurry this along. Satisfied?" He stomped off.

"It's probably not a good idea to leave him alone with anyone," Robert commented, watching Simon.

"No," Simon agreed. "Shall I follow him?" He turned as if to do so.

Robert stepped in his path to stop him. The noise of the busy office behind them created a small bit of privacy. "No," he said. "We can't go on like this, Simon."

"Oh, dear," Simon said, a brief, amused smile quirking the corner of his mouth. "It sounds as if you are giving me my congé. Over so soon, is it?"

"Simon," Robert said, chastising him with that one word.

Simon had the grace to look abashed. "Sorry. You're right, of course. Damned awkward, though, isn't it?"

"Yes, it is. So let us be gentlemen about it and simply agree to let it pass. It happened, and it won't happen again. We were both…"

"Yes?" Simon asked curiously as he hesitated. "What were we, exactly? I've been wondering that, too."

"Half asleep," Robert concluded, knowing it was a lie.

"All right, we'll agree to that," Simon said. "Why not? It's as good as anything else."

"I could have been anyone," Robert said.

"Oh, well." Simon looked as offended as he sounded. "That's what you think of me, is it? Good to know."

"It's the truth, isn't it?" Robert asked, confused. "I mean, we hardly know one another. I'm a married man. I'm married to Christy, the woman you—" He broke off, shocked at what he'd almost said.

"Yes, there's that. The woman I…well, then." Simon looked away. "You needn't worry that it will happen again. With you or with Christy. I promise I will keep my promiscuous ways to myself while under your roof." He looked over Robert's shoulder. "If I find myself unable to deny my baser instincts, I will seek out Hastings."

"Here, what?" Hastings asked from over Robert's shoulder, startling him.

"Nothing," Robert said quickly. "Simon was attempting to be funny."

"He shouldn't," Hastings said. "He could get hurt that way."

"Too late," Simon said with a laugh. "I've let my poor humor lead me to disaster too many times to recall already."

"Well, stop it," Hastings said, looking at both of them. "We've just got to find the Dutchman and stop an assassination, and I can be shot of the two of you. Keep your heads on straight until the job is over. Christ almighty, I'm not being paid to nanny you."

"I don't know what you're talking about," Robert blustered. "I am perfectly fine."

"Right as rain, sure thing, Constable," Hastings said sarcastically. "I may not be the best spy here, gentlemen, but even I can spot that lie with my limited skills. Come on. Let's find a ship."

. . .

THERE WAS ONLY one ship that stood out among the fourteen detained by customs the day before. A Turkish cargo vessel that came into port half empty, carrying a small cargo of rugs. Customs had flagged the ship because they had no manifest, no port of origin for the goods, nor any details about their cargo other than the most basic: rugs.

"Well, that's certainly suspicious," Robert agreed.

"With no authentication for the rugs, they are worthless in the British market," Simon said. "They might as well have listed them as destined for the black market right on a forged manifest."

"Doesn't that rule them out?" Hastings asked. "It would seem that someone who was trying to sneak into the country and was operating a spy ring would try not to attract the attention of the authorities."

"If they know what they're doing, that's true," Simon said. "But the more we discover about this case, the more I begin to doubt that. Nothing about this seems to follow the usual protocols, does it? A spy network of boys? A partnership with a madam? Assassination? Nothing about this seems right."

"I know we must find the Dutchman and stop whatever he has planned," Robert said. "But my objective is still the same as it ever was. To find and bring to justice the person or persons responsible for killing those boys. In all that has transpired in the last day or so, their deaths seem to have been forgotten."

"You work for Sir Barnabas now," Hastings told him. "Your objective is whatever his objective is."

"I will find his spy," Robert said. "But I did not seek his employment, nor did I have anything to say about it. So he shall simply have to accept my objectives or learn not to be so high-handed in the future."

Simon's laughter sounded delighted. "Oh I am going to enjoy this game of cat and mouse. You do realize those boys, as you call them, were spying for a foreign power? That's treason."

"You heard the Dutchman. He admitted that they were ignorant of what they were doing, innocent couriers. They were boys and they died horribly." He stopped and looked at Simon and Hastings. "No one else is speaking for them. So I shall."

"So you shall," Simon said quietly, staring back at him. "No, Robert—*we* shall. Isn't that right, Hastings?"

"I used to be one of them." Hastings took his hat off and wiped his brow with his handkerchief. "Damned hot, isn't it?"

"Yes, it's still hot," Simon said. "What do you mean, you were one of them?"

"Oh, I wasn't a boy traitor, but I could have been." Hastings barely stopped to check for traffic before he stepped out into the busy street. "I was one of those orphans, running around the streets, no family, no education, no one to care. It was Sir Barnabas who found me and recruited me, but it could just as easily have been someone like the Dutchman or Alice Gaines." He looked at Robert over his shoulder. "So yes, I'll help you find the she-devils who killed those boys. It's the least I can do for my own kind, isn't it?"

Robert didn't know what to say to that. A life like that was foreign to him. He'd been raised privileged, perhaps not among the aristocracy, but well-to-do, the son of a prosperous businessman. His father had died when he was young and he had been overindulged by his mother, but he'd been well educated and wanted for nothing. Yet another reason why his current situation baffled so many. Why lower himself to do police work? But cases like this were exactly why.

The Turkish ship sat out in the harbor, still waiting for an available docking but cleared by customs, who had inspected the goods and found nothing unusual about the rugs. The customs man had made a note: *poor quality/not Turkish.*

But it was the note below that one that had sent them looking for the ship first: *Dutch captain.*

"It would be too simple if the Dutchman we seek is this captain," Robert said.

"Yes," Simon said. "And I don't trust simple."

"Neither do I," Robert said.

"I love simple," Hastings said. "That's why I like the jobs where I get to just kill someone. That's easy. Here's a name. Go kill them. Good job. On to the next. None of this tramping all over town and making nice with the locals and trying to figure out who did what. It doesn't matter who did what. Sir Barnabas says they need to go. I make them disappear. Now that's simple."

"You are very frightening," Robert told him, and he meant it. They had reached the ferry landing where they were joined by a group of Sir Barnabas's men, who would board the ship with them.

Robert hadn't even known men like Hastings existed. He certainly hadn't known his childhood friend and schoolmate Daniel was one of them. Finding out about Daniel's secret life had been a turning point for Robert. His life had gone in extraordinary directions ever since he'd been pulled into Daniel's affairs. He was married now, a father, he'd had…whatever that was with Simon this morning, and here he was tracking spies for the Home Office. He wasn't sure he particularly cared for the last, to be sure. He liked being a constable, solving crimes, protecting the populace.

As for Simon, he had mixed emotions. He'd been friends with Daniel, and been aware of his predilection for men, for too long to be shocked by his own encounter in that regard. But he was shocked at how easily he'd fallen into the passionate interlude with Simon. He'd never been tempted by another man before for all he was aware that men acted in such a manner.

He knew he was boring and staid in comparison to Daniel and Simon and men like Hastings. He was content to pursue his livelihood, seek a wife and family, and live his life simply. He had never sought excitement, or wanted to live a less mundane life. He thrived on order, duty, organization. The disorganized life of a spy did not appeal to him in the slightest. Nor did the abnormal affections of same-sex love. Other men might be able to live with the inherent disorder of a life like that, but not Robert.

And yet...and yet he'd married Christy, who was a contradiction of all he believed in from the moment he met her. Married to one man, pregnant with another's child, on the run, lying about her identity, having a love affair with Simon— Robert had known all of that and he'd still asked for her hand. He'd been ready to beg for it. And he had never regretted marrying her. Not for one second.

He looked over at Simon. Were his confusing feelings for Simon just a result of his love for Christy? He knew she still cared for Simon, she'd admitted it to him earlier. Was he simply trying to get ahead of a possible complication on the horizon? His mind balked at where his thoughts were leading. He couldn't imagine disrupting his well-organized life in such a fashion.

Perhaps the solution was more complicated than that. Perhaps in a convoluted way Robert was making sure there would be a place for him in Christy's life, no matter what happened.

The thought made him stumble, and Simon reached out a hand to catch him before he fell. Robert shook it off, Simon's touch like a splash of cold water, sending goose bumps along his arm.

Was that it? Was he trying to prepare himself to accept the inevitable? Christy had wanted Simon, and it was apparent that Simon still wanted her. What man wouldn't? After the last two days, Robert could plainly see that no matter what had caused Simon to reject Christy last year, he was a good man at heart. Did Robert have the right to stand in the way of their love?

"Are you coming?" Simon asked. Robert looked over at him,

startled. Simon was standing with one leg on the ferry, the other on the dock, his hand held out to him, a quizzical look on his face. "Are you all right?"

"Yes," Robert lied. "I'm fine. I'm coming." He motioned Simon ahead and followed him onto the ferry. They would have to see this thing to the end, wherever it might lead. To the Dutchman, and possibly to the end of Robert's marriage.

CHAPTER 14

"Ahoy there," the ferry man called out. "Customs to board!"

Simon did not want to board the ship. He didn't like the feeling. He hadn't wanted to do parts of the job before, of course, but mostly for reasons of laziness or foreboding. What he felt now was fear. Fear because his jailers had been Turks and the men negotiating his release had been Dutch. A fine partnership that had lasted hundreds of years along the Barbary Coast, with or without treaties or international agreements.

And just knowing he would be on their ship again, that there was a possibility, remote though it may be, that he could be captured again, made him break out in a cold sweat. Why did the first case upon his return have to involve this devastating combination? It was a heavy blow that knocked the breath out of him and made him lightheaded and nauseous.

"You don't look well," Robert said to him quietly. Of course Robert would notice. He noticed everything. "Is it the water?"

It took a moment for Simon to comprehend what he meant.

He shook his head and then wished he'd said yes. It was a fine cover.

"Stay here," Robert ordered him. That did the trick.

"I'm fine," Simon said. "Quit being an old woman."

He glanced over and saw the second ferry making its way around the bow. While they had the attention of the crew, the rest of Sir Barnabas's men were going to board quietly on the starboard side. By the time they reached the deck and announced their real intent, they should be able to subdue the crew handily.

"Customs?" a man shouted down at them from the deck. Perhaps the captain, he sounded Dutch. But not the Dutchman from Alice Gaines's. "We have been inspected already."

"Still have some questions," Hastings shouted back. He held up a slim leather portfolio with papers sticking out. "Paperwork, I'm afraid," he called apologetically. The captain's curses were carried away by the wind but he motioned them on board.

"Can you climb the rigging?" Robert asked.

"Yes," Simon said through lips tight with anger. He knew Robert was asking for his own safety and that of the others. They didn't need a man going up who couldn't pull his own weight and might need rescuing if things got rough. Simon had never been that man and never would be.

He came up in the rear. He could do it, but he wasn't the strongest or fastest and he was man enough to admit it. He hoped his days of doing second story work weren't behind him.

By the time he climbed onto the deck, Sir Barnabas's men were in place with the crew under control and Hastings was interrogating the captain. Robert had waited to help him onto the deck.

"I'm fully capable of climbing over the rail myself," he grumbled, taking Robert's hand.

"Of course you are," Robert said. "But there's no need to reinjure yourself at this point with needless heroics. Come on."

His brisk tone was businesslike and cooled Simon's temper. As soon as his feet were firmly on the deck, Robert dropped his hand and walked away without a backward glance. So much for sentimentality.

"Where did you pick him up?" Hastings was asking the captain.

"Algiers," the captain said in disgust. "And if I had known he would cause so much trouble, I would have turned down his offer."

"What offer?" Hastings asked.

"He said he knew a man in London who would be interested in buying this ship."

"Did he have other business in London?" Robert asked.

"I didn't ask," the captain said. "And he didn't offer. He said he needed to go to London and knew someone who would be interested in my ship, we came to a mutually satisfying arrangement, and here we are."

"And are you in the habit of transporting spies, no questions asked, captain?" Simon queried.

The captain grew pale at the question. "How was I to know he was a spy?" he argued. "A well-dressed Dutch businessman. The last time I checked, the English and the Dutch were friends, yes? Ask the Bey in Algiers, who is still trying to rebuild his city that you destroyed together not too long ago."

"You are Dutch, and yet you captain a Turkish ship," Robert said.

"This is true," the captain said with a shrug. "But this is business. I own the ship, but she sails out of Algiers. That's why I have no papers. I only recently acquired her and am in the middle of sorting out the particulars. My Dutch papers are in process. I have the bill of sale. It satisfied customs."

"And the crew?" Robert asked.

"They came with the ship." The captain shrugged again.

Simon beckoned one of the agents over. "Go with him." He

turned to the captain. "Fetch the bill of sale." The captain hurried away. Simon turned to Robert and Hastings. "The captain seems to be telling the truth. I have a sense about these things. But something is amiss here. I can feel it. I don't think the captain knows what is going on aboard his own ship." He looked around at the crew, all of whom were eyeing them sullenly. "We need to search this ship."

Less than an hour later they were staring at a square-shaped hole cut in the middle of the pile of rugs. It had been not so cleverly concealed by several rugs laid on top of the pile. "I shall have to send a sternly worded note to customs about the obvious lack in their searching techniques," Robert said gravely. "What do you suppose they were smuggling in?"

"Not they. He," Simon said. "Clearly the Dutchman was bringing more than himself to London. Question the crew," he said without looking at the agents behind him.

Belatedly he realized he was sounding and acting more and more like Sir Barnabas, just expecting his will to be carried out. He turned around only to see that the agents had melted away, obeying his orders. It was a bit heady. No wonder Sir Barnabas seemed drunk on power half the time.

"Do they sit, stay and fetch with such alacrity?" Robert asked quietly. He sounded amused rather than upset, which was good. Stupid, simple Simon didn't want to upset him because he was an idiot who was obviously infatuated again with the wrong person. When would he learn? The answer was clearly never.

"I never learned," he replied lightly. "That's why I don't work for him."

"I hate to be the one to remind you that you're working for him now," Robert pointed out gently. "And showing a remarkable resemblance to him, I might add. In this case I believe familiarity has bred similarity."

"Ouch," Simon said, wincing. "I probably deserved that. But never fear, you shall keep me humble."

"I'll do my best." Robert squeezed his shoulder as he walked past, headed for the ladder out of the hold. Simon ignored the frisson of awareness that skittered across his back at the touch. Not here, not now, not ever. *Again.*

When they emerged on deck, it was just in time to see a man go over the side. "Man overboard!" one of the agents yelled.

In the ensuing chaos, several agents began to struggle with various crewmembers who rushed them in a coordinated attack. Robert pulled his pistol out from under his jacket, attempting to shove Simon behind him with his other hand.

"For God's sake," Simon shouted at him. "Let me go! I'm highly trained in this sort of combat, and can probably kill faster with my bare hands than you can with that gun. Now stop being so ridiculous." He shoved Robert out of the way and pulled a stiletto out of a sheath in his boot. "You go that way," he yelled, pointing left. "Bludgeon, don't shoot. We need answers, not dead men."

"I'm not Hastings," Robert said, affronted. He took off running, and Simon saw him bash a sailor on the back of the head with the butt of his pistol. It stunned him long enough for the agent he'd been struggling with to subdue him, and Robert moved on.

Simon ran toward the rail where he'd seen the sailor jump over. Another sailor tried to grab him and he slashed at his hand, cutting him. The sailor fell away with a cry, holding his hand, and Simon ran on as another agent jumped at the sailor.

Simon could see that men on other ships anchored nearby had also seen the man go overboard. At least two small dinghies were rowing toward him where he was treading in the water. He had one leg up on the rail before he took even a moment to think about what he was doing. He shoved his knife back in his boot and grabbed a rope to pull himself up onto the rail.

"Simon, no!" he heard Robert shout, but he ignored him and jumped.

He thought he was prepared for the water, but he wasn't. It was much farther to fall than he'd estimated, and when he hit the water it wasn't feet first, but at an angle, and his back bore some of the brunt of the impact. The searing pain momentarily stunned him and he sank in the cold, dank, stinking water of the harbor. He gasped and took in a mouthful of that awful stew, and immediately spewed it out and kicked for the surface, his shock dissipating, but the pain remained.

Simon was handicapped by his tight jacket and what he now remembered to be a serious lack of swimming experience. The Turkish sailor, on the other hand, looked to be half fish. The odds were distinctly against Simon, but he set off after the sailor.

He had a bit of luck when the sailor suddenly turned around and began to swim back his way. The dinghy had gotten too close to him and nearly caught him. They had him surrounded, and he'd clearly decided Simon was the lesser threat. Simon chased him down, grabbing his pant leg and hauling him back. The sailor proved as adept at grappling in the water as he was at swimming in it, and Simon was losing the struggle. Suddenly the sailor shoved Simon's head under the water, holding him down, and Simon knew he meant to drown him.

He heard the dull echo of a shot ring out. The pressure eased and he was able to jerk his head free and rise to the surface where he gasped and coughed, not caring if he ingested the disgusting water around him. He couldn't think about that when he was so relieved just to have air.

When he regained his senses, he saw Robert standing at the rail above him, his pistol still pointing at the water. When he looked to his left, the sailor was floating on the water, and he reached out, grabbed the sailor's shirt and began to drag him toward the nearest dinghy. Once there, he let the boat's occupants take charge and gladly accepted a ride from the second dinghy back to the dock, where he met Robert and Hastings.

Robert had somehow procured a blanket for him. He waved it away. "It's so damn hot I don't need it. I stink more than anything. Did you kill him?"

"No," Robert said calmly. "I shot him in the shoulder. He'll most likely never use that arm again, and frankly with a wound like that in this water it will probably fester and he'll die anyway, but at least he'll be able to answer some questions first."

Simon turned to stare at Robert with wide eyes. "I had no idea you could be so ruthless."

"You, sir, do not know anything about me." Robert's gaze was cold and enigmatic, and Simon felt a disturbing sort of confusion, as if someone had told him he didn't know his own name.

"I am beginning to think I don't know very much of anything at all," he said honestly.

"It's a start," Robert told him. "A good start, I should think. Now, what in the hell did you think you were doing jumping into the water like that? We'll be lucky if you don't start to fester as well."

CHAPTER 15

"**G**ood heavens, Simon!" Christy exclaimed as he came through the door. He was limping, looking like a drowned cat, filthy and wet and stinking. "What on earth happened?"

Robert was beside him, and she could tell he wanted to help Simon but was resisting the urge. No doubt Simon was being stubborn about his injuries.

"He jumped in the harbor and had a fight with a Turkish sailor," Robert told her. "Believe it or not, he won."

"I don't believe it," Christy said, her hands on her hips as she looked him over from head to toe.

"You should see the other fellow," Simon said. She could hear the pain in his voice.

"You need a hot bath," she declared. "Nell," she called. The young maid appeared almost instantly, giving Christy the impression she'd been eavesdropping just out of sight. "Fill the tub in the bathing chamber. Hot water, if you please. And as soon as Mr. Gantry gets out of these clothes, they are to be washed. Immediately. I know it isn't wash day, but if we leave them, they'll be ruined. Go on, now."

She ignored her misgivings and reached out for Simon's arm. "Come on," she said without an ounce of pity. "Let's get you upstairs. Robert, help me get him out of these wet things."

"What?" Simon asked, looking appalled. "I can undress myself."

"You don't look like it." Christy looked over her shoulder at the agents who were guarding the front door. They were peering through the door watching them with interest. "Shut the door and mind your business," she told them briskly. One of them immediately pulled the door shut.

"You are a martinet," Simon complained as he leaned on her support and let her lead him upstairs.

"You may call me whatever you like," she said. "But this is my house and I make the rules." She realized what she'd said and cleared her throat as she looked at Robert. "That is, we—I mean, Robert and I—make the rules. With his permission, of course."

"Too late," Robert said, sounding amused and not a bit put out. "You can't put any of the blame on me. This is your doing, not mine."

They reached Simon's bedchamber and Christy ushered him inside. "Robert, close the door behind you." She let go of Simon, who started to sit down on the bed. "No," she nearly yelled at him, and he froze halfway. "Not in those clothes. Not on my linens. Robert, help me."

"Shouldn't we be doing this in the bathing chamber?" Robert asked. He stepped in front of Simon and began to unbutton his jacket.

Simon slapped his hands away. "I can unbutton my own jacket," he insisted. "I'm not an invalid."

"Of course not," Christy said. "But it's as obvious as the nose on my face that you've hurt your back. Oh, Simon, what were you thinking?"

"I was thinking that a man who clearly knew something about our investigation was getting away and if I didn't go after him he'd be gone," Simon snapped. "And I should be at head-quarters questioning him and not here being coddled like a child."

He tried to jerk the jacket off over his shoulders and gasped and nearly fell over. Robert had to catch him with an arm around his waist. He pulled Simon up and caught him against his chest, and Simon just hung there for a moment breathing heavily. Christy wanted to cry for him.

"Are you all right?" Robert asked, concern etched on his face. Christy adored him at that moment.

Simon nodded, the motion jerky. "Fine," he said, the word short and sharp. Robert slowly let go.

Christy moved behind Simon. "Let me," she said quietly. "You just stand there." She pulled the jacket down his arms and off as gently as she could, but its sodden condition made it more difficult than it should have been, and she knew it was hurting him. Robert stood there in front of him with his hands on Simon's upper arms, helping him to stand while she did it.

"I feel like an imbecile," Simon muttered.

"You are an imbecile," Robert told him.

"Your sympathy is duly noted," Simon replied politely.

"Robert," Christy chastised. She dropped Simon's stinking jacket to the floor and wrinkled her nose in disgust.

"Don't bother to launder it," Simon told. "It's ruined. We might be able to save everything else, but the jacket is beyond redemption."

"You should have thought of that before you jumped." She pushed it farther away with the toe of her shoe. "Hold on," she said, realizing the dilemma they now faced. "I'll be right back."

She ran down the hall and grabbed an old linen sheet from the washroom for Simon to sit on so they could remove his boots and trousers. When she got back to the room she found that Robert had already dispensed with Simon's boots somehow, and as she came through the door he was pulling Simon's shirt off. Christy's hand involuntarily flew to cover her mouth and stifle her exclamation of horror as Simon's back was revealed to her for the first time.

It looked horrendously painful. A dark read angry slash of puckered skin from his right shoulder blade to his left side, just above the waist of his trousers. There were other scars there, too. They looked like whipping scars.

"Oh, Simon," she whispered.

He froze in place, his arms still locked in the sleeves of his shirt, bound in front of him, his back exposed, his weaknesses exposed. She wanted to fall to her knees and wrap her arms around him and press her cheek to his scarred back and will her own strength into him.

Robert had been standing in front of Simon, but at Christy's pained whisper he walked slowly around to look at his back. He didn't say a word. He simply reached over and took the linen from Christy, opening it up and holding it high. "Here, hold it like this."

She did as she was told, blocking Simon from her view. Robert walked back around in front of Simon, and she heard him say, "Let me help you get these off, too." The rustle of clothing told her he was helping Simon get his trousers off.

"This is embarrassing and awkward and feel free to add any adjectives you care to contribute," Simon said.

"I believe awkward doesn't do the situation justice," Robert agreed in a strained voice. "There." He immediately came around the makeshift curtain and dropped the rest of Simon's stained, smelly clothes on the floor.

"Close your eyes," he told Christy. She did so, and then he took the sheet. "All right," he said, and when she opened them, Simon was wrapped in the linen, only his bare shoulders visible.

"Now I must head back to the Home Office," Robert said. He

and Simon were avoiding looking at each other, and it was all Christy could do not to roll her eyes. Men were so odd about their privacy and nudity. "Simon, once you are cleaned up, rest, and I will fill you in at supper."

"Now you really are making me feel like an invalid," Simon complained.

"I do not mean to," Robert said, frustration in his voice. "The fact is I am trying to avoid just that. You have been home for less than a week. You are not completely healed from your ordeal. If you continue to push yourself this way, you may very well end up an invalid, and no one wants that. So we must use common sense. I am trying to do what is right, and what logic dictates must be done. Surely you can see that."

"Tomorrow will be a week," Simon said. He readjusted the linen. Christy stood there, her arms wrapped around her middle, letting Robert handle the situation. He seemed better able to handle Simon in this mood. She just wanted to either yell at him or smother him with hugs and kisses, neither of which was appropriate or helpful.

"Fine," Simon finally agreed. "I will rest. And I concede that you are right. I am trying too hard to deny that anything is wrong and pretending that nothing happened to me. There? Are you happy? So I shall be a good boy and take a hot bath and go to bed."

"Yes, I'm happy," Robert said. He sighed and started to leave but then, almost as an afterthought, remembered Christy and came to kiss her cheek goodbye. "I shall be home for supper," he told her.

"That's fine," she said, the awkwardness they'd spoken of suddenly finding its way to her. "But we need to talk about something that happened today while I was out shopping."

"Yes, all right," Robert said, clearly distracted. "When I get home."

The irony that Robert was leaving her alone with a naked Simon expecting her to bathe and take care of him was not lost on her. He either had a great deal of trust in her or he was the world's greatest fool.

CHAPTER 16

"What happened while you were shopping?" Simon asked as he stood next to the steaming tub of water. A cold bath would have been better. Standing naked in a room with Robert and Christy had pushed his endurance to its limits. It was probably a good thing his back was screaming or he'd surely be wearing a tent for trousers.

"Nothing really," Christy said dismissively. "I was approached by a strange man, a couple of strange men actually, and a blonde woman. It was all very odd. The agent seemed quite agitated about the whole thing." She shrugged. "But nothing happened. The woman was yelling at me to run, the little man lunged at me, and the other man, the tall one, dragged him away. Then they all disappeared. It couldn't have lasted more than a minute or two. I was frightened at the time, but now I think it was all a tempest in a teapot."

Simon's blood ran cold at her tale. "Christy you must promise me not to go out again unless it's absolutely necessary, and then only with more than one agent. Promise me."

"What a lot of fuss," she said, with a little huff of annoyance. "But if it will get you in the tub, then I promise."

"I can wash myself." He looked again at that steaming tub of water and wondered how the hell he was going to climb into the damn thing and wash without howling.

"We made it too hot," Christy said, her voice wavering. "I didn't think. I mean, I didn't realize—"

"I'll just let it cool off." Simon eased down to sit on the chair beside the tub. "It will be fine."

"Let me wash your back while you sit there," Christy said. Her voice was getting stronger, like it had been downstairs. She was different than she'd been last year. More sure of herself. But then, this was her house, as she'd said. She had a place at last, as Robert's wife.

She could have been yours, that harsh little voice in his head whispered. *This could be your house.* When that voice had belittled his cowardice in rejecting Christy, when it had taunted him with what might have been as he'd lain in that stinking cell in Africa, rotting on the floor, he'd slapped his own face to shut it up. He couldn't do that now. He also knew he couldn't wash his own back, damn it.

"Please," he said with a sigh, turning slightly.

He listened to her dip her cloth into the tub water and ring it out. Every nerve in his back that wasn't screaming in pain was standing at attention anticipating her touch.

"You'll have to lower your cover," she told quietly. "I want to clean this wound thoroughly. I know it's healed, but we should still keep it as clean as possible so as not to invite a relapse."

Simon knew she was right, but he also knew the whole situation was wrong. What they were all inviting here was trouble. What was Robert thinking, leaving Simon and Christy alone together like this? And what was Simon thinking letting him? He wasn't thinking, that was what. He was feeling, and what he was feeling were things he definitely oughtn't to be feeling about Christy or Robert or anyone else in this house.

His thoughts were crashing around in his head, careening

off one another as his shoulders grew tense waiting for Christy's first touch. When it came, it broke him. Not with pleasure, but with pain. He cried out and shied away from her hand.

"I'm so sorry," she said, sounding near tears. "I didn't mean to hurt you. Is it the cloth? Shall I just use my hands?"

Simon wanted to cry, not at the pain, but at the injustice of it all. "Yes," he said, his voice strangled with bitterness and longing and a whole stew of emotions he'd rather not name or feel. "The cloth is too rough right now."

When her hands, slick with lather, gently touched his back, he did cry. Silently so as not to alarm her. He cried because it still hurt and he didn't care.

Christy ran her hands up and down his back, gently cleansing it and massaging it, and it felt divine, as if the hand of a goddess had reached down and anointed his ravaged back with some secret elixir. She scooped up water from the tub and rinsed his back, and then she lathered it again. This time she washed his arms as well, and he sat there docile as the child he'd proclaimed himself not to be and let her. When she was done, she moved around in front of him, and only then did he realize he'd closed his eyes. He opened them and looked up at her.

She was watching him closely. Her gaze traced his face and came back to his eyes, and they stared at each other. She cupped his cheeks and ran her thumbs under his eyes, wiping his tears away, and it thrilled him, these simple things.

"Oh, Simon," she said sadly. She ran her thumb over his lips. "I'd kiss you, you fool, but to be honest, you still smell disgusting."

Simon burst out laughing at her unexpected comment. "There's my practical Christy," he said. "God, I've missed you."

She let go of him then. "Have you?" she said with a sad smile. "I've missed you, too. I wish I didn't."

Their situation came back to him like a blow to the chest then. "Yes. I wish that, too."

But he didn't. Not really. She was the only thing that had gotten him through Africa. The only thought that had kept him sane. He'd promised himself that when he came back he'd apologize to her. He'd tell her that he loved her, but walk away because it was the right thing to do. But he didn't want her to think that he hadn't loved her enough to offer for her. He'd loved her too much.

Now the words stuck in his throat. He could see that telling her would only make matters worse for both of them. For Robert. He cared for Robert now, too. Why was he always hurting the people he cared for the most? The few people that seemed to give a damn about him, too. That seemed to be his lot in life.

"I'm sure you do," she said. She stepped back. "Can you take care of the rest? I think the water is cool enough now."

He looked away from her and tested the water, although he didn't care about the physical pain anymore. He welcomed it. It drowned out the much worse pain inside of him. "Yes, it's fine. Thank you." He looked at her then. "Thank you for everything."

"I haven't done everything," she said, brushing away his thanks. "But you're very welcome." She went to the door, not looking back at him as she opened it. "I'll lay out some clean clothes for you." She closed the door, still not looking at him.

He dropped the linen sheet and stepped into the cool tub, wishing it was hot enough to burn his sins away.

WHEN HE RETURNED to his room wrapped in a fresh linen sheet, he caught Christy unaware. She was leaning against the bedpost, her face buried in one of his shirts. At first he thought she was crying, but then he realized she was smelling it. Inhaling it might be a better description.

He understood completely. It was what he wanted to do to her. Every time he was near her, he could smell the faint but distinctive perfume of her, and it was branded in his mind as clearly as the mark on his back was in his skin. Did she feel the same way about him? Although Lord knew he didn't smell as good as she in the godawful heat of this unusual summer.

"Christy?" he asked quietly. He half shut the bedroom door. He didn't want anyone else to see what she was doing.

She straightened and dropped the hand holding his shirt to her side. She was blushing furiously. "Simon," she said. "I didn't see you there."

"I'm sorry." He rather thought he'd be saying that to her for the rest of their lives.

She bustled about, putting his shirt on top of a pile of clothes on the bed. "I've gathered what I could. You came with a minimal wardrobe. I assume you thought you'd only be here a short time. The case must be turning out to be more difficult than you all imagined. I sent around to Daniel's for some things. The agent in charge at the door said it wasn't a good idea to go to your apartment for anything since they might be watching it and we didn't want to put anyone else in danger. Although apparently we are watching it, too? It's all very confusing. But I thought Daniel would probably have something of yours since you were always there so often when I was staying with him." She stopped abruptly and her gaze cut over to him.

He licked his lips. Her chatter was most likely meant to distract him, but it was having the opposite effect. He was sharply conscious of the fact they were in his bedroom alone and he wore nothing but a sheet wrapped around his hips.

And now she brought up Daniel's and the two of them together there. It was where they'd fallen in love. Where they'd made love.

He couldn't have stopped his feet from moving toward her if he'd nailed them to the floor, and Lord knew he was no martyr.

"Don't," she whispered, but she didn't move away.

When he stood in front of her, he stopped. He leaned down

and lay his nose against her hair and inhaled deeply. He felt her shiver. "Simon," she whispered.

"It's not as I remembered," he said, his lips touching her silky hair. "At night I'd lay on the floor and I'd imagine the way you smelled. Like violets and cinnamon, and freshly laundered clothes. You still smell like that a little. But now it's..." He sniffed again. "Roses. Is it roses? I like that, too."

"Violets are for girls," she said, her voice so low he could barely hear her. "I'm not a girl anymore. I wasn't then, either, but I didn't know the proper way to be a lady. I do now."

"I hope not," Simon said. "I never met a proper lady I liked."

Christy laughed, as he hoped she would, and she turned her face up to him only to discover how very close they were, how simple a thing it would be to close the distance between them in a kiss. "I don't suppose you have," she whispered breathlessly.

"Can't abide the breed," Simon told her. He stole his arm around her. She felt so good, so right there. *I shouldn't, I shouldn't, I shouldn't.*

He pictured Robert, trying to guilt himself into letting her go, but all he could see was a sleepy, aroused Robert kissing him passionately. That didn't help. He pulled Christy against his chest and she put her palms on the bare skin of his shoulders, and it was like a match to kindling.

He wasn't sure who moved first, but suddenly they had their arms wrapped tightly around each other and they were kissing hungrily, a year's worth of passion and longing and misery pouring out of their mouths without words.

When he needed air more than he needed to kiss her, he broke away with a gasp. She was breathing as heavily as he was, but neither wanted to forgo the taste of the other. Simon rained kisses across Christy's cheek to her ear and bit her lobe, eliciting a moan from her while she kissed his chest and his chin, any part of him she could reach.

"How I missed you, my darling," he whispered. "How I

dreamed of you at night. How I cursed myself for a fool for abandoning you. I loved you, Christy. You must believe me. I loved you too much to ruin your life by marrying you."

"Simon, Simon," she moaned. "I dreamed of you, too, my love. I cried each day you were gone, sure you were dead and my happiness with you. Never leave me again. You must promise me." She dragged his head down to hers and kissed him again. Her mouth was like a drug, and Simon allowed himself to get lost in the haze of pleasure for a moment, but eventually he forced himself to pull away.

"I have to leave you, Christy," he said, his voice breaking despite his attempt at fortitude. "You belong to Robert now. I made my choice and so did you. He is a good man and I will not betray him."

Christy ripped herself out of Simon's arms at his words, and one look at her face told Simon all he needed to know. She looked horrified, ashamed, grief-stricken. "What have I done?" she whispered.

She wiped the back of her hand across her mouth, and that gesture more than anything broke Simon's heart in two. "I love Robert," she whispered. "He *is* a good man. He is the best man. I will not betray him. I swore I would not. Not even with you, not for you. Never. This can never happen again."

She turned away and hurried to the door, stumbling only once. When she got there, she stopped, her back to Simon. She smoothed her hands over her hair and down the front of her dress, composing herself. Simon let her have her moment, standing silent as he watched her. He had nothing left to say.

"Supper will be at six," she said. Then she walked out the door and closed it behind her.

ROBERT BARELY HAD time to duck into Hastings's empty bedroom before Christy walked out of Simon's room. He leaned against the wall next to the door and prayed Christy wouldn't decide to come into the room where he was hiding. He was trembling. He wasn't sure if it was rage, or grief, or perhaps shock.

He'd known that Christy and Simon had a past relationship but had never really understood the nature of it. He'd assumed Christy had been the one with feelings for Simon that were not reciprocated in kind, which was why he had rejected her. And why he and Simon had had their own passionate encounter the other day.

But Simon and Christy were in love with each other. Robert had not expected this. He had not expected it to hurt quite so much, either. And it wasn't just Christy's betrayal, but Simon's as well that hurt, which was laughable.

Christy wouldn't betray Robert, Simon wouldn't betray Robert, but hadn't Robert betrayed them both? Were they both using Robert to somehow be close to one another? The thought was sickening.

He put a hand to his churning stomach. He didn't want to be anyone's consolation. Christy said she loved him, but she had never passionately declared herself to him the way she just had to Simon. Her love for Robert was a pale imitation of what she felt for Simon. And whatever Simon felt for Robert, it was nothing compared to what he felt for Christy. He had dreamed of her every night in Africa. Robert knew what that meant. He knew Christy must have been the one thing that helped Simon survive the hell of his captivity there.

Robert stepped away from the wall, straightening his spine. He knew what he had to do. He clenched his hands into fists and then relaxed them. One deep breath before he opened the door and left the room.

He'd meant to talk to Christy about the attack this morning. Barnabas's man had just filled him in. He was sick at what might have happened to her. And now this. He would talk to her about it tonight, and he would handle the Simon problem, too.

CHAPTER 17

R obert got home later than anticipated. It had taken longer to get the information out of the Turkish sailor than they'd thought it would. He'd been surprising loyal to the Dutchman. But they now had a name—Lucas Van de Berg. A common enough Dutch name, but it was a place to start.

And they knew he was looking for a ship. He'd removed a small cargo of explosives from the Turkish vessel they'd seized today, and he wanted another ship to put it on. The sailor did not know why. As far as he knew, Van de Berg was still in London. It wasn't the answers to all their questions, but it was more than they knew this morning. There were actually two of Van de Berg's men among the remaining crew. The rest were exactly what they seemed, simple sailors who had fought with the agents out of fear and a sense of misplaced loyalty to their fellow Turks, and not as part of the Dutchman's plot.

Explosives for an assassination seemed a messy business. Hastings and Sir Barnabas agreed. Robert had offered to bring it up with Simon before they returned to the Home Office tomorrow to sort through it all. The perfect opportunity to address that other situation as well. And he still needed to talk to Christy about the attack this morning. He'd been trying all day not to think about how close he'd come to losing her.

But when he walked in the house, he knew everything would have to wait until the morning. The house was quiet and the lamp was turned down low in the hall by the door. He headed for the kitchen and a bite to eat. There was a plate covered by a cloth, left for him by cook or by Christy.

He pulled off the cloth and knew it was Christy. She'd sliced two pieces of bread and the butter dish was there, as well as the honey. Cook only left him one slice with butter. He smiled sadly. Soon he'd be back to a one slice of bread life.

After he'd eaten, he slowly made his way up the stairs. Tonight was definitely different than the other night, when he'd come home late and Christy had waited up for him. She'd most likely cried herself to sleep tonight. Or given in to temptation and crawled into bed with Simon. Robert was too much of a coward to go and check.

His own hypocrisy wasn't lost on him. Hadn't he spent the night in Simon's arms just two days ago? God, it seemed longer than that. So much had happened since he innocently offered Simon comfort, and yet he couldn't blame Simon. Was he to blame? Perhaps. Maybe he had been testing himself and Simon.

He went straight to his own rooms, unable to think about it anymore. He was too tired to think at all.

When he entered his bedroom, he stopped short at the sight of Christy curled up in his bed. She looked peaceful and angelic with her pretty dark hair fanned out across the pale sheets. Her hands were tucked up under her cheek. She looked as if nothing bad could ever touch her.

Robert knew it for the lie it was. Her life had been harder than most. Unloved, unwanted, orphaned, tossed aside by a self-absorbed husband, an uncaring lover, and then rejected by Simon, who swore his love at the same time he said he could not be with her. Why? What was it Simon had said? That marrying her would ruin her life. Robert didn't understand that. His past as a spy certainly made him less respectable than most, but so did Robert's profession.

"Robert?" Christy's sleepy voice pulled him from his thoughts.

"Yes, dear?" he asked.

"Come to bed. I tried to wait up, but I was too tired." She reached out a hand blindly to him, a sleepy smile on her face while she stayed curled up, the covers kicked to the end of the bed in the heat, her eyes closed. She looked…happy. But how could she be when who she really wanted—Simon—was in the bedroom next door? Wasn't he?

"Stop thinking about the case," she chastised. Her eyes were open now. She came up on all fours and crawled to the end of the bed. She kneeled there to face him, one hand on the bedpost, still looking sleepy and disheveled, her unbound hair falling around her shoulders. "Come to bed," she said again.

"Why are you here?" he asked quietly.

"Shut the door," she whispered. She put a finger to her lips. "Don't wake everyone." She had a devilish gleam in her eyes at odds with her angelic looks. She wore nothing but a simple, shapeless nightshift, yet she was temptation itself. He resisted.

"Why are you here?" he asked again. It was a question he'd been asking himself all day. Why had she accepted his proposal? Was it desperation? She could have stayed with Harry; he'd told her so. But she'd opted instead to divorce Harry and marry Robert. Was it merely for the marriage bed? Surely not. She could have taken lovers, even kept Simon as her lover had she stayed married to Harry. His head had been spinning all day trying to make sense of her choice. Why him? Why choose Robert?

"Because I wanted to see you, silly," she said. "We haven't had enough time together the last few weeks with this awful case and everyone coming and going. I miss you. Don't you miss me?"

She pouted, a very pretty pout, a flirtatious pout. She didn't flirt with him. They'd never needed it. Although perhaps at the beginning they had flirted. Or she had. He'd never been any good at it.

He knew why she was here tonight. Because she felt guilty about what had transpired with Simon this afternoon and she was here to make herself feel better by being with him. And he was just weak enough tonight to let her.

He took a step closer to the bed, and she reached out and pulled him closer still by tucking her fingers in the waistband of his trousers. "Well?" she asked. "Didn't you miss me?"

She had no idea how much. How frightened he was by the attack on her this morning. He didn't answer her with words. Instead he closed his fist in the hair on the back of her head and kissed her hard, trying to both punish her and force all thoughts of Simon from her mind.

She wouldn't play by his rules, however, and pushed her arms up, forcefully making room so she could wrap them around his neck. She imitated his embrace, closing her fist in his hair and kissing him just as hard, upping the ante by biting his lower lip and sucking it like a piece of sugar candy. Robert's head began to spin as if he'd had too much brandy and he had to pull away from the kiss to catch his breath.

"Yes," Christy whispered, kissing his throat as he gulped in air. "That's exactly how I want you tonight. Please, Robert. Take me like that."

Robert grabbed her arms and had to pull hard to break her hold on him, dragging them down and off him. He shoved her and she fell back on her hands on the bed, panting. At first she looked angry, but when he began to unbutton his jacket roughly, almost tearing the buttons in his haste, she smiled like a self-satisfied cat.

Robert didn't take his eyes off her as he undressed hastily, tossing his clothes aside. He never did that. He was normally fastidious to a fault. But he saw no reason to be like that tonight. There was no benefit to it and every advantage to getting in that bed with Christy as fast as he could so he could forget his misgivings and make her forget any she may have. That was all he knew, as far as he could reason in the moment.

When he had nothing left to remove but his trousers and small clothes, Christy sat up and slowly pulled her shift up and over her head, tossing it aside as carelessly as he'd been doing. While he finished undressing, she kneeled naked and unashamed on his bed, waiting for him, her head cocked to the side as she watched him, as if to say, *Here I am. Come and get me.*

So he did.

He crawled on the bed in front of Christy on all fours and he kept advancing, forcing her back awkwardly. She didn't complain. She scrambled to untangle her legs so she could lay beneath him. She was panting, and he knew it was from want. She liked this. How had he never known that? Married for months and he'd never realized she wanted to be hunted, stalked, won. She was a prize to be won.

He reached down and hooked a hand under her arm, pulling her with him as he moved farther up the bed, almost dragging her, and she laughed in delight. The sound both pleased him and saddened him. She had never laughed like that in bed with him before.

To mask his reaction, he swooped down and kissed her again—hard and possessively, the way she seemed to like. She tasted warm and sweet. Her mouth was so wonderful, soft and tender. Vulnerable.

He lowered his weight onto her so that her breasts were pressed against his chest and he could feel each breath pushing her softness against him. He slid both hands into her hair and cupped her head holding her where he wanted her, directing the kiss, controlling it. She purred in her throat and wrapped her arms and legs around him, rubbing her quim against him like a cat in heat. He dragged his mouth away, across her cheek.

"Oh, yes," she said breathlessly. "Like that. I like this." She dug her nails into his back. "I want you."

"I like it too," he whispered in her ear. He licked the delicate whorls there, then bit her lobe, and she purred again. "I like not worrying about hurting you or frightening you. I'm not sure where those ideas came from." He rubbed his nose against her cheek and then kissed her again, giving free rein to his passion. He hadn't really understood until just now how much he'd been controlling it. "I've been holding back so much," he murmured against her lips.

"Don't hold back," she whispered back. She bit his lip and it stung. She licked the sting away. "I can take it." She leaned up, and right against his ear whispered so quietly he barely heard her, "Fuck me, Robert. Like I know you want to."

Her words ignited something in him, something he hadn't even known was there. He had always desired Christy, but this feeling burning him up inside was so much more than mere desire. It was elemental, a need to take her and possess her, to be one with her. To carry her with him into the abyss of this thing that had got hold of him.

He kissed her again and then slid down to worship her body as he had not done properly since he had promised to do so in his wedding vows. He understood it now, those words he had spoken. *This. This is what it means to worship her with my body.*

He kissed her skin, licked it, tasted the salt of the day's heat on her and relished her spice. When he traced his tongue down the path between her breasts, she shivered and he travelled next to her hard nipples, kissing and sucking them, gently nipping them, and she gasped, her legs tightening around his waist, her fingers clenching in his hair as she held his mouth on her. He had never dared do this to her, though he had longed to. What a fool he'd been. What a misguided fool to think respecting one's wife meant you could not treat her like an object of sexual desire. He desired her in so many ways; this was only one of them. To deny her this act of worship was the height of disrespect. Tonight he would atone for his sins.

He let his hand glide down from her hip to her thigh, massaging it as he went. He pulled it from around his waist, and she moaned in protest. "No," she begged.

"I want to kiss you everywhere," Robert told her, sucking on the side of her breast, leaving a mark, licking it. He liked his mark on her. He'd heard men talk of kissing women on the quim, and he'd seen pictures of it, naughty illustrations when he was in school. He'd never done it. He had a gorgeous, willing, passionate wife, and he'd never done it. He refused to let one more day go by without doing that for her, too.

"Oh, God, yes," she said enthusiastically. She quickly pulled her legs down and spread them, feet braced on the bed. "Please." She pushed his head down toward her sex. "I've been dying for you to do it."

Robert was a little nonplussed. Clearly Christy had done this before. Well, then he'd better make sure to do a damn good job of it.

He pushed himself down with one last kiss on each breast, a playful kiss on her stomach, and then he was there. The scent of her was the world's most exotic aphrodisiac. He cupped her derriere, leaned down and delicately licked her slit—her moisture was salty and earthy and divine. She pressed his mouth harder against her.

"Kiss it like you did my mouth," she whispered. "I like it like that down there, too."

Robert was grateful for the guidance. He followed her advice and kissed her passionately, shoving his tongue inside her, fucking her with it, lapping up her salty sweet passion, and she moaned, arching her back, pushing her quim against his face, wordlessly begging for more. Robert smiled, pulled back and teased her with the tip of his tongue. When he nudged the hard little button of flesh at the top of her slit, she gasped and fisted the covers.

"Right there, then?" he asked with satisfaction. "Good."

"Robert," she moaned. "God, please."

"What?" he asked, then he teased her with the tip of his tongue in that special little spot again. She sobbed a little.

"Put it inside me," she begged.

His cock was so hard he could feel his heartbeat there. At her words, the beat intensified and he felt it leak a little. Clearly his cock liked the idea very much.

"What?" he asked. "This?" He slid his finger inside her. "God, you're so wet. You've never been this wet."

"Fuck me," she begged. She pumped her hips, riding his finger, and moaned in frustration. "More," she demanded. He obliged by leaning down and tickling that sensitive little knot with his tongue while he moved his finger in and out. She purred and thrust against his mouth and hand. "More, more," she said again.

Robert couldn't tease her anymore. "Yes," he said. "I've got to have you."

He came to his knees and shoved her legs apart, staring at her wet, dark pink, swollen quim. He'd never taken the time to really look at it before. To admire it and memorize it in amazement that it was his to fuck.

"I never thought a man fucked his wife," he told her. His voice was rough, a little breathless. She watched him with glassy, passion-drunk eyes. "I never thought of what a man and wife did as so earthy or carnal. I'm sorry. I'm sorry I didn't understand that this was what you wanted, that this is what I should have been doing all along."

"I should have told you," Christy said. She reached out and wrapped her small, delicate hand around his hard cock. Her grip was surprisingly strong. "So now I'm telling you. Fuck me, Robert. Fuck me like a man should fuck his wife."

She stroked his cock, and when she let go he kissed her and adjusted his weight before he finally pushed into her. She moaned and slid her hands up his arms to his shoulders and dug her nails into him as she lifted her hips off the bed and met his thrust. "Just like that, husband," she whispered.

"Like that?" he asked. "Or like this?" He gripped her hip with one hand and fucked into her harder. She gasped, her nails digging deeper.

"Yes," she hissed. He felt her sex clench around him. He did it again, a little bit harder. She moaned, and bent her legs so that she was gripping him with her thighs. "More," she whispered.

"I see," he said, his chest heaving. He wasn't going to last much longer, but he teased her nonetheless. "What you really want is to be fucked."

She laughed breathlessly. "Didn't I say so? Fuck me, Robert. Fuck me now."

He obliged her. He thrust into her hard, steady, pushing her up the bed so that she had to put a hand against the headboard behind her to keep from sliding into it. Robert loved every minute of it, and from the sounds Christy was making, so did she

He knew the instant she came. Her back arched and her quim strangled his cock, pulsing around him as she threw her head back and moaned loudly and long. He kept going even as she came, and with each thrust she shivered and cried out again. When he came, he buried his face in her neck and his cock in her hot, quivering passage and held on for dear life, shaking and sweating and falling apart in her arms.

CHAPTER 18

"I'm sorry."

Christy stroked Robert's hair as he lay beside her, his head on her shoulder, his arm around her hips. They were both sweaty and sticky, and neither cared a bit. She'd never had this with a lover, this kind of after-the-fact affection and closeness. Harry had cried and confessed he loved Daniel. John Coachman had rolled over and gone to sleep, ignoring her. And Simon...well, theirs had been a hurried affair, clandestine, with no time for affectionate cuddles like this.

If she wasn't so thoroughly satisfied, she'd be angry on her own behalf for what she'd been denied. But then, she hadn't demanded it, had she? She was learning that she had to ask for what she wanted.

"Why are you sorry?" Robert asked in that sleepy voice she loved so very much. No one else got to hear that voice. Just her. It was an intimacy she cherished.

She brushed his hair out of the way and kissed his forehead. "For not telling you sooner what I wanted."

"Ah," Robert said. He was quiet for quite a long time. Then he asked, "Why didn't you tell me?"

She let her fingers dance across his broad shoulders. "I have always been the girl no one wanted, you know," she told him, trying not to sound pitiful. "When my parents died and I was stuck with my aunt and uncle, I tried not to ask for too much or make myself a nuisance because I wanted them to like me. When I was engaged to Harry and he came back from Portugal to marry me, I didn't say anything and just did what I was told because I just wanted everyone to like me and to finally have a place. And then for ten years I lived alone in a little house in a little village where no one liked me and no one bothered to get to know me because I was an outsider with no husband present. I practically had to beg John Coachman to be my lover, and once again I never asked for anything, I just took what he was willing to give because I was so desperate to be close to anyone. How sad I was."

Robert had opened his eyes and was looking up at her now, his hand stroking her hip. She bit her lip and then decided that Robert deserved the truth.

"And Simon...I did ask Simon. I asked him to be my lover, but I didn't have to beg, not like before. He wanted me. And, well, he showed me what it was like to be wanted. And I liked it. I liked how it felt. And I wanted it again. I wanted it with you." She cupped his cheek. "You believe me, don't you?"

"Yes," he said. "I believe you." There was something in his eyes, something lurking there that she couldn't decipher. "You shall always be wanted by me, Christy, and this will always be your place if you want it." He took her hand and kissed her palm. "Tell me what happened this morning. I almost lost you."

"Nonsense," she said with a chuckle. "There was just a strange little man who hailed me, and then a tall, thin man grabbed him and pulled him away into the crowd."

"I believe those strange men were assassins," Robert told her. "The first one most likely meant to kill you, my love."

She felt lightheaded for a moment. "What?" she whispered.

"From now on there will be more men stationed out side, and you will only leave in a carriage with a full armed guard, and only when necessary. Understood?" he asked.

"Yes, I understand," she agreed. "I promised Simon as much earlier. But who was the other man? The one who stopped him?"

"I'm not sure. I dare not hope one of them is actually on our side," he said. "For now, we will treat them all as hostile. My main concern is keeping you safe. You and Christian."

"Oh, Robert," she whispered.

She was about to kiss him when there was a shout from Simon's room. Both she and Robert sat up immediately, their intimacy torn apart by the broken cry.

"Simon," she said, though it was clear Robert knew it as well as she.

In seconds he was off the bed. He grabbed his robe and was out the door so quickly she was sure he hadn't had time to put it on. She was clumsier than he, unable to spring into action from the lethargy of sexual satisfaction with such alacrity. Her wrapper was securely tied before she dashed from the room and down the hall to Simon's.

When she entered Simon's room, shock stopped her in her tracks. Robert was sitting on the bed and Simon was in his arms, and Simon clung to him, both arms wrapped tightly around his shoulders. It took a moment to register that Robert was murmuring soothing sounds to Simon, rocking him gently, almost like he did with Christian when he woke in the night.

She caught Robert's look above Simon's head and she could see he was distressed. When she cautiously came closer, she could see that Simon was shaking, and his hair was plastered to his head with sweat.

"What's wrong?" she asked quietly.

"N-nothing," Simon stuttered, pushing away from Robert. "A

stupid dream is all." As he twisted away, he gasped and his hand went to his back.

"Your back," Christy said, concerned. "Let me see it."

"No." Simon awkwardly gathered the sheet around him, looking pale and sweaty and miserable.

"Don't be an idiot," Robert said sharply. "Come here." He held out his hand and stared Simon down. To Christy's surprise, Simon relented, but on his terms.

"Fine," he said. He pointed behind him. "Take a look."

Christy looked at Robert, who nodded. She lit the lamp on the nearby table and walked around the bed. She'd seen it earlier, in the bath, so she was prepared for the sight of the angry red, puckered slash. But the cruelty of it still hit her like a fist in her stomach. She swallowed with difficulty before speaking.

"It looks...dry, I guess you would say. Tight. Is that how it feels?" she asked. She tentatively reached out and touched it lightly with her fingertips.

Simon flinched. "Yes," he said. "Tight. That's a good word for it. It feels like it's going to tear apart every time I move."

"I have some wound salve," Christy said. "Not much. Or some kind of hand cream?" She really wasn't sure what to put on it, but she knew it needed something with moisture.

"I have something. In my bag," Simon told her. "The doctor gave it to me. It's in a little glass jar."

"I'll get it," Christy said. She set the lamp down and went to get it from his bag.

"How long since you've put it on?" Robert asked. "I doubt you can do it yourself."

"No, I'm no contortionist. I guess since I got back." Simon sounded tired. Not just sleepy tired, but bone-weary tired. Christy didn't like the sound of him.

"I wish you had told me after your bath," she said. "I would have applied it for you." She blushed at the memory of what had occurred after his bath, hoping that Robert couldn't see.

"Yes, well, I didn't think of it at the time," was all Simon said, bless him.

Christy started to put some salve on Simon's back, but every time she touched him he jerked away.

"Here, lay down," Robert said impatiently. "She can't put it on with you flinching away like that."

"Robert," she chided.

"No, he's right," Simon said.

He slowly went down, first onto his hands and knees and then he was about to go to his stomach when both men realized that Robert was in the way. Simon was lying almost crosswise on the bed. Robert started to get up.

"No," Simon said. "Stay there."

Robert slowly sat back down where he'd been, his back up against the headboard.

"Put your feet up, too," Simon said, gesturing.

Robert did as he was instructed. Christy didn't say a word. Simon finally lay down, gingerly settling himself with his head resting on Robert's thigh, his arms wrapped loosely around his waist. Robert had the look of a hunted deer, wild about the eyes as he looked between Christy and Simon.

"Not a word," Simon said. "If I have to endure this torture, so do you. Hold onto my arms so I don't flinch so much."

Christy was trying very hard not to think about the fact that Robert was nude under this robe. She was quite sure Robert was trying very hard not to think about it either. The thought almost made her laugh.

"Um, I'm going to have to climb up on the bed to apply this," she said apologetically. "I'm far too short to reach your back now."

"I forgot what a little thing you are," Simon muttered,

sounding utterly relaxed now that he was in Robert's lap. "Go ahead."

She peeked and could see that his eyes were closed. That made climbing up on the bed in her wrapper much easier, since she, too, was nude underneath. After she climbed up, she readjusted the robe to cover her exposed breasts and thighs. She looked up and met Robert's amused gaze, and shrugged with a smile.

When she began to rub the salve into Simon's back, he tensed beneath her hand. For several minutes his muscles were so tight he began to shake again. Christy was as gentle as she could be. Eventually she felt the tension leaving him as she massaged the thick unguent in. It smelled like lavender and honey, with the underlying unpleasantness of calendula, which wasn't awful.

She looked up and saw that Robert wasn't just holding Simon's arms, he was rubbing them soothingly. A quick glance at his face convinced her he wasn't even aware he was doing it. But he was watching Simon resting in his lap with the oddest look on his face.

"That feels good now," Simon mumbled.

"What?" she asked, confused at first. "Oh, good."

"Tell us about the dream," Robert told him quietly.

Simon tensed under her hands again. "Just a stupid dream."

"I don't think so," Robert said. "Try again."

"My back feels better."

Simon moved as if to get up. Christy quickly straddled his thighs, preventing it.

"Simon, tell us what upset you so," she urged him. "We want to help."

"No one can help," he said harshly. "Get off of me."

"Tell us about the dream," Robert said again. "It will feel better if you tell us. It will lose its hold on you."

"What do you know of dreams like that?" Simon asked

angrily. "Damn it, Christy, get off me. I don't want to hurt you."
He moved his legs and then froze. "Christ. Are you naked under
that?"

"Well, I was in bed," she said. "What did you expect? That I'd
taken the time to get fully dressed? Have you any idea how long
that takes?"

He laughed in disbelief. "Ever practical." He slumped back
down and then his head popped back up. "Oh my God, Robert.
Are you…"

"Yes," Robert said. He ran his hand through Simon's hair and
pushed his head back down into his lap.

Christy was bemused by the affectionate gesture. It was one
she'd expect of Daniel or Harry. She'd never seen Robert do that
to another man before.

There were undercurrents here she didn't understand. If
these were any other two men, she'd say it was attraction. She'd
been around Daniel and Harry and their friends enough to
recognize it. But Robert had never shown any interest in
another man. And while she knew Simon had a rather colorful
romantic past, he hadn't shown an interest in Robert before.

But they'd been working together quite closely on their
current case. Had something happened between them?

Was something happening now?

And if it was, how did she feel about that? She'd been so
pleased to finally be the one someone wanted, both with Simon
and then Robert. She wasn't sure how she felt about possibly
having to share her newfound place.

But as she watched Simon lay his head down in Robert's lap
and Robert lay his hand on Simon's head and stroke his brow
with his thumb, she realized she might not have a choice.

CHAPTER 19

"**N**ow tell us about the dream," Robert said.
"Tell me first about your dream," Simon demanded. "The one that lost its hold on you when you shared it."

"Of course," Robert said. "But first, do you need more salve?"

Simon nodded reluctantly. "Please. It felt...good, when you massaged it. My back, I mean." He wasn't usually so clumsy with words.

"Of course," Christy said. Simon could hear her amusement. She knew very well the other places that felt good when she massaged them.

A wave of longing crept over him, and he kept his eyes closed as she slowly and gently massaged his back while he hugged Robert's waist, his head in Robert's lap. It felt so intimate. It *was* intimate. They were both nude under their robes, and Simon wore nothing but his small clothes. It was hot and close in the bedroom, stuffy, even with the windows open. The curtains were still; no wind at all.

He knew Christy and Robert had made love tonight, before

they came to him. He knew it from their state of undress and he could smell it on them. It added another level of intimacy, another, deeper level of desire, at least on his part. Why did he still want them? Why, when it was surely self-destructive and would lead to nothing but misery? God, he was a damn fool. He buried it, like he did everything else, down deep, where it would wait for alcohol and mindless sex with faceless strangers and finally death. Because that was what his life had become, hadn't it, before he'd been kidnapped?

Then why, that annoying little voice in his head asked him yet again, *did you let the memory of Christy keep you alive in Africa?*

"When I was a boy in school, my father died," Robert said quietly, blessedly breaking into Simon's thoughts. "We had not been particularly close, but we shared a bond, of course, as father and son. He had always taken me to his study on each holiday home and discussed my studies and what his expectations were of me, what his plans for my future were, that sort of thing. He was a banker, you know."

He cleared his throat and gave both Christy and Simon a fleeting smile. "Anyway, he died unexpectedly—an apoplexy struck him down and he died a few days later." He shifted in the bed, and Simon understood that kind of discomfort brought on by memories.

"After the funeral," Robert continued, "I went back to school. I was about eight at the time. I started having terrible nightmares about my father's dead corpse coming to me from the grave and discussing my future as a banker."

He laughed, but there wasn't much humor in it. "I'd wake screaming. The other boys were quite cruel about my night terrors, and I didn't dare tell them what the dreams were about. Eventually I was sent home in disgrace, but the dreams intensified. I felt I had failed my father. I began to study with Daniel's father, and one day I told Daniel about the dreams. It was as if a huge weight had been lifted off my shoulders. Daniel, of course, being older and wiser, said there were no records in the history of the world of a corpse rising from the grave to talk about anything, much less my future as a banker, which seemed to be of very little consequence in the scheme of things. He put it all in perspective for me. But the experience made banking a rather distasteful career choice."

During his story, Christy had stopped massaging Simon's back, and she sat back on his legs, disregarding her nudity. "You never told me that," she said. She didn't sound angry. A little hurt, perhaps.

Simon wasn't surprised that Robert hadn't shared something so personal. It made him vulnerable. On the other hand, Robert was telling her now. *Her and Simon*, a little voice in his head reminded him. Simon crushed the seed of hope and longing that sprang from the thought.

"Trust Daniel to point out that you are quite unimportant in the larger scheme of things," Simon said with a forced chuckle. "Yes, he's very good at that."

"He's a dear man for whom you would both take a bullet," Christy said wryly. "And you both know it."

"That's the truth," Simon said with a sigh. "What a bother he is."

"Indeed," Robert agreed. "Now tell me about your dream, or I shall send for Daniel."

"Now you're playing dirty," Simon accused him. "Fine." He took a deep breath and let it out. He knew this story would kill any feeling they might have for him. It would show him for the monster he was. "I was married before."

Christy's hand slipped on his back, and she very nearly fell over face first into him. Simon pretended not to see the sharp warning look Robert gave her. Simon had called Christy a martinet the day before, but Robert was the one in control when they were alone. Simon could see that. Even Simon danced to his tune. Wasn't he even now telling them things he'd never told anyone else because Robert demanded it of him?

"Were you?" Robert asked calmly. "I assume you are a widower."

"Yes." Simon didn't say anything for what seemed like endless minutes. He didn't care if he made them wait. He needed to tell this story in his own time.

"She died," he was finally able to bring himself to say. "We were both young. Too young." He sighed and pulled his arms from around Robert's waist. To his regret, Robert let him. But Simon didn't sit up. Instead he rolled to his side, unseating Christy. Simon lay with his face buried against Robert's stomach now, hidden from their searching eyes.

He could hear Christy moving on the bed until she settled next to Robert. He turned his head a little so his voice wasn't so muffled.

"It's really an old story," he continued, as if they were talking about the weather. "We married young, Giselle and I. We grew up together, neighbors, and everyone said we were foolish and the marriage was doomed. I would say cursed, but in the end the result was the same. Because of my selfishness—my unmitigated thoughtlessness—Giselle died."

He took a shuddering breath. "She's in the dream. She's always been in the dreams, of course. They used to be about the war, but those never frightened me. I went to war to die, you know. Bought a commission right after I buried her with every intention of joining her as soon as possible."

"I'm glad you didn't," Robert said. Not exactly words of love, but they warmed Simon all the same because he was pathetic. "How did she die?"

"I see," Simon said, finally sitting up because he had to move. He couldn't lean on Robert anymore. Not for this part of his story. He immediately missed Robert's stalwart support. "You're planning to make me go through the whole thing."

"Yes, I'm afraid so," Robert said apologetically. "Sometimes you have to reopen the wound to let out what's festering."

"That's a thoroughly disgusting analogy," Christy said. Her unexpected comment made Simon laugh, and she smiled as she lay down and took his place, her head in Robert's lap. Simon was struck by the unintended symbolism of it. She hadn't taken his place. He had momentarily occupied hers.

Robert immediately began smoothing her hair out, pulling it from behind and under her, spreading it out to the side, running his fingers through it. She did have beautiful hair. Christy hummed a little in the back of her throat in contentment. Simon understood. God, how he understood.

He went on with his story.

"We were out walking in the woods on a crisp fall day, flirting, enjoying each other's company, when I realized that she was my wife and I had every right to take her right there in the woods," Simon said. "Giselle protested, of course. She was a gently reared girl, only seventeen, quite modest, not yet used to the physical side of marriage. I wasn't doing a very good job of being patient with her about it. I was a randy nineteen-year-old boy, too immature to understand how to handle the situation. Anyway, I seduced her into it. Took her right there against a tree despite her misgivings. And she loved me. What was she going to say?"

He paused, lost in the memories. At that moment he felt every blow, every cut, burn, blade, and yes, near drowning he'd experienced in the last few months. He felt old and worn down.

"She wasn't going to say no," Christy said softly, breaking into his grim reverie. "I've been where she was, Simon. You are very persuasive." She smiled at him. Simon was shocked. "Robert knows," she said, surprising him again. "I told him."

Simon looked at Robert then, asking without words if he had also told Christy about them. He had never felt like such a knave as he did at that moment. He had sullied them both, perhaps ruined a marriage that had so much promise. He ruined everything he touched. So many undercurrents and revelations this night. And still they were not over.

"As to that," Robert said, sounding very strange. He cleared his throat nervously. Simon tried to silence him with a look, but Robert ignored him. "I, too, have been there, and he is quite persuasive."

At his casual confession, Christy slowly turned her head in his lap to look at him. At least he had the courage to meet her gaze. When she turned to look at Simon, he looked away.

"Well, well," he murmured. "Aren't we all being so very honest tonight?"

"Apparently," Christy said. "But I'm ill-equipped to handle more than one thing at a time, so I shall deal with that later. Finish your story. Giselle."

"Always practical," Simon said. He didn't know why that appealed to him. Perhaps because of Giselle and what he was about to tell them.

"Maybe it's cowardice," Christy said. Simon could not let her believe that.

"I know you think you're weak and easily swayed, changing your colors and character to suit people's expectations and situations as needed. But I have seen your core of iron, forged perhaps by loneliness and abandonment. Your ability to adapt and compartmentalize and move on from heartache and rejection are the characteristics of an iron will, not a weak personality."

Christy seemed stunned by his praise.

"Yes. You do know her well. I agree." Robert sighed. "I can see that you two have a deeper connection than I thought. I have no right to stand between you."

"Robert," Christy said, alarmed, grabbing his arm.

"I'm not good enough for her," Simon said bluntly. "I never was and I never will be. You were always the right man for her."

"That is not true," Robert argued.

"What?" Christy seemed as confused as Simon was.

"Are you actually trying to convince me to run off with your wife?"

"You don't have to run," Robert said. He wouldn't look at Christy. "I'm saying if the two of you want to be together, I won't stand in your way."

"What about what I want?" Christy asked.

"Yes," Simon said, pointing at her. "She already made her choice."

"You didn't give me the option of choosing, not really," she threw back at him. "But I did, and I don't regret it."

"But it's obvious you still have feelings for him. You told me you did."

Robert's words cut Simon as cleanly as a sharp-edged sword. He'd known it already, of course. This afternoon had proven he and Christy still burned for one another, that she still ached for him the way he ached for her. But it was not meant to be.

"I cannot," Simon said. "I am not meant to love again. Not because I don't care for Christy, I do. But because I ruin everything I love. I kill and destroy. It's what I do, without even trying. And I won't do that to you. To either of you."

"Simon, what foolishness is this?" Christy said impatiently. "I have seen how you treat your friends. How you care for them, take care of them. They needn't even ask and you are there for them. You'll do anything for them. And none of them are dying. On the contrary, I know for a fact that you have saved the lives of several of them at one time or another. You do yourself an injustice to deny yourself love based on one unfortunate tragedy in your past. People die, Simon. They just die."

"Giselle didn't just die. I killed her." Before they could protest, he pushed into the tragic end of his story.

"Giselle was very cold that day in the woods. I can still see her shivering, like it was yesterday. Her hands were so cold. She was small, like you, Christy. Did I tell you that? But blonde. I promised her I'd warm her up from the inside out, thinking it such a great joke, so bawdy and mature. And then it started to rain. But I hadn't finished, so I just laughed at her shivers and kept at it until I was satisfied. Her lips were near blue with cold by then. But she still kissed me. Still told me she loved me."

He stopped. Looked away. He realized he was picking at the sheets and made himself stop. "We were soaked to the skin from the rain by then. I had to carry her the last mile home. She had a fever before nightfall. By morning she was delirious. Two days later she was dead."

When he looked back at them, he felt haunted by her ghost. "I did love her, you know. Very much. She was far too good for me." He took a shuddering breath. "I have not been back home since her funeral."

"I'm so sorry, Simon," Christy whispered. She didn't give him platitudes. She knew him well enough to know he didn't want them. "But you didn't kill her."

"Did you force her against her will?" Robert asked. "That day in the woods. Did she say no? Fight you?"

"No, of course not," Simon said, shock on his face. "I would never do such a thing to any woman, least of all a wife I loved, no matter how young I was. But I should have known. I should have listened to her complaints about the cold and the rain."

"Complaining about ill weather is rational," Robert told him. "I'm sure you did the same. But I'm also sure that she wanted you, probably just as much as you wanted her. The conditions weren't ideal that is true. But I'm sure the passion was mutual. You were both young and in love, Simon. As Christy said, people die. Sometimes they just die, as tragic as it is."

"Don't you think I know that? After everything I've been through?" Simon asked, stubbornly refusing their kindness and sympathy. "But I also know that she'd still be alive if I hadn't been so selfish."

Robert sighed. "Now tell us about the dream," he urged Simon, changing the subject, obviously deciding not to argue the point. "Do you dream about that day?"

"That's right, the dream. I'd almost forgotten that was what started this whole thing. Yes," Simon said. "It used to get it mixed up with the war and I'd see Giselle cold and shivering on the battlefield, or dying in Portugal. That seems so long ago. Now...now I see her in Africa. And it's so bloody hot, but there she is with her blue lips, and cold hands and dead eyes, lying in the dirty sand in that stinking hole. And I promise to warm her up and then...and then..." His voice broke and he stopped talking.

Christy reached out and grabbed his hand. "It's just a dream, Simon," she told him. "It never happened."

"It happened to me," he whispered, clutching her hand. His back ached all over again. *Burning.* "I brand her. I brand her back with that red-hot piece of iron, and I'm laughing." He shook his head, unable to go on.

"Simon, you know you would never do such a thing," Robert told him. He put his hand over his and Christy's joined hands. "You're just...transferring something awful that happened to you onto someone you loved, into another situation, another awful situation. It's not that uncommon, I believe. Our minds do terrible things to us sometimes. Especially when we are at our weakest."

"No," Simon said. "It's a warning." He looked at Robert and Christy, and everything felt bleak and hopeless. "*I* do terrible things to people, especially to people I care about. You both should be very wary of getting too close to me."

"I think, perhaps, your warning comes a bit too late," Robert said.

Christy pulled Simon's hand to her and kissed the back of it before pressing it to her cheek.

"My back feels better," Simon said, gently extricating his

hand from Christy's. It was both a physical and an emotional pulling away, like building a wall between them. It was for the best, even if it didn't feel that way. "I'm sure that was part of what brought the dream tonight. Thank you, Christy, for helping me."

"Of course." She rose awkwardly from Robert's lap, making sure to keep her robe closed. Robert got up to stand beside the bed. Simon was grateful they accepted his change of mood without protest.

"We should all get some rest," Robert said. He sounded as tired as Simon felt. He helped Christy off the bed, lifting her down and setting her on her feet beside him. He put his arm around her and pulled her close.

Simon kept his expression blank as he watched them, but it hurt. How quickly they went from the intimacy of the three of them sharing secrets in the dark to Simon feeling odd man out to Robert and Christy's easy pairing.

Christy looked exhausted, as if she had been the one who had the dream, not Simon. "I am not forgetting what you told me," she said to both men. Then she yawned. "But I cannot talk about it tonight. Christian will be up with the sun. But rest assured, we *will* talk more about it tomorrow."

"Of course," Robert agreed, as he pushed her toward the door.

Simon said nothing, and after just a few steps Christy planted her feet and refused to move farther. She turned to face him. "Did you hear me, Simon?"

"I heard you," he said. "I don't need to remind you that you have no hold over me nor any right to make demands of me."

"You may remind me all you wish, but unless you'd like me to make a very long overdue scene, I suggest you make the time to have a discussion," she said firmly. She'd been blindsided, but he could already see her mind working the problem, figuring out how to handle the situation, figuring out what was required of her, as she did when faced with adversity of any kind.

"He'll talk, don't worry," Robert said. His tone made it very clear that it wouldn't be necessary for Christy to make a scene. Robert seemed quite willing to do so instead.

That was fine with Simon. He was an expert at avoiding them. He wasn't best friends with Daniel for nothing.

CHAPTER 20

Christy knocked on Daniel's front door again. She knew she was being impatient and most likely impolite, and she didn't care. She needed to talk to someone, and Harry and Daniel seemed like the most logical choice given they were most familiar with her situation.

Christian began to fuss in her arms and Nanny Beth reached for him, but Christy shooed her away. "I don't mind," she told the nanny, not wishing to upset the girl with her brusque manners. "Shhh," she told Christian, kissing his cheek, which was damp with tears.

She knew how he felt. Robert and Simon had left early that morning after a tense breakfast. Simon had barely spoken a word to her other than polite pleasantries. She recognized that behavior. He was trying to push her away again. She hadn't had the time to deal with him this morning since Christian had decided to take exception to his father leaving him again when he'd barely had time to say good morning. It was all Christy could do to pull him away from Robert and hold his squirming body while he screamed and cried. Christy could see how the baby's tantrum distressed Robert, and she knew he would have stayed if he could. Simon gave no indication at all that Christian's tantrum bothered him. He had merely watched the drama from behind his teacup, the merest of smiles on his lips.

As soon as Robert and Simon had gone, Christy had bundled Christian up and they'd set off for Daniel's. Sir Barnabas's men accompanied them. They had wanted to take a carriage, but Christy had needed to walk to give herself time to think, and Daniel and Harry only lived a short distance away.

Daniel had inherited his father's house, and Robert lived just down the street from him as a boy. The elderly Mrs. Manderley still lived there. After he and Christy married, Robert hadn't wanted to move too far from his mother since he was all that she had left, even if she barely spoke to him now and she'd have nothing to do with Christy and the baby. As far as Christy was concerned that was her loss, but she did feel bad for Robert, who cared for her and felt a filial responsibility for her welfare. But Christy had got on just fine without parents her whole life, so she didn't feel as if Robert's mother's desertion was a great tragedy.

Daniel and Harry hadn't seen Christian since they'd returned from Africa, and she knew Daniel especially was probably missing him. The two had a very special bond. Christy was quite glad that her baby would have so many strong men around him as he grew up. Role models were so important to a boy, and Robert, Harry and Daniel were some of the best men she knew. Simon was as well, whether he knew it or not.

The thought of Simon and his sad tale last night made Christy pound the knocker even harder against the door. Where was the butler, Matheson? It was unlike him not to answer the door promptly. She could see the agents frowning at the bottom of the stoop and their concern made her nervous.

When Matheson finally opened the door, he was uncharacteristically flustered. "Mrs. Manderley," he said, relief in his voice. "How good of you to come." He stepped aside, and Christy and Nanny Beth stepped in. Two of the agents followed them in and two stationed themselves outside.

"Was I expected?" Christy asked in surprise. Now that they were inside, Christian stopped fussing, looking around in wonder at the shining gilt and mirrors everywhere. Christy passed him to Nanny and took off her bonnet, handing it to Matheson.

"Yes, ma'am," Matheson said. "Mr. Ashbury sent for you this morning."

"We must have missed the note on our way here," Christy said, concern beginning to overtake her own troubles. "What's wrong?"

"It's Mr. Steinberg." Matheson shook his head, his lips tight with unspoken concern. "I'm afraid his leg isn't healing as quickly as he'd like."

Christy's heartbeat tripled in the space of a second. She'd teased Daniel about his gunshot wound, never imaging that it would lay him low. He had always seemed invincible to her.

"Have you sent for the doctor?" she asked. "Where is he?"

"He is right here and he is fine," Daniel snapped. Christy turned to see him in the study doorway. He was leaning on a cane, obviously favoring his wounded leg. He looked pale and he'd lost weight in the last week.

"You don't look fine," Christy said flatly. "Matheson, get the doctor."

"Matheson, do not get the doctor," Daniel told him, a warning in his voice. "I will sack you."

"I will hire you," Christy shot back, staring Daniel down with narrowed eyes. "Get the doctor."

"Thank God, another voice of reason," Harry said from inside the study. "Matheson is more afraid of Daniel than of me." He came to stand beside Daniel, arms crossed. "But he likes you better than either of us, Christy. So I thought you might be able to persuade him."

As soon as he'd seen Daniel, Christian had started making delighted, gurgling noises and reaching for him. Nanny looked at Christy uncertainly.

"Bring me my nephew," Daniel demanded as he turned back into the study.

"I will do no such thing unless you agree to let a doctor take a look at that leg," Christy told him. "And what's more, I'll tell Sir Barnabas."

Daniel spun around and glared at her. "You wouldn't dare."

Christy just crossed her arms and smiled at him.

"Matheson, fetch the leech," Daniel said from between clenched teeth. "There, happy?"

"Very," Christy said. She took Christian from Nanny. "I'll send for you," she told her. "You two stay here," she told the agents, and she followed Daniel into the study.

"I need help," she said a few minutes later as they waited for the doctor.

She sat on the floor with Christian, piling up his blocks so he could knock them down. It was his favorite game. Normally Daniel would do it, but he just sat in his chair, his leg propped up, watching them. Harry was lying on his side on the sofa, leaning on one arm, helping her stack the blocks. He was pretending a relaxation he was far from feeling. Christy could see the strain around his eyes. He was terribly worried about Daniel. So was she. She hoped her dilemma would be a welcome distraction.

"Again? Does this have anything to do with the Home Office bullies in my foyer? I can't do much about them in my present condition." Daniel asked.

"I don't need help with them," Christy said. "What I really need is advice."

"You?" Daniel asked, surprise in his voice. "You usually give advice. Unsolicited, I might add."

"Quit being a baby about the doctor," Christy said mildly. "I need advice about Simon. And Robert."

Harry glanced at her, alarm on his face. "You aren't thinking of leaving Robert, are you?"

"She better not be," growled Daniel. He was glowering at her from his chair. "When I let you marry him, it was with the very strict edict that under no circumstance were you to break his heart."

"I wish someone had handed down such an edict about my heart," Christy said without rancor. "If you'll pardon my saying so, I don't think Robert needs or wants your interference in our romantic life. That having been said, I have no intention of leaving him. Your edict, however, is not the reason why."

"So you say," Daniel grumbled. "In that case, what has Simon done now?"

Christy took a deep breath in an effort not to lose her temper at Daniel's casual assumption of Simon's guilt in the matter. No wonder Simon walked around with guilt as his constant companion with even his closest friend always assuming the worst of him.

"Oh, the usual," she said. "He just been so incredibly wonderful that he's made me fall in love with him again and apparently my husband as well."

"What?" Daniel said, drawing out the word, with heavy emphasis on the "t".

"You mean, making you fall in love with him and your husband again?" Harry asked, confused.

"No," Daniel answered for her. "That is not what she means." He grabbed the cane next to his chair and stood up. "Damn that man!" he exclaimed.

He thumped the cane on the floor, startling Christy and little Christian. The baby's lip began to tremble.

"I suggest you tone down your temper," Christy told Daniel, "unless you wish to calm down the baby when you make him cry."

Daniel began to pace. No easy feat with his cane. He winced with every step. "I sent him to help Robert solve a murder, not to debauch him."

"I doubt very much there has been any debauchery," Christy said drily. "This is my husband we are talking about." She paused. "Although I think there was some talk of seducing."

"Perhaps you shouldn't jump to conclusions faster than a squirrel up a tree, and let Christy explain what's going on," Harry suggested mildly, waving his fingers in front of Christian to distract him. He let Christian capture one and promptly use it as a teething toy. "Ouch." Harry extracted his finger and substituted a block. "I don't think that pacing is good for your leg," he admonished Daniel.

"Well, sitting around on my posterior for a week hasn't done it any good, either," Daniel snapped. He sighed and stood still for a moment. Christy and Harry let him gather his composure. "I'm sorry. You're right. I'm just tired, and my leg hurts, and I feel like whatever you're going through with Simon is my fault because I sent him to Robert."

He thumped a fist against his thigh and then doubled over with a gasp. "Well, that was stupid." He straightened and made his way back to his chair. He sat down again. "If it wasn't for this damn leg, I'd have gone to help solve that murder."

"Murder has now become something much more dangerous," Christy said with a frown. "They are both working for Sir Barnabas directly, chasing down some sort of spies, and my house is overrun with agents who are there to protect all of us. Simon and Hastings are staying with us, too."

"What?" Harry asked. He sat up on the sofa. "Why didn't you tell us? Why did no one come and get us?"

"Because of me," Daniel said flatly. "And this leg. I couldn't do a damn thing."

"We could have moved them in here," Harry said. "This house is a damn sight safer and easier to protect than Christy and Robert's little house."

"I will choose not to be offended," Christy said. She was ignored.

"I'm sure it was much easier for Simon to cause mischief when not under my watchful eye," Daniel said.

"True," Harry agreed.

"That is enough," Christy stated as she stood up. She put her hands on her hips and glared at both of them. "Simon Gantry is a man of virtue and integrity, and I will smite the next one of you who says differently."

She looked between them, daring them to contradict her. They wisely stayed quiet.

She pointed at Daniel. "He came to help Robert at your request, when he had no business even being out of bed, much less traipsing around London looking for traitors or spies or assassins or whatever evil lurks in the hearts of men. For God's sake, he had to jump over the side of a ship and grapple with a Turkish sailor in the water, nearly drowning, just two days ago in order to get vital information, and then could barely walk up the stairs he was in so much pain. I had to bathe him like a child and put him to bed."

"Turkish sailors? Who are the Turks after?" Daniel said with interest.

"Argh," Christy growled. "That's the first thing you ask? Not about Simon's welfare?"

"Well, he must be all right. He seduced Robert, didn't he?" Daniel asked defensively. "And that had to take a great deal of effort. Robert has always been unimpeachable to the best of my knowledge. Trust Simon to ruin that, too."

Christy grabbed a pillow from the sofa and threw it at

Daniel, and Christian laughed and clapped his hands. "You are insufferable," she told him. "Simon hasn't ruined anything. What I'm trying to tell you is that he thinks he can't love anyone *because* he ruins everything. He's got some foolish notion in his head that he kills or otherwise destroys everyone or everything that he loves. So he has decided if he just doesn't love anyone, then everything will be fine."

"I know."

CHAPTER 21

Daniel's response took the fight out of Christy. She stood there dumbly staring at him. Daniel sighed. "I know about Giselle," he said. "Fetch me a drink, would you, love?" he asked Harry.

"It's tea time," Harry said.

"I don't want tea," Daniel told him. "I want scotch."

"I know," Harry said. "You get tea."

"When I am mobile again, you will pay for your impertinence," Daniel promised.

"Yes, well, we shall see," Harry said. He rang the bell. "Who is Giselle?"

"Simon's late wife," Christy said, watching Daniel. He had the grace to look slightly abashed. "You've always known about her?"

"Yes. He told me. During the war. He was reckless. When I confronted him about it, he told me why. He wanted to die. The damn thing was, he's got a bit of a sixth sense, you know. He can sense trouble before he walks into it. He saved quite a few lives during the war with it, including his own. As many times as he claimed he wanted to die, he never could bring himself to do it."

"Because he doesn't," Christy said. "Can't you see that? And can't you see how much love he has to give? How much he cares for you and for all of his friends? He deserves a love of his own. Even if it isn't me."

"And you think Robert is that love?" Daniel asked. "How does Robert feel about that? Are you willing to give them both up?"

"Don't be an idiot, of course not. I intend to have them both." Christy sat down on the sofa and picked Christian up, who had begun to fuss with no one on the floor with him.

"I feel like I've had this conversation before," Daniel said wryly. "Why am I not surprised?"

"You of all people shouldn't be," Christy said. "After all, you're the one who introduced me to all your friends who enjoy such unusual relationships. Didn't we spend weeks with the Duke and Duchess of Ashley and their lover, Mr. Haversham, last year? Really, Daniel, I'm beginning to think you had this planned all along."

"What?" he said, aghast. "Me? What are you talking about? I would never do such a thing. As you said I, of all people, know the hardships of such relationships. I have seen it among my friends. And it would be worse for you and Robert and Simon."

He nodded at her protest. "Oh, yes. You are not a duchess, my dear. And the middle classes are even more parochial about that kind of thing than the aristocracy. You would be shunned by one and all. Robert would be lucky to keep his job, much less rise above a lowly constable in the department."

Christy felt a little queasy, but then she remembered Simon's distress last night and she straightened her shoulders. "We will manage. There are other jobs. Other places."

"Yes, there are," Harry agreed, cutting off Daniel's argument. "And you know it, too, Daniel. Sir Barnabas would give them both a job. Hasn't he already?"

"Don't you want Simon to be happy, Daniel?" Christy asked.

He slumped in his seat. "Of course I do. The problem, Christy, is that I'm not sure he can be." He looked up at her. "Simon is so afraid of being happy, so afraid of being hurt again, that he will do just about anything to avoid loving someone. I'm worried that if he really is in love with you or Robert, or both of you, that he will start running and he won't stop until he's dead."

"Oh, Daniel," Christy said, trying not to cry. "That's what I'm afraid of, too. How do I get Simon to understand that he deserves to be happy?"

"What does Robert have to say about all this?" Harry asked.

"I don't know." Christy threw her hands up in the air. "Both of them told me so much last night. Simon and his story about Giselle and his nightmares, and then Robert admitting that Simon seduced him, right after he and I openly talked about my previous relationship with Simon for the first time. Things with Robert are so perfect." She clasped her hands together. "I'm finally able to be *me*. Do you know what that means to me? And he's happy with me. The real me. Not the me he thought he married. And the physical side of our marriage is…"

She paused, blushing. "Well, anyway, everything is going so well, and I don't want to jeopardize that. But I will always love Simon. And Robert knows that. I told him that. And he doesn't seem to care. I mean, he told me that he will always want me and that I will always have a place with him." She paused to take a breath.

"But…it's sounds like there's a but coming," Daniel said.

"But last night he said that it was obvious Simon and I loved one another and that he didn't have a right to stand in our way. Simon and I both disagreed. I told Robert I loved him, too. And that was when Simon told us about Giselle."

"I have a feeling there is a great deal you are leaving out." Harry held up a hand. "Which is your prerogative." He sighed. "It is a muddle, Christy. I'm sorry."

"You should be," Daniel told him. "Somehow this is all your fault."

"Mine?" Harry exclaimed. "How so?"

"If you had stayed married to her, none of this would be happening."

"If I were still married to her, all of this would be happening in your house," Harry disagreed.

"Good point," Daniel said. He yawned and rubbed his leg. "When is the doctor coming?"

Christy knew she wasn't going to get the advice she'd sought. Daniel wasn't feeling well enough, and Harry was more concerned for his lover's welfare than about her romantic entanglements, and rightly so.

"I guess it's up to me to figure out a happy ending to my own troubles," Christy said. "I shouldn't have bothered you."

"Nonsense," Daniel said. "I shall have a talk with Simon. Tell him to come and see me."

"Of course I will," Christy lied. "I'll see about the doctor."

She picked Christian up and headed for the door, wondering exactly how she was going to take care of Daniel, fix Simon, keep Robert, and stay sane. A woman's work was never done.

She needed to go see Veronica Tarrant.

CHAPTER 22

"**G**ood afternoon."

Veronica Tarrant was formidable, in every sense of the word. She dominated a room. Any room. Anywhere. Any time. In a gorgeous morning dress of sea green that highlighted her chestnut hair and brought to mind the Greek goddess Artemis, she made Christy feel ridiculously inadequate just by standing there in the doorway smiling politely at her.

"How do you do, Mrs. Tarrant?" Christy replied just as politely.

"Oh, I do all right," she said. "Some days are better than others."

She closed the door firmly behind her, right in the face of a very curious, curly-headed blonde girl who looked tall for her age. That must be one of her children. If memory served Christy right, she and Mr. Tarrant and their lover, Lord Kensington, had four children. Five if you counted Lord Kensington's oldest child with his wife, who also lived here in the Tarrant household with her lover, noted abolitionist Mrs. Grimshaw.

And yet, somehow, Mrs. Tarrant still managed to interfere in everyone else's business on a regular basis, or so Daniel claimed with great affection. She was just the woman Christy needed to take over some of her burden.

There was a tremendous crash in the hallway outside the parlor door, and suddenly several children were screaming at once and a man was bellowing and then a woman began scolding in French. Mrs. Tarrant's smile did not waver an inch.

"Pay them no heed," she said mildly. "I hid the rapiers." There was a polite knock at the door. "Ah, I've requested tea. Come in," she called.

The housekeeper wheeled in the teacart. "I'm sorry for the delay, ma'am," she apologized calmly. "We had to clear the debris from the doorway."

"Naturally," Mrs. Tarrant said, as if it was indeed natural. "Thank you, Mrs. Goose."

The housekeeper left, and Mrs. Tarrant sat down and began to pour. "Well, don't just stand there," she said. "Sit."

Christy sat.

"Her name isn't really Mrs. Goose. Honestly I can't remember what it is. But the children started calling her that and it stuck. Luckily she doesn't seem to mind."

Christy took the proffered cup of tea. "I would imagine that if the pound notes make it into the right bank account, she doesn't care what you call her."

Mrs. Tarrant choked on her tea and started coughing.

"Oh dear," Christy said, putting her cup down on the table. She felt like a country idiot. "I'm not supposed to talk about money. I forgot."

Mrs. Tarrant was wiping her eyes with the tea cloth. She waved off Christy's apology. "No, no, it's fine, really." She laughed. "Daniel told me we'd get along splendidly. He was right." She reached over and took Christy's hand. "I'm so sorry I haven't been to see you since you got back to London. There never seem to be enough hours in the day."

"Oh." Christy was taken aback. "Well, we've never actually met, so I never expected you to visit, despite our mutual acquaintances. As a matter of fact, it's Daniel I'm here about."

"Well, you should have expected it," Mrs. Tarrant said. "You must hold me to account. I'm told that is the only way to keep me in line." She took a sip of tea, and there was a calculating gleam in her eye that made Christy nervous. "I'm surprised you're not here about Simon."

Christy felt her cheeks warm considerably with what must be a formidable blush. "Simon, I mean Mr. Gantry, is working with my husband on a mission right now. For the Home Office."

"Is he?" Mrs. Tarrant leaned forward, obviously very interested. "When I saw him last week, he looked quite poorly. He'd just gotten off the ship from Africa. I'm surprised he's already working a case for Sir Barnabas." She flopped back against the sofa, lips pursed. "That devil. No wonder he was at Simon's when we got there. He didn't even let his boots dry before he pounced."

"Oh, it wasn't Sir Barnabas's idea. It was Daniel's," Christy corrected her.

"Daniel's?" Mrs. Tarrant looked confused.

Suddenly the door burst open and a woman rushed in. She was out of breath, and still wearing her bonnet. "I got here as fast as I could," she said, untying it. The butler stood stoically behind her. She passed the bonnet back without looking and began to pull her gloves off. She had beautiful dark red hair and a splash of freckles across her nose, which only made her more attractive. "What did I miss?"

"She's an utter delight and very practical," Mrs. Tarrant said. "Do hurry up. She's about to tell me why Daniel sent Simon to work on a mission with her husband for Sir Barnabas at the Home Office."

The woman shoved her gloves at the butler and closed the door in his face with a "So sorry." Then she hurried across the room and sat next to Mrs. Tarrant. She stuck out her hand. "Mrs. Sophie Witherspoon, how do you do?"

"How do you do?" Christy said. "Christy Manderley."

"Oh, yes, I know. Very sent a note over to say you'd unexpectedly come to call and were either very impertinent or there was a delightful mystery to be solved." She grinned. "Things have been rather dull, so I rushed right over."

"I see," Christy said.

"Really, Sophie," Mrs. Tarrant said, rolling her eyes. "You are the one who is being very impertinent. You have been with Derek too long. He's rubbed off on you."

"I should think so," Sophie said. "He's been training me for years." She turned to Christy. "So, to summarize. You are delightful." She ticked it off on her fingers. "Daniel sent Simon to help your husband with a case." Tick. "They are working for Sir Barnabas." Tick. "Sir Barnabas is a rascal. I added that part." Tick. "Although I do like him."

"Me, too," Mrs. Tarrant said. "One of my favorite people, but don't tell him that. Go on," she said to Christy.

"What kind of case?" Mrs. Witherspoon asked. "I thought your husband was a constable, not an agent."

"He is a constable," Christy said. "Let me start at the beginning."

"Oh, yes, that's usually best," Mrs. Tarrant said. "Start when you met Simon."

"I...what?" Christy looked at her in shock.

"I don't think we're at that level of confidences yet," Mrs. Witherspoon chided her. "Excuse her *impertinence*," she said to Christy, while glaring at Mrs. Tarrant. "Start wherever you like."

"Well, there was a series of grisly murders in London. Young boys with their throats cut," Christy began.

Both the ladies gasped. "Stop right there," Mrs. Tarrant said, aghast.

She rang the bell and the butler appeared at the door within seconds. "Send for everyone else," she said dramatically. "Except the children."

He closed the door. She turned back to Christy. "My husbands would never forgive me if I didn't include them in a conversation that started like that."

"Derek will kill me," Mrs. Witherspoon said, her face alight with equal parts morbid curiosity and horror. "But I'll tell him about it later."

A few minutes later the room was filled with Mr. Tarrant and Lord Kensington standing behind the sofa and Lady Kensington and Mrs. Grimshaw seated across from Christy. More tea and biscuits had been brought and poured, and children had been shooed from the room and all eyes turned to Christy.

"Do start again, Mrs. Manderley," Mrs. Tarrant said.

"I...I've forgotten where I began," she said, a little flustered by the attention of so many strangers.

"Grisly murders," Mrs. Witherspoon reminded her.

"Oh, I say," Lord Kensington said with interest. "This sounds interesting."

"*Mon dieu*," Lady Kensington said in alarm. "Are the children in danger?" she asked in a charming French accent. Mrs. Grimshaw took her hand.

"No, no, not at all," Christy assured her. "You see, my husband is a constable. He was working on a case involving the, ah, well..."

"Grisly murders, go on," Mrs. Tarrant encouraged her. "We're all adults here."

"Yes, well, grisly murders of several boys around London. He had reached an impasse and he went to Daniel for assistance. You see, they are old school friends. Since childhood."

"Of course," Mr. Tarrant said. "Very read us Daniel's letters from Scotland. We are aware of his, and your, history with Daniel and Harry. You needn't explain." He accompanied his comment with a friendly smile, so Christy wasn't worried they condemned her for her divorce and second marriage like some in society did. But they could hardly cast stones, could they?

"It makes perfect sense that he'd go to Daniel, after all," Lord Kensington said. "He has more than his share of experience with that kind of sordid thing."

"Indeed, you are correct," Christy said, nodding. "But Daniel couldn't help. So he sent Simon to help. But Simon shouldn't even be out of bed. Honestly, he's not fully recovered from what happened in Africa."

"What happened in Africa?" Mrs. Tarrant asked with a frown. "He didn't tell me anything. Just said they threw him in a dungeon and fed him poor rations until Daniel and Harry showed up, and so he blew up their compound in retaliation." The others nodded and murmured in agreement.

Christy stared at them all in amazement. "And you believed him? That he was held by Barbary pirates for months and the only thing they did was feed him substandard fare?"

Mr. Tarrant and Lord Kensington began to look uncomfortable. "We didn't wish to pry," Mr. Tarrant said.

"I would have pried," Mrs. Tarrant said in indignation, "if you had indicated that there might have been more." She turned to Christy. "What's wrong with Simon?"

"I have Simon under control," Christy informed her, silently fuming at the carelessness of his so-called friends. How long had they been so involved in their own lives that they had neglected his? According to Sir Barnabas, Simon had been on a downward spiral long before Africa and yet no one had noticed, including her. But in her defense, he had spurned her and she had been in Scotland. They had been here, in London, and they had let him self destruct.

"What does that mean?" Mrs. Tarrant asked sharply.

"Very," Mrs. Witherspoon murmured.

"It means that she is taking care of 'im," Lady Kensington said matter-of-factly. "And that she does not want you to interfere."

"I don't interfere," Mrs. Tarrant said with an affronted sniff.

"Yes you do," several voices said at once.

"I do need your help," Christy said loudly, not wishing to spark an argument.

"You just said you had Simon under control," Mrs. Tarrant said loftily. "I'm sure I don't know what we could do."

"It's not Simon, it's Daniel," Christy said. That got their attention.

"What's wrong with Daniel?" Lord Kensington asked.

"Wait, you said he couldn't help your husband," Mr. Tarrant said. He reminded her very much of Daniel and Simon. She knew he had worked with them during the war, another spy.

She turned and directed her words to him. "Yes, that's right. You see, he was shot in Africa."

"What?" Mrs. Tarrant exclaimed. "No one told us!" She stood up. "We have to go see him immediately."

"Oh, good," Christy said with a relieved sigh. "I just can't do it all, you see. Daniel's leg isn't healing, and I had to force him to let the doctor come, but the doctor was useless. Terrible. And I still have Simon to worry about. And this case isn't just murder anymore. Robert and Simon are working for Sir Barnabas now..."

"The Home Office? Why do they care about the murders of a few boys?" Mr. Tarrant asked sharply.

"The boy were spies, you see. And now they are all trying to foil an assassination. It's all very complicated." She put a hand to her head. "And the baby's teething, and so I'm trying to fix Simon, and keep Robert, and heal Daniel and deal with Christian, and stay alive because apparently there are assassins that might possibly try to kill me and so I've got an escort of agents everywhere I go. It's all just too much." She let her hand drop to her lap only to see everyone staring at her.

"I think you left some of the story out," Lady Kensington finally said.

"Where are the agents?" Mr. Tarrant asked, stone faced.

"Outside," Christy told him. "They agreed to wait out there because you were in here. And honestly, nothing has happened at all the last few days, so they're beginning to think it was a false alarm."

"Michael." Mr. Tarrant indicated the door with a tip of his head. Lord Kensington immediately got up and left. He came back a moment later and nodded. Mr. Tarrant relaxed.

"They're still there," Lord Kensington said.

"We will go armed," Mr. Tarrant said. "Aurelie, you and Agatha stay here with the children." Lady Kensington nodded, looking quite relieved. "Sophie, we will drop you at home."

"Of course," Mrs. Witherspoon said. "And then we will meet you at Daniel's."

Mrs. Tarrant came over and knelt in front of Christy, taking her hands. "Don't worry, my dear. We'll take care of Daniel. You take care of Simon and your husband. I do believe that you can handle that." She grinned and patted Christy's hand.

Christy felt as if a huge weight had been lifted from her shoulders. Now she could concentrate on Simon and Robert and what on earth she was going to do about the two of them.

CHAPTER 23

"Are you sure the Dutchman is here?" Robert whispered.

"No," Sir Barnabas replied. They were standing in an alcove of the George hotel, hidden by a curtain, observing the lobby of the hotel. His answer surprised Robert.

"Then why are we here?" he asked.

"Because this is the best information we've received so far, and I'm hoping we have a bit of luck today and the Dutchman falls into our grasp."

Robert was even more surprised by that. "Luck? You have agents all over the hotel based on luck?"

Simon was leaning against the wall nonchalantly, lightly slapping his thigh with his gloves. "You'd be surprised how many disasters are avoided by happenstance and a lucky fall," he said.

"You nearly drowned," Hastings said, sounding bored. He, too, was leaning against the wall looking as if he'd rather be anywhere else.

"See?" Simon said. "I was lucky I didn't. There's the luck."

"Simon," Sir Barnabas said with a sigh.

"Am I wrong?" Simon asked.

"Simon." Robert silenced him with a look. To his shock, Simon winked at him.

He turned away quickly, not sure what to do in response. Whatever was going on between him, Simon and Christy seemed far easier to deal with in the dark of night than the light of day. Or the dark of a crowded alcove. Hastings was watching the exchange with interest.

When Robert looked back out into the lobby, he nearly exclaimed out loud. Instead he grabbed Sir Barnabas's arm and nodded at his inquiring look.

"You have got to be joking," Hastings said, leaning over Robert's shoulder. "Is that him?"

Simon leaned over his other shoulder. Where Hastings's nearness hadn't affected him, Simon's breath on his cheek made him shiver despite the heat in the close confines of the alcove. "That's him," Simon said. "I'll be damned."

"What now?" Robert asked as they watched the Dutchman walk across the lobby to the stairs. He was trailed by his body-guard. Other than his size, he didn't offer much in the way of guarding, looking neither left nor right for possible surveillance or ambush.

"We wait," Sir Barnabas said. He made a small hand signal. "All exits are covered, and the outside as well. He cannot leave the hotel without being followed. I'd like to wait and see if anyone comes by to meet with him. Kill two birds…"

"A bird in the hand," Hastings argued. He straightened. "I think we should pick him up now and simply beat the truth out of him. Why wait? We know he's the ringleader. If we detain him, we cut off the head of the operation and in all likelihood we put an end to whatever he has planned."

"'In all likelihood' is not the same as definitely," Sir Barnabas said. "And I would prefer that we definitely put an end to what-ever he has planned."

"As I'm sure we all would," Simon agreed. "But do you think we could do that somewhere else? It is stiflingly hot in here, and we are beginning to stink like overripe fruit."

"It is stiflingly hot everywhere," Sir Barnabas said. "And there is the chance that whoever he is meeting may recognize one of us if we do not remain hidden."

"You think he has another accomplice here in London other than Alice Gaines?"

"I always think anything is possible," Sir Barnabas said. "It's why I'm still alive and why I'm in charge."

"You know what else is possible?" Simon asked. "That you are insufferable."

Robert had to turn away to hide his smile as he stifled his laughter.

"*You* are overripe," Sir Barnabas said. "Go stand in the corner."

"We're in an alcove," Hastings reminded him. "There is no corner."

"Why do I put up with you two?" Sir Barnabas grumbled.

"Because without these two we wouldn't even be here," Robert told him. "If I'm man enough to admit it, so should you."

"I jumped into the harbor for you," Simon added.

"You jumped into the harbor because you let an important witness get away," Sir Barnabas fired back. "And because you knew I would have flailed the skin off your back if you hadn't chased him down, whether in the water or out of it."

Robert noticed Simon turning a little pale and he started to lean against the wall again, but as soon as his back touched the wall he straightened with a wince. Neither of the other two men noticed.

"Could we leave backs out of it?" Simon asked. Robert was amazed for a moment how fearless he could be when it came to his own vulnerability.

"My apologies," Sir Barnabas said. "I promise to throw my

glove in your face and leave your back alone should your performance be as disastrous as Hastings."

Simon laughed quietly, and Robert was struck at the easy comradeship between him and Sir Barnabas. It was obvious they had known and worked together for a long time. Also evident was their obvious, if grudging, affection for one another.

"I heartily object to that description," Hastings said. "I got him to talk, didn't I?"

"No, I did," Robert said. "I shot him."

"Well, I convinced him he was going to die," Hastings argued, "and that he ought to cleanse his conscience first."

"I actually think it was the pressure you were applying to his wound at the time that may have coerced him to spill his secrets," Robert said drily. "Let us agree that it was a combined effort."

"Agreed," Hastings said politely. They shook hands.

"Now you are all insufferable," Simon said.

"Be quiet," Sir Barnabas whispered. He was looking out the slit between the curtains. A man had just walked in the door. He glanced around the lobby, his eyes alighting on the alcove. Almost immediately he was hailed by the Dutchman's bodyguard. He hurried to the stairs and went up without a backward glance.

"Do you know him?" Robert asked Sir Barnabas.

"I think so," Sir Barnabas said. "I believe it is Thomas Naismith. Damn." He cursed under his breath. "This affair gets more confusing with each new revelation. Naismith was involved with that business on the Gold Coast, with the African Company of Merchants. Now he's here with the Dutch and the Turks. What the devil are they up to?"

"None of them seem connected," Hastings said. "I mean, the African Company of Merchants was dissolved. You said yourself, Simon, that a legion of boy spies or couriers or whatever they were hardly seemed legitimate, nor did an alliance with a madam, and now we find him working with the Turks, who haven't the nerve or the manpower to launch an assault against Britain. And we've had no indication anywhere from anyone that there is a threat imminent from those areas. So, here's a thought: maybe they're working alone? Maybe they're malcontents who are planning to sow chaos and rebellion and nothing more?"

"Why?" Robert asked, puzzled.

"Why not would be a better question to someone like that," Sir Barnabas asked. "Because they can, that's why. Because they want to see us in chaos, panic-stricken, the fabric of British society ripped apart by their nefarious plans, no doubt."

"Slow down, Barnabas," Simon cautioned. "You're getting a little ahead of yourself there. We don't know enough yet to make that assumption. They might very well be doing it for money. I find the simplest explanations are often the right ones."

"I second Simon's observation," Robert said.

"Yes, well, you would, wouldn't you?" Hastings said.

Both Robert and Simon looked at him sharply.

"What do you mean?" Robert asked.

"Just that you two seem so in tune you're practically finishing each other's sentences," Hastings said in disgust. "So, is anyone going to go up and try to find out what they're meeting about? Or are we just going to speculate all night? As much as I'm enjoying this little tête à tête, I'm willing to sacrifice myself for the greater good and go snooping."

"Go," Sir Barnabas said, and Hastings slipped out. "Come on." He gestured for the others to follow him.

"Where are we going?" Robert asked. He wanted to know, of course, but he was also worried about Simon's abilities. His back seemed greatly improved this morning and he had said as much when Robert and Christy had quizzed him, but he would, wouldn't he? He'd also push himself to the point of reinjuring it, as he nearly had yesterday.

"The idea of a group of malcontents appeals to me in this case. Hastings is correct, it fits the lack of a pattern we're seeing. But the whole thing does seem to center around this Dutchman. I've sent a note to the Dutch ambassador for any information he has on this Van de Berg. In the meantime, I'm putting full-time surveillance on this hotel. My gut tells me we haven't long to wait for the denouement of this drama."

"Yes, but where are *we* going?" Simon asked. They were stealthily making their way out a small delivery entrance at the back of the hotel.

"Sir?" An agent materialized in front of them.

"Round the clock, McNally," Sir Barnabas said. "Apprehend, very quietly, everyone on the way out."

"Yes, sir." McNally dematerialized, ostensibly to carry out his orders.

"And now we three are going to put our heads together. I have a detailed list of events going on in and around London over the coming week, from the smallest gathering to state affairs, that involve anyone worth assassinating. We are going to go through it and try to narrow it down."

They followed him along a labyrinth of alleyways, and when they came out Sir Barnabas's carriage was waiting. Robert started to walk over to it, but Simon's arm shot out and slammed across his chest, stopping him. Just in time. The whistle of the thin stiletto could be heard as it swung through the air right where his throat would have been.

"Two more!" Sir Barnabas shouted.

Robert heard Sir Barnabas's weapon as he pulled it from his walking stick. Simon pulled his lethal knife from his boot again, but Robert was left to face his would-be assassin with nothing but his wits and his bare hands.

"You have lost the element of surprise, ladies," he told them, squaring off with a woman of average height and size. She wore men's attire, all in black. The other two were similarly dressed.

"Don't need surprise," she answered him in a smooth, uncultured accent. "I like a bit of a tussle anyhow."

He heard Simon scuffling with his attacker but dared not take his eyes away from the woman in front of him. He had to trust that Simon could handle himself.

"Are you the one who attacked my wife? And killed those boys?" he asked coldly, determined to stop her before she harmed anyone else.

Her eyes narrowed but she didn't answer. Instead, she swung the stiletto at him again and Robert blocked it with his arm, stepping into the attack. The knife was sharp and cut through his jacket and shirt, but it was only a small cut and a bit of a sting. It gave him the leverage he needed to grab onto her arm and twist it roughly, forcing her to drop the weapon. She cried out in fury and attempted to slash his face with the nails of her other hand, but he caught that hand as well. She began to twist and kick like a wild cat, but there was little finesse to her tactics.

Robert didn't hesitate to handle her roughly, spinning her around and shoving her to the ground on her stomach. He held her there, capturing both her hands in one of his, and looked up in time to see Sir Barnabas neatly knock his assailant unconscious with a punch to the jaw.

Simon was not so lucky. It was he who ended up on the ground as his attacker took off running down the nearest alleyway.

"Simon!" Robert called out in fear.

"I'm fine," Simon said breathlessly, slowly getting to his feet. "Just my dignity is wounded. She wasn't armed, but she caught me in the stones with a well-aimed kick."

Sir Barnabas had the audacity to laugh. "Lesson one in self-defense, Simon. I can't believe you fell for the oldest trick in the book."

"Yes, well, a practitioner of the oldest profession ought to know the oldest trick," Simon joked. He was standing, but he was bent over, still catching his breath. "I am not having a good week," he said sadly.

Robert had to fight a grin. His heart was pounding and he realized it wasn't from the fight he'd had but the fright when he'd thought Simon had been injured. The situation was becoming more precarious, and he didn't just mean the assassins—he meant what was happening with his emotions.

"Sir!" Sir Barnabas's coachman called back at them. "Are you all right?"

"Fine," Sir Barnabas called back. "Stay with the carriage."

"Let's take these two back with us and find out what's going on," Robert said.

"As if I'd tell you a thing," the woman he held sneered at him. "If I get loose I'll still slit your bleedin' throat."

"Check her for more knives," Simon advised him. He stood up and adjusted himself gingerly. "I shall sing harmony slightly higher from now on."

"Miss," Robert said politely, because he always found he got more cooperation by being unfailingly polite, "we shall both find this a much easier and far more pleasant situation if you would stop resisting and hand over your weapons."

Sir Barnabas was looking at him as if he had two heads. "Does that ever work?" he asked incredulously.

Robert had to yell to be heard over the cursing of his prisoner. "I have found it to work once or twice, and I'm ever hopeful in situations such as this one."

"'Hope springs eternal'," quoted Simon.

"Indeed," Robert said. He managed to find two more stilettos hidden in various crevices on his would-be-assassin. "I need something to tie her hands."

"Use your cravat," Sir Barnabas told him.

Robert had trouble holding the squirming woman with one

hand and untying his cravat with the other. Simon came over and knocked his hand away. "Let me," he murmured. He had it undone in an amazingly short time. Then he tied her hands with a complicated knot that she could not undo. She twisted and squirmed and tried, but it only seemed to get tighter.

"How did you do that?" Robert asked, ignoring her complaints. She had tried to kill him, after all.

"I'll show you later."

A shockingly erotic scene flashed into Robert's mind at Simon's simple words, and the image left Robert breathless and slightly embarrassed. He looked at Simon, who was looking at him as if he'd been about to say something, but he stopped at the look on Robert's face. Then Simon blushed. Robert was relatively sure he was blushing, too.

"Oh, good God," Sir Barnabas said in disgust from beside them. "Really, Simon? You had to corrupt the constable, too? Is there no one you won't shag?"

"We have not," Robert protested.

"No, no one," Simon said at the same time, as if it was a great joke. "You know me."

"Simon, that is not true and you know it," Robert said, offended on his behalf. "You don't go around shagging anyone and everyone. Perhaps at one time, but not anymore."

"Is that what he told you?" Sir Barnabas said snidely. "And you believed him? Ah, to be that innocent again." He hoisted the unconscious woman over his shoulder. "Simon, your cravat."

"Use your own damn cravat," Simon snapped.

"It would be unseemly for me to be seen at the Home Office improperly dressed," Sir Barnabas said primly. "And I'm very attached to this particular cravat. It is my lucky cravat. So give me yours."

"Apologize to him first," Robert demanded.

Sir Barnabas turned and stared at him incredulously. "Do

you know who I am? I do not apologize. And you work for me. Start acting like it."

"I did not ask to work for you. I believe we have been over this before. And you have disparaged Simon and hurt his feelings, and what's more it isn't true. If he and I were involved, then first of all it would be none of your business, and second of all it would certainly be more than shagging for both of us. The very idea." He sniffed in disapproval of the very notion.

"I simply have no words," Sir Barnabas said. "I have never encountered someone like you, Manderley. You defy categorization."

"I will take that as a compliment."

"I'm not sure I meant it as one." Sir Barnabas turned away and started toward the carriage.

"I am quite sure you did not," Robert said under his breath. "And I did not hear an apology."

"And you never will," Sir Barnabas called back.

"Don't bother," Simon said when Robert started to respond. Simon was already taking off his cravat. "He always gets the last word."

CHAPTER 24

Sir Barnabas sat in a chair facing the woman who had tried to cut Robert's throat. Simon still got chills thinking how close he'd come. Thank God his intuition had not failed him. Too many times to count during the war—and after when he prowled St. Giles with Daniel meting out vigilante justice in their foolhardy and reckless past—Simon's intuition had saved his life and the life of his friends. He'd always had it, that sixth sense of…something. And he always listened to it. It had failed him with Giselle and so he had never trusted it, not even after all these years. But lately he'd been giving it a bit more credence, and today he was willing to swear by it.

He glanced over at Robert for what must have been the one hundredth time that day, just to watch him breathing, and catch the slight vibration of the pulse in his neck, visible now that he wore no cravat. It was taking every ounce of self-control Simon possessed not to cross the room and put his mouth on the heartbeat in Robert's neck. He felt like a foolish, infatuated idiot.

He tore his gaze away from Robert's neck only to find Robert watching him. The knowing little smile Robert sent him made his own heart skip a beat, and Simon quickly looked away, embarrassed by his ridiculous reaction.

He blamed it on his weakened state. He never should have agreed to do this for Daniel and then for Barnabas. It was too soon. He hadn't even recovered from that nightmare in Africa yet. What on earth were they doing, expecting him to watch Robert and Hastings like this? This had turned into a very serious affair, a matter of state, of security and the safety of the empire. It should not be in Simon's hands, of all people. He could barely handle his own fate, let alone that of the empire, for God's sake.

Barnabas was sipping a cup of tea, his legs crossed, his pinky in the air like a right gentleman, as Hastings would say. The little harridan who'd nearly decapitated Robert was sitting facing him with her hands tied behind her, watching him drink the tea with a near feral look on her face. They'd been questioning her for hours and had refused all her requests for food, drink and even a moment's rest. The room was windowless. She'd lost track of time. Barnabas was merciless. But then, he was an expert at this sort of thing. He'd had many years to perfect the art.

"Now, my dear, you know I cannot give you anything until you tell us where the Dutchman plans to strike and when. I'm sorry, truly, you cannot know how sorry I am. But my superiors at Whitehall have been very clear about this. Only subjects who cooperate with our investigations receive complimentary treatment. I'm afraid the others…well, let me just say that I should hate to see you suffer as they have." He made a *tsk, tsk* sound that was almost believably sympathetic even to those who knew him. "Are you sure there's nothing you can tell us?"

He turned as the door opened. "Oh, look. A proper tea. Of

186 | SAMANTHA KANE

course, it isn't the time for it. Or is it? I'm just not sure. Here we are." The tea cart was wheeled in and placed next to Sir Barnabas, who lifted the lid on the covered dishes. "Oh, sandwiches. And is that jam? How delightful. Gentlemen, do come and have something to eat. You must be famished."

Robert pushed himself off the wall and accepted a plate of food from Sir Barnabas with a hearty thanks. He stood next to Barnabas's chair and stuffed a sandwich into his mouth, and his would-be assassin gave a little sob.

Simon forced himself to follow Robert's lead. He wasn't hungry at all, honestly. He'd always hated this part of the job. His specialty had been gathering information. He'd been able to infiltrate an enemies' camp and steal battle plans from right under their noses. And when need be, kill someone. Like Hastings, he preferred the clean kills. Interrogation had always been a necessary evil.

"I..." The woman paused to swallow. "I don't know much." It was a promising change from her defensive denials for the last few hours. Apparently Barnabas had at last worn her down.

"No?" Barnabas asked. He handed Simon a plate loaded down with food. "Tea?" he asked Simon.

"Please," Simon replied politely. "Milk and sugar."

"But of course." Sir Barnabas poured his tea and prepared it while the woman watched, fascinated. He handed Simon the cup and turned back to her. "What do you know, my dear? Every little bit helps."

"He needed the ship," she said in a rush. "He was bloody angry when he had to unload it and run."

"Did he?" Sir Barnabas looked as if they were gossiping over tea. He took a sip as he watched her, giving her all his attention.

"Yes, sir. They was plannin' to put the ship somewhere and blow it up. But now he's got to find another way to do it."

"They?" Sir Barnabas asked casually. "Who is they?"

"I...I don't know," she said miserably, shrugging as best as she could with her hands tied behind her back. "Some nobs, I think. And a Russian," she said in a rush. "Yeah, he was Russian. I heard him talkin'."

"Russian? Are you sure?" Robert asked. "Do you know Russian?" he sounded skeptical.

"I don't speak it," she said, "but I know what it sounds like. I do. Had some Russian sailors come in from time to time. It don't sound like no other language."

"Oh, I don't know," Simon said for argument's sake. "It sounds a bit like Polish."

"Does it?" Robert asked. They turned to each other and ignored her. "Do you speak Polish?"

"I knew a Polish officer in the war. Or perhaps he was Hungarian." Simon tapped his finger on his chin. "No, I'm mistaken. He was German." He nodded. "Yes, that's right."

"*Deystvitel'no?*" Sir Barnabas asked them with a raised brow. "Really?"

"That's it," the woman said. "That's what it sounded like."

"That's Russian all right," Barnabas said. "What else can you tell us?"

Like most suspects, once she began talking, she couldn't seem to stop. "There's an Englishman for sure, he's rich as can be but he ain't no gentleman, leastways not titled, if you know what I mean. Comes from trade or somethin', I heard her say."

"Her? You mean Mrs. Gaines?" Barnabas asked.

"Yeah, that's right. Fat Linnie. She's the one what introduced him to the Dutchman. Anyway, he says he can get them more explosives. They ain't got enough for the job now. 'Cause they lost the ship, like I said. They were goin' to smuggle more in."

"I thought they were going to blow it up," Simon said, acting confused.

"They are, I mean, were," she said. "But not before they used it to get more explosives."

"Interesting," Barnabas said. "What else?"

"Isn't that enough?" she cried. "I'm starvin', I tell you! I can barely talk I'm so parched!"

Robert took another bite of sandwich and spoke with his mouth full. "Well, I daresay I wouldn't be eating or drinking at all if you had managed to slit my throat."

"It was Fat Linnie what told me to do it," she said, whining. "I didn't want to, you being the law and all. But she said you were gettin' too close. So they were goin' to take care of that one at the hotel and we was to take care of you three."

"Hastings?" Barnabas said. He didn't actually move, but Simon could sense the tension in him. He turned to the agent at the door. "Has he checked in?"

"No, sir," the agent said.

"Find him." Barnabas turned back to her. "Who are they trying to kill?"

"Well, you three and that other one," she said, confused. "I told you."

"No," Barnabas snapped impatiently. "Pay attention. Whatever they are going to blow up, they are going to kill someone. Who is it?"

"I don't know nothin' about that," she said. "I s'pect they'll kill a lot of people with an explosion like that."

"Just how much explosive is the Englishman giving the Dutchman?" Barnabas asked.

"Not sure exactly," she said. "But I heard him say it will light up the sky so they'll see it clear to St. James."

"When?" Robert asked.

"Well, they were right angry about that, too. I guess it wasn't supposed to be for a very long while. Years even. But now they've got to do it soon because you're breathing down their necks. I heard the Dutchie say next week. It won't be as big of a dust up as they planned, but it will still make noise, he said."

"Years?" Barnabas put his teacup down and rose from his

chair. "That narrows our search, gentlemen." He waved away the tea tray.

"No!" the prisoner cried as it was wheeled out of the room.

"You shall eat the same fare as the other prisoners," Sir Barnabas said coldly. "And for the time being, count yourself lucky your head is still attached to your shoulders." He headed for the door and signaled Robert and Simon to follow him.

CHAPTER 25

"Mr. Naismith," Barnabas said pleasantly as they entered another interrogation room. "How nice to see you again."

They came straight to Naismith from the assassin. He'd been brought in quietly as soon as he'd left his meeting with Van de Berg. They'd left him to stew in the room for hours, but Naismith looked unperturbed. Simon could well imagine he'd endured such harsh conditions and boredom before, having spent so much time in Africa as a leading member of the African Company of Merchants.

"I told him no," Naismith said without being prompted. "He wanted a backer for some sort of harebrained scheme, and I said no. That's all I can tell you." He sat at the table, his legs crossed, tapping a calling card against the scarred, wooden top impatiently. Perhaps he wasn't as unperturbed as Simon thought. "What has that idiot Dutchman dragged me into now?" he asked in disgust. "Something that will cost me my head, no doubt, if Sir Barnabas James is taking a personal interest in it."

"What was his harebrained scheme?" Barnabas asked, taking

the seat across the table from Naismith. "Whether you and your head part company depends on the particulars."

"You don't know?" Naismith asked in surprise. "I don't either. I wouldn't even let him tell me. I knew it was trouble. I have been working very hard to regain my reputation since that African business and I won't risk that now over this Dutchman's asinine plans."

"Why don't you just tell us exactly what Van de Berg said to you?" Simon asked him. "Beginning with how he got you to agree to a meeting in the first place."

"Fine," Naismith said, eager to cooperate. Simon wished all witnesses were this helpful. "He sent me a note that said he was in London on business and he was looking for investors. That was his word for it. That it was an opportunity involving a situation here, in London, which he knew would appeal to me. Everyone knows I've been avoiding foreign investment, for obvious reasons."

"Of course," Barnabas murmured sympathetically.

"And so I went. It's been hard to get my foot back in the door here in London. So when opportunities arise, I can't pass them by. But as soon as he started to talk, it didn't sound like investment, it sounded like trouble, and so I left. Immediately, despite his pleas."

"How so?" Robert asked. "What exactly did he say, if you please?"

"Of course," Naismith said. "He said that he was looking for money to purchase explosives and that he already had a contact, but he wouldn't tell me what they were for or what exactly my profit would be. He just asked, wouldn't I like to get back at them all for that mess in Africa, and I said no and walked out. Into the waiting arms of your men."

"Them? Who is them? Who would you be getting back at?"

"I have no idea," Naismith said. "There were too many names to count involved in that fiasco." He shrugged. "I will say I got the impression that he already had investors. I was to be another, not the only one."

"And if he contacts you again?" Barnabas said.

"Naturally, now that I know you're after him, I'll try to get as much information as possible and contact you immediately."

"Naturally," Barnabas said. "You might be interested to know that he's joined forces with a rather notorious madam who runs a gang of female assassins."

Naismith sat there and blinked at him uncomprehendingly for a moment. "You must be joking."

"No, indeed we are not, Mr. Naismith. You should be careful," Simon told him. "There's nothing else you can tell us?"

"No," Naismith insisted. "Unless—he did mention something about foreign involvement as well, but I'm sorry to say I didn't get particulars on that, either. He's Dutch, after all. I assumed there would be a foreign component."

"I'll be in touch," Barnabas said. "About this, or perhaps other problems about which you might have useful information."

Naismith froze in the process of getting out of his chair and glared at Barnabas. "I see," he said. "That's to be the price of making a foolish mistake, is it? Informing for the Home Office?" He sighed and picked up his hat and gloves from the table. "So be it. I have nothing to hide, James. And if I can be of assistance to the Home Office, I will gladly do so." He put on his hat and left the room unimpeded.

"Do you trust him?" Robert asked.

"Not necessarily," Barnabas asked. "But I believe him. He fell into a bad situation, but he's no fool."

"And now you have another victim under your thumb," Simon said.

"I like to think of it as another lamb to the fold."

"Said the hungry wolf," Simon muttered to Robert, who quietly chuckled as they followed Barnabas out.

~

ROBERT TOSSED another paper down on the table with a frustrated sigh. "I can't make head nor tails of your secret codes, Sir Barnabas." He ran both hands through his hair and rubbed his scalp. He looked out the window at the moon halfway through the night sky. He'd sent yet another note to Christy telling her they'd be late.

Sir Barnabas got up from his desk and walked over to the table he'd had set up in his office. Robert, Simon and several other agents were going through papers and calendars trying to figure out the Dutchman's target while Sir Barnabas went about his usual business. His absence earlier in the day had put him behind on his paperwork.

He picked up the paper Robert had discarded. "*Pic* is obviously Piccadilly. *MPD w/sp* is clearly military parade with speakers. Really, constable, it's not that difficult."

"Well, that sounds like something that might be a good target," Robert said. "And that's next week, June 18th, the tenth anniversary of Waterloo."

"But they were supposed to blow it up years from now," Sir Barnabas argued. "That was always planned for next week."

"Yes, but they've got to settle for a secondary plan, haven't they? Whatever they were going to blow up won't be ready by next week, so they've got to find something else," Robert argued right back.

"He has a point," Simon said.

Robert was tired and hungry and short tempered. He was in his shirtsleeves, disheveled and overheated in the stuffy office. And upon their arrival they'd learned that Thom Longfellow had been attacked. He had fatally wounded his attacker—another one of Fat Linnie's operatives. Luckily Thom would live. But they were all on edge now wondering where the assassins would strike next.

Robert looked out the window. London never truly slept, but it was as close as it got tonight, quieter than he ever remembered. Probably because of the heat. No one wanted to be out in it.

Simon was tired, too. Robert could see it in the shadows under his eyes and the ache in his voice. He couldn't sit in his chair for long, and so he paced the room, picking papers up as he passed the table, alighting briefly on the windowsill and then taking off across the room again. He looked so exhausted Robert was sure he'd rather sit still than walk around, so it must be his back.

"How, exactly, were they going to get a ship to Piccadilly?" asked Barnabas.

"No one said anything about getting a ship to Piccadilly," Robert snapped.

"She didn't say they were changing the target," Sir Barnabas said. "Her exact words were 'It won't be as big of a dust up as they planned, but it will still make noise.' That to me indicates the same target, but an earlier timeline. Correct?" He looked at Simon.

"Yes," Simon said with a sigh. "I'm sorry, Robert, but he's right. They have an agenda, a very specific goal in mind. We heard assassination. That was what Alice Gaines said she intercepted in the communiqués taken from the original victims."

"Yes, what about those victims?" Robert said angrily, standing and confronting both of them. "I have not forgotten them. My original task was to find their killer, or killers. We have at least one, if not two, in custody. Will they be prosecuted for those murders?"

"Yes."

Sir Barnabas's simple reply took the wind out of Robert's sails. "Oh," he said. "Well, then, that's all right." He sat back down.

"Are you ready to listen to reason?" Sir Barnabas asked.

"I am always a reasonable man," Robert said. "Why have we not received any word on Hastings? It's been hours."

"Because there is no word on Hastings," Sir Barnabas said. He sighed, and Robert realized the spymaster was as worried about his young protégé as he and Simon were. "In this instance I choose to believe no news is good news." He paused and pinched his nose in that gesture he made when he was unhappy with something. "I wasn't going to tell you, but they've found two more of the female assassins not far from your house, Manderley. Dead. Their throats slit."

Robert stood up so quickly he felt lightheaded and had to grab onto the table. Now that he knew more about them, he understood the danger to be tenfold what he imagined it to be when Christy was attacked.

"Sit down," Sir Barnabas snapped. "I said they were dead. That means either they are turning on one another or we have another party at play. Either way, they seem to have shut off access to your house for the time being. I am hoping what- or whoever it is will keep Hastings from harm as well."

Simon came over and put a hand on Robert's shoulder. "Do we still have agents in place?" Simon asked.

"Yes," Barnabas said. "I'm not moving them. But I believe all of that is merely a distraction. They can't afford to lose more operatives. By my count they are down at least five. Two from the Manderley house, two from the attack on us, and one from the attack on Mr. Longfellow. It is more imperative than ever that we deduce their ultimate goal and stop them before more damage is done."

"My family's well-being is more than damage," Robert said. His insides churned with worry for Christy and Christian. He had not meant to put them in danger. He'd had no idea a simple murder case would turn into this.

"Of course it is, and you know that's not how I meant it," Sir Barnabas replied impatiently. "This bickering does no one any good. We must focus, and figure this damn thing out. Now, if they are keeping the same target, and it would not be ready for years—" He stopped suddenly. He began to search through the papers, tossing them aside.

"What are you looking for?" Simon asked.

"The bridge," Sir Barnabas said. "The plans for the bridge."

"The bridge? Oh, you mean the new London Bridge?" Robert sorted through some papers in front of him. "Here." He handed them to Sir Barnabas. "Why? Do you think they mean to blow the old bridge? Wouldn't it make more sense to blow up Waterloo Bridge? It's newer and considered one of the finest bridges in the world."

"Perhaps," Sir Barnabas said. "But the Duke of York is not going to be at Waterloo Bridge next week. And he *is* going to be at London Bridge, laying the first stone of the new bridge with the Lord Mayor of London, on Wednesday. They requested security for the event." He held up the paper. "They were going to blow up the new London Bridge. But now, they are going to blow the old one, and assassinate the Duke of York."

WHEN HASTINGS BURST into Sir Barnabas's office half an hour later and declared, "They're going to blow up London Bridge!" it was rather anti-climactic.

"Yes, we know," Simon told him.

"Damn it," Hastings said angrily. "What is the use of snooping around, risking my life, I might add—there's two more of those godawful women from Fat Linnie's downstairs in a cell—when you lot are just going to sit on your arses here and come up with the same information?"

"That makes seven down," Robert said.

"Because now our information has been confirmed," Sir Barnabas told Hastings without looking up from his paperwork, ignoring Robert's comment. He signed yet another order of some kind and added it to a pile of signed papers and then picked up another paper and scanned it while talking. "We deduced the target. I assume you overheard the Dutchmen and his accomplices talking about it?"

"I did," Hastings said. "And I was about to grab him and some Russian, name of Demetriev, when those two she-devils showed up and tried to—"

"Slit your throat?" Robert guessed.

"How did you know?" Hastings was beginning to look quite put out at not getting the reaction he'd expected to all his dramatic news.

"Same thing happened to me," Robert said dismissively. "This Demetriev must be the foreign contact Naismith told us about."

"You ought to think about starting a club or something," Simon told them. "A very small club, I guess. They actually seem to be very good at that sort of thing, so not many members, you know."

"Not amusing, Simon," Robert told him.

"No, but true," he said. He felt a pang of guilt at the frown Robert sent his way. "Sorry."

"Now what?" Hastings asked. He threw himself down in a chair in front of Sir Barnabas's desk. He casually put his feet up on the desk and crossed his ankles.

Sir Barnabas finally stopped working to stare at his dirty boots. "I have had men killed for less," he said in a dangerously low voice.

"I know," Hastings said, blithely unconcerned for his well-being. "I'm hungry. This snooping business is hard work. I haven't eaten for hours."

Simon felt as if he was looking in a mirror. Hastings reminded him of himself, not just when he was younger, either. It was how he'd been living his life for too long to remember. Good God, he'd been that devil-may-care only a year ago.

He'd lived an entire lifetime in that year. Fallen in love when he'd thought it would never happen again, lost her, nearly killed himself with drink and excess, then nearly been killed by those pirates because he'd let himself go so much he couldn't do the job anymore and he'd gotten caught. No one had said that to him, but it was a glaringly obvious omission. He thought he knew the game from every angle, but the truth was he'd never been tortured before. He'd never known that kind of pain and misery, and it changed a man. It changed him.

Was that why he found himself so drawn to Robert as well as Christy now? When he'd first met Robert, he'd found him insufferable. Too perfect, too naïve, too willing to follow the rules. But now his stalwart presence soothed something in Simon that had been awoken this year. His antiquated commitment to duty and honor and right and wrong—all the things Simon had forgotten about—appealed to him.

It appealed to Christy, too. Robert was a man who could be counted on, a man who would never desert you or turn his back on you. Not like Simon had.

"Simon?" Robert was suddenly standing beside him, looking at him in concern. "Are you all right?"

Simon looked around and saw that everyone was looking at him. "I'm sorry," he said with an apologetic smile. "I was woolgathering. Did I miss something?"

"I was just saying that our next step needs to be finding Mr. Demetriev. If he is a tradesman here in London, that shouldn't be too difficult," Robert told him.

"Yes, excellent idea," Simon agreed. "You're very good at this business."

Robert blushed, and Simon found it rather endearing.

"Well, it is my occupation," Robert said drily to cover his embarrassment.

"Please don't make me go with them," Hastings said in a pained voice, his head resting on the back of the chair, his eyes closed. "Their little mutual infatuation is becoming nauseating. I can't stand it for one more day." He lifted his head and glared at Barnabas. "I mean it. I *will* kill someone."

"You'll most likely kill someone anyway, so that is a moot threat," Sir Barnabas said. "But it is your lucky day because I have something else for you to do." He turned to Simon and Robert. "You two can go to the Russian section in London. I assume that would be where Mr. Demetriev has his business, whatever it is."

"I don't think so," Simon said, his brain suddenly deciding to join the investigation.

"I don't either," Robert said.

They looked at each other.

"The wharves?" Robert asked.

"They've got to have a ship," Simon said, nodding in agreement.

"What about the explosives?" Sir Barnabas asked.

"Where does the military store them?" Simon asked, already knowing the answer, of course. "If they don't have the money to buy the explosives, the next best thing is to steal them. Perhaps that is the contact Van de Berg was talking about."

"Woolwich. The Warren," Sir Barnabas said, already writing a note. "I can get you details and locations in an hour."

"We will be at home," Robert said. "We need a few hours of sleep and something to eat or we won't be good for anything. Come on, Simon. And Hastings you'll just have to put up with our mutual appreciation society for a little longer if you want something to eat."

"Damn it, man, you know my price," Hastings said, standing.

"Don't you want to know what your assignment is?" Sir Barnabas asked him without looking up.

"Do I get to kill someone without having to know why or ask any questions?" Hastings fired back, heading for the door.

"No." Sir Barnabas was sealing his note.

"Then tomorrow is soon enough." Hastings opened the door.

"Be here by six o'clock," Sir Barnabas told him. "Here. To the Admiralty." He handed the note to his secretary.

"You are cruel and I dislike you," Hastings called back to him.

"Good night, Barnabas," Simon said, suddenly so tired he could barely put one foot in front of the other. He yawned and let Robert take his arm and lead him to the door. "I don't hate you. But you can be cruel."

"Well, I've got to have some fun," Barnabas said. "All work and no play makes Barnabas a harsh task master."

Robert was laughing as he closed the door behind them.

CHAPTER 26

Christy paced the floor again. Christian was in her arms, his head on her shoulder. He hadn't been sleeping well with Robert gone at night these last few weeks. She hadn't told Robert because she didn't want him to feel any worse about his recent absences. She knew he wasn't at fault. But Christian was used to Robert playing with him and reading to him before Nanny took him up to bed, and the change in his schedule wasn't sitting well with him.

In a way, Christy didn't mind. She wasn't sleeping well with Robert gone, either, and she appreciated Christian's company. He was a sweet little boy, chubby with a head of light curls. Christy adored him. He was the first person, the only person, who was really and truly hers. He rarely cried, but he could be stubborn. Christy was relatively sure he got that from her.

He looked like his father, the long gone John Coachman, but she didn't mind that. When Robert held him, Christy could swear there seemed to be a resemblance between them. Enough so that people wouldn't question his legitimacy. Robert never brought it up. Of course he didn't. He wouldn't. He loved Christian like he was his own.

Christy hummed as she walked the floor with him. He liked to hold a piece of her hair in his little fist when she held him like this. He'd go to sleep holding her hair like that, and he'd fuss when she'd pull it free. She liked that. Liked that he didn't want to let her go. Too many people had been too willing to let her go. It was nice to have someone who didn't want to. He'd be one year old soon, and he'd start walking and then he wouldn't want her to carry him like this. Just thinking about it made her want to cry.

She heard them come in, and so did Christian. He raised his head from her shoulder and turned toward the door.

"Shall we go and say good evening to Papa?" she said to him quietly. He reached for the door with a wordless baby sound of happiness when he heard Robert's voice. "All right, then," she told him.

She found them in the kitchen, of course.

"Christy!" Robert exclaimed in shock. "And Christian." He put down the bread he was holding and reached for the baby, who was just as eagerly reaching for him. Christy handed him over with a smile. She loved to watch their affectionate greetings. It was clear they adored one another.

"Christian, this is Hastings," Robert said, pointing to the younger man who sitting at the table eating. Hastings raised a hand in greeting and the baby clapped. "He has atrocious manners. Do not emulate him."

"I'm starving," Hastings said in his defense as soon as he swallowed. "I haven't eaten all day. Don't listen to your father, Christian. I am a wonderful role model."

"He is also a liar," Simon said to Christian, looking very serious as he bent down to look in the baby's eyes. "If he says the grass is green, don't believe him."

Robert laughed. "And you already know Simon," he told Christian.

"No warnings about me?" Simon asked lightly as he turned away to get something to eat.

"Only that he should get used to your presence," Robert said, bouncing Christian gently and making a face at him.

"Hmm," was Simon's noncommittal response. Christy, on the other hand, had to resist the urge to cover her pounding heart with a shaky hand. She glanced over at Hastings, who was avidly watching the proceedings. Now was clearly not the time to ask Robert what he meant by that.

Christy realized that both Hastings and Simon were eating. "Oh, dear," she said, taking Christian back. He didn't fuss too much. "You must be hungry, too, Robert. Get yourself something to eat. I'll put Christian back to bed."

As she walked out of the kitchen, she stole a glance at Simon, only to find him watching her. He smiled at her and she could see the exhaustion on his face. She just smiled back. No, tonight nothing would be settled.

With a little encouragement, the baby put his head on her shoulder and took her hair in his little fist, and he was fast asleep before they even made it up the stairs. She put him in his bed and waved to Nanny, who had come in at their arrival, then she left the room quietly, closing the door behind her.

She stood in the hall, debating whether or not to go back down to the kitchen, when footsteps on the stairs froze her in place. She breathed a sigh of relief when Simon appeared and not Hastings. It wasn't until she'd brought Christian up that she'd realized how inappropriately she was dressed to be entertaining Hastings in the kitchen. She was only wearing her dressing gown and her hair was down, plaited, of course, but not neatly.

Simon stopped at the top of the stairs, one boot on the landing. He simply looked at her for a moment or two, his expression pleasant, warm even, but very, very tired.

"You look absolutely beautiful," he said quietly. "I know you aren't doing it on purpose. You haven't an ounce of artifice in you. And yet you've somehow managed to stand in the perfect shaft of moonlight to highlight your dark curls and alabaster skin."

Christy blushed at his compliments. Simon heaved himself up the last step onto the landing with a great sigh. "But I am so tired, Christy, I can hardly think, much less figure out what to do with you."

"I don't believe I asked you to do anything," she replied a little tartly. She had already decided no one was doing anything *with* her. This time she was going to figure it out and make sure she got what she wanted out of this mess, and fix everyone else up nice and proper in the process, Simon included.

"No, no, you didn't," he said with a laugh that sounded a bit delirious. "That's always been the problem."

"I'd argue that when the situation arose I asked plenty," she said, "but this is no time for arguments. Come on, Simon," she said, stepping forward and taking his arm. She pulled him toward his room. "Let's get you to bed."

"Do you know how many times I dreamed of you saying that to me?" he asked, letting her lead him.

She looked at him curiously. "No," she answered, surprised by the question. She hadn't imagined Simon dreamed about her at all.

"Well," he said as they entered his room, "perhaps it wasn't those exact words. Something more like 'Let's go to bed.' Or my favorite, 'Take me to bed.'"

"Simon," she said, a little scandalized, even after what they'd done together. Even knowing his reputation, and hers. "Let me help you get undressed."

"Why are you forever undressing me?" he asked, but he obediently turned around and let her tug his jacket off.

"Because you are forever injured or tired or heaven knows what else," Christy replied.

"Ah, Christy, you have no idea," he said in that smooth, decadent, rapscallion's voice of his. She wondered if he was even aware that he was trying to seduce her. He spun back around and took the jacket from her hands, tossing it aside.

"I should hang that," she argued.

"Never mind it," he murmured, stepping in close to her. "When do I get to undress you?"

He smelled so good, and even though it had been insufferably hot all day, she still wanted to be close to him, to touch the fire of his skin. But he was so tired he was almost punch drunk, and Christy knew that even though Robert had given his tacit approval, he hadn't meant it. Particularly now that he also had feelings for Simon. Did Simon reciprocate those feelings?

"What about Robert?" she murmured, letting herself put her hand on his chest. She was still separated from his skin by his shirt and waistcoat, after all.

Simon leaned against her hand, cupping her elbows as he leaned down and kissed her neck just above her dressing gown. "Robert?" he murmured against her skin. "He can help undress you. Or me. Or *we* can undress *him*." She felt him smile against her. "That sounds nice."

Christy was shocked at the decadence of the picture he painted. Although, honestly, it did sound nice. But she couldn't imagine Robert letting that happen.

"Shirt off," she said breathlessly, trying to get back to the task at hand. "Do you need me to rub your back tonight?"

Simon took her hands in his and placed her palms on his chest, then he ran them slowly down over his stomach to the top of his trousers and with his hands over hers bunched his shirt in their fists and tugged it out. "Maybe," he said, placing light kisses on her neck and cheek. "I may need you to rub me."

"Simon, you're being very naughty," she told him, her voice unsteady.

"There was a time you were very naughty with me," he said.

"Take my shirt off." She hesitated, and Simon pulled back. His gaze on her was no longer sleepy, though his lids were heavy. "My back hurts," he said.

She wasn't sure if you was lying or not, but she chose to believe him. She pushed his shirt up slowly, so as not to hurt him, while he held onto her hips. He had to let go so she could pull it off over his head, and she realized that he had taken advantage of her preoccupation to untie her wrapper. It fell open as she pulled his shirt off.

"Simon," she said firmly as she turned to put his shirt away. He wrapped his arms around her from behind. Her heart sped up because, even though she couldn't feel it, she knew he was bare-chested now.

"You're so beautiful, Christy," he breathed into her thick plait. "It's been so long since I've seen you."

"You very nearly saw me last night," she said, trying to sound sharp and practical and annoyed with herself when she could only manage breathless and aroused.

"Last night seems like years ago," he said. "A fever dream. This feels like another fever dream, too. Another dream of holding you in my arms, wanting you, but not able to touch you. Not really." She clutched his shirt to her chest to prevent herself from grabbing onto his hands and holding them against her.

"When did you dream that?" she whispered.

"A thousand…no, a million times in Africa," he told earnestly. "Every night, every waking minute. Christy, my Christy. My dream."

She dropped his shirt and turned in his arms. Wrapping her arms around his neck, burying her hands in his glorious hair and pressing her lips to his seemed like the only thing to do in response to a confession like that.

The kiss was shattering in its intensity. She'd thought the kiss they'd shared the other day had scorched her willpower. This kiss devastated it. Simon held her so tight she could hardly breathe, and he devoured her. She could feel the loneliness he'd endured, the pain and suffering, the ache of missing her. If he hadn't said so much in words, she would have known from this kiss.

He broke the kiss and panted against her lips. "Christy," he whispered.

She loved the feel of his breath in her mouth. That's exactly what she wanted, to breathe him in like air. He kissed his way down her jaw to her neck and then down her chest, and she realized he'd unbuttoned her nightgown. He slid it down off one shoulder, exposing her breast. When the tip of his tongue traced a circle around her nipple, she gasped and her hands clutched his head to her chest. He sucked on her nipple briefly and then pulled away to look at her.

He traced a finger along the side. "Robert?" he asked. Christy didn't understand what he was asking.

"Yes," Robert's voice came from behind her. "That's my mark."

Christy gasped and tried to turn, but Simon's grip on her prevented it. She stood there, shaking, uncertain, her skin only moments ago flushed with arousal now chilled with a rush of emotions too jumbled to name. Simon's hand slid up her back, and he wrapped it around the back of her neck. Then, to her horror, he bent her slightly back over his arm, exposing her bare breast to Robert.

She fought him briefly, but he was still strong enough to hold on to her, and the truth was she didn't want to get away enough to hurt him or herself. Simon's other hand rested between her breasts. She looked over and saw Robert standing in the shadows by the door. There was a sound on the stairs, and he glanced out in the hall in alarm and then stepped fully into the room, closing the door behind him.

"Hastings?" Simon asked quietly.

"Yes," Robert said. He was exposed in the moonlight now.

Christy was holding her breath. What would happen now? She'd wanted to resolve the situation. It looked like there would be some sort of resolution now.

Simon began to unbutton her nightgown further. He let go of her neck, which had been awkward, and simply supported her back with his arm wrapped around her. She had her arm around his back, and his skin was hot and slick with sweat.

"What are you doing?" Robert asked quietly.

"What we all want," Simon said. "The tension is killing us all. I can hardly eat, sleep or think wondering what it will be like."

"What what will be like?" Robert asked. His voice was still pitched very quiet, but it was also that lower timber that made her shiver the other night, the voice of arousal.

"The three of us," Simon said. He spread her undone nightgown until it fell open, exposing her entire front. "Christy?"

"What?" she asked, surprised by her name.

"I want to do something with you," Simon whispered. He leaned down and kissed the pulse in her throat. "Do you want to do something with us?" he whispered.

The question hung in the still heat of the room. Christy looked at Robert, who had taken a step closer to them. She wasn't even sure he was aware of it.

He wanted it. She could see it in his face, even if he didn't know it yet.

"Yes," she said, more sure of it than of anything else in their mixed-up life at the moment. Perhaps things weren't settled between them. No promises had been made, but then none had been demanded. All she knew was that this night was hers if she reached for it. She stretched out her hand to Robert.

He stepped forward and took it.

CHAPTER 27

"Now what?" Robert asked, amused in spite of himself. It has seemed like a huge step to take, but it had only been the beginning.

"Well," Simon said playfully, setting Christy on her feet, "your wife was undressing me." He looked at Robert expectantly.

Robert just stood there. After a moment, he understood.

"Surely you don't expect me to do that. Again." He could feel his cheeks heat up at the memory. When he'd stripped off Simon's trousers the last time, Simon had been in a great deal of pain and Robert had felt like a lecher because that morning's erotic encounter had still been fresh in his mind and he'd grown aroused even though Simon had not. It had been horribly awkward.

"I absolutely do," Simon said. "This time I am not attempting to play injured."

"This isn't cricket." Robert hated that he sounded like a grumpy old man. Christy actually coughed next to him, trying unsuccessfully to stifle a laugh. Simon didn't bother to stifle his.

"Duly noted," he said. "But, honestly, I do need help with my boots. And so will you." He looked at Christy. "See? You wanted us to undress Robert, and now I have given you your wish."

"And when did she wish for this?" Robert asked to cover his awkwardness as he tugged off Simon's boots and tried to avoid looking at the bulge in the front of his trousers.

"Just before you caught us being very naughty," Christy said breathlessly. Robert looked over at her and very nearly groaned at how decadent she looked. Her night clothes were parted just enough to see the deep valley between her breasts and the dark triangle between her legs. A hint of paradise.

"I would say you were being a bit more than very naughty," Robert said. "That sounds as if you knocked over the milk jug."

He now stood in front of Simon, facing Christy. Simon's laughter from right next to his ear surprised him.

"I think you're right," Simon purred in his ear. "Bad. We were being very, very bad. But it felt very, very good."

When Simon slipped his arms around Robert's chest, Robert nearly jerked away but stopped himself at the last second. Wasn't this what he'd been wondering about? Hadn't Simon been right? Now was as good a time as any to find out if what he'd been feeling around Simon was indeed desire, or merely curiosity spurred by Christy's feelings for the other man. Was what happened between them at Simon's apartment an aberration, not to be repeated? Or the beginning of something more? Robert was no coward, and he owed it to Christy and to himself —and yes, to Simon—to discover which one it was.

He knew that he'd been sending messages to Simon that might indicate an interest of a sexual nature, whether he'd been doing that intentionally or not. It would be unfair to him not to follow through on them, or at least try to, if he could.

Simon began to unbutton Robert's jacket, slipping each button out of its hole very slowly. Robert had never before imagined a button and hole could be so incredibly arousing.

"So, Robert," Simon said, resting his chin on Robert's shoulder. "Do you want to be very, very bad, too? I don't imagine a constable gets the chance very often." He chuckled, and the rumble of it went through Robert like a hot knife, making him shiver.

"I think I would like to see what you two find so appealing about it," he said softly, trying to play the game. He must have succeeded, because Christy's face lit up with excitement and anticipation. It was all worth it for that look alone.

"Excellent," Simon said. He had Robert's jacket unbuttoned, and as he began to slip it off, Christy stepped over, and she placed her hands on Robert's shoulders and glided them down his arms as the jacket slid down and off. Robert was nearly undone by that simple touch alone. Trapped between the heat of Simon and Christy's bodies, both of them half unclothed, and undressing him, their hands on him—he felt like a madman barely holding onto the merest edge of his sanity.

Christy leaned in and licked the hollow of his throat. "Why are neither of you wearing your cravats?" she asked, a little frown on her face.

"We had to tie up a couple of suspects with them," Robert told her.

Her eyes got quite big at his casual answer. "Oh, dear," she said. "Were they dangerous?"

"Not very," he lied. "But Simon knows a very clever knot that only gets tighter as you pull on it." Christy looked intrigued, but not, Robert was sure, for the same reason he had been.

"I plan to tie Robert up one night and have my way with him," Simon said from behind him as he reached around and began to unbutton Robert's trousers.

Robert caught his hand. "Not yet," he said. He wasn't ready for that yet, he knew that much. He felt Simon's chuckle against his back again.

"Fair enough," Simon said. "Shirt? Please."

The last was said in a nearly begging tone, and Robert found he liked it, liked being physically desired like that. He knew Christy desired him, but there was something special about a man like Simon—handsome, suave, well-dressed, lethal, seductive—wanting him.

He nodded. "Yes," Simon whispered with satisfaction.

He tugged the shirt loose from his trousers and then he let his hands play, gliding them around Robert's torso as he slid the shirt up and then over Robert's head. Christy stood in front of Robert, her fingers hooked in his waistband, watching his face as Simon played. Robert tried to remain stoic but finally had to close his eyes because he couldn't contain the shudder of desire and didn't want to see if Christy's noticed. He was embarrassed at sharing his reactions like this.

Christy laid a chaste kiss on his bare chest right over his heart, and Robert blindly reached up and cupped her head, catching her braid in his hand. She rose up then and her lips met his, and he pulled her in and kissed her the way he'd watched Simon kiss her earlier.

He'd watched them longer than they'd thought. He had been shocked, and then the arousal had slammed into him and he couldn't tear himself away. When he'd heard his name on Simon's lips in that intimate moment between them—and the way Simon had said his name, longingly—he'd spoken without thinking. And now he was reaping the reward. When he felt Simon's mouth on his back—hot, wet, open—it was one more thrilling sensation among a multitude, almost too much for him to take in.

Christy wrapped her arms around his neck, pressing her bare breasts against his chest. When Simon's hands slowly slid around his hips—slowly, slowly—stopping to rest just shy of his cock, framing it almost as they rested in the hollow of his crotch, Robert tore his mouth from Christy's with a groan as his hips thrust up against her.

He was overwhelmed, and he felt that if he didn't slow down he would embarrass himself further.

"Christy," he said, his voice a little ragged. "I would like to do something, if it's all right with you."

"This sounds promising," Simon said. He was probably trying to be flippant, but the breathlessness gave him away. He was as aroused as Robert and Christy were.

"What is it, my love?" Christy asked, kissing the corner of his mouth. Robert felt a thrill at the endearment.

"Come with me." Robert stepped forward, pushing Christy with him, breaking Simon's hold on him. It was almost a physical pain to lose that contact with him. Robert didn't look back. He couldn't. If he did, he would lose what willpower he had, and there were things that needed to be done, atonement to be made, homecomings to be celebrated.

Robert sat down on the edge of the bed. "Come here," he urged Christy, who had stopped to stare at him curiously, her head tipped to the side, her brow furrowed. He loved that look. It meant she was trying to figure out what was going on and what her role was supposed to be. He'd seen it many times. Christy rarely acted until she knew exactly what her part was in the scene.

"Trust me?" Robert asked, holding out his hand to her.

"You know I do," Christy said, taking his hand and quickly stepping forward until she was standing between his legs. Her answer gave Robert a deep satisfaction. He didn't believe that Christy had trusted that many people in her life, and with good reason.

She smiled at him, and suddenly she kneeled, one hand holding his knee for balance. She knelt there between his legs like a supplicant, smiling up at him.

"What are you doing?" he asked quietly, cupping her cheek, confused.

"Isn't this what you wanted?" Christy asked. "You've never asked for it before."

"Asked for what?" Robert looked over at Simon then, who'd been quiet through the whole exchange. He looked very amused, and very aroused.

Robert realized what Christy thought he wanted, and he blushed. He'd never had anyone do that.

"No," he said quickly. He pulled her up and she stumbled into his arms, her open night clothes slipping down off one shoulder. "No," he said, less urgently. He hugged her and kissed her exposed shoulder. She looked very enticing like that, like a siren from ancient mythology. It wasn't his doom she was leading him towards but rather, he hoped, his salvation.

"I know that in the past men have demanded much of you, darling," he told her in a whisper, "but tonight Simon and I will only give to you."

"Yes," Simon agreed. Robert met his look and he could see that Simon understood what he was doing.

Simon came over to them and cupped Christy's shoulders from behind. Robert had found being between Christy and Simon incredibly arousing, but this—the two of them surrounding Christy, both of their hands on her, the things that Robert was planning to do—this was desire like he had never known. He had never imagined that sharing a woman, sharing his wife, with another man would excite him so. But sharing Christy with Simon excited him beyond even his wildest dreams.

"May I?" Simon asked, gently gliding his hand down and pushing Christy's clothing off her other shoulder.

It caught in her elbow, but the damage was done. Her breasts were entirely exposed as she stood between them. Robert leaned forward before she could answer Simon and took her nipple in his mouth, roughly sucking on it. It was still slightly damp from Simon's kisses earlier, and it was another added dimension of decadence.

Christy exclaimed and her legs gave a little, so Robert reached around and cupped her derriere. He slowly pulled her in close to him, loving on her breast, and she moaned, clutching his head. He pulled away to enjoy the sight of her nipple damp from his mouth, then he leaned forward and sucked on the inside of the mound of her breast, leaving another mark. Her hips undulated in his hands as he did so, and she moaned.

When he stopped, he admired his mark and kissed the angry red spot. He put his hand between her breasts and ran it down over the soft swell of her stomach to her mound and lightly traced his finger through her slit. Christy gasped.

Robert held up his glistening finger. "You like it when I mark you like that."

"Yes." Christy ran her hand through his hair. He liked that she was honest about her passion now. He was sorry that it had taken so long for that to happen, that he had made her feel that she had to hide that part of herself. She hadn't hidden it from Simon.

He looked over at Simon. The he held out his hand. Simon didn't need to be told what to do. He leaned forward and took Robert's finger in his mouth, sucking Christy's essence from it. Robert's cock hardened at the sensation. Simon lightly dragged his teeth down Robert's finger as he let go.

"Oh, my," Christy said in breathy voice.

"I always loved the way you tasted." Simon straightened just enough to lean over her shoulder to look at the mark on her breast. He cupped the plump mound, rubbing his thumb over it. Robert searched within himself and could find no jealousy that Simon had kissed Christy's quim before him, or that he was caressing her bare breast now. On the contrary, Robert wanted to watch him, enjoyed watching it.

"If this is what you want to do to me," Christy said in a

breathless, uneven voice, "then my answer is most definitely yes."

"Good." Robert hardly recognized his own voice. He pulled Christy's clothes off and tossed them aside, then spun her around and sat her in his lap, hooking her knees over his, spreading her legs wide. Simon stepped back, giving him room.

"On your knees," he told Simon. It was less a command than a request.

"Yes, sir," Simon said. His obedient response thrilled Robert. It seemed an odd thing to arouse him, but then everything about this night had taken on a strange quality. He'd never imagined even an hour ago he'd be demanding that Simon put his mouth on Christy's quim in front of him, but here they were.

Simon went to his knees, pushing Robert's farther apart to accommodate his wide shoulders. He put his hands on Robert's knees, and the simple, innocuous contact suddenly took on sexual overtones because of what they were doing. Robert's knees were now the most erotic part of his body.

Simon leaned in, and at the first contact Christy gasped and grabbed onto Robert's arms. "Oh, God," she said, like a prayer. "Simon."

Simon took his time, licking and sucking and deeply kissing her there, exploring her, reacquainting himself with her, perhaps. Robert was fascinated and aroused. He loved to watch Simon fuck her with his agile tongue, keeping Christy just on the edge of her peak. It was masterful, and yet there was almost worship on his face as he loved her. He did love her. And still Robert felt no jealousy. He didn't want it to end.

Christy squirmed and moaned and gasped in his lap and he held her still, hushing her, soothing her. "Simon, please," she begged when he stopped at one point to gently hold her folds open and blow against her.

Her head was resting on Robert's shoulder, and she rolled it from side to side in agitation. Robert held her legs open, taking their weight for her, supporting her fully, and he turned to rest his lips against her ear, tendrils of her damp hair catching on his lips.

"Shhh," he whispered, licking her ear and then biting the lobe. She gasped and tried to thrust her hips at Simon, but Robert held her in place and she whimpered. "Let Simon please you," he whispered in her ear. "Let him apologize properly."

Christy bit her lip and nodded.

"Kiss me," Robert told her softly.

Christy looked at him and smiled. Her cheeks were flushed and her face was damp with sweat. Robert was suddenly aware of how hot he was, the sweat on his own body, the painful arousal pressing against the front of his trousers. He wondered if Simon could see it.

Christy cupped his cheek and turned his face toward her and kissed him. It was a sweet kiss that Robert immediately deepened. He wanted more. He needed more. He thrust his tongue into Christy's mouth, tangled it with hers, tasted every corner of her mouth as he imagined Simon was doing with her quim. Christy moaned into his mouth, and he wondered what wonderful thing Simon was doing to her with *his* mouth. Robert had never felt so alive, so decadently alive.

Christy's moans deepened, and her hips began to undulate in his lap and then Robert felt a caress on his cock and he tore his mouth from Christy's with a gasp. He looked down to see Simon watching him, his tongue flicking against Christy's slit while he fucked her with two of his fingers. His other hand was between Robert's legs, rubbing his cock through his trousers. Robert began to pant as if he were running a race.

"I've pleasured many couples like this before," Simon said. "I'm good at it. I teach them how to enjoy a third in their bed when one or both desire it."

It took Robert a few moments to understand what Simon

was saying. When he did, his arousal was replaced by an almost equal, simmering rage. He very carefully let go of Christy's leg and reached for Simon's head. He grabbed a fistful of his hair and dragged him off of Christy and up, until he was half standing, bent over at the waist, his face right in front of Robert's. His face was a blank mask. That alone told Robert all he needed to know.

CHAPTER 28

"We are not one of your random lovers from the past, Simon," Robert said very slowly.

Christy had turned her face into Robert's neck, and he could feel her tears on his skin. But she was stoic and said nothing. So be it. Robert would speak for both of them.

"Look at us. Christy deserves better, and you know it. How dare you come in here and speak words of love to her only to shut her out like this? Whilst at the same time you share a physical intimacy with her that is precious and rare and so perfect that you are undeserving of it until you admit your true feelings."

Simon ripped his head out of Robert's grip. "My true feelings?" he said angrily pushing to his feet. "Was this about feelings?" He pointed to the ground. "Making me kneel at your feet to apologize? The two of you together up there?" He paced away, and as always the sight of his ruined back made the muscles in Robert's stomach clench.

"You don't understand—" Robert began.

"Oh, I understand perfectly," Simon cut him off. "You wanted to make certain that I knew Christy was yours. Well, never fear,

I wouldn't dream of trespassing again." He faced them, his arms outstretched at his sides. "So here I am. Use me as you see fit. I am here to atone for my sins. And then you may cast me aside and consider my punishment fitting."

"Simon," Christy said softly. "Darling, you know I would never do such a thing." Her voice was rough with tears and emotion and unfulfilled desire, choked off at its peak. "Everything I have said to you since your return has been the absolute truth. You must believe that."

Simon wrapped his arms around his stomach as if he'd received a blow. "I thought…I knew that. I know it. But I can't blame Robert for what he's doing. I felt the same way when you accepted his proposal. I know that was my fault…God, let's not go through all that again."

He ran his hand through his hair and continued to pace, and Christy shifted in Robert's lap so that she sat on one leg and cuddled in close to him. He wrapped his arms around her. He needed her warmth and support right now, too, to help him do what he knew needed to be done.

"Simon, I want you, too," Robert said. Simon spun around and faced him. "You have to understand I don't have experience with…with any of this. I'm tiptoeing through unfamiliar ground, surely you must see that. And surely you know me well enough now to know I wouldn't intentionally hurt you like that, or seek retribution in such a manner. And I certainly wouldn't involve Christy like this, not when her feelings for you are so genuine and so deep."

He sighed and looked around, trying to find the words and gain his composure. "The truth is I never know what to say to you. Half the time I never know what to say to Christy."

At his confession Christy looked up at him and ran her hand down his cheek until her index finger settled on his lower lip. "Robert," she whispered. "You don't have to say anything."

"I know," he said with a desperate little laugh. "but I'd like to.

And lately, I felt like we were getting better at it. I do adore you. I love you."

She raised her face for a kiss, and he obliged her with a kiss that was sweet yet arousing as their lips clung. Christy lightly sucked on his bottom lip and smiled at him as they pulled apart.

"I have never been good at discussing my feelings," Robert told Simon, still looking at Christy. He finally looked at Simon. "When we are together I'm confused by feelings I've never had for any other man. You excite me, arouse me, challenge me. I breathlessly anticipate your touch in the same way I do Christy's. What does it mean? I don't know. That's why I agreed to this. Am I falling in love with you? What does that even mean? Are my feelings an extension of Christy's? Am I so afraid of losing her to you that I've imagined these feelings for you to make a place for myself in your lives? Based on the things I was feeling before your foolish comment, I don't think so. My feelings appear quite genuine, as does my desire for you."

He laughed ruefully. "But fair warning. I am only just learning my way around physical intimacies with Christy. What you were doing before, kissing her quim? I have only done once, last night. I still have a great deal to learn." He paused, licked his lips and confessed, "When she kneeled between my legs to… well, I imagine she was offering to take my penis in her mouth. I've never done that."

"I'll be gentle." Christy playfully bit his jaw and he laughed.

Simon had been silent through his entire confession. Robert looked at him, unwilling to bare any more of his soul until he knew what Simon was going to do.

He was unprepared when Simon strode over, cupped his face in his hands and kissed him hard. When Simon's tongue probed, seeking entrance, Robert opened his mouth. He had kissed Simon before, that morning in his apartment. But it was a hazy memory, dimmed by sleep. This was a burst of rough desire in his mouth, as Simon drank his inexperience and his passion and gave him a lesson in seduction and leashed eroticism.

When Simon ended the kiss, he dragged his thumbs along Robert's cheekbones while he stared into his eyes. "God," he said, his voice a low rasp. "There is so much I'm going to teach you."

"Thank God," Robert told him sincerely. "I've been fumbling in the dark."

Simon laughed and stepped back, leaving one hand on his cheek. He placed the other on Christy's. "I'm on shaky ground," he admitted. "It's been a very long time since I've done this with meaning and significance." He looked at Christy. "I guess, perhaps, when we were together it had those things, but I didn't realize it."

"I know it did for me," Christy said. "You made me fall in love with you. I'd never been in love before."

"God, how I must have devastated you. How you must have hated me," Simon said. "I'm sorry. I can't say it enough."

"You say it too much." Christy got up from Robert's lap and slid into Simon's embrace. "I never stopped loving you. That, I think, is what it means to truly love. I thought you had not wanted me, which was nothing new to me, was it? I had grown accustomed to being rejected by the men in my life."

She turned and held out a hand to Robert, who rose and came to stand behind her. She was such a small thing, between him and Simon, and again Robert felt the thrill that came from that. Why, he didn't know and didn't care to explore it tonight. Perhaps another time. Tonight he would just enjoy it.

"You taught me that it didn't have to be that way," Christy said to Robert. "That men could be honest and true and not leave. I needed to know that men could just...not leave." She turned back to Simon. "And I don't mean that as an indictment of you."

"I think I understand that," Simon said. "I've just carried that guilt about Giselle around for so long…it's not going to be an easy task to let that go." He sighed and hugged Christy close, burying his nose in her hair. "This is complicated and hard." He looked up at Robert. "I didn't expect you."

"Well, that makes two of us," Robert said.

Christy laughed in delight. "That makes three of us. You have no idea how this delights me."

"Does it?" Robert asked worriedly. "I don't want you to feel like you aren't still very important to me, Christy. I love you. I always will. You are my first love."

"And I have already told you how I feel, Christy. I have dreamed of this. Of us. Of you. You got me through Africa. Without you…" Simon's voice broke. He cleared his throat.

"I know," she said, looking between them. "I fell in love with both of you almost from the first moment I met you." She faced Simon. "With you, I could be myself, from the very beginning, and you accepted me as I am. No one had ever done that before. It meant the world to me."

She turned to Robert. "And you…you saw me as perfect. I had never been perfect to anyone before. I had tried, so many times, but I always fell short. For you, I simply had to breathe and I was perfection. There was a freedom and wonder in that that still amazes me."

She stepped out from between them to stand beside them and took each of their hands. "But back then, neither of you loved the same woman. Now I think I am a combination of both, and to have men such as you love and care for me is a wondrous thing. No, I do not mind if you also have feelings for each other. After all, I can completely understand those emotions, since I am still in love with you both and I always have been."

Robert bent down and swept Christy into his arms. She squeaked in surprise and threw her arms around his neck. He turned and tossed her onto the bed, and she laughed.

"Where were we?" he asked Simon.

"Right here," Simon said, crawling on the bed between Christy's legs. He kissed her thighs. "I'm sorry for the interruption, my darling," he purred. "I was an idiot."

Christy spread her legs and guided his face to her quim. "Apology not accepted. Deeds, not words, will win fair maiden's heart."

Robert sat down on the bed beside Simon and watched as he began to lick and kiss Christy's quim again. It was just as exciting as the last time, except he didn't get the added thrill of Simon's hand on him at the same time, which was probably a good thing.

"Come here." It took Robert a moment to realize Simon was talking to him. Simon moved over a bit and indicated the bed next to him. Robert maneuvered next to him, and Christy put her leg over his shoulder. She was completely exposed and completely unselfconscious about it. He loved that about her right at that moment. They were going to be able to do anything they wanted with her, and she would be an enthusiastic bed partner. He shivered at the possibilities, most of which he probably didn't even know about.

"Don't just look at it," Simon teased. "Taste it."

Robert realized Simon had stopped and was waiting for him to take his turn kissing Christy. It was the most lascivious thing he had ever done, or could even imagine doing. He kissed like he had her mouth, ending by sucking on one of her soft, slick swollen lips. She moaned and her hips jerked.

"You don't need much guidance here," Simon said, amusement in his voice.

"It's pretty instinctual," Robert agreed. "She tastes so good."

"She does, doesn't she?" Simon took his turn and licked her from the soft flesh at the bottom of her slit all the way up to the little knot at the top, where he stopped to play with the tip of his tongue, making Christy thrash her head on the bed and clutch the bedcovers.

Robert noticed a bead of sweat rolling down Simon's temple, and he leaned over and licked it off. Simon turned to him and kissed him lightly on the lips. The taste of Christy in their kiss was more erotic than Robert could handle. His mind simply shut down and his senses took over. The salty smell of Christy, and sweat, and summer flowers from outside, the creak of the house, the call of an owl.

Simon moved and Robert kissed Christy again, this time using his tongue as Simon had. Simon pushed two fingers back inside Christy and began to fuck her with them, hard thrusts, his fingers buried inside her to the base, and she fucked them back, grinding her quim on Robert's mouth. Robert focused on the top of her slit, on the knot there, since Simon was busy below, and in moments Christy came apart beneath them, gasping and moaning as she arched her back and reached down to hold Robert's head in place.

When her peak had passed, she collapsed on the bed and pushed Robert away. "No more," she gasped.

Simon gently took her leg off Robert's shoulder and moved it to the side. "Do you mind?" he asked. "Robert and I have unfinished business."

"What?" Christy looked at them with dazed eyes. Comprehension dawned. "Oh, yes." She rolled over onto her stomach and out of the way, watching them, still breathing heavily from her climax.

Robert was nervous, but so aroused he feared the scrape of his trouser buttons was enough to make him come. Simon didn't give him time to think too hard about it. He pulled Robert close with an arm around his shoulders and kissed him, rough and deep, the way Robert liked it. Simon had learned that quickly. Or perhaps it was the way he liked it, too.

Robert kissed him back. The rough scrape of their whiskers

was incredibly exciting. He could taste Christy everywhere on both of them. That was exciting, too.

Simon pushed his hips away but at the same time kept kissing him. Robert hesitated when he felt Simon's hands on his trouser buttons, but he didn't resist and he let himself fall into Simon's kiss again. Simon just unbuttoned his trousers and nothing more, and it was a relief.

A moment later Simon pressed their bodies closely together, and Robert let out a cry into his mouth when their hips came together and his bare erection met Simon's bare erection. Simon was gripping him tightly, his arm wrapped around Robert's back, so Robert couldn't move far away. He didn't want to, not really.

"Tell me this is all right," Simon said breathlessly when he finally broke the kiss. He kissed Robert's jaw and then his collarbone and shoulder. He bit Robert's shoulder, and the sting went straight to Robert's cock. It felt hard as rock and he thought he was going to ejaculate any moment.

"Fine," he gasped. "Fine." His hips jerked, bumping his penis into Simon's, and it felt so good he moaned.

"This will feel better, lover," Simon told him. He pulled his hips away and Robert protested.

"No," he said, grabbing at Simon's hip, not willing to give up that penis next his. He never thought he'd feel that way, but right now Simon's penis was as essential to him as Christy's quim.

"Let me," Simon said, slapping his hand away. "Watch."

Robert opened his eyes and saw Simon aligning their cocks again. Then he wrapped his hand around them both. It didn't quite fit. "Damn," Simon muttered. "You're bigger than I thought. Up."

He went to his knees and pulled Robert up in front of him. Robert understood what he was trying to do now. He pressed his cock to Simon's without being told, and the contact caused a shiver throughout his whole body. Simon noticed and looked up at him with a grin. Then he wrapped both hands around their cocks and began to pump.

Robert shouted at the bolt of pleasure that shot up his spine. He wrapped his arm around Simon and pulled him close, pressing his mouth to Simon's shoulder to silence his sounds of pleasure so as not to wake the whole house. Simon was sweating and shaking and pumping his arms, and Robert didn't care, he held onto him. As his orgasm got closer and closer, he bit into Simon's shoulder to stifle it. Simon just grunted at the pain.

Then Robert came and it was glorious. His cock throbbed with each pulse of pleasure and his semen slicked down Simon's hand, making his grip slippery, and then Simon came, too, and when his hot semen hit Robert's stomach, he thought he might die from the pleasure of it. It was the same way he'd felt the first time he'd lain with Christy.

When it was over, when his thoughts, which had scattered across the universe during the onslaught, came back to settle in his head again, he reached out blindly and felt Christy take his hand in hers. She kissed his palm and he clasped her dainty hand in his and held Simon to his breast. He took a deep breath and felt everything fall into place inside him.

CHAPTER 29

"What are we to do now?" Robert asked.

They were lying in Simon's bed, the three of them. Christy was between Simon and Robert, her head on Simon's shoulder. Robert had his head propped up on his arm, cheek resting on his palm. He'd taken Christy's hair out of the braid and now was smoothing it out across the pillow. Occasionally he glanced up to give Simon a sleepy, satisfied smile which Simon returned. But his question was one Simon had been dreading.

"I don't know," Simon answered honestly. At his response, Christy lifted her head from his shoulder and frowned at him. "I thought you were asleep," he said.

"No," Robert told him, chuckling. "She has this breathy little snore when she's asleep." He imitated it.

"Robert Manderley," Christy said in shocked disapproval. "I do not. Take it back." Robert just made a face.

Simon forced a little laugh. Christy turned back, and he could see she wasn't fooled. She put her head down on his shoulder again and rubbed her hand along the top of his stomach, the firm line of muscle that separated chest from belly. She seemed fascinated by it. Simon was a little fascinated with Robert's, to be honest. He was the fittest man Simon had ever seen.

Christy snuggled closer and her breasts pressed against his side and the new distraction pulled his mind back to her. She felt soft and smooth and utterly feminine, and she smelled divine.

"Simon?" she asked. He glanced down and her face was tilted up so she could see him. She was watching him with a worried, expectant sort of expression.

"Sorry," he said. "I've done it again, haven't I?" He sighed. "Ever since I got back from Africa I frequently tend to get lost in my thoughts and miss the conversation around me. I don't mean to be rude."

"That's all right," Christy told him.

"No, it really isn't," Simon said. "And I know it. I can't help it. Getting lost in my own thoughts is how I made it through that nightmare. I guess it's a habit I can't break."

"I just asked what your feelings were about us, about where we go from here," Christy said. "And just so you know, I'm not willing to watch you walk away again. I don't think it's in your best interest, and I definitely know it isn't in mine or Robert's."

"Isn't it?" Simon asked sadly. He hugged her tightly for a moment and then let loose, keeping one arm around her while he stared at the ceiling. "There's Christian to consider. It isn't just the three of us."

"Do you dislike children?" Robert asked with a frown. He stopped combing Christy's hair with his fingers.

"No, of course not," Simon assured him. "I rather like them, actually. But I didn't lay with Christy for a reason. I don't want to get her pregnant."

"Why not?" Robert asked. His casual acceptance of the possibility of such a situation astounded Simon.

"Is that what you want? Your wife heavy with another man's child?"

"It wouldn't be another man's child," Robert said. "It would be your child. That's completely different. And it would be Christy's, too. Any child Christy bears is perfect, as far as I'm concerned, and I'd be quite thrilled if she bore yours, frankly. I think you'd make remarkable children together."

"That's not what I mean," Simon told him.

"Then what did you mean?" Christy asked.

She pulled away from him despite his attempts to hold her, and sat next to him. Her leg was still touching his, so it wasn't a complete abandonment. He didn't think Christy was capable of abandonment, actually. Perhaps she'd known too much of it herself and so was determined not to make someone suffer it on her account.

He put his hand on her thigh and she smiled at him, a quick, familiar sort of smile. The kind he'd seen his friends share. The kind that said *don't worry, I'm still here* and *I haven't forgotten about you.* The kind of casual smile he'd always wanted from someone, a level of intimacy he had aspired to. What a complete and utter fool he was for these two.

Robert didn't move. He just continued to lie there, entirely relaxed as he watched them. Instead of reassuring him, Robert's apparent acceptance of this intimacy caused Simon's muscles to clench in distress.

"Look at us," Simon said, pointing between him and Robert. "We look nothing alike. If Christy were to have my child, it would be painfully obvious. No one would mistake him for Robert's, not like Christian."

"I will shut down anyone who has the temerity to ask questions," Robert stated unequivocally. "Any child of Christy's is a child of mine. Our vows make it so, as well as our tender feelings. I imagine it would be the same with your child as it is with Christian. And I know that you would feel the same. You don't know him, but I'm sure that in time you will care for Christian as I do."

Simon's heart was racing. He resisted the urge to get up and leave, to run away—from them, from his feelings, from the future, from commitment. It had always worked for him in the past.

But wasn't this what he wanted? Wasn't it what he'd dreamed about in Africa? A life with Christy? And his new feelings for Robert weren't a passing fancy. They felt nothing like the shallow infatuations he'd had in the past.

For some reason known only to God and perhaps, someday, Simon, these two people had broken through decades of defenses and stolen his heart. And here, now, they were offering things he never thought he'd have. Things he thought he didn't deserve.

"Why are we talking about children?" he asked.

"Because it is a consequence of what we are doing, or are going to do," Christy said. "I, of all people, ought to know that."

"Always practical," Simon said, casting a half smile her way.

"Always, from now on," Christy said. "You're right. I have Christian to consider now. Every decision I make—"

"We make," Robert interrupted to say.

"We make, has to be made with his best interests in mind." She looked at Simon. "This"—she pointed at each of them— "was not done lightly. We both considered the ramification and made our decision based on what we thought was best for all involved, Christian included. Isn't that right?" she asked Robert.

"Yes," he said. "At one point, when you first came back from Africa, I thought that I would have to give Christy up. I thought that she would be happiest with you, and I was willing to let her and Christian go with you. I would not have even considered it if I did not find you worthy."

Simon ran his hands through his hair and pulled his leg away from Christy's in the guise of bending his knees. "I think you both give me too much credit," he said. "I have a rather colorful past, you know."

"So I gathered from things that others have said. From what you said, earlier," Robert replied cautiously. "I think you should know I have a very colorless past. What we did tonight was… quite extraordinary for me."

"What we did tonight was very tame," Simon said with a laugh. "But…" He rolled over to face Robert and mimicked his position. "I found it more satisfying than the most meaningless debauched evening I have ever wasted in my past."

"I'm afraid I'm like Robert," Christy admitted. Her cheeks were flushed a becoming pink. "Although I have a bit more experience, it hasn't exactly been full of variety." She bit her lip in embarrassment. "What you two did tonight is most certainly the naughtiest thing I've ever done."

"Are you both in a hurry to learn all you can from the infamously debauched Simon Gantry?" Simon asked wryly. "I've had quite a few people seek me out for just such a purpose."

"Oh, Simon," Christy said sadly. She took his hand and squeezed it. He held it tight. "I'm so very sorry."

"I don't think anyone has every been sorry for my sordid sexual escapades before," he said. "This is a new experience." He was trying to make light of it, but the fact was her sympathy lightened a burden he hadn't even realized he'd been carrying.

"I'm sorry, too," Robert said. "I've only known Christy, and now you. And both experiences have been sensual and satisfying, but also wondrous because I shared them with you two. I cannot imagine being so vulnerable with a stranger, or experiencing such joy and not have it be a sharing of souls as well as bodies."

Simon's heart did an odd sort of stutter that made him lightheaded and short of breath. "Is that what that was?" he asked quietly. "A sharing of souls?"

"Yes," Christy answered. "For me as well. The first time we were together I felt it, Simon, though I'm not sure you did."

He covered his eyes with his hand because they were burning. "I have not been with anyone else since you, Christy. Not willingly." He took his hand away and met her surprised gaze. "I know everyone thinks I have. I let them think it. I tried, but I couldn't go through with it. It wasn't the same. All I could see was your face."

He glanced briefly at Robert and then back at Christy. "And now I know why. Now I know why I saw your face in my dreams every night. Because you have a part of my soul and I have a part of yours. Inside me."

CHAPTER 30

C hristy carried Christian on her hip as she poured a cup of tea for Simon. The sun had barely risen, but the men had to get back to the Home Office.

"Where is the nanny?" asked Simon, after thanking her. He took a bite of toast. Christian was fussing on her hip and she bounced him a little.

"She left at first light," Christy said tightly. She was still furious about the young woman's desertion.

"Why?" Christian tried to grab Simon's toast, and Christy scolded him. She very nearly dropped the teapot.

"I imagine the three of you and what you got up to last night probably scandalized her," Hastings said, grabbing a piece of toast from the tray on the table.

"What did you say?" Simon asked, putting his tea down.

Christy was so tired she couldn't even take offense. "He's right," she said. "She informed me she wouldn't live in a 'house of ill repute'—her words—and that if people found out she'd never get another job. So I wrote her a letter of recommendation and she left." Christy tucked a piece of hair that Christian had pulled loose back into place. "And now Cook has taken to her room, as well."

"Christy, I'm sorry," Simon said. He looked devastated. "Here, let me." He reached for Christian, and Christy handed him over gladly. She loved him, but he was quite impossible this morning since he hadn't slept enough last night either.

"Why is he drooling?" Hastings asked with a frown. "Is there something wrong with him?"

"He's teething." Simon tore off a chunk of toast and handed it to Christian, who immediately began to gnaw on it happily. "I remember when one of Very's was going through this. She said the toast worked wonders."

He took a bite of what was left of his toast and watched Christian. The baby reached for his nose and Simon dodged his little fist with a laugh. "Oh, no. I'm wise to that trick," Simon told him.

Christy felt tears prick her eyes, and she turned away before Simon could see them. Robert was quietly standing in the door, watching them. He smiled at Christy, and she knew he was thinking the same thing. How wonderful it was to see Simon and Christian together. The baby was just what Simon needed. Someone new and innocent and trusting. Someone who would love Simon as they did, with no judgment or hesitation.

"So Nanny Beth has gone?" Robert said as he entered the room.

"You don't need her," Hastings said, surprising Christy with his vehemence. "She was far too judgmental. She would only have warped little Christian, mark my words." He tossed down his napkin. "I'll find you a nanny."

Robert and Simon both got a very alarmed look on their faces. "No, really, that's not necessary," Robert said.

"I'm sure Christy would prefer to hire her own nanny," Simon added. "Isn't that right, Christy?"

Christy hid a yawn behind her hand. "Oh, yes, of course," she said. "But I do appreciate Mr. Hastings's offer of help."

"You should both be ashamed of yourselves," Hastings said, glaring and Robert and Simon. "These gentlewomen haven't got that kind of stamina, you know." He stood up. "Here now, you and the baby should have a rest today. Come on, lads, let's go find some villains."

He marched out of the kitchen and Christy looked curiously at Robert, who looked at Simon, who just shrugged.

"I haven't any idea what's gotten into him today," Simon said. He took a sip of tea and Christian tried to grab the cup, but Simon expertly dodged that, too.

"You're very good with children," Christy told him.

"You have seen how many children Very has, haven't you?" he asked. "I was trained by the most devious brats in London."

"Actually I only just met Mrs. Tarrant yesterday," Christy told him. "I went around to see her because I needed her help with Daniel."

"What's wrong with Daniel?" both men said at the same time. They looked at one another in dawning comprehension.

"Do you think Daniel had anything to do with this?" Simon asked suspiciously. "He did send me to help you."

"I asked him yesterday and he said no," Christy told them. "He claims it was the furthest thing from his mind. But you know—"

"Daniel," Simon finished for her. "Yes, we do. Why did you need help with him?"

Christy bit her lip. "Well, I wasn't going to tell you because I didn't want to worry you, what with this mission and all, but his leg isn't healing and he's not doing well. I sent for the doctor yesterday, but he was an ineffectual potion peddler, as Daniel called him. And I was at my wit's end. So, I went to see the infamous Mrs. Very Tarrant. From her letters she sounded as if she could handle Daniel. You know Harry lets Daniel walk all over him, and with everything going on between us, and Christian, and the agents, I just couldn't take on one more thing. Does that make me a bad person?"

"No," Robert said. He came over and kissed her brow. "I don't know Mrs. Tarrant, but I'm sure she can handle Daniel. He'll be fine."

"Very could handle Armageddon, and probably does on a daily basis around that house of hers," Simon said as he got up, carrying Christian. He came over and kissed her cheek. "Daniel can be a beast when he doesn't feel well. I've been on the end of that whip of a tongue of his. Let Very and Harry handle him and I'm sure he'll be up in no time."

He handed Christian back to her. "I'm sorry, love. We've got to go. You know," he said as he was leaving the room, "I was wondering why Daniel hadn't shown up to inquire about the investigation. It's not like him not to interfere. I should have gone by to check on him."

"I should have as well," Robert said. "Perhaps later today we'll have time to stop by." He kissed Christy's cheek. "Hopefully we will see you tonight, but I can't make promises. This case is a mess, I'm afraid. But I'll send a note if we're delayed again."

After they left Christy sat down at the table, feeling as if all the air in the room had rushed out with them and she needed to sit down to catch her breath. She was going to have to take a nap with Christian today to make up for the sleep she'd lost the night before. But as soon as she had her wits about her, she'd direct her thoughts toward putting her house in order. And that definitely included Simon.

CHAPTER 31

"I'm honestly not sure if we should bother looking for the needle that is Mr. Demetriev here, or just sit on the Royal Ordnance at the Warren and catch whoever shows up and tries to steal the explosives," Simon said, looking at the busy dock that stretched out in front of them.

"I have a feeling that it's too soon," Robert mused. "If it were me, I'd steal the explosives at the last minute. Too soon, and you've given fair warning. We may suspect something, but if a large cache of explosives were to suddenly go missing from Woolwich, then we'd know, and double our efforts. And then we'd have the full support of the Army and the Navy to back us up. No, Mr. Van de Berg and Mr. Demetriev and their conspirators are biding their time and planning. They know the explosives aren't going anywhere."

"Hmm," Simon said. He didn't sound convinced.

"Well, how would you do it?" Robert asked.

"I would take the opposite approach," Simon said. "I'd steal the explosives months or even years before I needed them. Then I'd store them somewhere safe until it was time. After the rush and intensity of the initial investigation, as long as I wasn't found out, interest would fade, and by the time of the attack no one would be looking for me or my explosives any more. I could just walk in and blow up whatever I pleased."

"Which is exactly what they had planned originally," Robert said in appreciation. "Perhaps we are not dealing with amateurs after all."

"Not completely, no," Simon said. "My guess is that Van de Berg has some experience in the intelligence game or the military. As for Demetriev, I can't say. But he's Russian, so anything is possible."

"Demetriev was a last-minute substitution for the original plan," Robert reminded him. "I wonder if he knows he's going to be an unfortunate casualty of this scheme?"

"Because naturally Van de Berg needs to kill any witnesses," Simon said.

"Naturally," Robert agreed.

They walked along in companionable silence for several minutes, looking for all the world like two gentlemen strolling along the wharf with no pressing business, curiously looking in windows and watching the stowadores. There were actually quite a few people down on the docks doing exactly the same thing. Robert suspected they were hoping to catch even the tiniest breeze off the water in the heat of the day. He couldn't recall a hotter summer in all his years.

Simon drew his share of attention but didn't even notice it. Robert supposed he must be used to it. He wore a honey-colored jacket and matching vest with a white shirt and matching white cravat tied in a simple, loose knot in a concession to the heat. The jacket complemented his blond hair beautifully. Robert was proud of himself for refusing to study Simon's trousers with such detail.

"Do I pass inspection?" Simon asked, clearly amused. They had stopped to look in the window of an import business and Robert met Simon's gaze in the reflection.

"Yes," he said simply.

Simon chuckled and turned to walk on. "No wonder you and Christy get along so well," he commented. "You are evenly practical with your words."

"Do you require more words?" Robert asked, unsure of himself. "I'm afraid I am not very good at wooing. You may ask Christy. I am better at simply stating the facts and then logically moving on from there."

"No, I do not require more words," Simon said softly as several people passed them on the sidewalk. "Not from you. I have had too many empty words from people who did not mean them and did not care."

Robert tipped his hat to a lady, trying to act like this was a normal conversation. "I care."

Simon set his walking stick on the sidewalk in front of him in an exaggerated movement and then lifted it again as he walked by. It was a jaunty sort of move that made Robert smile. "Now those were not empty words," was all he said in response, but Robert knew what he meant was that he cared, too. He didn't need a codebook to decipher Simon.

"So what exactly did you mean when you said you had a great deal to teach me?" Robert asked at last. The possibilities had been driving him mad. He had some rudimentary knowledge of the baser physical acts, but not enough to even imagine doing any of them with Simon or Christy. He wasn't even sure he wanted to, to be honest. So far everything they had done had seemed honest and true. He had no desire to destroy that between them with foolish and unsatisfying mucking about.

"A better question would be, what do you want to learn?" Simon countered.

"I'm not sure," Robert said. "I liked what we did last night. It seemed natural and genuine."

"Genuine," Simon said thoughtfully. "Yes, that's a good word for it. I like that."

"What I'm trying to say is that I don't want to do anything that doesn't feel the same way."

"I think that has more to do with us and our feelings than whatever physical acts we are enjoying," Simon told him.

"I don't want to do anything that will hurt Christy. Physically, I mean." This was one of Robert's greatest fears.

"Is that what you're worried about?" Simon asked. He looked around and then guided Robert off the sidewalk to quiet spot near the edge of the wharf by the water. "I would never hurt Christy in that fashion."

"I know. At least not knowingly. But if we were to do something you hadn't done before—"

Simon interrupted him with a disbelieving snort of laughter. "Sorry, sorry," he said. "It's just, if I haven't done it, no one's thought of it yet."

Robert tilted his head, staring at Simon, not laughing.

"Oh, dear," Simon said. "Not funny, hmm?"

"No," Robert said. "It's not that. It's just...that doesn't bother me. It should, shouldn't it? That you've so much experience. And yet, I don't care. Just as I didn't care that Christy carried another man's child when I fell in love with her. It's as if nothing in the past matters once you're—" He'd been about to say *mine*, but then the presumptuousness of it hit him and it stuck in his throat.

"Once I'm what?" Simon asked. Robert didn't answer, too embarrassed now to say it aloud. "No? Hmm. I'm quite sure I would have been interested to hear that." He looked back at the street. "I'm in an awkward situation," he confessed after a moment of silence. "We have been intimate, and yet I don't really know your boundaries or preferences on language when it comes to sexual acts."

He glanced briefly at Robert, and Robert saw him blush. This conversation was as difficult for him as it was for Robert. *Good.*

"Just speak as you would be spoken to," Robert said. He was

rather relieved because it would give him a chance to learn Simon's preferences, too.

"All right." Simon shot his cuffs and straightened his cravat. "We can fuck, you and I. Do you know how?"

He looked right at Robert. It took a moment for Robert to realize he was waiting for confirmation. He nodded.

"Good. It can be uncomfortable at first, but it definitely has its rewards. Christy can also be fucked the same way."

Robert's eyes grew large at that.

"Never thought about the tit for tat, eh? A lot of men don't."

"Well, I suppose it is logical," Robert said, considering it.

Simon laughed. "Indeed," he said. "So let your imagination run wild, my dear. Take any one individual act, say me sucking your cock." The last was said in a soft, intimate voice. Robert had to lean in to hear him, and his eyes darted up to meet Simon's heated gaze. "I could do that while I was lying down, with you over me, and Christy could ride me, fuck me, at the same time."

Robert's breath was getting a bit shallow. It was a good thing it was so hot out or people might notice how overheated he was becoming.

"Or I could fuck Christy and you could fuck me," Simon suggested. Robert had difficulty swallowing as he imagined it. "And last, but not least," Simon said, building up Robert's anticipation, "We could both fuck Christy at the same time, one of us in her delicious cunt, and one in her very pretty bottom."

Robert had to put a hand on the nearby railing for support.

"So you see, my dearest, darling, innocent Robert, if you want to learn it, I can teach you." Simon whispered the last in his ear as he walked by, heading back to the sidewalk.

Robert wondered how he was supposed to walk when he had an obvious erection. It took him several minutes of staring out at the water and thinking about the gruesome details of the murders he'd been investigating before he could turn and follow Simon.

He didn't have far to go. Simon was just a few doors down, leaning against the corner of a warehouse, observing a building across the street. "Do you see what I see?" he asked. Robert looked.

"Demetriev Imports, Limited," Robert read off the window. "There can't be more than one down here."

"Perhaps in St. Petersburg, but not in London," Simon agreed. He straightened and started walking toward the warehouse.

"Where are you going?" Robert asked, following him.

"I'm going to speak with Mr. Demetriev," Simon said.

"And you think he'll just give you the information we seek?"

"I am ever hopeful in situations such as this one," Simon said, winking at him. "Isn't that what you said? We'll start with this and hope it works, and if it doesn't we'll just have to find another way to get it out of him."

"Hope springs eternal," Robert muttered.

"Exactly," Simon said cheerfully. He stepped through the open door into the dusty and overly warm empty offices of Demetriev Imports. "Greetings," he called out. "Is anyone here?"

A young man came out of a back office and closed the door behind him. "Yes. Good morning. Can I help?" He had a thick Russian accent, although his English was rather good. He sounded quite nervous.

"We are looking for Mr. Demetriev," Simon said pleasantly. "Is he in?"

"May I inquire who is asking after him?" the clerk said, trying to be very formal.

"Mr. Gantry and Mr. Manderley, presently with the Home Office."

At Simon's introductions the young man's face turned pasty white. "I will see if Mr. Demetriev is available," he said in a mumbled undertone as he backed into the office door behind him and opened it just enough to slide through into the back office.

Robert turned to Simon, and they looked at one another for a second. "Well, that wasn't suspicious at all," Simon said.

"I believe I have to disagree," Robert said. "Sorry, old man, but I found it most suspicious."

"Well, then the best was to settle this is to go in there and see what they're up to, I suppose. We can't be arguing about it all day."

"I couldn't agree more. I would find that most irritating." He waved a hand in invitation in front of him. "After you."

"No, after you," Simon said, imitating Robert by waving his hand in invitation. "You are the constable."

"This is true," Robert agreed. "And I do believe I'm younger." At that, Simon pushed in front of him.

"Age before beauty," Simon muttered as he passed. Robert was about to protest when he realized it was a compliment, and he grinned in spite of the circumstances.

Simon didn't knock, he simply opened the door and walked in. It was clear he'd taken the room's occupants by surprise. The young clerk was holding a satchel that was half full of papers, and a man behind a large desk currently held a large pile of papers in his hands which had obviously been destined for the overfilled satchel.

"Well, how do you do?" Simon said. "You must be Mr. Demetriev. And I assume those papers must contain information on your misdeeds. I do love it when villains do all the work for me."

"I win," Robert joked as he took a step toward the desk, intent on apprehending the ridiculously inept Mr. Demetriev. The sudden, sharp pain in his side came just a moment before Simon's shout of "Watch out!"

Robert grabbed the hand holding the knife in his side as he spun around. The pain caused his vision to waver, but he gritted his teeth as he faced his attacker. He'd expected another one of Fat Linnie's assassins, so he was surprised to encounter a rather large Russian fellow who did not look inept at all. As a matter of fact, when he pulled back his fist, Robert was relatively sure the Russian had very good odds of winning this particular fight.

"Use the knife," Simon called out to him. It was enough of a distraction to delay the Russian long enough for Robert to pull the knife from his side and, ignoring the searing pain, slice it out in front of him. He didn't connect with his opponent, but he did make him jump back out of the way, giving Robert some room to breathe and assess the situation.

Simon was engaged with another Russian on the other side of the room. The clerk was in an unconscious heap on the floor, and Mr. Demetriev was gone.

Robert and his opponent circled one another, but Robert realized he was trying to gain access to the door, clearly so he could escape. That was unacceptable. He'd only be another asset to Demetriev if he did. For all Robert knew, he was a necessary part of Demetriev's escape plan.

He stopped and feinted a lunge, staying out of reach of the Russian's long arms. As the Russian went to grab him, Robert spun out of the way and shoved him with a well-placed kick to the posterior. It was a move Thom Longfellow had taught him. He cried out in agony as fire spread from the wound in his side. The Russian stumbled and went head first into the corner of the ornate desk. He fell down and his head slammed into the floor.

Once he was sure the Russian was down, Robert turned, intent on helping Simon. But Simon had his opponent in a choke hold and the poor man was turning blue.

"Don't kill him," Robert said, panting. He put a hand to his side and was dismayed to feel how bloody it was. This jacket was ruined. He sat down on the edge of the desk.

Simon immediately let the Russian drop to the floor. "Are you all right?" he asked. He looked as if he might be sick.

"I'm fine," Robert said, fairly certain he was right. He held up the knife. "It's not very large and he didn't get a good thrust in." He winked at Simon.

"I cannot believe you are making tawdry jokes at a time like this," Simon said, sounding a bit on the edge of hysteria. "He could have killed you."

"Yes, but he didn't. Come on." Robert stood up, ignoring the pain. "We've got to catch Demetriev. I don't think these idiots will be able to tell us much." He limped over to the door, took the key out of the lock and held it up for Simon to see. "I'm always amazed how many people simply leave them in there during the daylight hours when they are in residence." He shook his head. "Let's lock them in for now."

Amazingly enough, when they came out of the office it was to find Demetriev waiting in a carriage on the corner for his associates. They each climbed in from a door on opposite sides of the carriage.

"Well, we meet again," Robert said. Simon was uncharacteristically grim. "Let's start over, shall we? I'm Mr. Manderley and this is Mr. Gantry, and we are both here as representatives of the Home Office. We'd like to ask you a few questions about your association with a certain Dutchman by the name of Van de Berg and, of course, about that little fracas in your office where your associates just tried to kill us."

Demetriev pulled a gun from his satchel, but before he could fire a shot, Simon grabbed his arm and twisted it roughly. Robert heard a bone snap, and Demetriev screamed as he dropped the gun. Robert caught it in midair and gingerly unloaded it, thankful it hadn't discharged in the struggle.

Simon let go of Demetriev's arm, which hung limp in his lap at an odd angle. He yanked Demetriev's head back, shaking him a little. The poor Russian looked as if he might faint.

"Don't you dare," Simon growled at him. "Not before you tell us everything we want to know."

"I will tell you nothing," Demetriev said in a quavering voice. Robert doubted his denial, which was weak.

"I know exactly where all the bones in the human body are located and how to break each one," Simon told him menacingly. "Trust me, you will tell me everything I need to know, and quite a bit I don't, by the time I'm through with you."

"It doesn't matter what I tell you," Demetriev said with a smug smile. "You cannot stop it."

"Stop what?" Robert asked, pretending more interest in his wound than in Demetriev's words.

"What is happening. Not just here, but everywhere."

That got Robert's attention. "Everywhere? You're planning to blow up multiple locations?"

Simon yanked on Demetriev's hair to get him to answer. "Yes! Our movement will grow. Soon the world will burn and the proletariat will rise, displacing imperialists such as you and your king."

"Oh, dear God," Simon said in disgust. "Revolutionaries. When am I going to be free of them?"

"Where exactly are the explosives, Demetriev?" Robert asked.

"Where they belong," he answered. Simon picked up Demetriev's hand on his broken arm, making Demetriev scream. Then he snapped his little finger. Robert winced. Demetriev cried out.

"Try that one again," Simon told him. He moved on to the next finger and held it, waiting for his answer.

"Where are the explosives?" Robert asked grimly, hating the process as much as he knew Simon did, but knowing it was necessary.

"They are already in place," Demetriev said, his words slurring a bit.

"At the bridge?" Robert asked. Demetriev's head swung around, and he stared at Robert.

"So we were right." Robert looked at Simon, thinking. "They need a great deal of black powder to blow the bridge. I doubt they have enough as of yet to blow it, much less another location. They only have the explosives from the ship."

"Let's take him to Barnabas," Simon said. "He'll get answers. We need to get your wound looked after, too. Then we can go and inspect the bridge."

"Why would you already have the powder on the bridge?" Robert asked, something bothering him that he couldn't put his finger on. "If you don't mean to blow it until next week, it seems foolhardy to risk the explosives so soon. A stray spark could set them off. A good rain could ruin them, although the weather is on your side right now, that's true. But still, after all this planning. And you have a limited supply of explosives."

Demetriev looked smug and calculating even through the pain, not the look of a man whose nefarious plot had been foiled.

"You've already stolen more explosives," Robert said, the light dawning. The victorious look on Demetriev's face said it all.

"Damn it, man, let's go," Simon said, throwing open his door and dragging Demetriev out of the now-driverless carriage. "We haven't a minute to lose. We have to tell Barnabas."

CHAPTER 32

When they arrived at the Home Office, Barnabas and Hastings were in Barnabas's office looking at maps of London Bridge along with several other men. Sir Barnabas waved them over.

"We expect they will try to blow the bridge here, here and here," he said, pointing to areas on the map. "Philips"—he indicated one of the men—"is my best engineer. He tells me these are the weakest spots. Taking out these sections will effectively destroy the bridge. The damage will be irreparable."

Simon took Demetriev by the nape of the neck and shoved his face toward the map. "Is that right, Mr. Demetriev? Is that where you've placed the powder?"

"It's already in place?" Hastings asked.

"Yes, I suspected as much," Barnabas said. "The Admiralty informed me this morning they had a large shipment of black powder go missing several months ago. Mr. Demetriev was just waiting for an opportunity to use it when Mr. Van de Berg came along."

Demetriev began to laugh. "He thought he was being so clever to hire me to get his powder. And all along I use him. He and the whore set the powder and take the blame." He frowned. "He couldn't even do that right. He is huge failure."

Barnabas handed Demetriev off to two other agents. "I will be there directly," he told them. He turned back to Simon, Robert and Hastings. "I will get more information out of him and his compatriots, particularly if there are more targets, as well as the whereabouts of Van de Berg and Mrs. Gaines. But I want you two at the bridge. Start searching for the explosives. As soon as he tells me where he's hidden them, I will send word. If we're lucky we'll find them ourselves."

"We need as many agents as you can spare," Simon told him. "The three of us cannot cover the entire bridge."

Just then there was a knock at his door and his secretary came in. "Excuse me sir, but there are some...ladies here to see you." His hesitation was odd.

"I'm an entirely too busy to see some ladies right now, Cranley," Barnabas said.

His secretary disappeared, yanked out of the way by a woman wearing men's clothes, dressed all in black. She was tall and thin, with a long, thin face to match. Her nose was sharp, and she had shrewd, dark eyes. Simon recognized her immediately as one of Mrs. Gaines's assassins. The very one who had unmanned him in the alley with a well-placed kick.

She hadn't even stepped into the office before several guns and as many knives were pointed at her. She put her hands out.

"I'm unarmed," she said. "I come of my own free will, didn't I?" A petite, rather bedraggled blonde pushed her way in front of the larger woman.

"Don't kill her," she implored. "I made her come. We've been at the constable's house. It's us—well, Essie, really—and a few of the other girls what's been protecting the lady with the baby."

"We come to tell ya they've rigged the bridge. They're going to blow it early. Tomorrow, I think. Saturday," the assassin said grudgingly. "Some of us, Linnie's girls, I mean, we didn't want to do what she told us. We didn't kill them boys. We did other work for her, see? But now she's got this idea in her head. She's gone mad, I tell ya. Blowin' London Bridge."

Barnabas waved off the weapons pointed at them. "Who are you?" He pointed at the mousey blonde.

"Oh, I kept house for her," she said. "The washing and cleaning and so on. But I didn't want no part of this. And I told Essie she couldn't, neither. It isn't right, killing a lady and a baby."

"What?" Robert said in alarm.

Simon put his hand on Robert's arm. "They just said they wouldn't do it," he told him grimly. "And it appears they've prevented others from trying. She must be the one who saved Christy before. I believe we owe them our gratitude."

"My sincerest gratitude," Robert said, bowing his head respectfully. "Are you sure they're safe?"

"Oh, aye," the one named Essie said. "I left Cal in charge. No worries. Fat Linnie's pulled all the others off anyways. Trouble's brewin'. That's why we come."

"I swear we won't let no harm come to 'em," the little blonde said. "It ain't right, hurting a baby."

"There you go, Manderley," Hastings said. "I've found your new nanny."

"Don't be ridiculous," Robert scoffed. "It takes more to be a nanny than a lack of desire to kill the baby."

"Watch what you say about my girl," Essie the assassin said menacingly." That brought the room to a momentary standstill. Essie was oblivious. "They tried to get you, eh?" she asked, pointing at Robert's side.

"Bloody hell," Barnabas exclaimed. "Someone fetch a doctor. Why didn't you say something?"

"It's just a scratch," Robert said, gingerly picking at his bloody clothes to try to see the wound. "We haven't time to worry about it."

Barnabas pinched the bridge of his nose again. "Fine." He took a deep breath, let go of his nose and looked around. "You." He pointed at an agent in the corner. "Give Manderley your coat. You're about the same size."

The agent immediately stripped his coat off and came over and helped Robert off with his.

"You three." Barnabas pointed at Simon, Robert, and Hastings. "Take her"—he pointed at Essie—"and go to the bridge. Find the explosives. Expect a large contingent of men to meet you there."

"I can signal the rest of my girls to meet us there," Essie said.

"No," Simon said sharply. Essie clearly didn't like that. "How are we to tell the good from the bad?" he asked, indicating her clothing. "You all dress alike. I'd hate to kill a friend and not a foe."

Essie's expression cleared. "Aye," she agreed. "I see the problem."

"We will start in the middle of the bridge and work our way toward the South Gate," Simon said to Barnabas.

"I will have my men spread out and report to you as they clear sections," Sir Barnabas said. "Go."

"What about me?" the blonde girl said.

"You?" Barnabas looked at her in consternation, and then he grinned. "You are indeed the new nanny. Go to the Manderley's and stay there until this is over. If you recognize any of your friend's former associates, let my agents know." He snapped his fingers at one of the agents. "Take her and stay there. Send word if there's trouble."

In the carriage on the way to the bridge, Simon watched Robert closely. "Stop worrying. Christy and Christian are in good hands. They have more people watching over them than the king at this point."

He wasn't going to admit he was worried, too. But his sixth sense wasn't telling him anything today. That could mean everything was going to turn out well, or it could just mean it was taking a holiday and who knew what was going to happen.

Essie sat in the corner, warily eyeing them all. "Cal's still there, watching the house for ya. And I killed the two what had the best chance of killin' 'em," she offered helpfully. "The others are still just learning, although Dorcas can throw a knife through a pig's eye from fifty paces. But she doesn't have the arm strength to slit a throat yet. But a baby—"

"I highly recommend that you be quiet for the next few minutes," Robert said softly. "I am trying very hard to remember you are not the enemy right now."

Essie crossed her arms and stared sullenly out the window. "Fine," she muttered to herself. "Try to help a body and this is the thanks I get. Probably swing for it, I will. A pretty little bum led me astray again." She shook her head. "Do anything for my girl, won't I? Ha! Well, next time she begs, won't I say no? Yes, yes I will. No, I'll say. I won't do it. Won't save nobody's life who's just going to gut me for it, no matter how good she tastes."

"This is absolutely fascinating," Hastings said. "I have never felt closer to, nor understood a woman more."

"Do you know where they were planning to put the explosives, Essie?" Simon asked.

"Not really," Essie said. "I wasn't part of that plan. I heard some of the others talking, though. They were scared of it. They didn't want to be the ones to do it. So I think it's probably Dilly and Laura. They's Fat Linnie's favorites." She pointed at Hastings. "Dilly's the one what tried to gut you when you snuck into the house."

Hastings swallowed and put a hand on his stomach. "Yes, I remember the delightful Dilly."

Carriage traffic around the bridge was congested as usual, so they got out several streets from the gate and ran the rest of the way.

"They were originally going to blow a ship under the new bridge," Simon said. "And one of the women we caught said they needed a ship, that they were very worried about getting a ship." He looked over the side of the bridge. There were several crafts waiting their turned to pass under the bridge.

"Don't be daft," Essie said. "You've got to blow the supports. Everybody knows that. I think they've got several little boats filled with the stuff."

At her words, Simon and Robert just looked at one another. Simon felt like a fool. "Of course," he said. "The supports. Why are we up here? We should be down there." He turned to Hastings. "Stay here. When the others arrive, send them down." Hastings nodded.

Robert grabbed Essie's hand. "Come on," he said pulling her with him. "Let's go find your old friends."

CHAPTER 33

They found the first small skiff full of black powder right away. It was tied up next to the support under the South Gate. It was just covered with a tarp, no guard or anything else to draw attention to it. Simon simply waded out to it and hauled it ashore. Robert looked around and couldn't see anyone suspicious. Not Fat Linnie's assassins or Van de Berg's bodyguard or the Russians.

"There weren't none on the other side," Essie said when she ran back after checking the support on the opposite side of the bridge.

"We each need to find a boat and locate as many of these as we can," Robert told Simon and Essie. "We need to haul them away from the bridge."

"But where to?" Simon asked in consternation. "We can't group them together. That creates a hazard of another kind. And we can't simply leave them floating out there."

"One of us needs to stay here and take them," Robert said. "They'll be together, but harmless. We can get the other agents when they arrive to dispose of it quickly, so that danger is minimal." He looked down the waterway, away from the bridge. He pointed. "Down there. See that small dock? We'll bring them there. Even if they were to ignite, at that distance they couldn't do any harm."

"I don't like the idea of splitting up," Simon said. "I have a bad feeling about it. Not my special sort of feeling kind of feeling, but all the same I'd rather keep you in my sights." Essie was looking at Simon as if he was crazy.

"Simon, it is the most efficient way to gather as much powder in as short a time as possible," Robert said, impatience creeping into his voice. "We are very close to finishing this. The other agents will be here shortly." He took Simon's shoulders in his hands and looked him in the eye. "I'm going to be fine, Simon. I promise."

"God, don't do that," Simon said. "That's the one thing that will bring disaster down on our heads."

"I've got to agree with 'im," Essie said. "Promises are made to be broken, my mum always said." She nodded and tapped her hat into place on her head. "I don't make 'em meself."

"You are a very interesting person," Robert told her, almost as fascinated with the creature as Hastings had been. He was meeting all sorts of people he hadn't even known existed before on this mission. He thought as a constable he'd seen and heard it all. He was only realizing he'd barely scratched the surface. He supposed that could apply to himself as well, he'd changed so much in the last week.

"Fine," Simon agreed. "I don't like it, and I'm reserving the right to say I told you so to one and all."

"Agreed. Come on." Robert led the way to a small dock where there were several small skiffs tied up. "Each of you take one. We will compensate the owners later."

"Hey, you!" There were shouts from people nearby as they each set out in a borrowed skiff. It was soon painfully obvious that Essie had never steered a craft before in her life as she struggled with the oars and uselessly rowed in circles.

"Essie!" Robert shouted. "Return to shore and wait for us to return with the other skiffs."

"Thank God," Essie called back. She inexpertly turned the skiff around and began a meandering, jagged course back to shore.

Simon made it to the next support first and waved that he'd found the skiff. He turned and headed for shore. They continued in this vein for some time, and it wasn't long before Robert noticed that there seemed to be agents doing the same from the opposite shore.

As he headed toward one of the middle supports, he could see that an agent had gotten there before him. "Ahoy!" he yelled, not sure what the protocol was in this particular situation. "Is this the last one then?"

The agent didn't answer and Robert pulled alongside him. When the agent turned, Robert realized his mistake. It was Van de Berg.

Simon watched with horror, his shouted warning too late, as Van de Berg pulled a gun and shot Robert.

Robert tumbled backward out of the boat into the water. Simon was too far away to do anything. He rowed as fast as could, and he could see several small boats doing the same from every direction. But they were all too late. Robert was dead.

Simon could hardly think as those words repeated themselves in his head over and over. *Robert was dead. Robert was dead.* His heart had stopped at the gunshot and now raced so fast he was lightheaded as he rowed and rowed, his vision blurry as tears streamed down his face.

All he knew was he had to get to Robert. And he had to make Van de Berg pay.

He watched as Van de Berg grabbed Robert's boat and climbed into it. Then, looking away, he pointed his gun at the little skiff loaded with powder and prepared to shoot. Simon felt helpless. After everything, all they'd done, all they'd accomplished, to get this close and fail? To lose Robert? For nothing? How was he to tell Christy? How were they to go on?

He bellowed in impotent fury and pulled his knife out of his boot, prepared to throw it at Van de Berg. His shout drew the Dutchman's attention, and the villain had the stones to smile at him.

Just as Simon was about to let his knife fly—and he was sure that Van de Berg was going to pull the trigger—a figure surged out of the water and grabbed Van de Berg's arm, yanking him out of the boat. The gun flew out of his hand into the water as Van de Berg fell. Robert clung to the side of Van de Berg's boat as the Dutchman tried to swim away.

Simon dropped his knife and began rowing again as fast as he could. By now several other agents were closing in on the Dutchman. Robert simply clung to the edge of the little boat and did not join the chase. That alone told Simon he was injured. He let the other agents worry about Van de Berg. He could do no harm now. He headed straight for Robert.

"How bad is it?" he asked grimly as he pulled up alongside him.

"It hurts like the very devil," Robert said. "But I don't believe it's going to kill me." Then he let go of the boat and slid, unconscious, into the water.

CHRISTY HEARD a commotion at the front door and rose from the table carrying Christian. He had been in her lap while she was feeding him.

"I can get that, missus," the girl said.

She was washing dishes because Christy wasn't willing to let her out of her sight. She had quite a few things to say to Robert and Simon about her. The very idea, sending a complete stranger, and one with a very questionable background to say the least, as the new nanny. She'd been prattling on all morning about her work with the madam who ran a gang of assassins, and her "lady friend" Essie, who was apparently one of those assassins but had been enlisted to protect Christy and the baby rather than kill them.

Christy had thanked her accordingly.

She knew she could hardly cast the first stone as far as an unblemished past went, and she knew they might be a little desperate when it came to finding a new nanny, but if Very Tarrant could find Mrs. Goose, then surely Christy could find someone a bit more suitable than Mary Peppers. Poor Cook had taken to her room again as soon as the girl had arrived.

"Ma'am," Nell called. "Can you come?"

"Christy!" Simon yelled. "Hurry!"

Christy forgot her concerns about Mary. "Here," she said, shoving Christian at her. The girl hurried over and took him, and Christy picked up her skirts and ran to the front of the house. She saw Simon half carrying Robert up the stairs, and her hand flew up to cover her gasp of shock.

"What happened?" she asked when she got her voice back. She hurried up the stairs behind them.

"He's been shot," Simon said.

"And I think he was stabbed this morning," Mary Peppers called up from the bottom of the stairs.

"What?" Christy asked in dismay.

"We've had a rough day of it," Simon said. They got Robert into the bedroom and stopped.

"Well, put him on the bed," Christy said.

"I've been in the river, Christy," Robert said weakly. "Pull off the blankets."

"Oh, for heaven's sake," Christy said. She yanked the covers off the bed. "There. Put him down."

They gingerly set Robert down on the edge of the bed.

Christy could see now that he was wet. "Where have you been shot?" she asked, not sure where to begin. His hand looked bloody, and she reached for it.

"My arm," he corrected her.

"We've got to get his clothes off," Simon said.

"Not this again," Robert complained.

Christy smiled weakly at his attempt at humor. "This is not going to end the same way, I don't think."

"Well, that puts a damper on things, madam. Thank you, very much." Robert's voice was strained with the pain.

Christy turned to Simon and was struck by how ill he looked. "Simon, darling, have you been hurt as well?" she asked in concern.

He shook his head. "No. I'm just concerned for Robert."

"He has some damn fool notion that this is his fault," Robert said. Christy tried to take his jacket off, and he gasped.

"Wait a moment," she said, looking at the jacket. "This isn't yours. Whose jacket is this?"

"I borrowed it, after I got stabbed," Robert said. "Just cut it off."

"Lordy," Mary Peppers said from the door, holding Christian on her hip. The baby seemed content for now. "He sounds like Essie. If it's not one thing with her, it's another. Where is she?"

"We sent her to Daniel's," Simon said. "He's a friend who lives nearby." He looked at Christy. "I know Very's there, and she'll get us a competent doctor."

"I'm going to get my scissors to cut this jacket off," Christy said. "I'll be right back."

She stepped around Mary Peppers and hurried down the stairs to her sewing room. She closed the door behind her and slid to the floor. Then she bit the palm of her hand in order to keep from crying or screaming. She didn't want them to hear her doing either one upstairs. But she needed a minute, just a minute, to herself.

If Robert died...she couldn't even finish the thought. Yes, he was sitting up and talking, but she knew wounds got infected and could take even a man as strong and healthy as Robert.

She loved him so much. She loved Simon, too, but even so she couldn't imagine her life without Robert now, their life without Robert. And Simon was suffering, too. What would happen to him if Robert died, if he lost another person he loved?

She wiped the tears from her cheeks and held her hands out. They were shaking. She stood up and shook her hands out at her sides, hard. Then she held them up again. *Better.* She went to the table and grabbed her sewing shears and opened the door. Simon was standing there waiting for her. He looked like a lost little boy.

"He's going to be all right," she told him before he could speak. "You don't know him like I do. He won't let this take him from us."

"Sometimes they don't have a choice," he said.

"Robert Manderley makes his own choices," she said firmly. "Now get yourself together and let's get back upstairs. Mary Peppers is probably stealing my linen."

"Her name is Mary Peppers?" Simon asked, his brow wrinkling.

"You sent me a girl off the streets and you didn't even know her name?" Christy said. "I ought to...well, I don't know what I ought to do, but of all the nerve." She marched past him to the stairs. "She could have murdered us in our beds."

"The point was that they were supposed to murder you but didn't, you see, that's why we sent her," Simon said as if it all made sense. "And actually, Barnabas sent her. I don't think he knew what else to do with her, to be honest. Essie came with us, so he just sent the girl here."

"Well, then I'll have a few words for Sir Barnabas James," Christy told him.

"You know, I don't think Barnabas knew what he was getting into when he got himself involved with you and Robert," Simon said.

"I daresay he didn't," Christy told him. "The rest of the world may dance to his tune, but I most definitely do not." She stopped suddenly, and Simon had to grab her to keep from knocking her down. She turned in his arms and put her hand on his cheek. "But he did help us get you back from Africa, didn't he? So I do owe him that, I must remember."

"He did?" Simon asked. "But I thought that was Daniel and Harry."

"We went to Sir Barnabas for help," Christy said. "He gave us the papers we needed and some extra men. And he told me that it was my fault."

"What?" Simon held her back when she tried to go to Robert. "How?"

"He told me I ruined you when I chose Robert instead of you," she confessed. "That I'd driven you into a decline and that had led to your capture." Simon didn't say anything. "He was right, wasn't he?" she asked softly.

"You said it yourself, there was no choice," Simon said. "I didn't give you one. There was only Robert. He is twice the man I am."

"And he is bleeding in the next room, so I haven't got time to tell you all the ways that you are wrong about that. But I most definitely will revisit this conversation later," she promised. "Now, come on."

CHAPTER 34

"Halllooo!" The cry echoed up the stairs with a faint Irish lilt. "I've come from Daniel Steinberg's. I'm the doctor."

"I've brought them, Mrs. Manderley. It's Sophie Witherspoon. Are you upstairs?"

"Where's Mary?" Simon recognized that voice. Essie had returned.

"I'm up here, Es," Mary called down.

In moments, the room was twice as crowded. Two strange men had entered with Sophie. "Oh, Simon. Are you all right?" Sophie rushed to his side and gave him a hug. "We've been so worried about you."

So worried he hadn't seen them since the first night he'd been back, apparently.

"I'm fine, Sophie," he lied, because he knew that's what she wanted to hear. That's what they all wanted to hear. Except Robert and Christy. They'd confronted him on that lie.

Sophie made the introductions. "This is Dr. Alec McCain and his friend Lord Hawthorne."

Christy stared at the doctor. "Alec McCain? Harry's Alec McCain?"

The big, blond, bearded Irishman laughed. "The one and only. It's nice to finally meet you Mrs. Ash—I mean, Mrs. Manderley." He smiled to show there was no ill will meant by the mistake. "I showed up to visit Harry and found everything in a mess." He shook his head. "I've only just fished a bullet out of Daniel. So let's see your man." He looked at Simon standing behind Christy with his hands on her shoulders, and frowned. "He doesn't look shot."

"This is my husband," Christy said, taking Robert's hand where he lay on the bed. "Robert Manderley."

Simon self-consciously removed his hands. Christy wouldn't let him get away with that. She grabbed his hand. "And this is Simon Gantry."

"Are you sure you're a doctor?" Simon asked. He was a little worried. After all, Robert was lying there with bloody bandages on his side and his arm. It should have been obvious who had been shot. And with his full beard and long hair, McCain looked more like the rough American trapper he was than a doctor.

"That I am," Alec McCain said. "Before my trapping days. But I must admit, I'm a wee bit confused about these London marriages." He laughed again. "We should have visited sooner, eh, Hawthorne?" His friend just smiled.

"Not sure if you remember me, Hawthorne," Simon said, holding out his hand. "We met briefly in Portugal."

Simon was curious as to whether Hawthorne would speak. He'd gone mute in Portugal, after Salamanca, Simon thought, or perhaps it was Busaco. They all ran together in Simon's mind now. He was rarely on the battlefields. His fights had been in the dark of night, in the woods, where he had stealthily crept and killed.

He shook off the memories and met Hawthorne's gaze. He could see the same memories there.

"I remember," Hawthorne said, taking Simon's outstretched hand, and the words carried more weight than just acknowledging an old acquaintance. He said no more, just let go of his hand and looked away. So he was speaking now. And he'd grown. He wasn't as rough as McCain, but there was more American about him now than Englishman.

"You got shot twice?" McCain asked in disbelief. "A word of advice, son: after the first one, run."

Robert laughed, but it must have hurt because he grabbed his side. "No, knife," he said, pointing to the cut on his side. "Bullet." He pointed to his arm.

"And you're wet because...?" McCain asked, gently removing the bloody makeshift bandage from the knife wound.

"Fell off the boat when I got shot," Robert told him.

"You London lads lead very exciting lives," McCain said, glancing at Christy and Sophie. He pointed at Essie, who had her arm around Mary. "Not sure what to make of that one." Essie just made a rude gesture.

"Never you mind," Christy scolded him. "Just fix him."

"Yes, ma'am," McCain said with another laugh. "I like a woman with spirit."

"She's taken," Robert said. His voice was a little breathless as McCain poked at his wound.

"Yes, I noticed that." The doctor reached behind him. "Alcohol," he said. Hawthorne reached into the bag he carried and passed McCain a jug. He popped the cork.

"You're going to drink now?" Christy asked shrilly.

"Now never you mind," McCain said. "I know what I'm doing. I fixed Harry after that Pawnee took his eye, didn't I? And I fixed Daniel. Didn't I, ma'am?" he asked Sophie.

"Yes, actually, he did," Sophie said. "He's not going to drink the alcohol. Apparently it's some homemade brew he concocted in America, and it cleans wounds or something. Although he said you can also drink it." She shuddered. "I tried it. I think it peeled a layer off my innards."

McCain laughed again. His laugh was starting to get on Simon's nerves. He got the impression he'd laugh a patient right into the grave.

"It's not for the faint of heart, that's true," he said. "I need a fine needle, missus, if you've got one, please. I've got to sew him up." Christy stepped out and called for the maid, Nell. He dug around in his bag and produced some type of thread. He held it up. "Catgut," he said. He looked at the ladies, and Essie. "Not sure you want to see this, ladies," he said.

"Don't be silly," Sophie said. "I've seen many stitches before."

"I've stitched myself up," Essie said. The whole room turned to stare at her. "What?" she asked innocently.

McCain dipped the catgut in the alcohol, and then he poured a small amount of the stuff on Robert's cut.

"Damn it all," Robert swore. "That hurts." His face was pale and he was sweating.

Simon felt sick to his stomach. Robert's injuries were his fault. If he wasn't operating at half capacity because of his physical condition after Africa, he would have been the one to take down all the Russians and to find Van de Berg.

"Stop it," Robert ground out between clenched teeth. Simon looked at him and saw that he was watching him. "This is not your fault and I'm not going to die."

"From little scratches like this?" McCain scoffed. "I should hope not. And you brought in a decent doctor, unlike that fool Daniel. Could have lost his leg letting it fester like that."

"What?" Simon and Robert both asked in disbelief.

"It was that bad?" Simon asked.

"Simon," Robert said, a warning in his voice. "That was not your fault, either."

"Really? Well, whose fault was it? He was shot rescuing me in

Africa. Christ! How many people do I have to kill before I figure out that I'm cursed?"

"Simon, I've known you for over ten years," Sophie said. "You have not caused any unfortunate ills to befall anyone. On the contrary, you have saved many of us, me included. I will never forget the debt I owe you."

Simon couldn't look at her. It was that favor, done for Sophie, that had started him and Daniel on their path in St. Giles as vigilantes. They'd killed Sophie's brother, who had raped and abused her in her childhood and tried to do the same after she'd married their good friend Ian Witherspoon. Ian and her other lover Derek Knightley couldn't do it; they'd have been suspected right away. And so Daniel and Simon had done it. They had bided their time, and then they'd found the black-guard and slit his throat. It was what they were good at, what they'd been trained to do.

He looked over at Essie. How could he say he was any better than her or her cronies? He was an assassin, just like them. He could argue that his targets deserved to die, but then so could she, from her perspective. He and Robert hadn't even gone into that aspect of his past. As a constable Robert had a duty to uphold the law, and Simon had broken it, many times. And he didn't regret it.

"Here it is." Christy rushed into the room and immediately noticed the tension in the room. "What? What happened?"

"Simon is blaming himself for everything again," Robert said.

"Oh, Simon, darling, I'm sorry." She handed the doctor the needle and looked down at Robert's side. She turned a little gray and swayed a bit. "I really am sorry. I don't faint, you know. Daniel steals the whiskey." Her voice had gotten very weak.

"Catch her," McCain barked.

Simon dove for her and caught her as she collapsed.

CHAPTER 35

"**S**he did the same thing when she found out about your back," Harry said from the doorway. Simon glanced over, Christy now safely in his arms. "I've come to see how things are going. Daniel came around and asked for a report. You know how he is."

"Just a little stitching here," McCain said. "Looks like the knife didn't go in too far and the bullet just grazed him."

"Knife?" He looked at Simon and Robert. "You two have had a busy day. You can tell us all later." He turned to go. "Come on, Sophie, Derek is champing at the bit to get you back. I wouldn't let him come because I was worried there'd be an altercation with Barnabas's Home Office boys."

"I'm coming," Sophie said, picking up her skirts and hurrying after Harry. "We've got enough to worry about right now." She looked back and waved. "If you need me, just send a note."

"Put her next to me," Robert said. His voice was rough, and Simon saw that McCain had started stitching. He carried Christy over and carefully laid her next to Robert.

"I've still got to do the bullet wound," McCain told Simon.

"You don't know Christy," Simon said. "If I tried to take her away from his side, she'd kill me."

"I don't faint," Christy insisted weakly.

"Never," Robert said. "Put your head on my shoulder so you can't see what he's doing."

"I'll be fine."

Simon sat down next to her so he could see what McCain was doing. "Trust me, darling, you don't want to see. Put your head on his shoulder."

"All right." Christy curled up next to Robert, her head on his shoulder and her face against his neck. Christian started to fuss.

"I'm going to take him down and finish feeding the wee thing," Mary Peppers said. "I promise not to run off with him."

"Wait, what?" Christy started to sit up.

"Quit your shillyshallying, woman," McCain growled. "I'm trying to sew a man up here."

"I'm going with me girl," Essie said, and out the door she went. "'Ere, what are you doin' 'ere?" she asked a moment later out in the hallway.

"You are going to be a challenge," Barnabas said, "but one that I am up to. Off with you for now." A second later, he stood in the doorway. "Who have we here? Ah, Hawthorne, good to see you. And this must be the infamous Dr. Alec McCain."

McCain paused his needle and glanced over. "The very same. And who are you?" He went back to sewing up Robert's arm.

"Sir Barnabas James."

McCain's needle paused again. "I'm told I have to reserve judgment," he said. "We'll see."

"Indeed." Barnabas dismissed him with that one word. Simon could see Hawthorne fighting a smile. "You gentlemen will be glad to know that we have returned all the black powder to the Royal Ordnance at Woolwich. According to their records, give or take a handful or two, that was all of it. We do not believe they actually had enough powder to attack any more targets. So, well done."

"What was his plan?" Robert asked as McCain tied off the stitches in his arm. "His method of planting the explosives was not what your experts told us to look for."

"Yes, well, Van de Berg has some engineering experience. His plan was quite ingenious, although once we started picking off his co-conspirators, it was doomed to failure. He planned to blow the eastern side of each support at the same time, weakening the bridge support to such an extent along that side that the entire bridge would collapse. A collapse at London Bridge at noonday would have been a disaster of monumental proportions. Who can say whether it would have worked or not? I'm sincerely grateful to you both for your efforts to foil their plans."

He pursed his lips. "Their motives concern me, however. Van de Berg was being paid. An anonymous benefactor. And the Russians are heading toward anarchy with their proletariat revolutionaries. I do not like them invading our shores with their political propaganda."

He walked over and peered at McCain's handiwork. "We do have a surgeon on call at the Home Office, you know. The same one that serves Parliament, I believe."

"Then I'm sure he's not worth the paper his credentials are written on," McCain growled. "Are you questioning my work?"

"I would never presume, doctor." Barnabas straightened. "I believe you will need a few days to recover before returning to work, Manderley. I shall not expect you before Wednesday."

"Work? What is this you're talking about?" Robert said. He started to sit up but winced and lay back down. "I don't work for you."

"Indeed you do," Barnabas said. "I found your work on this case to be exemplary. You are wasted with the constabulary. I have informed your superiors as such."

"Now see here, Barnabas," Simon said. "Robert likes being a constable. He likes coming home to Christy and the baby each night. Lord knows in our profession that doesn't happen often."

"'Our profession'?" Barnabas asked. "I'm glad to hear you say that. I have also reinstated your position, Gantry. You now work for me again, as well. The two of you and Hastings made a very good team, and I am thinking of having you train the woman, Essie."

"Oh, God," Robert said. "Tell me I'm delirious."

"So you all stopped a madman from blowing up London Bridge?" McCain asked, frowning. "I had no idea I was sewing up a hero." He clapped his hands together. "But for now, everyone out. This lad needs to sleep. Best thing for him." He stood up and waved Barnabas out.

"Christy and Simon stay," Robert said. Simon could hear the exhaustion in his voice. He felt the same way.

"I just need to borrow Gantry for a minute," Barnabas said. "I'll send him right back."

"I'll be back to check on you and change those bandages tomorrow," McCain told Robert. "Don't be overexerting yourself."

"Sleep. I promise." Robert's tone said he was telling the truth.

"I'll be right back," Simon said softly, squeezing Christy's hand.

"And we'll be right here waiting," Christy said with a smile as she held his hand. He walked away and distance finally broke their connection.

CHAPTER 36

"I presume this is where I shall find you from now?" Barnabas said as he pulled on his gloves. "Wallowing in connubial bliss? Well, Manderley may rest, but I will need you to come in tomorrow and sign some statements—the usual protocol. And we have yet to find Alice Gaines or the rest of her gang of cutthroats."

"Is this what you were angling for all along? Me working for you again?" Simon asked. He followed Barnabas back down the stairs. "What I can't figure out is why."

"Does the why matter?" Barnabas asked.

"A little. I haven't made up my mind whether or not I'm going to dance to your tune."

"I do not require you to dance," Barnabas said. He sighed. "I find that what worked during the war is not what is needed here and now in most cases. Did you think today's crisis at the bridge was the only one I had on hand? I am on my way back to the office in an attempt to avert a financial disaster that will rock not only England, but perhaps all of Europe." He stopped in front of the door. "Take my advice, invest in property until further notice."

He put his hat on. "There are no throats to slit, no assassinations to resolve this situation." He looked at Simon. "There is subterfuge and second story work. And methodical investigation. Things in which both you and Manderley excel."

"And Hastings and Essie?"

"I didn't say there were never throats to slit." He opened the door. "I also find that I would like to have someone that I trust implicitly in my organization."

"Why, Barnabas, was that a compliment?"

"I do not compliment. I state facts." He grinned wryly as he stepped over the threshold. "And so I go to save England from her follies once more."

"How does Mrs. Jones feel about these late hours of yours?" Simon asked. "Does she complain?"

"Of course not. She understands that this is my career. Anyway, that is what Lord Wetherald is for. He can be there when I cannot."

Simon laughed in spite of himself. "I see. Eventually we all get what we need." He was thinking of all of his friends, who had somehow managed to find each other in war, a group of like-minded men who shared proclivities, yes, but who were also loyal and steadfast and true. And all of whom had somehow managed to find lovers who were willing to accept both the good and bad that they brought with them, the baggage of war, and of pain and loss, and the stigmatism of those aberrant proclivities.

"No, no we don't," Barnabas said softly. He put his hand on Simon's shoulder. "I myself nearly didn't. Your dunderheaded friends, myself included, somehow managed to find the most persistent pains in the backside in England who simply wouldn't give up on us. But rest assured, Simon, very few men are so lucky. Most people go through life alone. Perhaps surrounded by others who might as well be strangers, who will never know the secret heart that beats within their soul. And they will die alone, with their secrets and their heart and their soul locked inside, never known by another, never seeing the light, never tasting love or acceptance or joy. And that is the way it is."

Barnabas shrugged. "Life is a cruel and lonely journey. When given the opportunity to share the road, I highly recommend you not be an idiot about it."

Simon was shocked that Barnabas had opened up so much in his little speech and he could see that Barnabas was uncomfortable with it. "Well, that was extremely morose and depressing," Simon said. "You must be working on a canto."

"Yes, now that Byron's gone and gotten himself killed rather unfortunately in Greece, I thought someone needed to take up the torch," Barnabas said, clearly relieved that Simon had lightened the conversation.

"Your meter is dreadful," Simon told him.

"My rhythm is perfection," Barnabas said, with deliberate innuendo. "Wetherald especially sings my praises."

Simon laughed. "Love has changed you," he said.

"I should hope so. I shall see you tomorrow."

"You shall see me next week," Simon said. "I have things I need to take care of."

Barnabas paused on the steps and turned back one brow raised in annoyed inquiry.

Simon just smiled. "Goodbye, Barnabas. Take your agents away. We have Essie." He closed the door.

WHEN ROBERT AWOKE, he was naked and Christy was pressed up against his side, sleeping. The house was quiet and the sky pitch black, so he knew it was the middle of the night. He immediately grew tense and looked around for Simon, fearing he had left. He relaxed when he saw him sitting in a chair in the shadows in the corner of the room.

"You're awake," Simon said quietly.

"So are you," Robert said. "Why?"

"I couldn't sleep."

"Because you're in a chair?"

"What? Oh, no. I've slept in much worse places." There was a smile in his voice. "I was just thinking."

"That makes me nervous." Christy shifted on the bed, and Robert pulled her close with an arm around her shoulders. "This is new to us," he confessed to Simon.

"Well, to me, too," Simon said. "I've never attempted any sort of relationship since Giselle."

"No. I mean yes, that, too, but this, between Christy and I. We cared for one another, but for some reason we had trouble showing it, sharing it physically. I don't know why."

"Yours was not a normal courtship."

"No, it wasn't. And there was you. Always there was you."

"I know. I'm sorry."

Robert ran his fingers up and down Christy's arm lightly. She shivered in her sleep. "Don't be."

He kissed her warm forehead. The window was open, but there was no breeze and the heat was unabated. He would always remember the heat of this summer. The summer of Simon.

"We have always shared her, haven't we? From the very beginning."

"You actually met her before I did," Simon said. "I kissed her the next morning, before I knew anything about her except her name. She was just so perfect."

"Perfect?" Christy said sleepily. "You thought I was a pregnant prostitute."

Robert laughed in disbelief. "Did you? How ridiculous."

"Even more so since she was at Daniel's," Simon said, laughter in his voice, too. "She was completely wrong for the part. But I found her irresistible."

"I found you irresistible, too," Christy said. She propped her chin on her fist on Robert's chest. "How are you feeling, darling?" she asked Robert.

"Considering I was both stabbed and shot yesterday, not to mention taking an unexpected dip in the river, not too awful," he said. "My side's a little sore and my arm is stiff. I hate to admit it, but that doctor was right. The sleep did wonders for me."

"Mmm, me, too," Christy said, stretching. "Christian?" she asked.

"I had Mary Peppers put him to bed," Simon said. "He was very tired."

"Robert, you're naked." She sat up, as if just realizing it.

"I noticed," he said. "I thought you'd done it."

"I did," Simon said. "Your pants were still damp. I didn't think you'd want to sleep in them. I washed you off, too. You were so tired you slept through it. And yes, I enjoyed it thoroughly."

"Well, damn. I probably wasn't in any condition to do anything about it anyway." The idea of being unknowingly undressed and admired by Simon was intriguing. Robert liked the idea of it. It was exciting.

"What about now?" Simon asked. His voice was smooth, almost silky—the voice of a seducer. That excited Robert even more. He felt like he'd been waiting his whole life to be seduced.

Christy lay back down beside him and nuzzled his neck. She glided her hand down his stomach and his muscles clenched. By the time her fingers ran through the rough patch of hair between his legs and she wrapped her hand around his hardening cock, he was breathing fast.

"It feels like he could do something about it now," she said, her voice husky from sleep and desire.

"Good, because I've been sitting here like a very good Simon for hours just waiting to fuck you two," Simon said, and Robert's cock grew harder.

Simon dragged his chair closer to the bed, right up to the edge, and sat back down. He was illuminated by the moonlight now, and Robert was shocked and aroused to see that he had taken off his jacket and shirt. Simon's cock was already hard, jutting out of his open trousers, and as Robert watched Simon reached down and stroked it. The gesture made it clear he'd been doing it while he'd been sitting there watching them sleep, thinking about fucking them. Beside him Christy hummed in excitement and Robert's pulse quickened.

This was carnality, physical pleasure for pleasure's sake, and he liked it. He wanted more of it.

Simon reached out—slowly, as if his hand was moving through water—and laid his palm against Robert's calf. Robert felt his muscles tremble at the touch. Then Simon slowly ran his palm up the leg, dragging it along, tugging the thin layer of hair covering it. When he slid up over his knee, Robert thought he might explode from anticipation alone. He stopped on Robert's thigh, his index finger just touching the sensitive area where leg met groin. Simon let his finger gently rub along the crease there, and Robert couldn't hold back a little groan.

"You two are a feast," Simon said softly, staring at his hand. "And I am a starving man." He looked up then and met Robert's gaze, then Christy's. "This time, I want us all to be together."

"Yes," Robert said gruffly, his voice nearly failing him as he recalled all the things Simon had told him the day before. Was that only a day ago?

"Yes," Christy said, her voice breathless with excitement. "How can we do that?"

"I think, despite what Robert says, that the knife wound in his side means he needs to stay on his back," Simon said. He let his hand glide higher and ran one finger up the length of Robert's cock. Robert's back arched off the bed as he panted.

"It was hardly a scratch," he said breathlessly.

"Better to be safe," Simon said.

He stood up and pushed his trousers off, then he climbed on the bed, straddling Robert. He leaned down, one hand resting on the bed by Robert's shoulder, and licked Robert's lower lip. The tip of his hard cock pressed into Robert's stomach, and Robert couldn't stop the sound he made in the back of his throat, something between a growl and a groan.

Simon laughed softly, his breath hot on Robert's mouth. "You were ripe for the plucking, weren't you, constable?"

Robert reached up and fondled Simon's cock, learning the feel of another man's member in his hand. He liked it. "I do believe I was," he whispered in Simon's mouth.

Simon leaned in and kissed him then. It felt strange to have a man's mouth on his instead of Christy's soft one, to feel a man's whiskers scrape against his own. But the wet heat of Simon's mouth was just as exciting as Christy's, and Robert surrendered to Simon's experience and let him dominate the kiss.

Simon broke the kiss and laughed softly, grabbing Robert's wrist and pulling his hand away from his cock. "I waited this long to come inside one of you," he said. "Don't ruin all my plans." He pulled Robert's hand up and kissed his palm. "Another time."

Simon came up on his knees and gestured to Christy. "Get up, beauty. We need to get rid of those clothes."

"Move back, Simon," Robert told him. "Straddle me like he has, Christy. I want to watch him undress you. Face him."

She didn't do as he asked right away, and Robert looked over to see her watching him in indecision. "Are you sure about this?" she asked. "Don't do it for me, Robert."

"I'm not," he told her truthfully. "I would, though."

She looked shocked.

"I love you so much, Christy, that I would do anything for you." He reached out and took her hand in his. "When I first found myself attracted to Simon, I asked myself if it was only because I wanted to make sure there was a place for me in your life." He smiled a little sadly. "I knew then, I've always known, that you still loved him. But I've come to realize that I want this, too. Very much."

He grinned, and he hoped it was as inviting as Simon's smile. "I like it. I like being so physical, so sexual. I never knew I would, but you opened my eyes to it, Christy. And now I want it all." He tugged on her hand. "So come here. Climb on top of me and show me that luscious bottom, please. I want to watch Simon undress you."

"Oh, I plan to do a great deal more than that." Simon helped her straddle Robert and avoid his bandaged side. Simon loosened the ties on her dress, and he reached down and lifted it up over her head. She wore nothing but a simple muslin shift underneath. "I thought earlier today it looked as if you were half naked under there."

"It's so very hot," she complained. "I couldn't abide the thought of wearing layers of clothes. I didn't know half of London was going to be traipsing through my bedroom."

Robert slipped his hands under the shift and slid his palms up her thighs to palm her plump cheeks in his hands. "I don't mind at all. The faster to undress you, my dear."

"We are of a like mind, Robert," Simon said. He cupped Christy's face in his hands. "My dear," he said softly.

"My darling," she said softly back.

Watching them kiss was an epiphany for Robert. What started out as a soft rediscovery turned hot and hard and possessive in mere seconds, and he realized they had not been together without him. Not since Simon's return. They had not wanted to share this without him. What they did together now was for Robert as much as it was for them, just as what Robert and Simon did together, or what Robert and Christy did, was for all of them.

Just as the thought struck him, without looking at him, without breaking away from the kiss, Simon reached down and grabbed Robert's wrist, and he held on. Robert twisted his arm until he could take Simon's hand in his, and then he rose up on one arm and, still holding Christy by the hip, kissed the back of Simon's hand.

Yes, he thought, *I'm here.*

When the kiss ended, Simon let go and he looked self-conscious. Robert just grinned and lifted the hem of Christy's shift and bit her gently on the bottom. She let out a little squeak. He felt a pull in his side and lay back with a grimace.

"I think you're right," he told Simon. "I'm not fit to do much else but lie here unless I want to get stitched up again tomorrow."

"Never fear," Simon said, pulling Christy's shift off over her head. "I know just what to do." He leaned back and just stared at her exposed body for a long moment. "I've never seen you like this," he said. He placed a hand on her stomach. "Without a baby in here."

"As you can see, I am normally much smaller," she said with laughter in her voice.

"Not for long, I warrant, with two men bedding you now," Robert said. It was out in the open now, the expectation that she was as much Simon's as his. "Are you prepared for that?"

"I'm prepared to be bedded right now, thank you," she said. "After that, we shall see what happens. I do want more children, and I can only have one at a time, no matter how many times you fuck me. So someone can get started right away, please."

Simon laughed. "I have spent most of my adult life avoiding any chance of getting a woman pregnant," he confessed. "I've fucked mostly men, or barren or pregnant women."

"Some would say that was prudent, unless you wished to be married," Robert said carefully.

"I think it's sad, because I don't think prudence had anything to do with it," Christy said. "You'll fuck me, won't you, Simon?"

"That's up to Robert," Simon said. "But not tonight. Because of his injuries, I have something else planned. I'm going to show you how I fucked women who might get pregnant."

"But you said..." Christy sounded confused. Robert was not.

"I said mostly," Simon told her. "Robert, show her."

Christy looked back at him. "Show me what?"

Robert slipped his hand between her legs. He would never not be thrilled that he had the right to touch her like this. Her curls were damp, silky perfection against his palm. "Here," he said, slipping the tip of his finger into her quim, "is where we usually fuck."

He pushed his finger deeper, and Christy gasped.

"Is she wet?" Simon asked. His voice was tight. "Please tell me she's already wet."

Christy slid up his finger and then pressed back down onto it, fucking it with natural eroticism. She was clearly as excited by Simon in their bed as Robert was. "I'm very wet," she said. She hummed in the back of throat. "More."

Robert added another finger and she fucked it harder and faster, so that Simon could hear how wet she was.

"Enough," Simon said, hugging her to him to stop her movements. He looked over her shoulder at Robert. "Now show her where I'm going to fuck her tonight while you're in her very wet cunt."

"I don't understand," Christy said. She was kissing Simon's neck. "Show me, Robert."

Robert slid his fingers out of her cunt, as Simon called it, and dragged them back along her crease to the puckered rosette of her bottom. He rubbed it with his damp finger, his pulse racing, his breath coming faster.

Christy had gone very still above him. "At the same time?" she asked. Her voice was equal parts trepidation and curiosity.

"Yes," Simon answered. She didn't say anything. "Robert, very gently slip one finger in there. Make sure it's wet."

Robert pushed his finger into her cunt again to make sure it was wet enough, and Christy gasped and he felt her shudder. Then he touched it to her bottom and pushed.

"She's very tight. I don't want to hurt her."

"Push back," Simon told Christy. "It will help him push his finger in." She did, and Robert's finger slid into her very tight back passage.

"Oh," Christy said, her hips moving a bit.

"Do you know the salve I put on my back?" Simon asked her. "I'm going to use that so it doesn't hurt you, and I'm going to fuck you in the bottom while Robert is in your cunt and we are going to fill you so full and fuck you so well, and you are going to love it, Christy, I know you will," he promised her.

"Can...can Robert use some salve now, so I can see how it feels?"

Simon immediately grabbed the jar off the bedside table. Robert gently removed his finger. Simon took a small dollop of salve and gave it to him. "Spread it around a little first," he advised.

Robert did so and Christy's hips quivered slightly. She spread her knees wider and Robert took that as an invitation. His finger went in much easier this time. Christy was panting.

"Fuck her with it," Simon told him. He took Christy's hair in his fist and kissed her as Robert pulled his finger almost out and then pushed it back in. Christy whimpered, but her hips moved slightly. He did it again, and this time she was clearly fucking him back.

God, the view he had of what he was doing, of Simon and Christy, he felt as if the whole thing was an erotic performance just for him, and it thrilled him. He feared he wouldn't last long enough to get inside of Christy.

"Oh, God, Christy, that's it," Simon said roughly, watching

over her shoulder. "You love to be fucked, don't you? I knew you would."

"It does feel good," she said. "I didn't think it would. Oh, Robert."

He couldn't stop his hips from lifting off the bed, his cock seeking comfort from one of them. He found hard, hot flesh—Simon's leg—and stroked it with the tip of his cock, and had to stifle a groan.

Simon still held Christy's hair in his fist. "This is how men fuck, too, Christy," he whispered in her ear, his gaze holding Robert's.

"This is how you like to be fucked, isn't it?" she asked breathlessly. Robert immediately imagined it, him fucking Simon, his cock tunneling in and out of him.

"Yes," Simon told her, kissing her ear. "Yes, it is."

They were toying with him, using his obvious desires to torture him, and he loved it. He let go the groan he'd been holding back, fucked Christy deeply with his finger and rubbed against Simon's strong thigh with abandon, the pain in his side merely heightening the pleasure in contrast.

"I'm going to put my fingers in your cunt now, Christy," Simon said softly, "so you can see how it will feel when both our cocks are in there, all right?"

"Yes," she breathed out on a sigh.

Robert could feel Simon's fingers sliding inside her. He gasped, and Simon laughed softly.

"That's right," Simon said. "We'll be able to feel each other inside her while we're fucking her."

"It's like we'll all be fucking," Christy said. "Simon, that's perfect. Now. Do it now."

CHAPTER 37

"Let me turn her around, Robert," Simon said, and Christy felt her heart start beating so fast she thought it might just jump right out of her chest. But it already had, and these two had caught it.

"I can't believe I'm so lucky," she murmured as Robert slipped his fingers out of her bottom. She shivered at the erotic sensation. "I never imagined I'd enjoy something so depraved but, honest to God, I cannot wait to have both of you inside me."

She dug her nails into Simon's shoulders as Robert gave her back entrance one more caress and then kissed the plump cheek of her bottom, sucking on it hard enough she knew she'd have one of his marks there.

"You love leaving your marks on me," she said to him.

"If I have my way you'll both have them by morning," Robert said in the gruff, growly voice he'd only recently discovered. *She'd* only recently discovered. Had they really known each other, or themselves for that matter, before Simon came back? She was beginning to wonder.

"God, you two are perfect," Simon said.

He cupped Christy's cheeks and kissed her again. His arms

snaked around her, and he hugged her tightly as he kissed her, his hands roaming her back until he finally cupped her bottom and pulled her hips tight to his. She thrilled at the feel of his hard cock pressed against her stomach. That was going to be inside her bottom.

As if reading her mind, he slipped the tip of one finger into that untried entrance, and she moaned into his mouth and spread her legs wider as he manipulated his finger, igniting sensations she'd never felt before, the sting of entry giving way to the bliss of pleasure. And the whole time Robert's hands were running up and down her thighs, holding her hips so she couldn't move until she whimpered, and then letting her go, sliding around her stomach to tug on her pubic curls.

She deepened the kiss, sucking on Simon's tongue and then biting his lip, the feelings overwhelming. She *needed*.

"Please," she whimpered into his mouth.

Simon had the gall to laugh softly. "Are you begging, my Christy? Tell us what you want."

"I need you," she said.

"That's not enough," Robert said. He leaned up and bit her bottom again, and she moaned. "Tell us exactly what you need."

"I need you to fuck me," Christy said breathlessly as Simon toyed with her bottom. Robert's hand was now between her legs, his fingers rubbing along her lower lips, gliding through her slick cream. She gave a sob, desperate to have him push inside.

"All right," Simon said. He pulled his hands away and Robert did as well, and then Simon helped her turn around so she was facing Robert.

"I'm going to enter you first, then Robert," Simon told her. "If it hurts at any time, I want you to say so, or if you want us to stop. There's nothing wrong with that. Some people need time to adjust to it and can't do it until the third or fourth or fifth try, and some never like it, and that's fine. All right?"

"All right." Christy was nervous, but she wasn't going to tell them that. She did want to do this. She liked the idea of all them being together like this. Of being the one that brought them together. Would Simon and Robert be together if it weren't for Christy? Maybe. Maybe not. But here, now, in this special way, she gave them something extraordinary, just as they gave her.

Simon pushed her down gently, until her head rested on Robert's chest, her bottom sticking up in the air. "I feel very exposed," she complained only half-jokingly.

"That's because you are," Simon said. "But you trust me, don't you?"

"Absolutely," she replied without hesitation. "Do your worst."

"I'd rather it be his best," Robert said, stroking her hair across chest as he liked to do.

"Oh!" Christy couldn't stop the little exclamation of surprise when Simon slipped a finger inside her bottom again.

"Just a little more of this salve," he said. "And just so you know, I may not last very long. Like I said, I was sitting there thinking about this for several hours. I'm ready to burst. You two are so bloody gorgeous and—"

He stopped and just gripped Christy's hip so tightly she knew she'd be bruised, and she didn't care. She loved it. Loved seeing that someone wanted her, someone cared for her, she belonged to someone.

"Yours," she said, understanding dawning. "You were going to say yours."

"Yes," Simon said, his voice choked up. "Mine."

"We are, you know," Robert said, tucking loose strands of Christy's hair behind her ear. "I didn't realize it back when I first met you both, but I think even then I knew this day would come. We have always been destined to be together."

"Do you think so?" Simon said. He ran his free hand up and down Christy's back. "I certainly fought it hard enough this last year. But I think you're right."

His finger disappeared and suddenly his cock was there, seeking entry. She did the same thing she'd done when it was their fingers—she pushed back against it and the tip slipped in, like a key in a lock. Christy gasped at the sting, and Robert hushed her and smoothed his hand over her hair.

"I'll wait," Simon said breathlessly. "I'll let you adjust a minute."

Robert came up one elbow. "Robert," Simon said warningly.

"Be quiet," he said. "I want to kiss my wife while you fuck her bottom." Just hearing those words ignited the pleasure she'd been waiting for. She had them both, Robert *and* Simon, in her bed, loving her, fucking her. Robert's mouth found hers, and all she could think was, *mine, mine, mine.*

He kissed her with exquisite slowness and attention to detail, outlining her lips with his tongue, tickling the corners so she opened wider, delving inside and tasting every inch, licking and sucking her mouth like a confection, like he'd done to her cunt last night with Simon.

Was this what her life would be like from now on? Decadent, pleasure filled nights, her every wanton fantasy fulfilled by the two men she loved more than words could express? Two men who loved her equally, who loved her enough to love each other.

She moaned into Robert's mouth as Simon pushed deeper into her waiting, wanting passage. She needed him to fill her. Needed them both so badly now.

Simon was moving in her now, fucking her, *actually fucking her*, in her bottom, and she laughed breathlessly against Robert's mouth. It ended in a moan of pleasure.

"It feels good?" Robert asked, nuzzling her temple. He fondled her breast, pinched her nipple, and she gasped as a bolt of sensation traveled between her breast and her cunt and her bottom. She felt her muscles contract.

"So good I might come if you do that again," she told him, panting.

"I felt that," Simon said, as out of breath as she was. "Hurry, Robert, fuck her. Let's try to come together this first time."

Robert lay back down and gripped his erect cock. "Help her take me," he told Simon gruffly. Simon wrapped his arm around her waist and lifted her, pulling her torso up, changing the angle of his cock inside her and she trembled, trying not to come.

"I don't think I'm going to last," she said. "It's so good. It's so good to have you inside me again."

She reached over her shoulder to cup his head and feel his gorgeous hair, and he put his mouth on her shoulder and bit her just this side of too hard and she gasped and her orgasm receded just enough. Simon cupped her breasts in his palms while she arched her back, holding onto a fistful of his hair, his cock in her bottom, while Robert pushed his into her tight cunt.

"Oh, God," she moaned. "It feels so full down there, so tight. He's so big."

"With both of us in there, it's going to be tight," Simon told her. "Is it too much?"

She shook her head. "Never. I like it. It hurts, but I like it."

"I think you like it when it hurts a little," Robert murmured. He'd been going slow, pushing into her, but he was almost all the way in. He shoved in the last inch and she gasped at the sharp sting of it, and immediately felt her orgasm coming.

"Oh, God," she gasped. "I'm going to come."

"So am I," Robert ground out between clenched teeth. "I can feel him. I can feel his cock against mine inside you, Christy."

Robert put his hands over Simon's on her breasts and squeezed, and then he moved just a bit, his cock pulling back and pushing in just an inch or so, but it was enough. Something inside her felt so good where his cock was rubbing, and she pressed down on him, twisted and rolled her hips, reached back and held Simon inside her with a hand on his thigh, and the pleasure broke inside her so hard, like an explosion.

She cried out as colors burst behind her closed eyelids into stars in the night sky. When she heard them both moan, heard Robert saying Simon's name, and felt the heat of their release inside her it ignited another wave of pleasure so intense she couldn't even hold herself up anymore and Simon had to wrap his arms around her.

Robert found her knot of pleasure between her legs and pressed on it, rolling it, his cock still semi-hard inside her, and she had a smaller orgasm that made her moan and smile and stretch and throw both arms back and around Simon's head. Robert cupped her breasts again, and pinched her nipples while she rocked on both cocks until they softened and they all sat or lay there, breathless and sated.

There was so much Christy wanted to say, so many things she needed to tell them, but as Simon gently laid her down beside Robert, sleep overtook her and she drifted off to the gentle ministrations of her men, and their murmured words of love.

CHAPTER 38

"Mmm," Christy said, waking slowly to the warmth of a strong, naked male body curved around her back. There was a kiss on her neck. *Robert.* Funny how she could tell them apart even with her eyes closed.

She reached out for Simon but found only empty sheets. She rolled over and put her arm around Robert, kissing whatever was in front of her lips, eyes still closed. It felt like his chest.

"Where's Simon?" she asked sleepily. She stretched and instantly regretted it. "Ow," she said. She laughed ruefully and opened her eyes to see Robert watching her with a very serious face. "I'm all right. Just a little stiff and sore. I'll be right as rain by tomorrow, I'm sure." She eyed him warily. "Regrets?"

"None." His words and his tone of voice said one thing, but his facial expression said another.

"Then what's wrong?"

"Simon's gone."

It was the defeat in his voice more than the words that got through to her. She scrambled out of bed. "What do you mean, Simon's gone?"

Robert slowly climbed out of bed. Bruises surrounded both

of his bandages. "I mean he left before cock's crow and he took Hastings with him."

"But why? More Home Office business?"

"No." Robert sounded tired. "His note said he had something personal to take care of."

Christy searched the floor for her shift, and yanked it on. She found Robert's shirt, but it was a bloody mess. "I hope you're going to get a clothing stipend for this new job of yours," she snapped.

Robert smiled weakly. "I really don't know why he left. Last night..."

"I'm sure there's a perfectly good explanation," Christy told him, praying she was right. She opened up the wardrobe and pulled out something to wear. "Get dressed. I'm going to go bathe, and then we are going to track the blackguard down. If he thinks we're letting him run off again, he is very much mistaken."

"Maybe we should just let him go," Robert said sadly. She looked over and he was just sitting on the bed looking out the window. "If he's that determined to run, we should let him run. Maybe he just doesn't want us, Christy."

"Don't you see that's what he expects us to do?" Christy told him. Robert looked at her quizzically. "No one has ever gone after him before," she explained. "It took me a while to figure that out, but he's let us in the past week, Robert. I think he's told us more about himself than he's told anyone, possibly even Daniel. He may not have said it in so many words, but if you think about what he did say, you can piece together what he didn't. You're a detective, aren't you? Then put the puzzle together.

"He's never had a real relationship since Giselle. He only takes people to bed who won't expect a commitment, only teaches people his erotic little lessons and walks away. And they let him. Where are his friends, Robert? Off with their own families and their own loves now. He's alone. Everyone has always let him walk away. And he thinks we are going to do the same. Didn't we say last night that we have never done these things together"—she gestured at the bed—"never been this physically intimate before he came back into our lives?"

"We said other things as well," Robert reminded her. "We told him we cared about him. That the three of us were destined to be together from the beginning."

"Words," Christy said. "Nothing but words. Easily spoken, and easily forgotten. He deserves deeds, too, don't you think? I think he's worth going after. Do you?"

Robert stood up. "Yes, I do. I think…I think this is his way of giving us a chance to change our minds if we want without making it awkward for us." He shook his head. "Damn."

She looked at him, wide eyed. Robert rarely if ever cursed.

He smiled ruefully. "He's a tangle, but yes, I think he's worth it for all those reasons and more. He makes me feel alive just like you do, and when I'm with him, that doesn't feel strange or wrong."

Christy ran across the room to hug him. "Exactly. I couldn't have said it better." She looked up at him. "You know I love you, don't you? Just as much as I love Simon? I fell in love with you both at almost the same time. I won't lie, I thought I wanted Simon, and when he didn't offer for me, I accepted you. But I'm so glad I did now because you were what I needed. I think in my heart I knew that, or I never would have accepted you. I didn't have to. Harry had already told me he was more than happy to stay married to me. But I wanted someone of my own and I chose you, just as you chose me. Don't ever doubt my love for you."

"I don't. I won't lie either. I did doubt you, especially when Simon came back, but I didn't blame you. I always knew you and Simon were meant to be together. It just took me a while to figure out that the puzzle had three pieces." He kissed her, and it was sweet and tender. "Now let's go find that idiot," he said softly.

"I'm going to kill him," Christy vowed. "But yes, let's go find him."

"Where do we start?"

"Where else? Daniel's."

"OF COURSE HE WAS HERE, my dear," Daniel said, turning his cheek up to be kissed by Christy and making room beside him for Christian. He was holding court in his bedroom, his leg elevated on a stack of pillows. "He came by to see how I was, the rotten little baggage. Hasn't been here since I saved his hide in Africa. Look at me! I nearly died for him, and he couldn't be bothered to come and see how I was doing."

"You sent him to help me solve a murder which turned into treason and assassination and Sir Barnabas James," Robert reminded him drily. "How did you expect him to come and see you as well?"

"Priorities," Daniel said without remorse. "And so you've lost him again, I see." He shook his head. "I don't know what has happened between you, but I can guess. What are you planning to do once you find him?" Robert could tell this was more of an interrogation than idle conversation.

"I don't see as that's any of your business," Christy replied tartly. "The very nerve, sending Simon to help Robert with a case when the man wasn't recovered from being tortured in Africa! You ought to be ashamed of yourself, Daniel Steinberg. Don't think I don't know what you were up to. No, don't even try to deny it again."

"Simon was tortured in Africa?" Mrs. Tarrant asked in horror. "Why didn't you tell me?" She reached over from her chair near Daniel's bedside and slapped him in the arm. Daniel shot a look at Christy.

"Yes, Daniel, why didn't you tell Mrs. Tarrant?" Christy asked.

"Very," Mrs. Tarrant insisted. "You must call me Very." Both women stared daggers at Daniel.

"All right, if you must know, because I was interfering. There, happy? Although I never expected you to fall victim to his charms, Robert. It was clear something needed to be done. The situation couldn't go on as it was. At the very least you might have reached a truce and Simon would have found an occupation." Christian chose that moment to climb into Daniel's lap, and he used the baby as an excuse to evade their dirty looks.

"I tried to tell him…" Harry muttered from behind his paper in the corner.

"Well, I, for one, am very grateful," Robert told Daniel. "I would not have solved that case and averted a horrible disaster and, *ahem*, found Simon, so to speak, had you not. But Christy is correct in saying that it is none of your business now. We'll take it from here, thank you very much. Now, where is he?"

"Ah, Mr. Manderley," Dr. McCain said, walking into the room. "Saving me the trouble of coming to you today, are you? For a man who was both stabbed and shot yesterday, you're looking as fine as a fiddle."

"What?" Daniel asked. "I thought you just got shot."

"Stabbed, too," Robert said, raising an eyebrow. "I guess some of us just have more stamina." Daniel frowned while the rest of the room laughed.

"Let's see those stitches," Dr. McCain said. Robert began unbuttoning his jacket.

"Here?" Daniel asked in surprise. "Don't you want more privacy?"

"We're in your bedroom," Robert said, frowning. "And I don't trust you and Harry not to share secrets with Christy behind my back."

"Robert Manderley," Christy scolded. "You know I'd tell you as soon as we left."

"Where have I heard that before?" he asked no one in general. He got his jacket and shirt off and let the doctor unwrapped his bandages.

"Do all constables look like him?" Very asked Daniel in a loud whisper. Robert looked over to see her staring at his bare torso with interest.

"No, they do not," Christy said with pride. "Robert is by far the handsomest constable in London. In England, I'd wager."

"I thought I said nothing too strenuous," the doctor chided Robert as he poked at the stitches in his side. "You've gone and popped a few here."

"Oh, God," Daniel said. "Don't even tell me." Christy was blushing.

"This falls under the none-of-your-business category," Robert said firmly. "Do you need to stitch me back up?"

"Just take a minute," the doctor said, reaching for his bag. "The arm looks fine. I'll put a new bandage on. After this, Mrs. Manderley, you should be able to handle it unless it starts to look infected, red, hot to the touch, puss, that sort of thing. Mr. Manderley, sit right there, if you would, please."

Robert sat on the edge of the bed and Christian crawled over to him. He held onto Robert's arm as he stood up, and Robert smiled at him. He got a smile back, with Christian's two new front teeth just visible.

"Look at that," Robert cooed at him. "Nice teeth, lad."

"Pa," Christian said.

Robert's heart stopped. "Did he just say my name?" he asked in wonder. He looked at Christy. Her mouth was open in surprise, and then she grinned.

"I do believe he did," she said. She came over and took Christian in her arms. "Who's that?" she asked, pointing at Robert.

"Pa," Christian said, clapping his hands.

"He's brilliant," Robert said matter-of-factly. "Wait until Simon hears him."

"Yes, a right genius," the doctor agreed. "Move your arm out of the way, please."

"He's on his way home," Daniel said.

"To his apartment?" Robert asked. That wasn't very far to run. And why take Hastings?

"No. His childhood home." Daniel was watching he and Christy closely, so he must have seen that both knew the significance of this news.

"He never told us where that was," Christy said carefully. "Just what happened there and that he's never been back."

"You are all talking in riddles and I don't like it," Very said. "What happened there?"

"If Simon wanted you to know, he would have told you, Very," Christy said, not unkindly. "It was something that profoundly affected him and he has harbored the pain of it all these years. He would not take it kindly we were to share it without his permission. You will have to ask him when he returns, and you will have to respect his wishes if he refuses to tell you."

Very mulled that over with a mulish expression on her face for a minute or two. "Very well," she finally conceded. "You are right. I shall ask him." Daniel looked surprised at her surrender.

"He is in Bury St. Edmunds, in Suffolk," he told them. "But he was going by way of Ashton on the Green. He said he needed to stop and see Stephen, Reverend Matthews."

"Was Hastings going with him?" Robert asked, still puzzled about that.

"The younger chap? Yes, I believe so, although he didn't tell me why."

Dr. McCain had finished the stitches and had rewrapped the bandage.

"Thank you, doctor." Robert slipped his shirt back on and went to Daniel's mirror to tie his cravat.

Christy went to the door and motioned for the rest of their party to come in. "Daniel, this is the new nanny, Mary Peppers" —the girl curtsied—"and her lady friend, Essie. We shall be leaving them here with you along with Christian while we go and fetch Simon."

"What?" Daniel asked in horror. "What, I mean, who is that?" He pointed at Essie.

"'Ere now," Essie said belligerently. "Who and what are you?"

"Essie, this is the Saint of St. Giles," Robert made the introductions. "Daniel Steinberg."

"I thought that was the other one, wit' you two," she said. "The other one I'm to work with."

"Work with?" Harry had put down his newspaper for this.

"We are going to train Essie to work for Sir Barnabas," Robert said, trying not to sound too grim. "She is a semi-trained assassin."

"Semi?" Essie said, clearly outraged. "I can kill you."

"Yes, but just with a knife," Robert said.

"Es," Mary Peppers said, taking her hand. "Don't mess this up for me, please, love."

"They are coming home with me," Very said, standing up. "I've been gone too long already."

"You've been gone two days," Daniel argued.

"And it's been deadly dull around here. Just wait until Agatha meets you," Very said to Essie, her eyes shining. She turned to Christy. "A bachelor's establishment is no place for a baby. Mary Peppers," she barked, "have you any experience as a nanny?"

"No, ma'am," Mary Peppers answered right away.

"Well, Mrs. Sunshine and Mrs. Goose will have you trained in no time." Very gathered her things and whisked Christian from Christy's arms and deposited him in Mary Peppers' before Christy knew what was happening. "Don't worry, my dear, he'll be safe with us. You can come fetch him after you find Simon. Come along, Mary Peppers. Miss Essie, do you perhaps have a surname?"

"I ain't got no man's name," Essie said belligerently. "Just Essie. I ain't a man, I'm a woman. I just like men's clothes. So don't expect me in no dress." Their voices faded as they walked down the hall.

"And I need a new cook," Christy called down the hall after Very. "And that's taken care of nicely," she said with satisfaction.

"You knew Very was going to take them all along," Daniel accused her.

"Of course I did," Christy said.

"When did Cook leave?" Robert asked in dismay.

"Yesterday, after you came home shot," Christy told him. "Nell gave me her note this morning." She turned to Harry. "I've left Nell in charge of the house, but send someone around to check on her every day, won't you?" She walked over and kissed her ex-husband on the cheek.

"Of course." He shook Robert's hand. "Good luck," he told him.

"Thank you," Robert said. The whole situation seemed very odd. Here he was about to go chasing after another man for love, and all these people were wishing him well. There seemed to be a whole secret society in London that most people knew nothing about, and in the last year Robert had become a member without even realizing it.

"When you do find Simon," Daniel said as they left, "be gentle. He's very fragile, you know, though he pretends not to be. I know I've failed him in the last couple of years—we all have. Be the ones who don't."

"That is exactly what we had planned," Robert told him. "And you didn't fail him. You almost died saving his life because you love him, and he knows that. I just hope chasing him down to Bury St. Edmunds is enough to convince him we do, too."

CHAPTER 39

"Simon? Oh, yes, he was here," Stephen, Reverend Matthews, said, shading his eyes as he looked at them from under the brim of his wide hat, his arms draped over the fence. He was in his beloved garden. The silly straw hat only enhanced his boyish charm, as did his freckled face and ruddy cheeks. "As a matter fact, he left something behind and I'm not sure what to do with it." He motioned them over to the gate.

"We've missed him, then?" Christy asked, dejected. It was probably her fault, mostly. She didn't ride very well and so they had taken the stage. Robert didn't care for horses, either, but he could ride if he had to.

"I'm afraid so," Stephen said. "Just, actually. He left not two hours ago." He opened the gate and they entered. "Why are you looking for Simon?" he asked curiously. "Is something wrong?"

"Yes," Christy said. "We love him very much and he's run away again, so this time we are chasing him down so he realizes how much we love him." She looked over at Robert to see how he reacted to her matter of fact pronouncement, and her inclusion of him in it. He looked surprising unconcerned.

"Oh, really? That's splendid. I daresay it's about time someone did. Poor chap's been wandering about in limbo for years, eaten up by guilt with no direction and nothing to live for. I was quite worried, I don't mind telling you."

"How was he when you saw him yesterday?" Robert asked, his brow furrowed in concern. Christy took his hand.

"Drunk," Stephen said. "With him."

They'd been walking toward a little lean-to sort of garden shed and Stephen pointed underneath it. Lying there wearing nothing but his boots, a burlap sack tossed over him all that was left of his privacy, was Hastings. He was sound asleep and snoring loudly. Christy covered her mouth with her hands to hide her laughter. Robert just sighed.

"Have you any idea who he is?" Stephen asked. "All I was told was that he was Hasten, the Killer of Men and Ladies' Virtue."

"That would be Hastings, not Hasten," Robert said. "He's one of Sir Barnabas James's men at the Home Office. Simon and I recently worked an important mission with him. What did Simon say when he left?"

"Not much." Stephen fanned himself with his hat. "He just asked me to take care of his friend here, who needed to learn there was more than killing. I assumed he was being facetious about ladies' virtues and whatnot, but now I think he meant it literally."

"He meant it literally," Robert told him. "Where are Hastings's clothes?"

"I do believe Simon took them," Stephen said. "To force him to stay, or ask for help. Who knows what was in Simon's head? I think he was still half drunk. I asked him where he was going and he said home. I thought he meant London, but he didn't go in that direction."

"No, he meant Suffolk," Robert told him. "Have we missed the last stage?"

"Not to worry," Stephen said. "Stay for nuncheon and I'll

send a note to Ashton Park. I'm sure Freddy has a carriage he can spare."

"I still don't understand why he's naked," Anne, Duchess of Ashley, said as she sat with the others in the shade of a nearby tree having lemonade and cucumber sandwiches. "That burlap must itch rather fiercely."

"I daresay you are correct, my dear," her husband Freddy, the Duke of Ashley, said, sipping his lemonade and peering at Hastings. "He certainly is well-formed."

"If you like that sort of thing," their lover, Brett Haversham, said from where he leaned against the tree.

"We like that sort of thing," the duke said, grinning at Mr. Haversham, who was quite well-formed himself, even though he was older than the duke.

"I think Simon is trying to teach Hastings a lesson," Christy said. "He has a hard time trusting people, you see."

"Ah," Freddy said. "Then leaving him naked and at Stephen's mercy makes complete sense."

"It did to Simon, apparently," Stephen said, reaching for another sandwich. "My clothes won't fit him. I'm not tall enough. You'll have to send something over, Freddy."

"I'm too thin," Freddy said.

"I shall find something," Anne said. "But there's no rush, is there?" She smiled and took a sip of her lemonade.

"So you're going after Simon are you?" Freddy asked.

"Yes," Robert said. Freddy waited for more, but Robert just ate his sandwich.

"You were always parsimonious with your words, if I remember correctly," Freddy said drily. "Christy, my dear? Have you anything to add?"

"No," she said. "We *are* going after Simon. And we are ever so grateful for the loan of your carriage, Your Grace. We would have to wait a whole day for the next stage otherwise, and Simon is travelling quickly."

"Why is he running?" Brett asked with a frown.

"Why do men always run?" Robert asked. "Because he fears the future, he runs to the past to escape the present."

"Oh, well said," Freddy complimented him. "Well said." He looked pointedly at Brett.

Hastings suddenly sat up and looked around. He jumped to his feet and then froze. The duchess covered her eyes with her hand, but Christy could clearly see that she had her fingers splayed and could easily see Hastings in all his glory.

"Where am I?" he asked. He was out of breath and obviously upset. "Manderley?" he said when he saw Robert, his face furrowed with confusion.

"Cover yourself," Robert told him. He pointed. "The burlap sack." Hastings reached down and grabbed the sack, and tried to wrap it around his waist. "Apparently you got drunk with Simon yesterday and ended up here, where you passed out in Stephen's garden."

"Your servant, sir." Stephen waved. "Stephen, Reverend Matthews. I'm an old friend of Simon's."

"What the bloody hell?" Hastings asked. He ran one hand through his hair and over his face. "Why am I naked in a field?"

"Garden," Christy corrected. Hastings glared at her.

"We have no idea," Freddy said. "I am Freddy Thorne." He left off his title. He liked to do that when he met people for the first time. "This is my wife, Anne." He twisted in his seat and pointed to Brett. "And that's Brett Haversham. You're in Ashton on the Green."

"Surrey?" Hastings asked in disgust. "I'm in bloody Surrey? Christ. I'm going to kill that bastard."

"Language, Hastings," Christy chided him.

"I'm in my altogether, ma'am," he said tightly. "I think I've got provocation."

Robert stood and held his hand out to Christy. "We are going to be on our way, if you don't mind," he said. Christy silently agreed and took his hand. The duchess nodded and smiled and sipped her lemonade, and Christy knew she'd make sure Hastings was taken care of.

"Wait, what?" Hastings came hurrying over, trying to hold the burlap in place to cover as much as possible. "Take me with you."

"You have no clothes, Hastings," Christy told him. "And I'm sure you're a bit under the weather. I think you should stay here with Stephen for a while."

"A while? How long is a while?" Hastings asked, trying to follow them to the gate.

"Just a bit," Christy promised as Robert helped her up into the carriage. "We'll stop and get you on our way back. Do what Stephen says."

CHAPTER 40

S imon sat with his back against a tree, his legs crossed, not too far from Giselle's grave. He'd been working his way closer all morning. He'd started by walking through the town center, making his way to the churchyard, sitting by the gate on the bench he'd paid for with the money he sent the rectory every month to care for the graves here.

His parents were here, and his younger brother Gavin, too. A fever had swept through the village during the war and taken all three of them. Simon had failed them, too, in a way, not being here for that. But for some reason their deaths—though they had saddened him—had not burdened him with guilt. He knew realistically there was little he could have done to save them from that fever. He had neither caused it, nor could he have cured it. More likely had he been here he, too, would have died from it.

The irony was that he'd gone to war to die and he'd have had a better chance had he stayed at home.

He looked around. He was the only one in the cemetery. It was a beautiful day. Hot as usual this summer, sunny. The birds were singing, there were bees buzzing about, the odd butterfly.

Many of the graves in the small cemetery had flowers planted around the headstones. His family's did not. They were clear of debris and in good repair, and Simon supposed that was all his yearly donations were worth. He would have sent more if they'd told him about the flowers. But then, he hadn't asked.

Still, it wasn't a bad resting place for all eternity, he supposed. It was quite tranquil and pretty, shaded with large trees. He could hear the steady stream of traffic at the rectory, so it wasn't boring for them, either, if they were still hanging about the place waiting for him to show up.

Well, here he was.

He slowly got to his feet, hat in hand, and walked over to his mother's grave. *Marissa Gantry, Wife and Mother* it read above her dates. His father was next to her, *Stanley Gantry, Husband and Father.*

Was that it? Was that the sum of their lives? He thought about Christy and Robert, how much they loved one another and little Christian, and he supposed that those epitaphs were not perhaps as simple nor as empty as they seemed. They encompassed a whole lifetime of experiences—joys and sorrows and shared adventures. He remembered the happiest moments from his childhood and recalled his parents' fondness for each other and for him and Gavin, and supposed that yes, that was the sum of their lives, and it told a full and rich story.

He walked over to Gavin's grave and squatted down in front of it to read it. *Taken From Us Too Young.* Gavin had only been seventeen and he'd died first. His mum had doted on Gav. When Simon left, he'd been only thirteen. According to the last letter he'd received Gav had been itching to buy a commission of his own and go to war, but both Simon and his parents had wanted him to go to university.

Simon wiped tears from his cheeks. They'd been gone so long. And when they died, he was at war. There had been so much death all around him, and theirs had just been three more.

He realized he had never grieved for them. What an injustice to them. They had loved Giselle, too, and right on the heels of losing her he'd run off to war, hoping to die, and they'd never seen him again. It was a wonder they had written to him at all, that they hadn't disowned him and cut him off, but that hadn't been their way.

He stood up and walked over to Giselle's grave. He shivered and crossed his arms, remembering the last time he was here, the day of her funeral.

He made himself read her epitaph aloud. "'Giselle Marie Gantry, Beloved Wife and Daughter.'"

He laughed softly at how hollow and inadequate those words were. Her loss had set him on a course of self-destruction that had lasted almost twenty years. Her mother had collapsed and had taken to her bed until the day she died, according to his own mother's letters.

"It's very nice here."

Simon's head came up at the sound of Christy's voice behind him. He didn't know why, but he wasn't surprised to hear it.

"The last time I was here was the day I buried her," Simon said, still not turning around. "It was so cold that day. The wind was blowing out of the east right off the North Sea, and it was raining. Nothing like today."

He knelt down and brushed some dirt off the headstone. "You know, I expected to be overcome with emotion when I got here. But…nothing. Not really." He sat down, one knee up, his elbow resting on it, staring at her name. "I guess I've spent so many years mourning her I haven't got anything left."

Christy knelt down beside him, and Robert walked over to stand in front of him. "You have memories. Good memories," she said. "Maybe now you can focus on those. You've tortured yourself with the bad ones for too long already. I think Giselle would agree."

"She wouldn't even recognize me now," Simon said. "I used

to be a wild, reckless boy. I never had a care for anyone else except for my own pleasures, and the world let me act that way. My world, anyway. But my pleasures in those days were hunting and fishing and riding fast horses, and Giselle. The prettiest girl in the county, and I'd fight anyone who said differently."

Christy reached out and wiped another tear from his cheek.

"Am I crying? I didn't realize," he said, capturing her hand and kissing it. Robert handed him a handkerchief. "Thank you." He wiped his face.

"I like fishing," Robert said. Simon laughed.

"You told me that you have a sixth sense about danger," Robert said.

Simon looked up at him in surprise. "Yes. Although this seems an odd time to bring it up."

"Did you always have it? Even as a child?"

"I suppose so," Simon said. "Although it failed me with Giselle."

"Did it? When did you first notice you had it?"

"Robert, stop interrogating him," Christy said sharply.

"Now that you mention it, I don't recall any incidents before the war," Simon said, frowning. "But then, I was never in a life or death situation before then."

"Except Giselle," Robert pushed.

"Yes, except Giselle," Simon agreed. "What are you getting at?"

"That maybe Christy and I owe Giselle a debt for keeping you safe all these years," Robert said. "Maybe, while you were blaming yourself and trying to die, Giselle was working very hard to keep you alive."

Simon looked at him shock. "Are you saying that my sixth sense comes from Giselle?"

"That's exactly what I'm saying," Robert said, sitting down

beside him, opposite Christy. They all sat and looked at Giselle's headstone for several minutes.

"Thank you," Christy finally whispered, "for keeping him safe for us."

After a while Simon reached out and grasped both their wrists. "You came for me."

"Of course we did," Robert said. "You belong to us now."

Simon didn't dispute his words. "How did you find me?"

"First we went to Daniel's," Christy said, surreptitiously wiping a tear from her eye. "And he told us you went to Ashton on the Green. Oh, Simon, what you did to poor Hastings."

"He'll be a better man for it, mark my words," Simon said with laughter in his voice. "Haven't we all gone to Ashton Park to heal ourselves at one time or another?"

"We were at Ashton Park when we found out you'd been kidnapped," Christy said quietly. "It was not a pleasant memory for us. Yesterday, at least we knew that we would find you today."

"I'm sorry, darling," Simon said. He pulled her into his arms and kissed her temple. "And how did you know I'd be here?"

"Daniel did tell us you were coming here, to Bury St. Edmunds. When we arrived we just guessed that this would be where we'd find you."

"You know me too well," Simon said, standing up.

"If only that were true, I would have known you were going to run after our night together," Robert said, standing as well.

"Running? Is that what you think I was doing?" He shook his head and affectionately ran his hand down Robert's arm, a gesture no one who might be looking would find too familiar. "I came to say goodbye. I never had, not properly. It was time."

Christy reached a hand up, and both men stepped forward to help her stand. "Simon, this will never do. We must find some flowers for all the graves. And I am going to have a stern talk with the rectory about this. We will arrange to pay them for the upkeep, and we will come a time or two each year if we can."

"I already pay them, Christy."

"Well then," she said in righteous indignation. "I can see that they have taken advantage of your absence to shirk their duties. Have you no other family to take care of them?" Simon shook his head. "We will find someone before we leave."

"Where is Christian?" Simon asked as they headed toward the rectory.

"With Very Tarrant," Robert said. He grinned and looked at Simon out of the corner of his eye. "Along with Mary Peppers and Essie."

Simon burst out laughing. "I am going to get a visit from Kensington and Tarrant as soon as we get back to London," he said. "So are we going to work for Barnabas?"

"What do you think?"

Simon had given it a great deal of thought on the way to Suffolk. "I think it's a good idea. The pay is better, and eventually we could find ourselves at a desk if we want. Things are changing, and we can change with them. And I trust Barnabas. He will always make sure we are taken care of. I don't think we could do better."

"You make some good arguments." Robert stopped and turned to him. "And I would get to work with you every day."

"That is definitely one of the favorable arguments," Simon agreed.

Christy stepped between them and took each by the arm, looking up at them. "So we are going to do this, then? We're going to be together at last?"

"We've always been together, from the very beginning," Simon told her. "We fell in love the first time we saw each other."

"Not true," Robert said. "I hated you. Your perfect hair, and handsome face, and heroic nature. I wished baldness on you."

When he stopped laughing, Simon confessed, "I hated you, too. You were always so perfect. Perfectly polite, beautiful manners, manly physique, immaculate past. I wished you to the devil many times." He touched his hair. "But never baldness. If something should happen, we shall look to you now."

"Do you think that two men who fall in love with the same woman are only a heartbeat away from falling in love with each other?" Robert asked.

Simon's heart stumbled in his chest. Was Robert saying he loved Simon? "Perhaps. I know I have seen it happen many times. Loving Christy has turned us from enemies to lovers."

"Not yet," Robert said, his eyes gleaming with intent. "But tonight, I plan to correct that."

CHAPTER 41

S imon moaned as Robert pushed another finger
inside him.

"How long has it been since you've been fucked?"
Robert asked, his voice rough and low in Simon's ear. He had
his arm around Simon's chest, holding him tightly against him.
Christy lay between his spread legs, his cock in her hungry
mouth, sucking and licking him, keeping him on the edge as
Robert prepared him to be taken just the way Simon had taught
him to prepare Christy.

"Not since Africa," Simon said breathlessly.

Robert stopped. He rested his forehead on Simon's cheek.
"I'm sorry," he whispered. "Should I go on?"

"This is nothing like that," Simon said. "You are nothing like
that."

"Simon," Christy said. She kissed his inner thigh. "Darling,
I'm sorry. I would take that away from you, if I could." She
rubbed his hips soothingly.

"You are," he said simply. "Take me. Fuck me. I want this,
please," he begged.

Christy took him in her hot, wet mouth again, and he moaned.

Robert covered his mouth with his hand. "Shhh," he whispered. "You'll have the innkeeper at the door."

Robert's hand over his mouth, the clandestine nature of their encounter, as well as this being the first time Robert would fuck him, the first Robert would ever fuck a man, made the whole experience that much more erotic for Simon. He bit down on Robert's palm and fucked into Christy's mouth, and they both gave low, quiet moans. Simon loved that, loved being able to please them both at the same time. He couldn't wait to fuck Christy while Robert fucked him.

As if they'd read his mind, Christy slid her mouth off his cock and Robert pulled his fingers out. Christy continued to lick the length of his erection and Robert fondled his stones. "Now?" Robert asked, kissing his nape.

"God, yes," Simon said desperately.

"Good, because I can't last long," Robert said. "I hope someday to fuck you both without feeling like an overeager schoolboy."

Simon laughed ruefully. "I'm afraid I'm guilty of that, as well. I'm ready to come just thinking about fucking into Christy's sweet cunt with your cock in my arse."

"Oh my God," Christy said. "Do it. Stop talking and do it." She slid up the bed and rearranged herself, legs spread wide so Simon was between them. He ran his finger down her slit and was delighted with how wet she was. He licked it clean, humming in satisfaction.

"Fuck me," Christy demanded.

He didn't wait for another invitation. When he entered her silky passage, he had to bite his lip to keep from coming immediately. Christy turned his face and kissed him roughly, biting his lip for him, and he thrust hard into her.

"Yes," Robert whispered. "Fuck her like that. Hard. She likes it hard."

Simon tore his mouth from Christy's. "Someday I will fuck her just for your pleasure and you can watch us all you like. But tonight I want to be fucked. So put your cock in me, now."

"I am married to two very demanding people," Robert complained.

"What did you say?" Simon asked, shocked.

"Consider this a wedding vow of sorts," Robert said. At that moment he pushed in between Simon's legs, and his cock found Simon's entrance. "Ask to be fucked, and I will fuck you."

He pressed against Simon's hole with his finger, and as soon as Simon opened for him, he replaced it with his cock and slid in. The head clearing the entrance made a satisfying sound as it slid home, and Simon gasped at the pleasure of it.

"More," he demanded when Robert stayed still for too long.

"It feels too good," Robert said, his voice tight. "I can't believe I'm fucking you. I'm fucking a man."

"Not yet. Give me your cock, damn it."

Robert shoved the rest in in one hard push, and Simon relished the sting of it. He reached back and grabbed Robert's thigh, and they stayed like that for a minute as they all adjusted.

Christy finally brushed her hand lightly over Simon's hair, getting his attention. He looked at her, and then she grabbed a handful of it in her fist and pulled him down for a kiss. Then she moved her hips.

"Fuck me," she said against his lips.

Robert was the one to obey the command. He pulled back and then pushed in, a gentle movement that brought all of Simon's senses to life and rocked his cock into Christy. Christy hummed in his mouth. Robert pulled out again, and this time his thrust was harder. Simon groaned at the same time Christy moaned, the sounds mingling in their kiss.

Robert took Simon's hip in his hand and held on for the next thrust. He began a steady rhythm that had Simon's head spinning. He devoured Christy's mouth in their kiss, a way to avoid making too much noise.

He wanted to shout and moan and cry out at the sheer pleasure of fucking and being fucked with Christy and Robert. How long had he wanted this? Fought this? Had he known even last year that eventually this would happen? Maybe. All he knew was that no cunt and no cock had ever felt as fine as these to him, and he would never want any others.

Christy came. She dug her nails into his shoulders and cried out in his mouth, a high, keening cry that he caught and swallowed even as he ground into her, intensifying her orgasm. Her sweet cunt clenched him so tightly, and all he could do was rock inside her.

At the same time she was coming all over his cock, Robert gave him no quarter. He continued to thrust into him, slamming home now, riding him hard, breathing heavy above him, owning him, pushing him, fucking him so well, so right.

"Yes, yes," Simon said just below his breath after he broke off the kiss with Christy. "Fuck me." His voice was high and tight. He was going to come. "Fuck me like that." His hips raised of their own accord, pushing back, fighting for more cock, harder, and Robert gave it to him. "Robert, yes."

When he began to come, he pushed back into Christy, wanting to come inside her, needing to. "Christy," he said.

She shook in his arms, and then he felt her coming again, fucking his pulsing cock, and he trembled at the storm that gripped him. He started to collapse, but Robert yanked up his hips.

"Now I'll fill you," Robert said gruffly. He held both of Simon's hips and fucked him harder for another minute, and Simon loved it. Loved being used like that by Robert. He fucked him back, giving it all to him, and when Robert came he sat back on his haunches and pulled Simon with him, holding him with a hand on his chest, his cock pulsing in Simon's passage, filling him, spilling out of him, owning him.

"I love you," Robert said when it was over, when they were panting and sweaty and stuck together like that. And he kissed Simon between the shoulder blades. "Say it."

"I love you, too," Simon said. And he meant it. "Christy, come here."

She came to them, kneeling in front of him, her hands on his shoulders, looking happier than he'd ever seen her. "I love you, too, silly," she said before he could say anything.

"I know." And he did.

The End

ABOUT THE AUTHOR

Reviewers have called Samantha Kane "an absolute marvel to read" and "one of historical romance's most erotic and sensuous authors." Her books have been called "sinful," "sensuous," and "sizzling." She is published in several romance genres including award winning erotic historical, contemporary and science fiction. She has a master's degree in American History, and taught high school social studies before becoming a full time writer. Samantha Kane lives in North Carolina with her husband and three children.

http://www.samanthakanebooks.com

facebook.com/AuthorSamanthaKane
x.com/skaneauthor
instagram.com/samanthakane125
pinterest.com/kane2993
reamstories.com/samanthakane
goodreads.com/Samantha_Kane
amazon.com/Samantha-Kane/author
bookbub.com/samantha-kane

ALSO BY SAMANTHA KANE

Brothers in Arms

The Courage to Love

Love Under Siege

Love's Strategy

At Love's Command

Retreat From Love

Love in Exile

Love's Fortress

Prisoner of Love

Love's Surrender

Love Betrayed

Defeated by Love

Fight for Love

For Love and Country

Mission to Love

Valor

Daniel and Harry

Mercury Rising

Cherry Pie

Cherry Bomb

Cherry Pop

Birmingham Rebels

Broken Play